DIAMONDS, FURS & MURDER

The Many Crimes of Mona Hayes

Tara Oldfield

Diamonds, Furs & Murder: The Many Crimes of Mona Hayes
Print ISBN: 978-1-76109-731-7
Ebook ISBN: 978-1-76109-926-7
Copyright © text Tara Oldfield 2026
Cover design by Graham Davidson
Author photo by Natasha Cantwell
First published 2026 by
GINNINDERRA PRESS
PO Box 2 Bentleigh 3204
ginninderrapress.com.au

*I acknowledge the first storytellers of the lands on which I write,
the Traditional Owners across Victoria, and pay my respects to
Elders past and present.*

1

Lined up like lambs for the slaughter. Twenty-five ushers stood in a row as theatre manager Edelman, thin moustache twitching, walked the foyer. An impatient crowd formed in Melbourne's wintery cold outside.

'Forgotten how to iron, Margaret?' The young woman blushed at the reprimand.

Edelman moved down the line identifying un-shined shoes and wonky bow ties. Finally, he came to Mona Hayes.

He looked down his nose. 'All girls must wear their uniform pressed, hair neat and their lips... what, Mona?' Mr Edelman asked.

'Raspberry red, Sir.' Mona rolled her eyes.

'That's right,' he spat, 'rasp-ber-ry red, and what colour is that?' He winced, pointing a skinny, ticket ink-stained finger at Mona's pretty pout.

'Rebel red Sir. It's more my colour. And you don't pay me enough for Guerlain.'

The other ushers giggled. One placed a reassuring hand on Mona's back. In less than a month she'd been scolded for her laddered stockings, messy hair, and of course, her lipstick shade. But upkeep was expensive. She preferred to spend her money on booze, getting by with finger-combed hair and lips obsessively licked. They weren't rebel red; they were red raw.

'Borrow from one of the other girls next time. I want you all uniform. Pristine. It's what the patrons expect.'

Ushers were chosen on appearance and presentation. They needed to be appealing and friendly. Mona could sell a ticket better than any salesman, but following rules in uniform just wasn't her style.

At the snap of Edelman's fingers, the ushers sprang into action, swinging open the heavy glass doors making way for the hordes. The theatre gave Melburnians a chance to escape the cold and rain and football, to dress in their finest suits and gowns, and applaud the talents of the few traveling artists who saw fit to add the far-flung southern city to their touring schedules.

Mona glanced down at the tickets presented by each theatregoer and motioned to the rows ahead of her. She admired their finery. Even in the shivering cold of winter, women were sheathed in silk dresses, fur shawls and velvet capes draped delicately over bare shoulders. The men wore grey and black suits with matching hats, cigarettes dangling from clean shaven lips. Mona inhaled the smoke as they passed and considered the outfits in her own wardrobe – a mix of handmade skirts and blouses with what she liked to call 'second-hand' coats and heels from the Midas factory where her friend Lawrence moonlighted.

'Excuse me, Miss. What time's the show start? Do I have time to run for more cigarettes?' A handsome gentleman in a charcoal three-piece waved a stub in her direction.

'You might want to wait until intermission. The show starts at eight sharp.' Mona shrugged an apology, shining her torch light onto his ticket. She led the man down the red-carpeted aisles.

'Here you are.' She turned around as his eyes darted from her backside to her face. 'D18. You might have found it yourself, had you been looking in the right direction.'

He laughed and caught her hand in his. 'Can't blame a man for appreciating a beautiful woman. Perhaps you have time after the show for tea?'

Mona smiled back at him. 'How 'bout I make you a deal? If Robson sings, *I'll Be Seeing You*, then I'll be seeing you.' She turned on her heel, tossing a grin back in the man's direction.

'Hang on, he doesn't sing that one!'

When playing movies on the projection screen, advertisements for local businesses and long opening credit sequences allowed extra time for latecomers to make their way in. Live shows weren't much different. As most performers didn't want to be interrupted mid-song or monologue, they'd start well after eight to give dawdlers time to find their seats. Some of the better-known performers would keep the audience waiting up to half an hour. Tonight's entertainment, Roy Robson, was an exception. Edelman had warned Mona and the other ushers that Robson started on time or not at all. Once, a theatre in Paris had the audacity to ask him to wait for a royal guest to arrive, he left without singing a note. He was also known for his short fuse on stage. In London, he'd sworn at a pianist mid-verse and stormed off stage when a chorus dancer stepped out of line. No one knew what would set him off next.

The lights dimmed and the velvet curtains parted.

'Direct from London's Covent Garden, it's with great pleasure that I bring to you one of the most acclaimed baritones of our generation. Ladies and gentlemen, please make welcome the magnificent and most estimable, the one, the only, Mr Roy Robson,' the compere announced, to grand applause.

Though sold out for weeks, Mona noticed some empty seats in her section. She waited at the back of the theatre for the tardy, torch at the ready.

The music swelled and Roy Robson's striking face and incredible voice captured everyone's attention. Mona paced back and forth imagining a world in which she was the one on stage. As a child she dreamed of one day being a successful singer. Then she grew up. Yet the occasional daydream, of the life she'd always wanted, sometimes crept in.

Robson was older than Mona had pictured. Listening to him on the wireless, she'd envisioned him in his late twenties, with cropped dark brown hair like her boyfriend Brown. Yet here he was, at least forty, his bald head gleaming under the lights. Robson was, however, more captivating and commanding then Mona could have ever imagined. Slim, yet he seemed to take up the entire stage. That was what they called star-quality. Something she didn't have.

Robson began his first number, a pitch perfect rendition of *Without a Song*, with a full orchestra and chorus of girls behind him. He sang it slow.

Soulful. His voice reached a powerful climax when he stopped short and bellowed, 'No, no, no. Would you please sit down!'

The orchestra screeched to a halt, the chorus girls' jaws dropped, and a spotlight hit Mona. All eyes landed on her.

She froze, not fully understanding what was happening. Slowly, she brought her shaky hand to her chest, and pointed to herself, 'Me?'

'Yes, you, the usher. Your incessant meandering back and forth is distracting the whole ensemble!'

Blood rushed to Mona's face. Embarrassment wrapped her head to foot and squeezed, like a boa constrictor.

'Don't just stand there like a moron. Sit down! I won't continue until you please sit down!'

The spotlight and the theatre patrons' shocked stares seemed to crack through her constricted limbs. After what felt like an eternity, to her and no doubt to Robson, she sat in one of the empty seats. Robson groaned and instructed the conductor to start the song again.

Mona endured the show in a state of utter humiliation. She couldn't make out a word nor a note from the stage, could only hear the pounding of unshed tears busting to emerge. She held them down. Head high, she did her best to avoid the pitying glances from the audience, thankful no one could see the flush of her neck and cheeks.

Finally, intermission arrived. Mona leapt out of her seat and straight for the door. She spent intermission in the alley swigging from her pocket flask. Stopping mid performance. She'd never seen a singer do such a thing. That's not the way she was taught. She'd always been told not to stop. Not if you fall, forget the words. Stop for nothing. Not this unprofessional prick. As intermission ended, Mona pulled herself together, bypassed the stage door and snuck backstage through the labyrinth of tiny rooms. 'Roy Robson' was scrawled in fancy gold ink on the door of the biggest dressing room. Mona looked from left to right down the hallway before knocking.

She cracked the door and peered in. 'Hello, anyone in here?' She couldn't be too careful. For all she knew, Robson could have a friend or agent sitting backstage waiting for him. But no, the dressing room was empty.

She entered, shutting the door behind her. She'd been in there before, offering visiting actors and singers drinks and reminding them of the time. But Mona had never seen it filled with so many flowers, chocolates and gifts from fans. She skimmed her hands over each item. Roses, daisies, Cadbury's. Her hands stopped at Robson's black walker hat, she ran her nails across the felt, leaving her mark on the material.

On Robson's dressing table sat a crystal carafe of yellow liquid. She knew it to be pineapple juice, a dietary staple of the singing elite. Sadly, there was no alcohol to be found. But there was a beautiful black woollen scarf and an All-American hand-laced wallet brimming with cash.

She sat in Robson's leather chair and looked at herself in the light-rimmed mirror. She daydreamed about being a star like Robson, sitting backstage like this – a real performer people paid money to see. She'd given the audience a show alright.

Mona startled as applause boomed down from the stage. Robson's performance was over. She gasped; she'd lost track of time. He wasn't known for giving generous encores, so she'd have to be quick. She wrapped the scarf around her neck, took the money from his wallet and spat in his pineapple juice. Her revenge hadn't quite erased her earlier humiliation, but it was a start.

Mona's pulse picked up as she heard people filling the hallways. His people. But she wasn't quite done. She picked up the walker and put it on her head. She checked herself in the mirror, pursing her lips and positioning the hat so its feathers stuck up like cat ears. A man's hat yes, yet it suited her.

She skipped out of the room as Robson and his staff rounded the corner. They headed towards her.

'Hey!' someone shouted. Maybe it was him.

Police had described Mona as a woman of low character, an exceptionally clever crook who ran with known cheats and thieves. A drunk, a cocaine addict, and more. But Mona didn't think of herself as a criminal. Simply put, if she saw something she wanted, she took it. Most women didn't do that. If the mark was deserving, even better.

Mona broke into a run. On her way upstairs, she grabbed her coat from the staff rack, gave her fellow ushers a wave and burst onto the street. She tripped over a beggar in a tattered soldier's uniform as she ran, apologising in the form of Robson's money, half of which she tossed into the poor man's tin can.

'Thank you Miss, very generous,' he said.

Yes, that was a better word for her. Generous indeed.

2

Brown and Guggenheim met Mona outside. They'd pinched two of her cigarettes while waiting for her shift to finish, their guilty grins glowing under the show lights.

Guggenheim thumbed the feather ears of Mona's new hat. 'Hey kitty-kat!'

She swatted him, pushing them away from the theatre as she wrapped her black ribboned coat over her usher's uniform for the last time. 'I hope you're planning on buying me another packet! Luckies don't come cheap you know.'

'Lesson be learned, Sweets, leave your shit with thieves, it's gonna get nicked.' Guggenheim was a lot older than Mona, though she never dared ask his age. He was an inconsistent man, Mona never knew how he'd react to her one day to the next. She'd normally fume at any man who took what was hers, but Guggenheim was not to be messed with.

'Where's Lawrence?' She asked of their missing member.

Guggenheim shrugged. 'Out with that bloke, Sharpe.' One of the few thieves in Melbourne she hadn't yet had the pleasure of meeting.

'I'm beginning to think 'that bloke Sharpe' doesn't actually exist. Am I ever gonna meet him?' Mona asked.

'Let's hope not.' Brown pulled his gloves on and tapped his watch. 'And if you're quite finished whining about your bloody cigarettes, we've got money to make.' He smelled of sweat and fish, his dark eyes framed by a permanent furrowed brow. His tone told Mona he hadn't had a very good day at the market.

She snatched her purse from him. 'Right now, my darling, you're *costing me money!*' No need to tell them she'd already scored off Robson. She turned on her heel and stalked towards bustling Flinders Street Train Station's famous clocks, buzzing ticket counters and draughty platforms.

Brown and Guggenheim exchanged smirks and trailed slowly behind her.

She'd barely made it to the station when she spotted an easy mark standing patiently under the clocks. May as well. Stealing was like eating cake to Mona. She'd ruined her diet with one slice already, what's a few more? A short toad of a man, his floppy hat looked like it had been caught in the rain one too many times. She surveyed his gleaming gold watch, fancy cufflinks and perfectly shined shoes. A man of money, deep pockets she knew how to pick.

She sidled up to him with a shy smile. 'Excuse me Sir, I don't mean to bother you.'

He beamed. 'That's quite alright Miss, something the matter?'

'You could say that. I've run out of cigarettes, and I'm already running late to meet my friends. You wouldn't have a spare I could borrow, would you?'

As he fished a packet out of his pants pocket, Brown came, as if out of nowhere, and grabbed him by the collar. 'You better not be hitting on my girl there, fella!'

'No I er... no, Sir.' The poor fool held up his hands, shaking his head.

'Calm down love, he's just loaning me a ciggie, I'm suddenly all out.' Mona pushed Brown aside and straightened the man's jacket. As she apologised profusely for her boyfriend's quick temper, her gloved fingers slid inside the Toad's pocket, swiping his wallet.

Guggenheim strolled behind to collect the contraband.

'Now you see, Browny, nothing to be jealous about.'

'Sorry mate,' Brown grumbled. He grabbed Mona by the hand and pulled her inside the station.

They vanished among the late-night commuters before the Toad ever noticed his wallet gone.

Mona first met Wilson Brown when she was just 19 years old. Seeking excitement, she adored the charming traveling showman the moment she laid eyes on him across a smoke-filled Melbourne dance hall. Only in town a few months at a time, she thought he lived off spruiking show tickets and tips. But she soon came to wonder how he could afford taxis wherever they went and an endless stream of beer, smokes and sweets. Finally, she met his friends, and all became clear.

Guggenheim approached the pair on the platform as the train pulled up. 'A fine performance Miss Hayes.' He tossed the wallet at her, as well as a fresh pack of ciggies.

'Why thank you.' She bowed before opening the wallet to check out their loot. Smiles lit all three faces when they saw how much they'd made. Almost enough for a whole night of cards and booze at their favourite sly groghouse. Brown picked Mona up and swung her around like a dancer. When her feet were back on the ground, she hugged him, ripped his hat from his head and ran to the train, knocking over waiting passengers as she went.

Mona and Guggenheim commandeered a row of seats on the second carriage. Brown stood, ensuring all the ladies in the car had a seat before joining them. Mona laughed. Brown was a gentleman alright; he could rob you blind and have you thanking him as he did it. Her smile grew even brighter as she took in the passengers around them. Well-to-do Melburnians loved nothing more than a fancy charity ball. A chance to dress up in glitter and fur, sip champagne and enjoy caviar by the spoonful all in the name of a good cause. They wanted to help people – the down-trodden, the broken soldiers, the less fortunate, otherwise known as half of Melbourne. Then, tipsy on top-shelf grog, they'd hoof it home by taxi, tram, or train, ignoring beggars as they went. Yes, they were all about helping people. And Mona and her men were all about helping themselves.

'All aboard for Sandringham. Stopping all stations,' The conductor shouted down the aisles.

As the train pulled away from the station, Mona lost her balance, landing in the lap of an elderly couple dripping in jewels. 'Oh, my goodness I'm so sorry.'

The couple chuckled, helping Mona to her feet.

'No mind, dear. Would you like a seat?' The old man attempted to stand.

Mona's hands met his chest, gently nudging him back down. Her slippery fingers found his wallet. 'No, I'm fine. I've been sitting all day. I just need to stretch my legs for a bit. So long as they'll hold me!' Mona turned and continued walking to the back of the carriage. Brown and Guggenheim followed, each taking a turn with the other passengers.

During the short trip to their favourite Richmond grog and gambling house, they gained four more wallets, a gold brooch and a lady's coin purse. But as usual for them, it was in one hand and quickly out the other.

It was almost dawn before they made it back into Fitzroy. Broke again.

Mona had seen her fair share of Australia. She'd travelled with Brown and the sideshows from Traralgon through Sydney, to Bundaberg and Rockhampton. They'd seen most of the east coast of Australia, and every type of person in it. They'd spent their days playing tricks, spruiking amusements and picking pockets; their nights boozing with boxers, or dining with performers; from the great tattooed woman to the tallest man in the land. On their way out of town, they'd stop off at a few shops and take what they wanted. Watches, coats, suits and ties, even shoes.

Mona loved the lifestyle, hated being stuck in one place for too long. Yet she always returned to Melbourne. She'd found no place she loved as much. The Yarra, the cable trams, the football and the theatres – so long as the performers behaved. And discounting the poor accommodations, Fitzroy of the inner northeast was no exception. She liked the unaverage. Whenever she came home to Fitzroy, the curiosities of the sideshows gave way to thieves and drug runners. There were at least twenty hotels and grog shops within walking distance. But there were families too. Children played in the street in the evenings and gave no care to who did what for a living or who got up to what on a Saturday night. So long as you were willing to throw a ball around or kick a can, you were alright.

The Exhibition Building was one of Mona's favourites. The first time she saw it, she was just a child, her family there for a picnic. They'd sat between the fountain and one of the ponds. While her siblings fought, and her parents drank, she'd watched the ducks, fascinated. They could see worms and grubs from above water, diving down to the bottom of the pond and re-emerging moments later with dinner already half eaten. They had waxy water-proof feathers and, according to her father, magic quacks, the only sound in the world incapable of producing an echo. She now lived within spitting distance. And on the way home from nights out, she'd pass the ducks and say hello. Sometimes they'd quack back, and she'd listen to see if her dad was right.

'Browney, Mona, always a pleasure.' Guggenheim kissed Mona lightly on the nose as he departed, leaving Brown and Mona on the corner.

As they approached their Hanover Street home, a voice came from one of the yards opposite their house. 'Late night you two.'

Their neighbour was lying in her front garden with her two toddlers wrapped in blankets beside her. A small fire burned in a makeshift pit.

'The rats taken over again, Liza?' Mona asked.

The toddlers shifted in their mother's arms. Mona saw her mouth a 'yes' before she headed inside with Brown.

Their house was one of the nicer ones on the street, which really wasn't saying much. Mona's mother had always said that a girls' ambition in life should be to find a nice man and live in a house with a white picket fence. Well Mona had the white picket fence, if her mother ever cared to ask. Her man may not be the definition of 'nice', but neither was she, she supposed.

Mona and Brown subleased the back of number 15 from Gerry, a Western Market grocer. His six family members spread themselves across the front room at night, while Mona and Brown had the back to themselves. They shared the kitchen, including the insects. The house would have once been the white beauty of the street, and it still was – on the outside. On the inside, its leaking roof, water-stained ceilings and rotten floors were damn near intolerable. At least there weren't any rats.

In the dark, Brown navigated the obstacle course of tiny bodies, leading the way for Mona. Once in bed, they laid the night's meagre winnings out under candlelight.

'We shouldn't have played those last few hands,' Mona said, discreetly slipping Robson's cash under her side of the mattress.

'I hardly sold any fish today. When's your next shift at the theatre?' Brown asked.

Mona ignored the question. She doubted her boss would call the police for her earlier misadventure – a thieving usher wasn't the kind of attention he would want – but she was fairly certain she was out of a job. What was the point of an honest living anyway? Crime came much more easily to her.

She scavenged under the bed for a familiar cold rounded glass, but felt nothing.

'Sorry love, drank it all earlier.' Brown rolled over and blew out the light.

<h1 style="text-align:center">3</h1>

Mona had never been interested in pursuing a life in the suburbs. She saw the way her parents existed – her father working seven days a week so the family could barely scrape by, dodging loan sharks he'd borrowed from and hadn't paid back, her mother with a sewing needle permanently attached to one hand, a never-ending glass of whisky in the other. If Mona ever made any money herself, doing odd jobs for the neighbours or singing concerts with her music teacher, her parents made her hand it all over to help pay down their debts and keep them in drink. No, Mona didn't want any part of that. Well, except the drink. And so, she'd stayed away from ordinary relationships and had never once had a traditional date. Not until Brown.

When Mona found out he'd asked her father's permission to take her to the pictures, she almost dropped him right there. She was unimpressed that the charming, cheeky, dangerous showman she'd met in town, had turned out to be so old-fashioned. The only permission he needed was hers. He redeemed himself when instead of paying for tickets, he snuck her in the theatre's side door, smuggling liquor in his pocket while he was at it.

When Brown first brought Mona to the Albanian Club to meet his mates, their eyes lit up.

'Well, well, well, this must be the famous Mona we've been hearing so much about.' A tall, balding, lanky man reached a hand out to her.

'Nice to meet you.' Mona coughed as he blew smoke from the ripe smelling cigarette dangling on his upturned lip. Brown's friends were gathered at one of six crowded card tables. Men loitered around the dark smoky room, drinking beer out of coffee mugs, waiting for seats to open up.

'Stanley, I'm Stanley Hutchison,' he said.

Brown sat Mona at their table, causing a grumble from men still standing nearby, and leaned in close as he introduced the others. 'James Lawrence, makes boots and shoes.' Brown kicked a heel up on the table to demonstrate.

Lawrence had a dark mop of hair, a nose like a hawk and a noticeable scar, like a birth mark, beside his left eye. Mona tried not to stare at it as she turned to look at him.

'Can get you a car whenever you need it too,' Brown added before moving to the last fellow at the table. 'And this is Daniel Guggenheim.' Brown lowered his voice to add, 'You'll want to keep your purse close at all times around *him*.'

'Is that so?' Mona questioned the man. He sat with his blazer buttoned up and top hat on. Very impolite. She liked him immediately.

With a smirk, he lifted his hand above the table and a gold-plated bracelet dropped from his fingertips. The men laughed.

Mona ripped the bracelet – her own – from his hands and fastened it back on her wrist. 'How'd you do that?'

The group abandoned their game as Guggenheim, mouth hidden behind fanned cards, discreetly shared his pickpocketing tips with Mona. Hutchison and Lawrence leaned into Brown. No one needed to say so, but they were delighted with the new addition to the team. Every gang worth their salt had a decoy used to scam easy money from unsuspecting, well-to-do, men.

In only a few short hours, Mona learnt how to distract and obtain wallets from back pants pockets, side hip trouser pockets and even inside vest pockets. She'd learnt how to slip fingers into handbags while striding beside a woman and how to lift a watch from a man with a flick of the wrist. She would make an exceptional thief.

'The only place safe for a man to keep his money is the soles of his shoes, isn't that right Mr Bootmaker?' Guggenheim said.

'Not true, not true.' Lawrence strode over to where the pair had been practicing on unsuspecting late-night gamblers. 'There's a special trick, but it requires a special kind of talent.'

'And what is that?' Mona asked, certain she could learn any trick she tried her hand at.

Lawrence leaned in close and asked, 'Can you charm a man, Mona?'

His closeness made Mona uneasy. She took a step back.

Brown sidled up and put his arm around her. 'She's the most charming woman you'll ever meet.'

Surrounded by four men staring intently at her, Mona asked 'What do I have to do?'

'You don't have to do anything, just tell these blokes to get lost,' Hutchison said.

'Shut up Hutch,' Lawrence said. 'See that bloke over at that table there? Playing poker?'

Mona looked towards the plump gentleman, sitting red-faced and jubilant, mountains of cash in front of him.

'He's been winning all night. Not that he needs the dough,' Lawrence said.

'Money finds money,' Brown muttered shaking his head.

'Works at the bank. Earns more than all of us combined.'

'You know him?' Mona asked.

The men laughed.

'Not at all,' Guggenheim said. 'Another lesson for ya, Sweets, make friends with the waiters, they're a wealth of information.'

He pointed at the handsome man wiping down tables. He had a crooked bow tie and a big smile. His name tag said 'Berktash', but she'd heard the fellas calling him 'Bebe' earlier in the night. Poor bloke probably had no idea he'd helped pick their mark. She gave him a nod and turned her attention back to the boys.

'All you have to do is go over there and flirt with him a bit. Give it a good twenty minutes or so. Then invite him outside to get to know you better, if you catch my drift.' Lawrence winked. 'Take him round the alley way where no one can see, and we'll follow soon after.' The ginger game. She'd heard of it.

'I sold him some dope earlier. He's well toasted. He'll go easy,' Hutchison said.

'Can't I just pick his pocket?'

'He's got a lot of pockets,' Brown said.

'Too many,' Lawrence said. 'Best to get him outside.'

'And then what, you'll attack him?' Mona asked.

'Don't worry about that, you just do your part, and we'll take care of the rest,' Brown said.

'Or maybe you're not up to it?' Lawrence challenged.

Mona studied the men's faces. Brown didn't seem a violent man; he had always been so gentle with her. On their first date he'd actually asked permission to kiss her. Hutchison seemed harmless enough, but she wasn't so sure about Lawrence and Guggenheim.

'Promise me you won't hurt him, and I'll do it,' Mona said.

Huffing and eyerolling came at her from all directions, but she didn't care. She wasn't a woman who could be used. If she was going to charm someone for money, it would be on her terms.

'We'd never badly hurt anyone. Long as he doesn't put up a fight, he won't be hurt at all. We just want the money,' Brown reassured her.

Mona took a deep, smoke-filled breath and headed to her mark. Self-conscious, she tugged at her lace collared dress, her tight girdle beneath the black fabric pinching her waist with every step. Her heels stuck to the liquor-licked carpet as she walked, giving her an excuse to slow down, take her time, catch her breath. Knowing Brown and his mates were watching wasn't helping her nerves.

Finally, she reached him. His blunt fingers, delicate and clean, twirled his dark moustache as he waited for the dealer to finish shuffling.

'Is this seat taken?' she asked. The stool beside him had been conveniently vacated a few moments earlier. Mona didn't know if it was a happy coincidence, or if Brown had something to do with it.

Her mark grinned. 'It is now.'

Mona's cheeks flushed and eyes widened. Up close, with a smile on his face, the man was much more attractive than she'd first thought. His eyes were deep green like the baize of the nearby billiards table, but with flecks of brown in them. When he moved his head back towards the other card players, they seemed to turn to moss. She wondered what colour they were in daylight.

'Deal her in,' he instructed one of the other three men at the table.

She pretended not to notice their groans. Not many women dared enter this level of the Albanian Club, let alone sit at a card table. Most of the women were downstairs, dressed in their finest frilly frocks, tearing up the dancefloor with the teetotallers. But those with a nose for booze knew the real party was on the second floor where beer and scotch were hidden under the floorboards and cards were played for cash.

Mona's eyes drifted to the open box of Matador Cigars on the table. They'd seemingly been shared around prior to her sitting down. She raised an eyebrow at the dealer who was still lighting his, he slowly, deliberately put the lid back on the box and threw it at his feet. Normally, she would have protested, but then he begrudgingly dealt her in. She took that as a victory and lit one of her Luckies instead.

'I'm Ruby,' she said, surprising herself with her unplanned alias. Ruby had been the name of a school bully Mona once creatively retaliated against. Mona framed her for stealing Miss Buckley's Cumberland pencils causing the girl to receive ten lashings of the strap and one hundred lines on the blackboard. Mona could still see the white chalk in cursive: 'I will not steal.'

'I'm George,' said Mona's mark. 'And this is Eddie, Walt and…'

'Rog,' the cigar-hogging dealer said.

'That's right, Rog, sorry 'bout that.'

Mona smiled. The men weren't well acquainted. She could work on him without having to worry about the rest of the table cottoning on.

As they played, Mona explained that she was single and had been stood up for a date earlier that evening. 'I've been trying to make the most of things. After all, I'm dressed in a new frock and my best lipstick. I may as well get some use out of it.'

She said she'd been having a lovely night chatting to strangers and learning to play pool and cards. If any of the men had noticed her with Brown and his friends earlier, she hoped this explanation would suffice. No one seemed to catch on that she was lying – something she'd always been good at. And the act didn't stop there. She laughed at George's jokes and feigned interest in his stories. She grazed his leg with hers, partly hoping he didn't notice the run in her stockings and partly trying to gain the courage to touch his leg with her hand.

'It sounds so interesting,' she purred. Though as it turned out, his green eyes and pockets were the only interesting things about him. 'I've been looking for a job to help my family. Do you have many women tellers at the bank?'

'Not really,' he admitted. Mona slumped prompting him to lean closer, coiling his left arm around her. 'But perhaps I could find something else for you, get you an interview at least.'

'Oh, that would be wonderful, thank you. You're so kind.' Flattery got you everywhere.

Even with her limited knowledge of poker, Mona won two hands. She squealed each time, George helping her scoop up her winnings.

'She didn't even know she had a straight,' Rog grumbled.

'Now, now, you can't begrudge the lady for having a bit of beginners luck,' George said.

'Oh, they're just jealous!' Mona sensed she was quickly wearing out her limited welcome.

Eddie unknowingly helped her along when he asked, 'Isn't it about time you two called it a night? You seem much more interested in each other than the cards.'

'True,' Mona said and turned to George with shy eyes. 'Would you like to go outside for a walk?' She finally took the plunge, sliding her fingers up George's leg.

He grabbed her hand and pulled her from her chair, leading her down the stairs, past the dance hall.

She glanced towards the back of the club as they stepped outside but couldn't see Brown, Guggenheim or Lawrence. Hutchison was exchanging coke for cash in the corner. He caught her eye and gave her a reassuring smile.

As soon as the door closed behind them, George lunged at her, the force of his lips almost causing her whiplash.

She pulled away. 'Perhaps we could go somewhere a little more discreet? I'd like to come back here and don't want everyone thinking I'm some immoral woman.'

George nodded.

Mona led him around to the lane as she'd been instructed. It was much darker than the main street, no lights.

George crashed into her again, pressing her back against the cold brick wall. He forced his tongue through her tight lips, probing every inch of her mouth.

Mona counted the seconds as she reluctantly kissed him back.

One … two … three…

It took at least 10 counts before a hand clutched George's neck and threw him to the ground.

He struggled as Brown, Guggenheim and Lawrence reached into each of his pockets to steal his week's pay and poker winnings. Guggenheim punched him.

'Hey,' Mona shouted, grabbing Guggenheim by the wrist.

He shrugged her away.

'Don't struggle, George, no amount of money is worth getting hurt. Just let these brutes have their way,' Mona cried.

George listened. The attack went easier then. No more punches. Once all his pockets were empty, Lawrence ripped George's shoes from his feet and grinned at Mona as he found even more cash stashed in the soles.

'That's it,' Brown said after what seemed like an eternity.

The three men ran from the laneway. It then occurred to Mona they'd never told her what to do next.

'Are you alright?' She knelt beside George and smoothed his hair, partly to maintain the charade that she wasn't involved, and partly because she was slightly concerned.

'There's a pay phone on the corner, go and ring the police,' he said, well enough to talk sense. 'Don't use the phone in the Club, or the coppers from licensing will show up.'

'All right.' Mona ran in the direction he'd told her.

She was one street away when she heard Brown's familiar whistle.

Catching up with the men, she slapped Guggenheim so hard his hat flew off his head. 'The one thing I asked was that no-one get hurt. There was no need to hit the poor man.'

'There was no need to hit me!' Guggenheim said rubbing his cheek. 'Besides, he's not poor.'

'He is now.' Brown laughed and wrapped his arms around Mona. 'Well done, my love.'

Mona was ready to lay into Brown, too, for taking so long to rescue her from a stranger's sloppy kiss, but Lawrence's cash-filled hand cut her short.

'You did alright for a first time. Here you go, your share,' he said.

She stared down at the money in her hand. She'd made more in one night than her father made in a week. Guggenheim was right – any man who carried that much money around certainly wasn't poor.

Not only had she made a killing, but she'd gained a few favours. Mona often ran into Eddie from the table, he worked at the Windsor Hotel. He'd won every hand after she and George left, said he owed her big time. Mona reminded him whenever she saw him but was yet to cash in.

That was 1933, four years ago. They'd all been together, on and off, ever since. Her friendships with Guggenheim and Lawrence seemed to mirror the hot and cold of her relationship with Brown. When she was fighting with him – usually over his wandering eye or love of her whisky – her bond with Guggenheim grew weak. He made it clear he was Brown's friend first. Lawrence was the opposite. Any time Brown and Guggenheim disappeared from Mona's life, Lawrence came around more often. He'd bring her food, booze, sometimes even flowers. He'd take her dancing. He'd talk to her until all hours of the night about life and love and heartache. Then when she mended things with Brown, as she always did, Lawrence disappeared with his mates, like 'that bloke Sharpe' from the other side of town. Drug dealer Stanley Hutchison was the only constant in Mona's life. It was in his best interest to stay on good terms with her, she quickly became his best customer.

4

Mona slept late, waking midday to a panicked conversation between Brown and Greengrocer Gerry outside her bedroom window. They used the backyard when they didn't want to worry Gerry's wife, Esther. Mona slipped on Brown's boots, wrapped a blanket round her shoulders and waddled out to meet them.

'What's the matter now?' Mona asked. There was always something. In truth, that's how she liked it.

Gerry wiped sweat, and maybe a tear, from the side of his face. 'Landlord's on his way.'

'Rent's not due for another week,' Mona said.

'I ran into Chas last night while packing up the market. He said Bill's been doing the rounds. You know what that means,' Gerry said.

Mona nodded. It meant the same thing it always did when Landlord Bill made a surprise appearance: he was increasing their rent.

Brown groaned wiping his forehead. 'We're so far in the shit.'

The three of them jumped as Bill's fist rapped against the leaded glass of the front door. Gerry cut round the side of the house to stop Bill from knocking a second time. He didn't want Esther answering.

'Bill, well isn't this a surprise.' Gerry gave a nervous laugh as Mona and Brown joined him.

'Good, you're all here,' Bill said. 'I won't beat around the bush. Rent's up another tenner next month.'

'You've already upped the rent five times in the last six months,' Brown spat.

Bill ignored him. 'Gerry, I know you have a fine young family, but you've been late with payment a couple of times. Anyone else'd be out on the street by now. And you know how many people would be willing to pay double for a place like this?'

'Pfft. It's falling down around us!' Brown's attitude wasn't helping matters.

'Now now, Bill's right.' Mona laid a calming hand on the landlord's shoulder, urging him to look into her pleading blue eyes. 'Bill you've been so good to Gerry and the family, and to us, since we moved in'—Brown shook his head at her, begging her to shut up, but she wouldn't have it—'However, I can't deny that never knowing when the rent will increase is hurting our hip pockets. So, I have a proposition. What if in two weeks we paid you three months' rent in advance at the current rate. Would you reconsider the increase then?'

Brown and Gerry's jaws hit the ground.

Bill laughed. 'You're not gonna to be able to do that.'

'Try us,' Mona begged.

Bill looked between the three of them, weighing up his options. Three months paid in advance was unheard of in the slums.

'Alright I'll give you 'til the end of August on those terms. But if you can't pay it, from then on, you'll owe me an increase of twelve shillings a month instead of the ten, or you're out. And I'll tell you what, I'm doing you all a favour now.'

'We know and we're just so grateful. Not everyone's so lucky with their landlords.' Mona smiled.

In the time it took for Mona to shake Bill's hand and send him on his way, Gerry had just about had a heart attack. He clutched his chest, barely able to keep upright. 'Are you planning on robbing a bank, Mona?'

'Better!' Mona said.

Back inside the privacy of the house, Mona told the men about a recent conversation she'd had with Miss Tilly, a local pawnshop owner. Apparently, she was paying double for diamond rings ready for spring, when men would come in and put rings on hold for Christmas Eve proposals. Brown liked the sound of that.

'Mr Jenkin's jewellery shop on Glenferrie Road has the biggest diamond rings I've ever seen,' he said.

'From what I hear, robbing shops ain't really your strong suit.' Gerry was nervous with good reason – the last time Mona and Brown robbed an actual bricks and mortar store was almost a year ago, and Brown had spent three months in Pentridge for it.

Since then, they'd steered clear of shops, preferring pickpocketing with Guggenheim instead.

'That was then,' Mona reasoned. 'I mean, we're talking expensive diamond engagement rings here. We'd never be able to pickpocket that kind of money. Enough to get us out of the shit.'

'But for how long?' Gerry was right. The walls were crumbling, cockroaches encroaching and water seeping through the upstairs ceiling, yet they were paying more than ever. But they had no choice. Rent was increasing all around them. It was this or the streets.

'It's worth a try,' Mona said.

'If we're gonna do this, we better bloody do it right,' Gerry said, his voice dropping as Esther entered the room.

'Soups up,' she said, wiping pumpkin-stained hands on her apron. She took no time taking Gerry aside while Mona and Brown helped themselves to lunch. With the children all playing at the neighbours, there was plenty to go around.

Esther ripped into her husband in the other room. She'd been listening through the kitchen wall.

Brown laughed. 'I think we'll be doing this one without him.'

'Yes, but not without his car.'

***

Mona, Brown and Guggenheim borrowed Gerry's old Ford and drove out to Malvern. The windows of Mr Jenkins' jewellery shop faced busy

Glenferrie Road. From across the street, they observed as customers walked in and out of the store. During their two-hour watch, the shop was hardly ever empty.

'The depression never hit Malvern,' Mona said.

The number of customers posed a problem. As did the number of staff in the store – a young woman and two men worked the counter, assisting shoppers as they browsed.

'You've not only got those three watching,' Guggenheim said, 'but you've got the shoppers and bloody passers-by looking in. I don't reckon there's any way to do it without being seen.'

Brown frowned. 'The weather might make a difference. Not as many window shoppers when it's wet, maybe waiting for the right day—'

'Hang on a second.' Mona leaned forward from the back seat.

Brown and Guggenheim followed her line of sight. One of the male shop attendants left the store and headed into the neighbouring cake shop.

'I'll be right back.' Mona leapt out of the car before the men could protest, skipping across the road and into the bakery. The young man from the jewellery store sat down to a cup of tea and a scone at a corner table.

'Can I help you, Miss?' An elderly man asked from behind the counter.

'Do you have any stale cakes, Sir?' Mona asked politely.

The man smiled. 'Let me see what I can dig up for you, love.' He left Mona alone as she turned her attention back to the young man in the corner, who was settling in to read the morning paper.

'Here you go, love.' The old man returned from out back and handed Mona a paper bag filled with day-old scones.

'Thank you very much. May I ask you'—Mona leaned in and whispered—'who is that fine looking man by the window? Does he come in here often?'

The old man chuckled. 'That's the young Mr Jenkins, Charlie. He works next door, son of the owner. Comes in every day round this time for morning tea. Has a wife, I'm afraid.'

'Oh dear, what you must think of me!' Mona said. 'I didn't even notice his wedding ring. The good ones are always taken. Thanks again, Mister.'

Mona had everything she needed: a break in the day when there'd be one less shop attendant in the jewellery store and a free lunch.

For the next few days, Mona and Brown honed their craft. They stole purses from Collins Street and coats from Bourke. Always the same way. One of them distracted the sales assistant, while the other pocketed what they could. They stole enough to keep their partying going, the booze flowing and occasionally indulge in a late-night meal at The Duke. But it was the rings that would get them over the line.

One more robbery, and they'd be able to call 15 hell hole Hanover Street home for three more months.

5

'What's this then?' Brown surveyed Mona's new fur coat, stolen from Wraight's Furs on Bourke Street, a final practice run before Jenkins' Jewellery. Mona spun around to show it off right there in the middle of the street. She was dressed up, ready to party with Stan and his Hawaiian Band.

As they walked through the city, one pub after another kicked the last of their patrons out the door. It was just on six o'clock, closing time. Drunk men in suits and ties littered the streets. Barmen tossed drunkards out on their asses and waited with hoses for the vomit soon to be spewed across tiled walls. Some men headed back to their offices, others went home to their wives and children. Mona and the boys picked a few drunk pockets, loose change, for the gig.

As a child, Mona discovered that her neighbour, Mrs Hart, was a singing teacher. Mona offered to wash Mrs Hart's windows each week in exchange for free lessons. Mrs Hart was in demand, reluctant at first on taking on a new student. She insisted on hearing Mona's scales. After one afternoon singing las and mees and does, Mrs Hart quickly agreed to the lessons. She said Mona had the best range she'd ever heard for a twelve-year-old girl.

Mona took those scales very seriously. One day she sang so high she fainted. She came to with a lick of Mrs Hart's white wine. Mona's head, which she'd hit on the baby grand piano when she fell, was bruised for weeks. She felt it worth the pain, to accomplish something not many people did. She didn't know for sure what note she'd hit, just that none of Mrs Hart's other students could reach it.

Mona spent three afternoons a week locked in that room singing mostly opera but sometimes modern styles including jazz and blues. For the longest time, she preferred to sing with eyes shut, which hindered her ability to share her talents beyond the confines of rehearsal.

Once, Mona invited her parents to come along. She wanted them to stay in the sitting room and listen to the lesson through the wall, but they insisted on sitting directly opposite the piano. Mona clamped her eyes shut, but when they fluttered open between verses, she saw something she'd never seen before. Pride. In her parents' eyes. And maybe dollar signs. She sang with her eyes open from that day on. And she'd gotten very, very good.

Now, anytime Stanley Hutchison invited her along to one of his shows, she knew exactly what he was up to. Hutchison was a man of many talents. Since returning from the war, he'd kept himself busy as a hairdresser to one third of Melbourne, cab driver to the other third and coke dealer to the rest – Mona included. Yet his true love was music. And any moment he wasn't cutting hair, driving or dealing, he was playing his ukulele and teaching Hawaiian music. As a self-made music teacher, he was always on the lookout for talent. They'd all be at a party and suddenly he'd have the host playing guitar or aspiring singers round the piano. More than once, he'd called Mona up on stage at his gigs. Sometimes she loved to sing for him, it gave her a bigger high than cocaine. Other times it made her feel a failure. She'd dreamed of being a singer, yet at 25, the only concerts she ever did were thrown her way last minute by a band too drunk and coked-up to finish their own set.

'Will you give us a tune tonight, Mona?' Guggenheim slipped her his hip flask as they arrived and settled in at the Apollo. There was a boy band on first, then Stan's group, The Royal Pacific Islanders, followed by a few solo singers.

'Not a chance,' she said, not in the right mood. The spotlight on stage was giving her flashbacks to the other night, embarrassment at the theatre. And her perhaps hasty attempt for more secure housing weighed heavily on her. No, she was in no mood to sing. 'But I've worn my dancing shoes if you fancy a spin later?' She crossed her legs, pointing her black heels in his direction.

Guggenheim laughed. 'Oh, watch out!'

They'd only been in the building a few minutes before Brown left to go for a wander. Mona was beginning to realise that 'wander' didn't always mean walking. They were both stalling on the jewellery store robbery, nerves causing them to put it off from one day to the next. Bands and booze a welcome distraction for a couple more nights at least.

The Apollo was tightly packed. Between sets, Mona stood on the table to spy a clear path to the bathroom.

While touching up her powder, a woman ran in, tears running down her cheeks. Her face was blotchy, smudged mascara lined her eyes. 'Sorry, the next act started so I thought the bathroom would be clear,' she said, backing away.

'No, don't go. The act is a friend of mine, I can hear him play anytime if you'd like some company, or a drink?' Mona pulled Guggenheim's flask out of her purse and offered the teary girl a sip.

The girl reached out with a trembling gloved hand. 'Thank you,' she said before downing almost the entire thing.

Mona regretted offering it. She took it back and peered down the nozzle. 'You must have had a really rough night,' she said.

The poor girl let out a laugh and a cry at the same time. She cried even more when she spotted her reflection in the mirror. 'Oh, dear God I look a fright,' she said, hands clutching at her cheeks.

'Here, I've got some powder. It's good stuff, nicked it off the dressing table of a Broadway star.' Mona handed her the slim shiny silver package.

The girl laughed again.

'You think I'm joking? Here let me help you.' Mona smoothed the lady's hair and used one of her own pins to clip it back on the side, while the young woman painted her face in Mona's powder.

'Are you going to tell me what the matter is?' Mona asked, curiosity getting the better of her.

She spoke in jerks between sobs. 'I had my first dance with my husband here. We come back as often as we can. Tonight, my husband told me this will be our last night out for a while. He lost his job. We're barely scraping by as it is.'

Mona helped her wipe her tears and reapply the powder once again. 'It's a bugger, isn't it? I'm out of work myself. But you'll get on. We just do what we have to, don't we? It'll all work out in the end.'

Mona didn't necessarily believe that. If she knew anything, it was that things got worse before they got better. But some people were better off with a lie. This woman, a rare being capable of eliciting Mona's last drop of alcohol, was one of them.

'Besides,' Mona added, 'in my experience, crying and worrying doesn't change a thing, so you may as well not. Save the tears for the debt collector – then they might do you some good.'

The woman chuckled. 'Thank you.' She straightened up and held out Mona's compact.

Mona waved it away. 'Keep it. I don't wear it much anyway.'

The woman beamed at Mona's generosity. 'That's so kind. Thank you again. Come on, I'm sure I've bored you enough. You're missing your friend.' She led Mona out.

Mona made it back to the table in time to see Stan finishing.

Guggenheim grinned. 'You're all right, aren't ya?'

'What?' she asked.

'Stan called out for you during *Akaka Falls,* and you were still in the ladies!'

Mona breathed a sigh of relief. She needed a night of entertainment, not to *be* the entertainment.

By the time Stan finished his set, the audience was all warmed up and ready to dance. There wasn't much room in the theatre. Some couples pulled a few moves in the space between tables, but Guggenheim and Lawrence decided they needed more room. They picked Mona up off her chair. She laughed hysterically as they stood her on the table and clambered up next to her. The table had uneven legs. Mona felt as if they would topple over at any moment.

Guggenheim held his hat to his chest as he danced beside Mona. Lawrence, on her other side, grabbed her hand and spun her around. She kept her eyes on the edge making sure she didn't fall over the side. Slowly, other audience members followed suit, dancing on their own tables. More than one person fell flat onto the floor, which only made Mona laugh harder. Lawrence was attempting to spin her around a second time when she finally caught sight of Brown in conversation with a petite red head by the staff door.

Mona tried to maintain her merriment while spying. He tipped his hat, the red head touched his arm, he whispered in her ear, red head laughed. A note was slipped from her hands to Brown's pocket.

Mona's heart and feet had had enough. Guggenheim and Lawrence lifted her off the table, back onto the floor as Brown finally re-joined them.

He handed out dope from Hutchison. 'He's necking some broad backstage. We won't be seeing him tonight. Besides, I think he's miffed you stood him up Mona.' Brown winked.

'Blow it up your arse,' she snapped.

'Well, what are we stickin' round for then? We only came to see him.' Lawrence said.

They gathered their coats, ready to head for the local groghouse.

Brown nudged Mona, nodding at the woman Mona had spoken to in the bathroom. The man she was with, no doubt her out-of-work husband, had left his wallet abandoned on his empty seat as they stood up to dance. Mona scooped it up and Brown smiled approvingly.

'Excuse me.' She tapped the man on the shoulder, and he turned. She held up his wallet. 'This must have fallen out of your pocket. Found it on the chair over there. You should be more careful.'

Brown's jaw dropped and he mouthed, 'What the heck?'

She shrugged. Enjoyed pissing him off. He may have a woman's number, but he wouldn't have this wallet. Besides, they were broke. Mona preferred stealing from those with more.

6

Mona kept her eyes trained out the window of the taxi as it pulled into quiet, narrow Gordon Grove on the corner of Glenferrie Road in Malvern, the street less crowded then when they'd visited weeks earlier.

'Wait for us here, we won't be long,' Mona told the driver.

It was a cool Thursday morning, and rain threatened to break through clouds gathered above the shop line. Mona couldn't feel the cold. Heat seeped out of every pore, her heart pounding fast, body buzzing. She removed her gloves and handed them to Brown to put in his pocket, only to find she had another pair on underneath. Black lace from the night before. Mona and Brown looked at each other and laughed.

'Still too drunk to dress yourself, not too drunk to shop?' Brown posed the question with a chuckle, knowing full well they weren't about to back out now, no matter how hungover they were.

Mona answered with a grin, dripping the kind of confidence that only comes from a cocktail of experience, whisky and cocaine. She nodded towards the glowing lights in the jewellery store that lined their path. Black velvet coated the spacious window displays, gold and silver shone bright in every imaginable style of ring, watch, necklace and brooch.

As they headed into the grand white corner store, Mona glanced up at the second storey windows. She wondered if the jeweller's family lived up there. She knew of his older son, but did he have little children like Bill's?

A little silver bell above the door rang out as they entered. Mona felt a familiar mix of excitement and trepidation, like going on stage.

The sales-clerk, a slight woman with dark ringlet curls, wore a baby blue dress with a white name tag stamped 'Muriel' in gold lettering and swirls. Mona found it hard to take her eyes off the woman's perfectly painted red nails as they tapped the top of the long glass jewellery case.

'May I help you?' Muriel turned towards Brown and smiled.

Before he had a chance to answer, Mona leaned in. 'Yes, I hope so. We've lost a diamond ring which belonged to my dear friend, Miss Towel, and we want to replace it.' Mona improvised, pulling the name Towel out of the air. 'We're putting in for the expense of it. Can we see a few options between 10 and 25 pounds?'

'Certainly.' Muriel floated across the room on black pointed heels, selecting an assortment of rings from the front window and then two more from the side.

A glint of ruby caught Mona's eye as she inspected the shop – red diamond-shaped earrings surrounded by gold, emerald and silver dangly necklaces; floral inspired clip-ons; opals; and pearls. Next, the small black leather watches grabbed Mona's attention. Then her eye ran along the back wall filled floor to ceiling with grandfather clocks. Dark wood, light pine, black numerals and a multitude of metallic hands all tick, tick, ticking in unison well past eleven o'clock.

Mona noticed the store owner, the famous Walter Jenkin, watching from the corner of the shop. His snow-white hair matched his crisp work shirt. He didn't have a name tag. He didn't need one. Mona remembered him from the papers. Ads promising the best value watches money could buy and editorials boasting 100 per cent Australian-made silver goods. She also remembered him saying 'business has never been better' and 'above-average trading' while other companies were going belly up.

Mona tried a casual smile before turning her attention back to Brown. 'You can put in a few pounds, can't you?' she asked him.

In view of Jenkin, Brown removed his wallet from his vest. Mostly filled to the brim with receipts, he flicked some of the paper inside as if counting cash. To outside observers, it would appear Brown was loaded.

To Mona it appeared he hadn't cleaned his wallet in quite a long time. Paper props. Perfect.

Muriel returned to the counter and placed a small selection of rings on the glass in front of them, varying quality, size and price. One solitaire was especially small, the others weren't much bigger, although one had stunning diamantes spread right around the band.

'I can't see the difference between these two.' Mona picked up a simple round cut 10-pound ring and similar 25-pound one inspecting them closely, calculating that more than three months' rent lay in the palm of her hand. Exactly the amount they'd promised landlord Bill.

Brown shook his head. 'Neither can I. Why is this one so much more expensive?' he asked Muriel as Jenkin sidled up beside her.

'I can show you the difference.' Jenkin nudged Muriel aside as he took the two rings from Mona's gloved hand. A laced fingertip caught on one of the diamonds. Jenkin shrugged a brief apology for the pulled thread and motioned for Brown to follow him to a back room.

Mona and Brown exchanged glances. They'd expected the man to go and get a magnifying loop. While he was out of sight, they'd take the rings and run, hoping that Muriel in her dagger heels and tight uniform would not attempt to catch them. They hadn't anticipated the old man taking Brown with him.

The wall of grandfather clocks seemed to tick louder. It was now twenty-five minutes past eleven. The younger Jenkin would be back from morning tea any minute.

'Come on, I'll show you in the optical room,' Jenkin said, leading a resigned Brown behind a curtain.

Muriel quickly lost interest in Mona, after all, Brown was the man with the money. As she attended to an elderly customer in the corner, Mona was left to mull over the remaining rings lined up on the counter.

Eleven twenty-eight, tick.

Three beautiful sparklers. Little paper price tags looped around each one.

Eleven twenty-nine, tock.

Both Muriel and Jenkin were distracted, just as Mona had wanted. But if she took the rings now Brown would have a hard time talking his was out of that bloody back room.

Tick, tock.

Heart pounding, she looked up again. Muriel was still chatting with the old woman about watches, and Jenkin still had Brown trapped behind the curtain.

The clocks ticked past eleven thirty. Any minute, Jenkin's fit salesman son would return from his tea-break. To have any hope of leaving the shop with the diamonds in hand, she had to move now.

Mona's heart leapt to her throat. She thought of the red head Brown had flirted with the night before. His potential new fling. To hell with him. She swore under her breath, swiped her hand across the counter, collected the three remaining rings and ran.

Muriel shouted after her, 'Wait. Stop!'

Mona almost raced smack bang into a confused younger Jenkin, Charlie, entering the shop, his hands full of scones and cakes.

'Quick Charlie, ring the police!' Muriel said.

Mona kept running. She made it round the corner. Jumping into the waiting Blue Top Cab, she said, 'Drive me back to the city, quick.'

The clocks continued ticking in her mind, as the driver folded up his newspaper and turned the key in the ignition. 'What about the other chap?'

'Never mind about him.' She had food, board, and an entire family to worry about.

Mona grew more nervous as they drove away. She wondered if Brown had gotten out. Perhaps he'd convince Jenkin he had nothing to do with it. They'd let him go, maybe even entrusting him to bring Mona back to the store to make payment. Yes, she had no doubt, by the time she got home he would be there.

She had the driver drop her at Tilly's pawn shop. Hurrying inside, she unloaded the rings onto the counter.

Tilly pursed her wrinkly lips and shrugged her bony shoulders a couple of times before saying, 'I'll give ya two pound ten for each one.'

Mona baulked. 'Try again. Not two months ago, you told me you were paying double for diamond rings. These are worth ten each and this bigger one is 25.'

'And I wasn't born yesterdee, these rings are hotter than the business end of a pistol. Two pound ten shillings is the best I can do.'

Mona pouted. She knew none of her usual tricks would work. There was no charming such a charmless woman. She slid one of the cheaper rings across the counter.

'Give me two pound ten for this one. I'll take the others elsewhere.'

'Suit yaself, but ya won't get a better price,' Tilly cackled, pulling jangling keys from around her neck and unlocking her cash drawer. She dropped the money into Mona's hand.

Mona took her time heading home. She dreaded facing Brown after what she'd done, particularly when the whole ordeal had only amounted to two lousy pounds. The remaining rings were like lead in her pocket, a reminder of what a failure she was.

She sat down for a sandwich at a city café. As she ate, she pulled out one of the rings and tried it on. She tried to imagine what it would be like to have a man buy her a ring like it. As hard as she tried, she simply couldn't picture Brown down on one knee. After all the years they'd been together, they'd never even exchanged 'I love yous' let alone jewellery that wasn't stolen.

When she finally arrived back at Hanover Street that evening, Gerry, Esther and the girls were all sitting down to stew, but Brown was nowhere in sight.

'Evening all,' Mona said, leaning over little Shirley's bowl. The young girl never finished her dinner. She handed Mona a spoon and nudged the bowl forward. Mona took a giant slurp.

'Where's Browney?' Shirley asked. 'He was going to teach me to play patience tonight.'

Gerry shushed the girl and motioned Mona out the back. Mona could see by the state of the room that Brown hadn't been there.

Gerry placed a rough hand on Mona's shoulder. 'He's been picked up by the coppers, so I spose we're buggered.'

Mona raked her fingers over her skirt pockets, two rings still contained within.

'Sorry Gerry,' she said, leaving the rings in place.

Gerry shook his head and placed his fist against his mouth to muffle his swearing. 'What am I going to tell them?' He pointed towards the kitchen door.

Mona knew he wasn't really looking for an answer, just putting the question out into the universe. Letting it sink in before composing himself and heading back out for dinner. Mona took her trusty bottle of whisky from under the bed and tucked herself in for the night.

She awoke in a panic around 2am. Brown's side of the bed was still empty. Unable to drink herself back to sleep, Mona crept out into the main room and crawled into the corner beside the sleeping children. She watched them. The littlest girl in pyjamas dotted with tiny bunnies, hand-me-downs from one of the kids round the corner. The child hadn't grown into them yet; her hands lost, curled inside the sleeves. They reminded Mona of her own pyjamas growing up. Her mother altered her brother's for her. She also turned his old pants into skirts and showed Mona how to cinch his old shirts in at the waist. Mona had told herself that when she grew up, she'd never wear hand me downs again. Yet here she was squatting in a share house, watching children that weren't hers in a nightshirt she stole from the Myers dressing room.

At dawn, Mona dressed and left the most expensive ring along with two pound ten on the kitchen bench with a note.

'I hope this will do for now. Love Mona.'

7

'Back again Mona?' Detective Collins greeted Mona at the door of Malvern Police Station, coffee in one hand, English muffin in the other. He was barely able to contain his amusement. His crooked grin and blue eyes seemed to light up the beige on brown on beige of the woodchipped Station.

'Anything to see you again.' Mona gave him her best sarcastic smile.

'Now, now, I wouldn't want your boyfriend to hear that.' Collins approached slowly, motioning to an officer to un-cuff her. 'He's in the next room, and from what I understand, you're already in his bad books. Come this way.' He finished the last of his crumpet and led her towards an interview room.

The police had found Mona on her way home pawning the third ring at another shop. Tilly was wrong, she got double. Not that it was any use to her now.

As she followed Collins across the station floor, Mona shot a glance in Brown's direction. In the same clothes from the day before, he paced back and forth behind the glass of one of the other interview rooms.

She turned her attention back to Collins. 'What are you doing here anyway? Malvern's not exactly your area.' Normally, he was based at the Criminal Investigation Branch, CIB, headquarters in Russell Street.

'Malvern boys called for your file.' He pointed at a manila folder with Mona Hayes and the numbers 165/33 emblazoned in black ink across the front on the nearest desk. 'Figured I'd stick around.'

Of all the police in Melbourne – more than 500 assigned to Russell Street alone – Mona always seemed to run into Collins. Over the last six months, he'd seen her drunk and high, he'd seen her swear, and far too often, he'd seen her end up in handcuffs. Even so, she had a soft spot for the handsome detective.

'Your boyfriend's been claiming he doesn't know you, Mona.'

'I'm shocked.' She could already see where this was going. Brown was turning on her, perhaps rightly so.

'Don't worry, you won't be going down alone. These guys in Malvern may not know you two but—'

'It's a good thing you're here then, I suppose.' Mona shivered. She'd left her warm new fur at the house. Without it, the interview room chilled her to the bone. The room smelled of coffee, smoke and feet. She wondered how many crims must have come in and taken their shoes off. She took her time taking a seat, leaning against the edge of the wooden table in the centre of the room. Collins was a lot taller than her, but he wasn't so imposing so long as she was standing.

'Now why don't you just save us all a lot of time and trouble and tell us what you did with the rings?' Collins folded his arms across his chest and waited.

Mona simply shook her head.

'Do I really have to search you, Mona?'

'You've just been dying to get your hands on me, haven't you? At least buy a girl a drink first.'

He laughed. 'I think you've had enough to drink today.' He poked his head out the door. 'Tracey would you come in here?'

Mona didn't often encounter the female police officers, though she knew there were a few. The young officer with a low ballerina's bun patted down Mona's pockets, while Collins searched her pearl purse.

He narrated each item he pulled out. 'Pack of cigarettes, half empty.' Mona rolled her eyes and shifted uncomfortably under Officer Tracey's hands. 'Flask of'—he opened and sniffed the contents—'whisky, half empty. Coin purse, empty. Matchbox, empty.'

'Loves the sound of his own voice, doesn't he?' Mona smirked as Tracey finished her search.

'Nothing Detective.' Tracey left Collins to finish his close inspection of Mona's personals.

'Well would you look here.' His smile grew wide as he scraped the bottom of her bag to find the receipt from Tilly's Pawn Shop.

Damn! Mona slumped in the chair, readying herself to make a statement. Hopefully, a confession, an admission she'd been drunk at the time, and a heartfelt apology would be enough to get her off the hook with a fine. It had worked every other time.

Collins stood and called in the Malvern detective. He then watched from the corner as the detective took Mona's statement.

'We believe you're the girl who stole three diamond rings from Mr Jenkin's jewellers shop in Glenferrie Road, Malvern yesterday, but I must caution you that you need not answer any questions unless you wish to do so.' The detective was a peculiar looking man whose eyes blinked one at a time.

Mona glanced over his shoulder and directed her gaze towards Collins' chiselled features instead. 'I will tell you the truth and make a statement, but I will not implicate my … friend.'

'Come on, Mona,' Collins said, 'you two are like falcons, one scattering the other birds while the other swoops in for the prey. You expect us to believe he wasn't involved?'

'Sometimes the swooping falcon collides with the side of a building, or power line—' Mona forced a smile— 'What do you suppose the other falcon does then?'

'Find another mate,' Collins concluded.

She enjoyed these conversations with him.

The other detective did not. He got straight back to business. 'We don't need you to implicate him, we caught him in the store.'

Mona shrugged and readied herself to make a statement, though it seemed they likely didn't need it. At least she could try take the heat off Brown. It was her stuff up, even if he did deserve it.

The impatient cop in front of her started again. 'What did you do with the diamond rings from the shop?'

'I pawned one at Tilly's for two pound ten. I pawned another at the Mont De Piete, Elgin Street, Carlton for four pound ten. I sold the other one, and I will get it back for you.'

The detective wrote down the name of the second pawn shop in his notes before retrieving a pair of ladies' gloves from his pocket. He laid them on the table, making sure to fan out the fingers so Mona could see them clearly.

'Are these your gloves?' he asked.

'Yes,' she said. They were the same ones she'd given to Brown upon entering the shop. She wanted them back but knew it was no good asking. They had enough evidence; she may as well give them the rest. She unbuttoned the top of her shirt and slipped her fingers into her bra, producing a half-torn scrap of paper and slamming it on the table. 'That's the ticket for the ring pawned at Elgin Street, Carlton.'

The Malvern detective left with his evidence, allowing a typist into the room. Collins watched intently from the corner as Mona relayed her statement.

'I am a domestic by occupation residing at 15 Hanover Street, Fitzroy,' she said.

Collins smirked, shaking his head. Domestic wasn't what he would have called her.

She continued. 'About midday on Thursday 19th of August 1937, I went to a jewellers shop in Glenferrie Road, Malvern, and I asked the girl in the shop to show me some rings. She showed me about half a dozen, and I took three of the rings and walked out of the shop, got into a car and drove away. The same afternoon, I pawned one of the rings at Tilly's for two pound ten. I pawned another today at Mont De Piete Elgin Street, Carlton, for four pound ten. The ticket produced is the one I received for the ring. The other ring I sold to a person, but I will not mention the name. I will return the ring. This statement has been made of my own free will, and I have been cautioned that I need not make this statement unless I wish to do so. Mona Hayes. 20/8/37.'

She signed the statement, and the typist left the room leaving Mona and Collins alone.

'You'll spend the night in a holding cell, you know the drill,' he said, moving to sit opposite her.

'Yep,' she replied.

'Nice hat by the way, I've never seen you wear it before.' He reached out to touch the felt.

She flinched. 'Given to me by a friend.' Shit.

Collins removed it from her head, stroking her hat hair flat as he did. Anyone else and she'd have slapped their hand away. Collins twirled the hat around his finger before peeking inside, under the top. He pointed out the label to Mona. 'R Robson.'

She'd become one of those idiots, wearing stolen goods to the police station. 'Yes. Given to me by my friend Robson.'

Collins smirked. 'Given, not taken?'

'That's right, given. Some of us actually have generous friends, not that you'd know anything about that,' Mona replied.

Collins looked at her as if debating whether or not to challenge her. Instead, he gently placed the hat back on Mona's head, asked her to stand and led her to her holding cell. She was surprised to find it empty. Must be less crime in Malvern. She wasn't quite ready to be left alone.

'Do you know why women wear diamond engagement rings on the fourth finger of their left hand?' she asked.

Collins leaned against the doorway and responded with an eyebrow raise and a shake of his head.

'It's the only finger with a vein that goes straight to the heart,' she said.

Again, he smiled. He had the whitest, straightest teeth Mona had ever seen. 'And how is it you know that?'

She shrugged.

'If only you used that clever brain of yours for better things. Life without crime doesn't have to be dull, Mona. Think about it.'

Collins had been singing the same song since they'd first met. It wasn't long after meeting Brown that she had her first run in with him. She'd spent one lovely summer afternoon pickpocketing solo up and down Bourke Street, securing enough money to stay out all night with Brown and his friends. She'd been so proud, eager to flaunt her cash in front of Guggenheim, whom she felt she was quickly surpassing in skill. After shouting one too many rounds at the local groghouse, she was right back where she started: bored, penniless and very hungover.

The next day, she headed back down Bourke Street to thieve more money to make her way home, when a red toffee apple shaped woman began shouting in the direction of a passing policeman. 'Officer, Officer, that lady is a scoundrel and a thief! I saw her yesterday on this very street pinching a man's wallet right out of his pocket.' The woman pointed her stubby red fingers in Mona's direction.

Mona's heartbeat quickened. Luckily, she didn't have one stolen penny left in her possession. Nothing could be proven. It was her word against Apple's. Mona turned and looked at the officer, handsome in his navy uniform.

'Thank you Marm I'll speak to the lady,' he said to Apple, which seemed to settle her. He smiled at Mona, tipped his bobby hat and led her into a nearby alley away from the prying eyes of passers-by.

'I'll have you know I've not stolen a penny. You can search me if you like,' Mona said.

'That won't be necessary, Marm. We had a couple of complaints yesterday of a woman pickpocketing in the area. Described as young, beautiful, with long brown wavy hair. Wearing a polka-dotted dress and wide brimmed hat,' he said.

Mona eyed him cautiously. 'Sounds like a woman of fine taste.'

'Didn't anyone ever tell you not to wear the same outfit back to the scene of the crime?' Collins asked, practically laughing at her.

'Officer—'

'Collins, Officer Don Collins,' he said. 'And before you start with your excuses, I know it was you. Tell me why I shouldn't walk you into CIB right now and present you to the detectives there.'

He was a smart man. Mona couldn't lie to him. Bend the truth? Maybe.

'Officer Collins, I'm merely a young girl of nineteen trying to get by. I recently came into the acquaintance of a man who promised he would love and care for me. I left my family home to be with him. Instead, he has ill-treated me and implores me to steal for my living.'

Lies come easy when tinged in truth.

Mona held her eyes open, unblinking, expertly causing them to burn and well up with tears. One rolled delicately down her left cheek. A better actress you couldn't find.

Collins caught the tear with his thumb. He surveyed her with narrowed blue eyes. 'What's your name?'

She wasn't sure why she did it. Brown and Guggenheim had drilled her more than once on this very point, but instead of giving an alias she told him her real name. Something deep inside her wanted him to know it. 'Mona. My name's Mona Hayes.'

'I thought you'd give me a false name, but you haven't, have you?' he asked.

She shook her head in reply.

'In the spirit of honesty let me tell you, there have been no complaints about pickpocketing around here, aside from the one just made of course. But without a victim coming forward we have nothing to charge.'

Mona looked to the sky, shame and frustration built up inside her. Tricked by a uniform. She worried about the ribbing she would likely receive from Brown and the boys after such a misstep.

'Look, I can see you're young, and in a rough spot. Everyone makes mistakes. Promise me you'll reconsider the company you keep, and I'll let you go with a warning.'

Mona let out a heavy breath she didn't realise she'd been holding. 'A taxi fare is all I need, and I'll be home to my folks in Frankston. You have my word.'

Collins shook his head. Mona could see he was already questioning his own judgment. He retrieved his wallet and handed over her fare.

Mona smiled, thanking him for his kindness.

'I'm no fool, Mona. And I will remember your name. By the end of this month, I'll have made detective, and if you go out thieving again, I'll know about it.'

He knew about it alright. Not long after, Mona received her first arrest.

Mona only saw two options in life: the exciting kind with booze and drugs and crime or the boring kind with marriage and babies and housework. Either way, this was the 1930s, she'd struggle to feed herself, keep a roof over her head, buy the things she wanted, just like half of Melbourne. If life was going to be tough, she might as well be tougher.

Unfortunately for Mona, when it came to diamond rings, the lower court wasn't as forgiving as Collins had once been. Both she and Brown were scheduled for the higher court in September. Gaol time was now on the cards.

8

Mona didn't dare go back to Hanover after making bail. Brown would be there, and now it was looking likely he'd be headed back to Pentridge, she wasn't sure she'd come home to a welcome reception. Instead, she headed out to Essendon to sleep on Stanley Hutchison's couch.

'Heard from Mary recently?' Mona quizzed him.

Stan swatted her behind in response as she crawled into her makeshift bed by the fire. Stan and Mary were married for more than ten years. They had two children, but no one had seen hide nor hair of the kids for a while. Apparently, Mary had grown tired of Stan's late-night occupations and had taken the kids to Rutherglen to start a new life. They were probably better off.

'You sure you don't want to come out with me tonight?' he asked.

'I'm sure. Better lay low for now. And get some beauty sleep.' She rubbed her tired eyes.

'Not that you need it.' He smiled and fluffed her pillow. 'I'm meeting up with Lawrence and that bloke Sharpe, you sure?'

As curious as she was to meet the infamous Albert Sharpe, she said, 'I'll meet him next time.'

She smiled and closed her eyes, unwilling to admit the prospect of serving real jail time made her nervous. Far too nervous to spend the night riding around in Stanley's cab. She didn't need a drug charge on top of everything else.

***

She couldn't stay cooped up for too long though. Not when a day at the Caulfield races beckoned, and who knows how long she'd be free to drink and gamble, prison sentence looming.

Mona had just walked through the turnstiles and was already lining her outfit with winnings, separating each note amongst her many pockets and undergarments. She had always been lucky at the races. But it wasn't just the money she loved. She adored the flurry of the betting ring, the shouting and scuffling over who could make better odds, the sound of the horses' hooves on the track.

The races also provided an easy atmosphere for Stan to sell his wares, although today he was making more money gambling than he was selling cocaine. He stood, towering over a slight little fair-haired thing. The girl wore a very grownup lace gown but the ribbons in her hair gave her away.

'Just how old are you?' Stan asked as the girl's little fingers dug through her purse.

'Old enough,' she answered, holding out her money.

Stan looked the girl up and down with a cocked eyebrow. She caught his eyes and held them for as long as she could, unwavering, waiting for him to reach into his pocket and produce a matchbox. He remained still.

'Fifteen,' she relented.

Stan scoffed and turned back towards the track.

Mona leaned towards the girl and whispered in her ear. 'Go on home now, your money's no good here.'

The girl huffed and slinked away, her ribbons trailing in the wind behind her.

'What are you two doing? Her money's as good as anyone's.' Lawrence sidled up beside them.

'Not to me it ain't,' Hutchison said, patting a pocket on his vest. Habit. He kept photos of his children in there: his son Stanley George, seven, and his daughter Elaine, ten. The girl they'd turned away wasn't much older than Stan's own daughter.

'All you've done is give your competition another customer.' Lawrence thumped Stan on the shoulder and headed towards the grandstand. He had no mercy, no boundaries – everyone was a target. He'd committed more crimes than Mona'd had hot dinners, but had yet to serve jail time on account of his strict rule: deny everything. Unlike Mona, he never cooperated with police, and was certainly never friendly with them.

She left Stan to his bets as the totalisator bell rang out. Walking towards the Leger, she saw the little girl bum a smoke from a group of young jockeys huddled near the saddling paddock. She was seconds away from telling the girl to go home when a loud click and a flash distracted her.

'Yes, that's it, you all look marvellous.' A press photographer was snapping the well-dressed madams congregating on the lawn. They were roughly the same age as Mona. Pretty. Fresh spring pastels the style of the moment. The women twirled, their floral skirts floating in the wind. One woman's neck was adorned with what looked like at least ten strands of pearls. Mona's hand danced around her own bare neck. She cast her eyes down the dark blue of her costume. The women wore flower crowns and beautiful veils. Mona had to hold her hat down in the wind. Men crowded around the women now, wolf whistling and offering their flasks and cigarettes. Mona walked inside, unnoticed by everyone except the photographer's assistant who motioned for her to move out of the way.

Sometimes it paid to be invisible.

The Caulfield Leger, otherwise known as the Guineas Grandstand, hosted fancy luncheons and afternoon tea at every meet. There was usually an entrance fee, but Mona never had any trouble getting past the staff.

While she hadn't planned to gamble on more than the horses, she couldn't help but be tempted by a dashing young gentleman with a silk red tie staring out the window towards the course. Unusual. The Leger was generally filled with punters more interested in the type of cream being served with the scones than what was happening on the track. But Red Tie seemed transfixed as the jockeys corralled the horses into the barriers ready for The Kambrook Trial. Half-way drunk, his rich chocolate blazer was wet with spilled drink stains and his wallet dangled out the side of his pocket. It was too easy. And it would heal her hurt feelings. Those women may know how to dress, but they couldn't do this – she pounced at the man's pocket.

Mona always imagined Guggenheim narrating her thefts as she performed them. Just as he'd done the first night he'd taught her how to steal. 'An ordinary trouser pocket is one of the easiest to pick. Sidle up beside your mark, closer, that's it. Now move your hand upside his pocket lifting his wallet to the top where you can see it. Do this very quickly now, before he notices. Once it's visible, pinch it out using just two fingers. That's it.'

She took the man's wallet with ease.

It was unusual for skirts to have pockets, but Mona sewed a small pouch to the inside of every skirt she ever wore, hidden places to carry stolen money. Just as she slipped Red Tie's wallet into her pocket, someone cleared their throat behind her. She turned and found herself face-to-face with Detective Don Collins. She stiffened. Eyes wide.

'Relax Mona. I'm not on duty today,' he said with a grin. She looked him over in his navy suit and tie. His outfit matched her own. But unlike her, he looked like he belonged. The photographer should have taken photos of him.

'Now why don't you give that nice gentleman back his wallet and we can all get on with our day?' he said.

'Why, I don't know what you're talking about.'

Collins stepped closer, his voice dropping to a whisper. 'Don't make me pat you down right here in front of everyone.' He motioned towards her hidden skirt pocket, his hand grazing the fabric.

She sighed and tapped Red Tie on the shoulder. 'Excuse me, Sir, I think you dropped your wallet,' she said, handing it back to him.

'Oh my gosh. Thank you, little lady,' he shouted as if unable hear his own voice. He clumsily, drunkenly, opened the wallet. 'What can I do to repay you? Here, let me give you some reward money.'

Mona raised an eyebrow at Collins, but he shook his head. 'No, no, not necessary,' she said.

'Well at least let me buy you a drink.' Red Tie headed to the bar without waiting for an answer.

Mona shouted after him, 'And one for my friend!'

Collins chuckled despite himself.

'So, what's this off-duty business?' Mona asked him. 'I thought you coppers were always on the job?' She made no attempt to hide her appraisal of his outfit as she straightened his tie.

'Drinking, gambling, not to mention consorting with criminals. And here I always thought you were such a square. Don't tell me you actually like breaking the rules?'

He removed her hand from his chest and smiled. 'Wouldn't you like to know.'

Red Tie returned with three champagne flutes, handing one to Mona and one to Collins.

'Cheers to the honesty, and beauty, of strangers,' he clinked their glasses and downed his drink in one mouthful.

'You're too kind.' Mona charged her glass.

She eyed Collins with caution yet intrigue. She'd never seen him like this, out of context, like spying on your teachers at the market or the theatre, when all that time you'd thought they ceased to exist outside the classroom. A slew of questions formed in her mind, if blabbering Red Tie would ever shut up.

Just as Mona found a pause and opened her lips to speak, Red Tie finished his breath and began again. Collins laughed at Mona's expression, seizing the next pause. 'It's been great to meet you, but I must get back to my party. Thank you for the drink.' Collins winked and added, 'See you soon, Mona,' before retreating to his table.

Mona ignored Red Tie's incessant blathering. She studied Collins as he returned to his friends. He was one of two men, three women. One of the women leaned into him as he returned. Mona thought she caught Collins say 'no one important' in reply to the lady's question. She wondered if the woman was his girlfriend. He didn't wear a wedding ring, but a man as handsome as Collins surely wasn't alone. Mona straightened her hat and fiddled with a ringlet of dull brown hair as she watched Collins' lady sweep her blonde bob behind diamond-adorned ears. She wore a pink hydrangea tied around her wrist with twine.

Mona knew more about flowers than she cared to, thanks to her mother who loved to be out in the yard in the warmer months – usually drinking, sometimes gardening. Mona's mother had once told her that the colour of a hydrangea depended on the soil. They are generally pink or white, but when the dirt is acidic enough, they grow to be blue.

When Mona was first in trouble with the law, she resented the comments and questions from police, judges and lawyers. 'But you come from a respectable family. You're a well-educated girl. Clever. Talented. Attractive.' As if they couldn't understand how a girl who hadn't grown amongst thieves could become one herself. But she began to see that the police had a point. Most people were like those hydrangeas – the colours of their petals a reflection of the surrounding soil. Unlike Mona, many of her friends were born into crime. Sons of robbers grew to be robbers, daughters of pickpockets became pickpockets, the poor stayed poor, the rich grew richer. Mona learned early, she was an exception. A blue flower born in pink soil.

Her parents drank too much, that was true, but not as much as she did. Her parents lied to themselves and each other, but they'd never cheat and steal. Mona's siblings had become labourers and housewives. But Mona had always sought a more colourful, less conventional life. She'd just been born in the wrong garden. She'd been looking for the right one ever since.

Mona skulled the rest of her drink, said a hurried goodbye to Red Tie and headed for the door. She felt Collins' eyes on her as she left.

Outside, she was confronted by a familiar sight. She'd thought a day at the races with Hutchison and Lawrence would take her mind off Brown, not to mention help her avoid him. Yet here he was. It seemed Mona wasn't the only one taking risks while out on bail. Guggenheim and Brown were picking the pockets of men who'd bent down to help a young blonde collect the contents of her spilled handbag.

'Thank you so much, you're all so kind. I'm so very clumsy,' the woman said.

Brown and Guggenheim finished their swipe and headed to the betting ring. Mona followed.

'Who's the girl?' she shouted after them.

They turned, stunned, not expecting to see her.

'Just so you know, there are coppers all round here today. Just had a run in with Collins myself,' she told them.

Guggenheim always looked handsome when he dressed up for the races. He wore pinstripes like the New York gangsters and shined shoes about two sizes too big, which made him walk like a strutting flamingo. He smiled and pulled Mona into a reluctant hug, eyeing Brown for permission as he did so.

'Thanks for the tip, Sweets,' he said.

Brown remained still. Cold. Wouldn't look her in the eye.

'You've replaced me already?' Mona asked. She felt she was dipping her toes into boiling water. Brown certainly bubbling.

'We needed a new decoy. Our previous one was … unreliable,' Brown finally said through gritted teeth. His eyes ran over Mona's face, prettied up using three-year-old makeup left behind by Stanley's ex. She was even wearing lipstick, a rarity for her. Brown noticed. His eyes stayed trained on her painted, pouted lips.

'I don't know how many ways there are to say I'm sorry,' she started. Shocked he hadn't already exploded. He was cool, calm, she'd take advantage.

'You haven't even tried one,' Brown raised his voice only slightly.

'Well, I am sorry. You know I wasn't in my right mind. I wasn't thinking.'

'You mean you weren't thinking about me,' he replied.

But she had been thinking about him. Him and the girl he'd been chatting up.

'I mean, what the bloody hell, Mona. You knew I'd get stuck there. We could have nicked something on the way out if you'd have waited. You never bloody think do you? Never think about anyone but yourself.'

'I know, I'm sorry,' she said. 'I was on the dope and…'

'Would you two just bloody kiss and make up so we can all get on with it?' Guggenheim said.

'Get on with what?' Mona asked.

'Nothing, we're done for the day.' Brown patted Guggenheim on the back and confirmed what Mona had warned moments earlier. 'Half the CIB are inside.'

'Righteo.' Guggenheim began stuffing his pockets. 'I'll take care of Elise,' he said and sauntered off to find the young blonde.

Mona wanted to ask again who she was but thought better of it. She didn't want Brown to take her back, just for him to forgive her. She didn't need enemies. Neither did he.

They stood in silence for what felt like an eternity. Brown gave into temptation, stepped towards her and reached out his hand. He lightly touched her lips.

'Looks nice,' he said of the orangey-pink colour now on the pad of his thumb.

'It comes off on everything. You should've seen my champagne glass earlier,' she said.

'Thanks for the warning.' He was softening now. She could see his whole body relax, joint by joint, muscle by muscle. His beautiful brown eyes finally met hers. 'Let's get outta here.'

Mona knew this would be their last night together. She savoured every moment. Skipping over a rat scurrying towards Nicholson Street. Walking hand in hand past the other slums of Hanover. Dodging the little breathing bodies of the sleeping children spread across the living room floor. The clatter of Brown's keys hitting the kitchen table. His hand around her waist as they shuffled drunk into the bedroom. His quick fingers on her buttons. The familiar taste of the sweat along the side of his neck. His moan as they fell on the bed. The feel of his calloused hands softly holding her hips. The scrape of her nails across his chest.

In the dark, Brown asked a question he'd never asked before. 'Do you love me?'

Mona wondered why he was asking now. Had her behaviour at the jewellery store revealed her true feelings, or lack thereof? She replied not by answering, but by returning the question, 'Do you love me?'

'Of course.' His voice turned to gravel as the sun came up. He often lost his voice towards the end of a long night on the grog. The room didn't smell like him, and she wondered how long it had been since he'd been home. While she'd been at Hutchison's, where had he been?

'You've never said it before,' she replied.

'Maybe I don't say it with words, but I tell you I love you every day. I've looked after you haven't I? I've taught you things. I've taken the rap for you many times.'

'Neither of us is going to gaol,' Mona said.

'We'll be lucky to get away with six months.' His voice was no more than a whisper.

She smoothed her hand over his hair in the way she knew he liked. It coaxed him to sleep. Mona lay motionless. Brown had done prison time before, and his stories about Pentridge made Mona nervous. She couldn't lay awake with those thoughts circling her head any longer. Spying her things boxed up in a corner, she cherry-picked her fur coat, makeup kit and a bundle of clean clothes and crept out of the room.

As she left, she realised she never answered Brown's question. She'd spent almost every day of the last five years with this man. But Brown wasn't her true love. He was her train out of the suburbs, her ticket to the sideshows, and a more exciting life. She was his sidekick, and he was her friend and lover but not her love. She assumed, rightly or wrongly, that when she met her true love, she'd know it. Right away. Like a lightning bolt from the sky. And she would have him and love him and he would love her back. Life would never be the same.

9

'This is it, Miss,' the taxi driver said. Mona remained frozen in the back. She watched as Brown walked right past the cab, tipping his hat to the Malvern policemen. They took that as their cue to stub their cigarettes on the wall of the courthouse and head inside. She couldn't see Collins amongst them.

'I said we're here, Miss.'

'Just one minute please,' Mona said. She craned her head to survey the street. The court loomed large, casting shadows across the road, ready to swallow her up. She'd never admit it to anyone, but she was terrified. She'd been to court before of course. That was part of life – the life she'd chosen anyway. Everyone she knew in Melbourne had been to court, served time, life is life is life. But serving time hadn't ever been her life. Now, she was about to lose at least six months to a prison cell. She waited for her brain to connect with her body. Willed her hand to open the door handle. Step outside. Face the consequences of the life she'd chosen. Instead, she said 'Drive on Sir, to Richmond please. I've changed my mind. I won't be going to court today.' She tried not to look at her driver, who was staring at her disbelievingly in the rearview mirror.

'Didn't think you could change your mind 'bout such a thing,' he said with some amusement. 'Are you sure Miss?'

'Yes, drive on.'

She caught a glimpse of Collins as she slunk down in the cab, and she thought, for just a second, that he saw her too. He stubbed his cigarette out in the gutter, checked his watch, fiddled with his tie, then turned to walk inside. She wasn't sure how she'd missed him before. He stood out amongst the crusty old lawyers, frantic journalists and crooked-looking crims milling about. His good looks set him apart from the cops of Malvern. Women walking out of the courthouse did a double take as they passed him, some even stopping to stare. It took everything in Mona not to stare too. The cab was at a crawl.

'Ya have an address for me love?' the driver finally asked.

Mona wasn't sure where she was going. The police knew her old place at Fitzroy, they also knew her friends. No doubt they'd be out looking for her soon and they'd stop in on Guggenheim first, then Hutchison's place at Essendon. They may not go to Lawrence, police found him notoriously difficult, but she didn't want to take any chances. After various unsuccessful stops at the doors of old friends and dealers, she had the driver drop her at Betty's groghouse. Perhaps if she offered to bring in some wealthy clientele, she could spend a few days on the cot in the kitchen. All she needed was to go unnoticed by police for another week or two. She could meet up with the showies in Flemington and go on the road with them. Parties with world-class acts, dancing and flirting with showgoers and the boys from the boxing tent were just what she needed. That was her way out. Maybe this time, she'd even find the nerve, and someone willing to allow her, to sing.

'Two pound fifteen Miss,' the taxi driver turned in his seat, reaching his long arm across the back, blocking her way to the door handle. It was almost as if he'd been expecting Mona to argue the fare. He was right.

'Can't be! You've jacked up the price,' she said, sliding to the other side of the cab. He caught her on that side too.

'I've been driving ya round all day and night. Two fifteen,' he said as he batted her hand from the door.

She'd spent most of her cash at the last stop, a cafe round the corner had sold her a night's worth of cocaine. Desperate times called for desperate measures. She shrugged herself out of her new fur coat.

'This coat is brand-new and worth far more than two pounds,' Mona said holding the beautiful brown fur out to him.

'What the bloody hell do you think this is? I take cash, not coats.'

'Consider it a deposit. See here, I work here. By night's end I'll have more than enough to pay you for your troubles. Meet me here in the morning, bring the coat along and I'll throw in an extra pound,' Mona was pleading now.

'Alright, alright,' he relented taking the soft fur in his hands. Mona opened the door and hopped out with a wave and a smile.

'See you first thing.'

***

She spent the night wandering around Richmond bringing gentlemen with full pockets into the groghouse. Lawrence stopped by late in the evening. He told her that Brown had defended himself in court and spent the trial trying to convince a hung jury that Mona had been behind the whole thing. He was just a pawn, unaware she'd planned to rob the shop all along.

Lawrence did his best Wilson Brown impersonation. Bowing his head, furrowing his eyebrows, softening his voice. 'I did not know she was going to steal the rings. I would not go and practically lock myself in a back room, where I would not be able to get out, if I thought she was going to steal the rings.' Mona could see that Lawrence was trying to get a rise out of her, but she wouldn't give it to him.

'That all matches up with what I told the police, I told them he didn't know what I was up to. So good, at least one of us should get off,' she told him. He seemed annoyed by her lack of anger and soon left for a more dramatic evening on the other side of town. Yet Mona was hurt deep down. Part of her thought Brown might have fallen on his sword for her.

The next morning Mona raced to the nearest newspaper stand. There she was, Page 14 in the Law Courts section, amongst articles about 17 year old 'lone wolf' thief Kenneth Raymond Jones and the tale of the drunken former police constable.

'Stealing charge, woman absconds from bail.' She skimmed through, aware she was already late to meet the cab driver. There was a warrant out for her arrest. Brown had pleaded not guilty, and blamed her, just as Lawrence said. The jury was hung, having failed to agree, and he was remanded for another trial. She folded the paper and held it in front of her, partly covering herself in Betty's borrowed silk slip. She hadn't even had time to dress properly. Her hands shivered in the morning cold as she fumbled around in her purse for four pounds. She was feeling generous and imagining her fur coat wrapped around her cold shoulders soon enough. But the taxi driver never showed.

***

Mona was surprised when Collins didn't take the seat in front of her. Instead, he circled the small space of the interview room. The fur coat she'd left with the driver was folded neatly on the table, he'd dobbed her in.

'Is this your fur coat Mona?' Collins asked, still standing.

Mona thought about Lawrence and how he'd never admit to anything. Yet she'd always found it impossible to lie to Collins. Besides, regardless of the coat, she was going to goal. So there was no point lying now.

'Yes,' she said.

'It's been identified as the coat stolen from Mr Wraight's fur coat shop in Bourke Street in July,' Collins said.

'I'll make a statement,' she said.

'Do you know how much this coat is worth Mona? With this on top of the rings, not to mention skipping your court date, you could be in real trouble here.'

'I said I'd make a statement.' Unexpected tears burned their way down her cheeks. It was as much a shock to her as it was to Collins, to see her cry. She swiped at her face. Collins reached out and stilled her hands.

'You know, in here, like this, it doesn't even look that pretty, does it?' Mona said of the offending item laid between them. Collins nodded. He retrieved a pad and pen from his top pocket and waited.

'I am a domestic by occupation and I reside at 15 Hanover Street Fitzroy. In July 1937, I cannot recollect the date, but I went to Wraight's Fur Shop in Bourke Street in the city and I saw a girl in the shop talking to another woman. In the shop I saw a fur coat hanging up. I picked it up and walked out.'

She then recalled how she'd used that same coat as payment for the taxi fare.

'Why did you do it Mona?' Collins asked. Mona shook her head. 'Come on, something to tell the judge, he might go easier on you.'

Mona was stunned. She was all ready to accept a prison sentence as inevitable, and here was Collins trying to give her hope. Maybe he was full of it. Maybe not. She chose to have faith. She'd never blamed her love of booze or drugs for her behaviour before. But it sure sounded better than simply admitting she liked the thrill of a steal. She wanted what she wanted when she wanted it. Yet she said:

'I have been mixing with the wrong type of people, a woman whom I know takes dope and I fell victim to it. I was not used to taking dope and this made me steal,' she said.

Collins put his pen down and read the statement over. Then he asked her again. 'Why really Mona?'

She sighed. She knew he was asking with honest curiosity. He couldn't understand her. How could he? He'd never felt that impulse, that compulsion that drove her.

'Don't you ever just want?' she asked him. He bowed his head. 'I want things,' she continued.

'Like warmth in winter?' he questioned. Mona didn't want him to feel sorry for her.

'Coats, rings, cash, some people have more than their share. Why shouldn't I get mine?'

While the Judge sentenced Brown to six months in Pentridge, Mona begged for leniency.

'I can only ask your Honour to give me a chance. I do not intend to carry on like this any longer.' Mona had no intention of changing, she turned on the best performance she could muster.

'You are a young woman who has, I would think, quite a lot of ability and good appearance, and if you can just separate yourself from some of your companions you would make good.' The judge looked in the direction of the gallery, a nun seated by the door nodded her head. 'Are you prepared to go to the Convent of the Good Shepherd if I think it proper to let you go there?' Mona hadn't anticipated this. A saving grace.

'If I'm not released on a bond, I would prefer to go there rather than prison.'

'I am very conscious of the effect upon a woman of a sentence of imprisonment and the danger of both moral and physical wrong which may follow. Considering the whole of your case what I propose to do is this, that on entering into a bond to enter the Convent of the Good Shepherd at Abbotsford and there to submit yourself to the direction and obey the orders of the Mother Rectress of that Institution for a period of six months I will suspend passing sentence upon you, but I warn you that if you break your bond, that is to say, if you do not enter the Convent or you do not submit yourself to the discipline there and you come before me I will send you to gaol. This is the last chance you will get.'

Mona was led to the back of the court where a nun waited. Without a word she turned, fluttered her hand beneath her long black robe, beckoning Mona to follow. Outside the court Mona could see Brown and a line of other men handcuffed, being led to a bus headed for Pentridge. She knew then, that would be the last she'd ever see of him, his head bowed, dark hair scruffy and grin crookedly aimed in another crim's direction. She felt lighter once he disappeared inside the bus. Maybe a fresh start at the Convent was just what she needed. Maybe her life could be different. She silently thanked the judge for seeing fit to let her off so lightly. While Brown was hitting bricks in the yard at Pentridge, she'd no doubt be taking things a lot easier with the sweet nuns of Abbotsford Convent.

10

Sister Leoni barely said a word in the cab. Mona gazed sorrowfully out the window as they passed more than one brewery on the way round the bend. She thought it must have been some twisted form of torture on Sister Leoni's part - to lead her straight past the lure of alcohol before delivering her to boredom.

A wall wrapped around the Convent grounds - like a prison. The nun accompanied Mona up a rocky path as darkness fell, leading her to the grand wooden door of the main building. When Sister Leoni knocked, a little peephole opened revealing two bright beady eyes on the other side. The eyes moved swiftly from Mona to Sister Leoni and back. The peephole slammed shut and the giant door swung open to reveal the puffy red face of an angry nun.

'You're late, you've interrupted supper.' The smell of baked bread, roasted meat and potatoes wafted out the door. Mona's empty stomach grumbled.

'Apologies Sister, I'll take her straight over to Sacred Heart and get her settled.'

The angry nun huffed and handed Sister Leoni a kerosene lamp before slamming the door. Sister Leoni led Mona around the side of the building, the lamp light barely illuminating the path in front of them. Mona lifted her head long enough to see mist rising off the river like a scene from *Island of Lost Souls*. Fitting.

The rattle of the Sister's keys cut through the uneasy silence as they approached a locked gate. Sister Leoni motioned for Mona to walk through first. They entered an enclosed courtyard. Mona's eyes trailed along the building in front of them as the Sister locked the gate behind. Her heart pounded with fear and regret now. This was just like a gaol, and Sister Leoni a guard.

Mona looked up at the building in front of her and spied a young curly-haired girl staring down from one of the second storey windows. Her angelic face and light hair lit up by the lamps inside.

'Come along now. It's almost lights out,' Sister Leoni ushered her into the building, Mona now knew was Sacred Heart, and up the stairs to the dormitories.

'Your bed is made up with clean white linens and your uniform has been laid out for you. Lights out in five. I'll take you through the rest tomorrow.' She nudged Mona into the long wooden hall lined with two rows of single white beds.

'They're all white. Which one's mine?' Mona asked but Sister Leoni was already gone.

The other girls pretended not to notice as she made her way to one of the few empty beds at the far end of the room, but she could feel their eyes on her.

'Wonder what she's here for,' whispered one.

'Drunk, trouble or crazy?' Others placed bets.

She changed into her bed clothes as it dawned on her; she may be all three. Mona tried to settle in as best she could, feeling every spring of the mattress beneath her.

'I know you.' A soft whispery voice came from the bed beside her. Mona turned and found herself face-to-face with the curly-haired girl from the window.

'Do you now?' Mona rolled her eyes. She guessed the girl would have been about 17, maybe younger. The girl's light eyes sparkled as she sat up, crossed her legs and tilted her head to examine Mona more closely.

'Yes, I think so, you were the usher who was working the night I sang with Roy Robson. Isn't that right?'

Mona felt the blood rise to her face. 'You were there? On stage?'

The girl nodded.

'I was in the chorus. Not that you could see me. I've a pretty decent voice but two left feet. They had me hidden up the back behind the better dancers. So, it *was* you, wasn't it?' she was giggling now, like a gossiping schoolgirl.

'My God, you have bloody good eyesight for a left-footed chorus girl.' Mona's voice dropped mid-sentence as a nun entered and dimmed all the lamps.

'I'm Mary. I'm here til Christmas – or so my folks say,' she declared reaching out her hand to give Mona's a shake.

'Mona.'

'And what name have the nuns given you then?'

'Huh?'

The girl explained that everyone who enters the Convent is given a saintly name they must answer to. Mona could already tell this was going to be an issue. There was a reason she could never stick to an alias, though she'd tried many in the past: Mona, Lena, Ruth. She had a shocking memory on account of all the drugs and alcohol. Maybe sober she'd do better, but she doubted it. Remembering two names for every girl would be near impossible.

'Mary, hey?' Mona mused. 'I'll call you Curly because I love your curly hair.' Not giving the girl a choice. 'Do you have a problem with that?'

'Surely not Moe,' Curly giggled and settled into sleep.

Mona lay awake all night, the thirst for alcohol keeping her up. She considered her options - as if she had any. She'd heard police chatter about girls escaping the Convent, it couldn't be that hard. Perhaps she could even just sneak out in the evenings without the nuns knowing, like she used to when she was little. Back then she'd be out the window the minute her parents' heads hit their pillows. She'd go out to parties, drink all night, get into all sorts of trouble, and be back sleeping soundly before her family woke. Just the thought of it was making Mona restless. She hadn't had a drink since a sneaky swig at the courthouse. There was no way she'd make it six months and she knew it. If the nuns didn't drive her to madness, Curly's snuffly snores sure would.

***

Mona's head pounded furiously as the assaulting early sun filtered through the windows to the tintinnabulation of bells. There was a flurry of activity as girls raced to get themselves ready for 6am Mass.

'We have prayers first thing before breakfast,' Curly explained.

'I don't go to church,' Mona mumbled and rolled over, burying her face in the pillow unable to dull the ache of withdrawals reverberating throughout her body. She'd sweated so badly in the night she'd gotten tangled in her nightdress. Every twist of fabric scratching against fiery skin.

'All our girls go to church Patricia.' Sister Leoni was by her bedside, peeling Mona's damp blanket back and nudging her out of bed.

'Patricia! Oh, I think I'm going to be sick.' Mona sat up and rubbed her eyes willing them open.

'You'll feel much better after breakfast.' Sister Leonie ran through the Sacred Heart schedule as Mona dressed.

Mass, breakfast, laundry, lunch, laundry, dinner, bed. Rules too. No gossiping, no asking questions, do only as you're told. Were they not meant to be in a place of God? It all sounded very much like hell to Mona.

All the girls marched silently, tiredly, behind Sister Leoni to Mass. Mona felt out of body, desperate for booze.

'You seemed distracted in Mass.' Curly whispered as they lined up for breakfast in the refectory later that morning. The occasion marked by more bells. Bells Mona would have to get used to in the Convent. They would ring incessantly, signalling a change in task, non-stop, throughout the day.

'I was singing the full *Strike Up The Band* set list in my head,' Mona said. She'd been trying every trick in the book to stop herself thirsting for alcohol. Remembering lyrics, imagining how she'd sing them, was the strategy she'd settled on for the morning.

Excitement built among the girls in line. Curly stood up on tip toes to see to the front of the pack.

'Oh my gosh, you came at the right time Moe, we have boiled eggs this morning. I haven't had a boiled egg since I've been here. Doesn't get much better than this.'

'God help me.' Mona moaned, splayed hands across her temples.

'He will if you let him dear.' One of the nuns floated down the line shushing the girls as they each took a table. Curly led Mona to a corner spot and motioned to a little drawer where the butter was kept in a dish.

Mona surveyed the room. Now that she was getting used to the dull throbbing of her head, and was out of song lyrics, she could properly appraise her surroundings. She guessed there were at least a hundred girls, but she wasn't about to count them to be sure. She was by far one of the oldest in the group. She wondered if many of them, like her, had chosen this place over Pentridge, and how many would make the same decision if given the choice again.

As the nuns settled at a table on a rise in the back, girls around Mona began whispered conversations to each other. Most trying hard not to move their lips as they spoke while the nuns watched on shushing every noise they heard. A tall red head plopped herself into the chair beside Curly.

'What's her story?' she asked Curly. Before Curly could respond Mona bit back.

'I'm not deaf or mute Red, you can direct your questions to me.'

The red head smiled but stayed silent until Curly formally introduced the pair.

'Moe this is Agnes, Agnes this is Mona - the nuns have called her Patricia.'

'Bad luck Patricia,' Red smiled. Mona didn't much care for the name 'Agnes' either.

'I've been called worse,' Mona replied.

'So, what are you in for? You've got to be what, thirty-one? Thirty-two?' Red asked leaning in to hear the answer.

Mona almost spat out her toast.

'I beg your pardon, I'm twenty-four years old!'

'You look older,' Red shrugged, dipping a toast soldier into her runny egg.

'Well, I suppose I've packed many more years into these twenty-four.' Mona had never been so offended in her life. But even she had to admit, the lifestyle she led had aged her quite a bit. Her skin sallow, eyes tired, wrinkles forming at the corners years earlier than scheduled. Maybe there would be some benefit to this break from drinking and smoking and drugs.

After breakfast Sister Leoni walked Mona past the laundry and steam rooms to the back of the building.

'As one of the older, stronger, girls in here, you'll help unload the sheets when they arrive and you'll fold, pack and load the fresh ones too. The truck pulls up here,' she motioned out the side door. 'It's important that sheets from each hotel remain separate, don't mix them up. Between trucks you'll be in the ironing room. Move onto the next task with the bell. Novice Anne will supervise you.'

Sister Leoni left Mona outside with Red, a scrawny 25-year-old named Cecilia, and the Novice Anne. Mona assumed that Novice meant Sister in training. She didn't wear the black habit like the other nuns. Instead, she was dressed all in white. They stood silently for a while, shuffling their feet. Cecilia spun in circles with her arms out. Red rolled her eyes and glanced in Mona's direction. They stifled their laughter.

Mona saw relief flood across Anne's face as a white van appeared at the gate. Anne strode towards the van unlocking the gate to allow it in. It did a u-turn so it could back in towards the loading bay where Mona and the girls were waiting. Two young, fine-looking men stepped out of the vehicle. The one who'd been driving stopped in his tracks when he spotted Mona. He had brown hair and bright blue eyes. His nose was crooked, as if broken in a fight. While the other young man opened the back doors of the van for the girls to start unloading, crooked nose cutie sidled up to Mona. 'Hi I'm Charles, or Chuck is what my friends call me,' he said, lowering his head shyly.

'Patricia,' Anne called from around the back of the van. Mona smiled at Chuck and went to help the others unload. There were mountains of sheets stuffed inside marked bags. Hotel Windsor, Menzies, Royal Mail, Chevron. Ships and hospitals too.

Once all the sheets were in the trolley Mona turned back to the men. 'I'm Mona - the nuns call me Patricia but I'd rather die than answer to that.'

Chuck smiled while the other man held out his hand to shake hers. 'Robbie. Guess we'll be seeing a lot of ya,' he winked.

'Patricia we're not here to socialise. Now please, we need to get this into the laundry and collect the fresh ones,' Anne admonished Mona and to the men, 'we'll be back in a moment.'

Chuck and Robbie leaned up against the truck and waited. Mona put all her weight into pushing the laundry cart inside. It took all her strength, alongside Anne, Red and Cecilia. They could have used ten girls, and it still wouldn't have felt enough. They left the trolley with the girls at the entrance of the laundry and exchanged it for another - this one packed with clean sheets. By the time they'd pushed it outside to the waiting van, Mona was exhausted and the day had only just begun.

11

Though Sister Leoni's first rule of the Convent was never to gossip, young Novice Anne didn't seem to monitor this too closely. Conversations were quiet and often chopped short by the bloody bells, but by the end of Mona's first day she'd learned a lot about the girls she was sharing a dorm with. Curly's parents admitted her after finding her in a compromising position with a boy well below her class, a gravedigger's son, the scandal! Red had been caught up in a brothel raid, and Cecilia was what Red called a 'lifer' at Abbotsford since childhood. Mona worked in the ironing room next to Martina, a scary looking young woman with long black spikey hair. She'd thrown her baby off a bridge some years earlier. And short-haired, four-eyed Philomena was a coin counterfeiter. While the youngest girl Mona met, Lucy, thirteen, had been branded a 'harlot' by her family when she fought off her married uncle as he tried to force his way into her bed.

That first day, Mona changed her own story with everyone she met. And did she have fun coming up with stories. An affair gone wrong, a case of mistaken identity in the courts. She couldn't tell whether Novice Anne knew the truth of her or not. Mona thought perhaps the no gossiping rule was more for the nuns' benefit - maybe they just didn't want to know. Mona couldn't blame them. She wasn't sure how she'd ever shake the image of a crying baby grasping for his mother's arms, being hurled like garbage into the swirling river below.

In the dinner line Mona noticed a couple girls sneak Jaffas from the hems of their smocks.

'What's that about Curly? Can you sneak stuff in here?' Mona asked.

'One of the nuns does. She has a little hole in the wall round the other side of the Convent.'

Mona's spirits began to lift as Red raced up beside them.

'Don't get too excited, it's just sweets, nothing more.'

'Why, you're just full of good news aren't you, Red,' Mona said.

Red laughed and approached a few of the other girls. She whispered in their ears and pointed to Lucy. One of the girls smiled and nodded handing a red ball to the little girl.

'The nuns don't just have Jaffas you know. There's Freddos too and Cobbers and…'

'Unless there's whisky on that list love, please shut up.'

With all these criminal and deviant minds around, how was it possible no one had figured out a way to get anything more exciting than Jaffas into Sacred Heart? Mona joined Curly and Red for soup and quizzed them further.

'So, there's no one selling ciggies or sneaking in anything other than sweets?' Mona asked.

'Well, there was one girl some years ago who handed out favours to the delivery drivers in exchange for dope. Apparently, the nuns figured it out pretty quickly. The coppers came and took the girl away and the blokes lost their jobs. That's why now all deliveries are supervised,' Red divulged in a low whisper.

'I never heard that,' said Curly.

'Like I said, was a while ago. Before our time. I heard about it from Helena, you know, that nurse that did abortions? She told me right before she left. She was the oldest duck in here, been around for years. Most of the nuns we're stuck with now haven't been here as long.'

Mona didn't want to let on just how interested she was to hear this.

***

Convincing young men to do things for her had never been a problem. And distracting a novice nun should be easy enough. It was winning over the other girls that would be a hurdle. She didn't have a lot of recent experience with female friends, her company dictated by Brown.

Curly, on the other hand, was beloved by each and every one of the girls in the Convent. In the last twenty-four hours Mona had seen one sneak her an apple, another offer her a chair and a nun allow her a fifteen minute break from the steam room. But Curly wasn't given these things by manipulation or trickery. She was simply pleasant and well liked. Mona saw potential.

'What are you thinking Moe?' Red's raised eyebrows said it all.

'Never you mind your pretty red head.'

'Oh come on, you're a schemer, I can tell,' said Red.

'All in good time.' The sweltering steam from the laundry had Mona sweating out the last droplets of grog and drugs from her body. Her skin tingled, breaking out in bumps she hadn't had since she was a teenager. But now, now she had hope. Mona went straight to work.

When the delivery truck arrived the next day, Mona was pleased to discover the same men behind the wheel. She smiled at Charles and he smiled back. Novice Anne watched on like a hawk.

'Patricia let's get moving,' she said.

Mona tried for days and could never seem to get any time alone with the men, Anne was always there, always barking orders. It didn't take Mona long to learn that if the sheets didn't get done before dark, the nuns would stay behind in the laundry, working into the night. The nuns tried to ensure this didn't happen often, so they ran everything like clockwork.

If Mona was going to sneak anything into the laundry, she needed to get around Novice Anne.

One morning Mona, Red and Anne were watching Cecilia put on her usual delivery dance, when one of the older nuns ran out in a fluster.

'Novice, we need you in the steam room,' she said. Not waiting for a response, the nun bolted back inside, expecting Anne to follow. Half in a run, Anne turned to Mona and the girls.

'Proceed as usual girls; I'll be back as quick as I can.' She disappeared inside.

Mona, curious to find out what was happening, instructed Red to wait with Cecilia while she went to look. As she snuck into the steam room, she could see about fifty girls crowded in a circle. Lucy spotted Mona and came running over.

'What's happening over there, little one?' Mona asked.

'Isabel's having some sort of fit,' she said. 'Do you think she'll be okay?'

The little girl looked terrified, her big green eyes wide with building tears and panic. Mona put a hand on the girls' head.

'I'm sure she'll be fine. The nuns will take care of her.'

With a wink Mona breezed back out towards the loading dock just in time for Robbie and Charles to arrive.

'Where's the Novice this morning Mona?' Robbie asked as he lifted a load of sheets onto the trolley.

'Inside. A girl's having a fit on the floor,' Mona said.

'Oh, is it Issy? She's had those before. She's sick in the head poor bloody thing,' Red said with a shrug. 'Anne was a nurse before she came here. She knows what to do.'

Mona tried to hide her smile, but Charles caught it.

'You don't seem very concerned for your friend,' he nudged her side with his elbow.

'Surely I am. And yet, this gives us a few moments alone for once. Can't help but smile at that.'

'You ladies like a smoke between loads?' Robbie asked pulling a tin of Egyptian tobacco from his pocket, three cigarettes already rolled.

Cecilia jumped up and down 'yes please,' she said clapping her hands together.

Mona popped a cigarette in her mouth and waited for Charles to light the match. He leaned in close and as she locked his gaze he blushed.

'You boys know Eddie at the Windsor?' Mona asked the men as casually as she could.

'Eddy Bye you mean? Works the kitchen?' Robbie asked.

'Yes, that's him. I imagine you run into him when making your deliveries,' she said and both men nodded, Charles looking uneasy. 'Do say hello to him for me the next time you see him.'

'He your fella Mona?' Robbie asked. Charles looked down and shuffled his feet from side to side waiting on her response.

'Gosh no. I'm a single lady,' Mona said. 'Mr Bye is a friend. And he owes me a favour. Tell him I expect to collect very soon.' Relief flooded over Charles, as did common sense.

'I expect the Novice won't be much longer,' he said.

The girls dropped their cigarettes and stomped them out with their feet. Robbie bent down and picked up the stubs. Charles was right, they'd run out of time. Novice Anne greeted the girls just as they wheeled the trolley inside. She didn't seem to notice the smell of smoke on their uniforms, nor did she question why they'd taken so long unpacking the sheets.

Over the course of the next few weeks, Mona went to work befriending the other girls of Sacred Heart.

She knew Red would be up for a caper, but could she keep her mouth shut and avoid word filtering back to the nuns?

'Red did you hear about Genevieve?' Mona cornered her on the way into lunch. Soup was on the menu again, thickened with the mornings' leftover oatmeal, and some of the girls were kicking up a stink at the front of the line.

'No,' Red leaned in, ready as always for any sort of gossip.

'Apparently, she got into Sister Winefred's snack cupboard. Nicked a whole jar of peanut butter. She said she'd let me have some with my bread tomorrow.'

Mona knew just how much this news would mean to Red who had been complaining about spoiled butter every day since Mona had been there.

'I love peanut butter,' Red said.

'Well you can't say anything to anyone, not even Gennie, not until she offers it herself. She doesn't want the nuns finding out. Promise you'll keep this under your hat?'

'Oh alright, but only if you promise to share, assuming Gennie doesn't give me any,' Red bargained.

'Of course,' Mona said. And she waited. She gave it a good twenty-four hours before testing the waters.

In the evenings a woman named Priscia, sentenced for biting a policeman, stood watch over the bath line. 'Mary, you're next,' her voice rang out through the dorms.

Mona wasn't sure whether the role of 'bath keep' was earned or self-appointed. This was just the second time since Mona had been at Abbotsford that they'd run a bath.

'Geesh you know things are bad when you can actually smell yourself,' Mona called over the partition as Curly got in the tub.

'You don't smell that bad,' Curly said. 'No worse than the rest of us.'

'Now don't lie to the poor girl,' Priscia said.

'Speaking of the finer senses - I don't know how much longer I can stomach that god awful butter in the refectory. Have either of you heard anything about peanut butter?' Mona asked.

Priscia snickered. 'You've been here no more than a couple weeks. You think you're so much better than the rest of us don't you?'

'Better than some,' Mona muttered under her breath loud enough for Priscia to hear.

'No point even dreaming of it,' Curly interrupted. She was out of the bath now, drying herself off with the same towel all the girls used before her.

Priscia continued 'Girls have been complaining about that bloody butter, not to mention the soup and rotten pumpkin for as long as I can remember. It's not going to change any time soon. Not for you.'

'So you've not heard about peanut butter?' Mona asked.

'My word no. But if anyone would have heard, it'd be Red. I'll ask her later,' Curly said. Mona watched her walk away with a smile. She made her way towards the bathtub, her tired, achy muscles screaming out for some soothing warm water. Priscia stopped her with a firm grip on the shoulder.

'Forget it Patricia. Joan, Hilary, Margaret, Dorothea and Crispina are all in before you.'

'That's everyone on the floor,' Mona said.

'That's right. Last in, last washed.'

Mona couldn't understand what the point of having a bath was if the water had already been used to clean at least twenty other dirty girls before her.

'I'd be better off jumping in with the sheets tomorrow!'

'Don't let me stop you,' Priscia said.

Mona got back to her bed and waited for Curly to curl up beside her.

'Where have you been?' she asked as Curly made it back just in time for lights out.

'I went over the far end to see Red. She said no way, hasn't heard anything about any peanut butter.' Suddenly Mona's cold, dirty bath wasn't plaguing her. She'd be bathing in booze and cigarettes soon enough.

12

Since Isabel's seizure in the steam room, Mona had barely had a second alone with Cecilia. The moment the girls were done with the morning delivery, Cecilia would be ushered away by the nuns to wash the dormitory sheets, clothes and undergarments, not just for the Sacred Heart dorms, but for the rest of the Convent too. A fresh round of bed linen finally meant a chance encounter. As the nuns busied themselves for lights out, Cecilia made her way around the beds handing out fresh folded uniforms.

'Tomorrow bring your old ones downstairs with you please,' she sang her well-practiced instructions to each girl.

Mona glanced around for the nuns as Cecilia approached her bed.

'Tomorrow bring your old ones downstairs with you please,' Cecilia said.

'Of course, Cecilia. Would you like to sit down for just one second and talk to me? We never get a chance to talk.'

'Talk about what?' Cecilia asked and sat down tentatively at the end of Mona's bed.

'Tell me something. How long have you been here in Sacred Heart?' Mona asked.

'I lost track of time. My parents brought me when I was little. Maybe eight.'

'And why would the nuns put a little eight-year-old in Sacred Heart, with the likes of us? And not over with the young orphans?'

'I'm not an orphan,' she said. 'When I was little, I liked playing with insects. Cockroaches, snails, I liked to pull them apart and look at their insides. Birds too and even a kitty once. My neighbour, Mrs Bray had a big fat cat. But it wasn't really fat was it? It was pregnant. It gave birth to five kittens. I suppose Mrs Bray assumed one just wandered off like kittens do. I watched and checked the hands of the clock. The little kitty only bled for a few minutes after I cut its head off. My little baby sister wasn't that much bigger than a cat. It made me wonder.' Mona hadn't spoken in a while, so Cecilia paused to check her reaction. 'Do you want me to continue?' she asked.

Mona cleared her throat. 'Maybe just skip to you coming here?' Like the nuns, she didn't want to know.

'We had an old white car, an Australian Six I think it was. Father told me to get out, walk over to the front door round the side of the Convent and knock. He said not to look back. The nuns must have been expecting me because they knew my real name - which I can't remember now - and they told me not to cry. But I wasn't sad. Just mad I suppose. Still am. And I never got to find out,' she said.

'Find out what?' Mona asked.

'How long. I never got to find out how long it takes for a baby to bleed out before it dies.' Mona tried not to fill in the blanks.

The whip of Sister Leoni's cane on the end of Mona's bed signalled Cecilia's cue to leave. As the nun moved down the room it occurred to Mona that her evening chat wasn't done. She grabbed Cecilia by the wrist and pulled her forward again.

'It was nice to get a few minutes to ourselves the other day, wasn't it?' Mona asked her. 'You know, when Novice Anne was called away.'

'Yes, I've never smoked a cigarette before,' Cecilia said, back to being the childlike dancer Mona knew.

'Can't help but wish the novice would get called away more often,' Mona said and Cecilia smiled.

'Yes, I think I'd like that.'

Outside the Convent, the nights seemed so short. Traveling between groghouses, doing drugs, running scams and planning thefts. Mona's pursuit of a thrill sustained her while sleep seemed dreadfully boring. Now all she wanted was sleep; yet every time she closed her eyes all she could see was Cecilia standing over her, knife in hand. The woman was more terrifying than any criminal she'd ever met. When brutes like Guggenheim or Lawrence beat a man, they did it for money. Or drugs. There was rhyme and reason to it all. Yet here was a woman whose sole motivation was desire to see someone die. Mona tossed this over in her head for nights on end. When the nuns instructed the girls to pray, Mona begged God, the Heavens, the Powers That Be, whoever they were, that she not make an enemy of Cecilia.

'Oh Isabel I've been so worried about you ever since the other day. Are you alright?' It took a week for Mona to work her way over to Isabel's bed. There wasn't a lot of time between dinner in the refectory and lights out and Isabel was on the opposite end of the dorm. Mona had to go out of her way to get a moment with her. The other girls noticed and were trying desperately not to look like they were eavesdropping.

'No need to fret over me Patricia I'm fine,' Isabel said.

'Please don't call me that. No nuns are listening, you can call me Mona.' She sat beside her on the bed.

'Alright. I have those fits every now and again, luckily Novice Anne is here now, she knows how to help me.' Isabel readied herself for sleep, attempted to pull her bed covers back while Mona still sat on them.

'It must be painful for you. Terrifying really. What if you were to hit your head on the concrete floor or burn yourself in the steam room? Such a scary thing to have to endure. It's a shame something good couldn't come out of it for you, for all of us.'

This stopped Isabel in her tracks. She glared at Mona.

'What do you mean?'

'Well I just couldn't help but notice that while Anne was assisting you, the back dock was left unsupervised. And I had a thought. What if we weren't unloading sheets, but delicious food, cigarettes and whisky? And no nuns there to see it. No one there to tell us 'no' because they're all with you.' Mona tried to paint a picture. A world where the girls could have anything they wanted. So long as Isabel was up for it.

'Patricia, I hope you're not suggesting pulling one over the Novice. She's the only one in here I like.'

'It's Mona, and I'm just asking you to mull it over.' She stood and walked away before the girl could say no. She was sure that a couple days to dwell on things would be more than enough to convince her. Strenuous, bloody, painful days slaving in the laundry room, refectory dinners of dodgy soup and rancid pumpkin, sleepless nights in a dormitory filled of unbathed, tired girls. They all deserved some creature comforts. Yet a week passed and Isabel hadn't agreed to help.

Mona found it almost impossible to hide her annoyance as the days wore on. She was tired, constantly hot and sweaty, every muscle in her body aching from the perpetually punishing manual labour. And the only thing standing in the way of her getting some booze was Isabel. And she was a thief just like Mona. Curly had told her all about it. She'd stolen sheets and linens, among other things, from a hospital when she'd been admitted for a seizure. Not her first conviction. Now she was washing those hospital's sheets every day at the Convent. Why would she act like she was above a little light deception?

Mona hadn't planned to bring Curly into her scheme quite so soon. But now she had no choice. Sometimes of a Sunday after prayers, the girls would be given free time to knit, sew, play basketball, or walk around the grounds. Mona sat with Curly and Red by the fence and watched as the orphan children went for their daily walk down to the river. Red scoffed at the sound of one of the nuns telling the girls not to look at the Sacred Heart girls.

'Yes one look at us and you'll be selling your souls on the street by supper. That's all it takes you know. Wouldn't want to consort with the low likes of us,' Red mocked. Some of the older girls trailing the back of the line laughed and one waved at them.

'I bet they'd love to talk to us if they could,' Curly said.

'Sure they would, we're the most interesting things in their orbit,' Red said.

'Want to make things even more interesting?' Mona asked. Red and Curly smiled, exchanging glances. Mona could see they'd been waiting for this. She kept them waiting a little longer. Picking at the grass beneath her feet.

'Oh come on, we know you've been scheming. What's your big idea, Mona?' Red asked.

'Well I just don't think it's right they treat us like slaves in here. Washing all those bloody sheets for well-to-do hotels, not a penny for it. Even Pentridge pays. To top it all off we get fed a shitty pittance…'

Curly cut her off 'No need to convince us Moe.'

Red laughed. 'Come on Mona, bloody out with it.'

'I have a friend who works for one of the hotels. If I can get Chuck and Robbie to agree to it, he could perhaps provide them with some whisky, maybe some cigarettes. When Isabel is having one of her fits and the Novice is called away, we can unload them from the truck, get them upstairs and be back down before anyone misses us. When the nuns go to bed, we can hand the stuff around.'

'And what do we get for the trouble, other than a couple sips of whisky? It's not like the girls can pay us for taking the risk, no one's got any money in here,' Red said. A true businesswoman.

'All about the money, aren't you?' Mona mocked. 'How about first bath? Or extra bread at supper? Or all the candy in the nun's cupboard? The girls would trade us anything. Would make our time in here a little easier.'

'What can we do to help?' Curly asked.

'The whole thing depends on Isabel and she's not too keen on the idea,' Mona started.

'If she won't do it can't we just get someone else? I could even do it, I've seen Isabel's fits, I know what they look like,' Curly said.

'I thought about that. If someone who's never been sick before suddenly starts having fits, out of the blue, they may be sent to sick bay or even hospital. A doctor could be called in. Or the nuns could figure out what we're up to. Since it's common for Isabel, we already know exactly what the nuns will do.'

'True, they never call anyone or send her off anymore. She's always ok after a bit of rest,' Red agreed.

'So you want me to convince Isabel?' Curly asked.

'Yes. I've already got Cecilia on board. Next, I need to arrange things with the boys,' Mona said.

'What about the other girls. Should I start drumming up business?' Red asked. This was what Mona had initially been afraid of.

'No, if they find out too soon and the nuns catch wind, this whole thing will be over before it begins. Let's wait 'til we have our stash and then slowly get the word out.'

Both Curly and Red nodded their heads in agreement.

While Curly worked on Isabel, Mona continued her charm offensive on the boys. She knew from their brief conversations that they didn't get paid much for their deliveries and that Robbie had a newborn to feed. She also knew Charles was single and easily dazzled. Any moment the Novice had her back turned, Mona would casually mention to Robbie how much she missed cigarettes. One day he slipped her one he'd rolled earlier and a match. She told Charles how much she couldn't wait for the day she was out. She'd take him to her favourite groghouse and have a drink with him. She could taste the whisky now. She quickly developed a rapport with both of them. Yet she couldn't make her final move without Isabel on board. Curly's gentle prodding was taking far too long for Mona's liking. Finally, Mona had had enough. She cornered Isabel in the courtyard on the way to church one Sunday.

'What do you want?' Mona asked her. Mona stood on tiptoes as she asked, crowding her, towering over her. Firm hands on each shoulder.

'What do you mean?' Isabel asked.

'Come off it. Everyone wants something. I want a drink and you're getting in the way of that. What do you want?'

Isabel shook her head. Her face stubborn, mouth pinched, eyes bulging. Mona tried again.

'I know you're a thief, Isabel. I know your last robbery was for stealing from a hospital. I heard it was sheets you stole, but I know better. What was hidden in those sheets? What is the only thing a hospital has worth taking?' Isabel lowered her gaze and Mona knew she had her. 'If I promise to smuggle in a bit of dope for you, would you be willing to take a few extra fits and falls for us then?' Mona asked.

Isabel's eyes refused to meet Mona's. She was hiding something. Was it shame? Mona didn't care. She just wanted to get the show on the road.

'Yes I'll take whatever drugs you can get,' she said, defeated. 'Just let me know when you want me to do it.'

Mona released her shoulders and without any acknowledgment, agreement, handshake or even eye contact, Isabel was gone. Of all the girls in the Convent it hadn't occurred to Mona that Isabel was most like her. A thief, an addict, and stubborn. If Mona had been asked by a stranger for a favour, she would have refused also. Not unless there was more in it for her.

Finally, the last piece of the puzzle. Her mates Robbie and Charles. Mona secured a piece of paper and lead pencil. She slipped them a letter.

'R&C, I have treasured our brief moments each day. The other girls and I spend the rest of our waking hours working our fingers to the bone in the laundry for no pay, nor comforts. We have all suffered. And we are not bad girls as they say, as I hope you well know after these many weeks in each other's company. I dream of being able to sneak these hard working, suffering girls the occasional cigarette or sip of whisky. Perhaps even a chocolate or two. Surely that's not so much to ask? If you would see fit to stock your van with a few of these items, the next time the Novice is called away to assist a sick girl, I can take them off your generous hands. No one will know and yet it would mean the world of difference to us. I'm sure if you would mention this to my friend Eddie he would compensate you most adequately. And if you could ask him to slip in something extra for me from our mutual friend Stan I'm sure he'll know what you mean. Please take the time to think this over. I do not want to risk your jobs and I would take full responsibility if ever discovered, and never implicate you my friends. Please give me some indication of your answer the next time I see you. If yes, I will arrange for the Novice to be called away the following Monday. Yours gratefully, M.'

The following day Mona, Cecilia and Red waited nervously for the delivery van to arrive. Cecilia, for once, stood still against the wall of the Convent. Mona and Red exchanged anxious glances, hoping the Novice wouldn't notice the change in Cecilia's behaviour.

As Robbie and Charles pulled in, they kept their eyes to the ground.

'Morning,' Robbie said to each of them as he walked round the back of the van and opened it up. The Novice was the first to start unloading sheets. Mona, Red and Cecilia hesitated before taking their own places around the cart. As Mona unloaded the last bag the Novice turned her back, ready to pull the trolley inside the laundry from the front. It was then Mona felt a gentle hand on her shoulder. She turned to meet the gaze of a smiling Chuck. He held open a small note between his chest and Mona's. It said 'Yes. Monday.' Mona's eyes grew wide and her grin even wider.

'Patricia!' at the sound of the Novice's voice, Charles tore the note in two and shoved it back inside his pants pocket.

'If I could, I'd hug you,' Mona whispered. She turned back to her task. Leaving Robbie and Charles behind, they wheeled the trolley inside.

13

Mona found it difficult to sleep without the lull of a drink. Nothing but cleaning, eating and going to bed at 7 o'clock was leaving her too much time alone with her thoughts. They were going round and round. Niggling, needling. They wouldn't stop. She would replay the diamond theft over and over dreaming up different scenarios for how she might have gotten away with it. When she'd exhausted that her mind would wander elsewhere. All the stupid things she'd said and done since childhood. The time she yelled at her father, right before his death, her stinging words the last she'd ever said to him. The time she knocked down an elderly woman while fleeing a shop in Queensland. She still wandered if the old broad was alright. Sister Leoni noticed the circles under Mona's eyes. She asked her if she'd been sleeping. When Mona explained her thoughts were keeping her awake, she half expected a sleeping pill, hot cocoa, anything besides counting sheep. She was told to pray. So she did. She prayed for booze. And it was on its way.

'Sleep well Patricia?' Sister asked as she floated down the dormitory stairs, leading the girls to Monday morning prayers.

'Very well Sister,' Mona replied. The nun surveyed Mona with a curious expression at first. Just as Mona began to regret her unusually chipper morning demeanour the nun smiled.

'I'm glad to hear it. Seems your prayers are doing some good.'

If Sister Leoni only knew what Mona's reformed mood was really about. She couldn't keep still from excitement through Mass. Her knees jiggled, her hands fidgeted. She licked her lips incessantly - a habit she'd thought broken since arriving at Abbotsford.

Breakfast was accompanied by nervous glances between Mona, Curly, Red, Cecilia, Isabel and back again. Mona ate absentmindedly, scraping her bowl of porridge. She noticed the other girls did the opposite, too anxious to eat. Mona took Red's bowl for herself followed by Curly's. The food helped calm her butterflies, and all going well, it would be best to line her insides. Today would be her first drink in two months.

Mona and Red left Curly in the laundry and held each other back from running towards the back door. It was amazing the difference a day made. Mona couldn't help but appreciate the beautiful sunshine streaming through the glass windows alongside the laundries. The view of the girls she'd grown so fond of over the last two months all working together, helping each other, warmed her too. She thought about her cosy bed upstairs, her full stomach. Until today she'd felt like she was sleepwalking through each day in the Convent. Now she had excitement back in her life. Delectable anticipation. The feeling that came along with doing something bad. Even if they were caught it would be worth it for this moment. The 'right before' moment. It meant everything to Mona. Like stepping onto a stage.

Mona, Red and the Novice stood watching Cecilia dance in circles the same as always. Red rolled her eyes the same as always. They were playing things perfectly. The Novice stood straight, eyes trained on the front gate as usual. Mona stifled a squeal as the van approached. Robbie smiled from behind the wheel. Charles in the passenger seat. When the van pulled up, Red eyed Mona with terror. The Novice hadn't been called in yet.

'Morning,' Robbie said and walked round the back. He took his time opening the doors. He looked at Mona and she knew. The boys had loaded the contraband in last, to allow for a quick handover. Cecilia was still dancing, side stepping from foot to foot. Mona lifted her right foot and kicked Cecilia in the back of her shin. Mona didn't know if her knock had worked or whether Cecilia had taken it as a hint, but sure enough, she fell.

'Ow!' Cecilia groaned.

'You right love?' Robbie abandoned the van doors and bent down to Cecilia's aid. Charles followed suit as did the Novice. It was at that moment Curly appeared at the door.

'Novice we need you, it's Isabel again.' Curly huffed and puffed as if she'd run from the furthest corner of the laundry.

'I'll be alright.' Cecilia dusted herself off and stood up urging the Novice 'you should tend to Isabel.'

'Patricia, Agnes, make sure Cecilia is able to walk on her ankle alright before you start unloading.' And with that she rushed inside. Curly waited at the door, wanting to see the results of their labour. Robbie and Charles went back to unlocking the van.

'That was close, we've got the stuff right here at the front,' Robbie said. A netted shopping bag with three silver flasks, five packets of Marlboros and matchboxes was the first thing they saw as he swung open the doors. Charles leaned in handing the bag to Red. Red and Curly rushed upstairs while Robbie pulled Mona aside.

'This is the something extra you asked for from your mate,' he said. Another matchbox. Mona slid it open and looked inside. Coke. Isabel's dope.

'It's not for me,' Mona said. She considered it could be, some of it at least. But no. she'd only ever liked the stuff, as it allowed her to keep on drinking. With so little booze to go through, and so many girls to share it with, what was the point? She lifted her grey smock and slid the matchbox into the waistband of her undergarments. Robbie whistled and Charles nudged him not to look. Mona smiled. She couldn't help but enjoy the attention. When she'd travelled with the sideshows she occasionally filled in for the dancing troupe. With each dance move she'd lift her skirt a little higher, and a little higher again, revealing just enough but not too much. The men paid extra for that show.

'She's coming back,' Cecilia hissed a loud whisper from the doorway where she'd been keeping an eye out for the Novice.

'Can you stall her? Your ankle, tell her it's hurt,' Mona ordered.

Cecilia headed inside to catch the nun before she reached the exit. Mona, Robbie and Charles went to work unloading the sheets onto the trolley. Mona kept glancing back at the doorway. She couldn't see Cecilia anymore. She hoped the Novice had taken her into the office beside the laundry. That way they wouldn't run into Red and Curly as they came back downstairs.

Red and Curly soon appeared red faced and panting.

'What took you so long? The Novice is on her way back out, you almost ran right into her,' Mona said.

'Sorry Moe, we may have taken a couple swigs on the way back down. Had to test the merchandise didn't we?' Red laughed. 'Good stuff. Hope Mona's mate is paying you decent enough,' she said to Robbie and Charles.

'We're being paid quite handsomely. So there's more where that came from. Next Monday?' Robbie asked Mona.

'I'll let you know,' Mona said barely getting the words out before the Novice walked out.

'I've sent Cecilia to the infirmary to get a bandage for her ankle. I think she sprained it quite badly. Mary will you assist us with the deliveries today?' She asked Curly.

'Yes, I thought as much,' Curly replied.

They each grabbed a corner of the trolley and rolled it inside.

The thought of what was waiting for Mona when she reached bed that night made the day race by. Sister Leoni commented on Mona's productivity.

'Finally gotten the hang of things Patricia?' she said. Mona smiled in reply. Her mind wasn't on the hotel-stained sheets, or on the washing or ironing. She'd gone into autopilot. Her mind was upstairs, drunk, surrounded by beautiful clouds of smoke. She noticed some of the other girls go more quiet than usual. Give her eager looks. Red had already spread the word. Perhaps not such a bad idea. The nuns were so far oblivious to what was going on, so any advance interest could only do them good. Mona's hunch was confirmed when Priscia approached her on the line for dinner.

'Nuns say we're to have baths tonight,' she said matter-of-factly.

Mona sighed, shaking her head. 'So what are you telling me for?'

'Well Red thought you might be up for negotiating on bath order,' Priscia replied.

Mona paused causing a hold up at the front of the line.

The girls behind started to walk around them, pushing in front.

'Soup and bread for dinner, what a delightful change,' Mona said, sarcasm dripping from her starving lips. 'I'll give you a nightcap and fag for first bath.'

Mona wasn't about to mess around.

Priscia grinned. Her brown stumpy teeth on full display.

'You're not so bad after all are ya?' she said to Mona and headed inside. By the end of the day she'd added two bread rolls and an extra blanket to her first bath. Red had also made her own bargains. The moment the lights were out, Red struck a match and dove under her bed. She lifted a loose floorboard and pulled out the string bag. All the girls crowded around oohing and aahing.

'Shhh, shhh, the nuns will hear,' Curly whispered. As the day had progressed Mona had watched Curly grow more and more anxious. She wasn't a natural risk taker it seemed. Mona pulled on Curly's plait playfully trying to loosen her up.

Red laid all the items out on her bed. Five packets of pre-rolled cigarettes, five matchboxes, a block of Nestle Nut Milk chocolates and three silver flasks.

'Whisky,' she announced to the room which was followed by even more ooohs and aahhs. Curly's eyes again drifted from the girls to the wooden door between them and the sleeping nuns.

Mona opened the block of chocolate and snapped it into pieces. One for each girl. She began handing them around. Much to Curly's relief, the room went silent, filled with the quiet of salivating mouths chewing crunchy, creamy, chocolate. Mona then took one flask and one packet of cigarettes and gave them to Priscia.

'Share this with Gret, Lily, Kay and Yvette,' she said. Each girl she owed for favours from throughout the day. She then took one flask and one packet of cigarettes to share between herself and Cecilia. 'The rest is yours to sort out Red.'

Red divided up the cigarettes amongst those she'd made deals with. So long as they didn't go through too many at once, the smell and steam of the downstairs laundry overpowered the smell of smoke. She gave the last flask to Curly who had a couple of sips and then passed it along the line. That night all the girls in the dorm sat up on the ends of their beds taking sips and smoking cigarettes. Whispering stories of parties they'd been to before winding up at the Convent. Priscia revealed she made a habit of stealing items she liked from every house she visited. After one party she walked out with a lampshade on her head. It matched the drapes at home, she couldn't leave without it.

Isabel, now high on cocaine, stayed up all night entertaining the girls with whispered songs and limericks she'd written on her all-night benders. Mona harmonised while Curly said 'I love yous' to the ceiling.

'Who exactly are you talking to?' Mona laughed, ready for bed.

'No one. I don't know. I just like to say it sometimes I spose. I like to imagine a day when I can say it to someone every night and have them say it back to me. Is that so strange?'

'Well, I've gone 25 years never having said it to anyone, perhaps I'm the one who's strange. Next time don't say it to the ceiling, say it to me.'

'Alright then. I love you Mo,' Curly said tentatively, almost, afraid she'd been tricked.

'I love you too,' Mona said. She'd never been able to say those words before. For some reason they now came easily.

'I love you too girls,' a cry came from across the room. Red. Her outburst was followed by laughter and a succession of 'I love yous,' 'good nights,' and 'sleep tights.'

If the nuns hadn't heard the girls indulging in their contraband, they surely would have heard the cacophony of love being declared ever so loudly, but for some reason they never came in. Mona couldn't remember the last time she slept so soundly but she did, from then on. Drifting off each night with love in her ears, a smile on her face, warmth in her heart, and a flask under her pillow.

The knowledge that smokes and whisky were never too far away improved the drudgery of the laundry. They'd gotten bolder. Initially Mona had been reluctant to smuggle goods in once a week as she thought the nuns may grow too concerned for Isabel and send her off to hospital. But Mona's concern for getting caught gave way to her thirst for drink. Rather than continuing to use Isabel, Mona snuck Jack another note convincing him to wrap the bag up in one of the sheets they were unloading and put it in a separate sack from the Windsor. Once they passed the sheets onto the girls in the washroom and took a trolley of fresh sheets outside, one of the wash girls would find an excuse to run upstairs with the contraband and hide it in the usual spot under Red's bed. All done right under the nun's noses. It was brazen all right. And so much more fun.

'Well, well, well, look what the boys snuck in.' Mona held up a copy of a country magazine one night. She'd never been more excited to see reading material that wasn't the bible. While the other girls turned their heads in disinterest and went back to readying for bed, little Lucy jumped up into Mona's lap.

'Read it to me won't you?'

'It won't be very interesting Lucy, it's over a year old. The cheap bastards must have snaffled it from hotel reception.'

'But I haven't read it before,' Lucy whined.

'You've never read anything before,' Red shouted from her corner of the dorm and the other girls snickered.

'You haven't learned to read?' Mona asked, stroking her hair.

'No.'

Not so unusual. Not everyone got to have the education Mona did. She settled in close and opened up the well-worn pages of the white woman's bible. By the time she got to the body beautiful tips for lovely hands she had a captive audience.

'No hands are so unattractive that they cannot be made beautiful,' she read aloud prompting each woman to examine their own laundry battered, dried stubs and chipped tips. 'Sun, wind, dirt, grime, and housework all detract from hand beauty if not counteracted.'

'Would you just get to the part where it says what to do about it?' shouted a chorus.

Mona laughed. 'Oh, we're all interested now, aren't we? Here, Lucy, why don't you give it a try?' Mona handed the rag over and Lucy began reading, with Mona's prompting, about good soap, hand cream and gloves.

By the time the nuns returned to turn out the lights all girls were in agreement. Next time the boys brought in the goods, they would happily go without cigarettes, even liquor, if it meant getting their laundry-wrecked hands on some cream. Mona was floored. She was as vain as the next person but to give up her other vices for the sake of silky fingers was not her idea of a fair trade.

Mona lay awake that night rereading the paper in her mind. If the pages were right, it was pretty fingers, expensive makeup and fancy clothes that made a woman. Mona had wanted those things, stolen those things. Now she was without all of those things. Is that what the nuns intended? For her to forget everything she'd always wanted? Forget she was a woman just like any other? And re-emerge a clean slate, ready to be good? Even without men around, the women wanted to feel beautiful. Was it so wrong to want that? To want to look and feel good? To be able to stand the sight of your own hands? The nuns seemed to think so. For pretty hands did not make clean sheets.

14

Mona's temporary relief courtesy of smuggled goods and improved relations with the other girls was interrupted by the introduction of Sister Margaret. Moved from the orphanage across to Sacred Heart. Mona thought perhaps it was punishment of some kind. She soon learned that Sister Margaret had been brought in to keep the girls in line. Where Sister Leoni, the Novice and company had turned the other cheek to whispered conversations in the refectory and laundry, Sister Margaret did not. Where the other nuns had allowed the girls to choose their own activities on Sunday, Sister Margaret preferred to delegate appropriate pastimes. And she wielded her cane wherever she went.

Philomena was the first to feel the brunt of the thick wooden instrument. It was Philomena's turn to read prayers aloud during breakfast. She stopped between verses for a piece of bread. Sister Margaret shouted from the altar, and swung her cane down on the table causing a loud thwack. So loud that every girl in the room practically jumped from their skins.

'No pauses!' she shouted at Philomena.

'When am I meant to eat?' Philomena made the mistake of retorting.

Thwack again went the cane on the table.

'Enough you insolent, insufferable girl. You'll not ask questions, you'll eat when I say you can eat and you'll do as you're told.' She stood from the altar and walked the row of tables thwack, thwack, thwacking the cane in the air with each step.

'We've always been allowed to eat while reading,' Philomena said. Curly coughed and muttered. Other girls shushed her. They'd heard enough of Sister Margaret to know what was coming.

'Well I don't know how my fellow sisters have been running things but talking back is *always* frowned upon in my book.' She towered over Philomena now. She was a tall woman, like a big black cat poised over a tiny mouse. 'Pull your smock up and bend over,' she said.

Mona could see Philamena biting back her impulse to refuse. To argue. To do anything but what she'd been asked. But she relented. She bent over and lifted her grey smock inch by inch. With a flick of her finger Sister Margaret pulled Philomena's under garments down so her bottom was bare. She thwacked the cane across her backside five times, harder and harsher than any cane Mona had ever seen a teacher wield growing up. Mona knew it wouldn't be long before her own turn came.

The rising tension from Sister Margaret's move to Sacred Heart was soon matched by Curly's unusually sour mood. Perhaps it was the heat getting her down? Even Mona, who usually ran a few degrees cold, had noticed the change that summer had sprung. Melbourne had only gained a few degrees here or there leading up to Christmas yet behind the walls of a steaming hot laundry the difference was like that of a cold bath and a scolding hot one. The steam from the laundry rose throughout the day and lingered. The girls could feel the heat trapped between the walls of the dorms at night.

Or maybe it was the advancement of Christmas affecting Curly's mood. The prospect of spending Christmas Day saying prayers and putting on plays for the nuns wasn't Mona's idea of a good time. Though on the plus side, at least they were guaranteed a good meal. The Novice had let slip while waiting for a delivery that they would be having ham, turkey and Christmas pudding. Curly didn't know that. Mona thought the news would bring a spark back to her eyes.

'Did you hear me Curly? A right feast,' Mona said.

After the deliveries, Mona had negotiated her way into the sorting room so they could talk. But she didn't have long. No doubt Sister Margaret would be doing the rounds shortly and figure out she wasn't in the laundry, steaming, like she was meant to be.

Curly shrugged. Her mood unchanged.

'Not impressed? Don't tell me your mum's Christmas lunch is better?' Mona asked.

'I hope so, since that's what I'll be having,' Curly said.

Mona let the news sink in. Curly's birthday must be before Christmas.

'You're leaving soon?'

'I turn 18 on Wednesday. Sister Leoni said my pop will be round early that evening to take me home.'

'Why aren't you swinging from the rafters? You're free.'

'Who said anything about being free? I'll be back home with my parents. They'll have me under lock and key. I'd be better off here. At least I have friends here. At least I have you.'

'Well,' Mona was taken aback at the compliment. 'Why do you have to go back and live with them? I wasn't much older than you when I left home.'

'I can't survive on my own. I've no skills, no fella, I've never lived out in the real world, never even been in the city without holding my mother's hand.' Curly's voice cracked, yet it was loud enough for Sister Margaret to hear as she walked up the corridor.

The nun announced her arrival with her cane and a brow so furrowed her eyes were barely visible between the wrinkles.

'Why are you not in your correct place Patricia? And why are you talking Mary?'

Mona went to speak and the nun thwacked her cane on the table again. This time so close to Mona's fingers that they stung.

'That was rhetorical. Or perhaps you don't know the word?'

Mona didn't answer.

'Well?' the nun shouted this time.

'I'm sorry I assumed that question was rhetorical too,' Mona smirked. She couldn't help herself. She clenched her buttocks, ready for the inevitable caning she was no doubt about to receive. She just hoped Curly wouldn't also be on the receiving end. Instead, Mona's smirk was met by one even more sinister on the nun's face.

'Go and see Sister Winefred and ask her for two toothbrushes. By the look of the dorm floors, the way these nuns have been running things, they probably haven't been scrubbed since last Christmas. By the time you're both done I expect to be able to see my own reflection in the floorboards.'

That's how Curly was to spend her last week in the Convent. Their knees were sore, red and bloodied. Their hands cramped. The toothbrushes bent from continual pushing and pulling back and forth over the hardwood.

They weren't allowed to join the other girls in the refectory. Instead, Sister Winefred bought Vegemite sandwiches to them. They sat on the ends of beds and ate as the Sister stood and watched over them, waiting for the plates so she could take them back to the kitchen.

Curly begged forgiveness every time Winefred or one of the other nuns came to check on them. Mona begged on her behalf too. She didn't have much longer to spend in the Convent, did she have to spend it separated from the other girls? Holed up in the dorms, day in, day out? The nuns wouldn't go against the word of Sister Margaret.

The only benefit was that for hours each day Mona and Curly were left in peace. Though their punishment was to silence them, in fact it had done just the opposite. They sang softly together so as not to be heard downstairs in the laundry. They talked and plotted, all the things they'd do to Sister Margaret given half the chance. Not to mention the fact they were left alone all day with their contraband. By the time the girls came in to go to bed they were all talked, and smoked, out.

Deliveries continued. Red made sure of that.

By the following Tuesday they were on their last few floorboards. Sister Leoni said she'd spoken to Sister Margaret and tomorrow they'd be able to join the other girls in the laundry.

'Oh joy, just in time for my last day,' Curly said as Sister Leoni left the room. Mona waited for the sound of footsteps to disappear down the stairwell. She sat up straight, cross-legged, her bloody knees hot against her resting hands.

'I've been thinking,' she said. Curly stopped scrubbing, wiped her hair from her face and sat opposite Mona ready to listen.

'If Robbie and Charles can smuggle things in, surely they can sneak us out,' Mona said.

'Do you really think the boys would be up for that?' Curly asked.

'Maybe not. Being found with a grocery bag is one thing. If caught, they can just say the stuff is theirs, accidentally mixed in with the sheets. But sneaking us out … that won't go unnoticed. They'll lose their jobs.'

Curly chewed on her lip, mulling over the idea in her head. 'I heard about a girl some time ago who jumped from the window after lights out.' Curly pointed to the glass pane in front of them. 'Her plan was to climb the fence.'

'Didn't she break both her legs?'

'Well, could've worked otherwise. Girls have gotten out before, I'm sure of it.'

'No, the boys are our best bet. All anyone will know is that we're missing. They won't know for sure why or how. And if we keep the boys in the dark it will make it easier for them to deny any involvement when questioned,' Mona said.

'How do we keep them in the dark?' Curly asked.

'Once we've finished with the deliveries and they're getting back into the van we simply jump in with the sheets. They won't know until it's too late.' Mona grinned. Something more to look forward to. Another rule she could break. And a way to help Curly in the process. She had it all figured out.

'And then what?' Curly asked.

'What do you mean and then what? You'll be free of your parents, and I'll be free of this hell hole. I mean you didn't actually want to leave me in here alone, did you?' Mona said.

'I just worry about what happens once we've escaped. We'll still be in uniform. We'll have no money…' Curly's worries rolled out of her in waves.

Mona cut her off. 'Let me worry about the particulars. And after we've unloaded tomorrow make sure you're at the side door ready to go.' Curly nodded, jaw tight.

'Ready to go where?'

Mona and Curly spun around startled. Cecilia's eyes glistened, she'd been listening the whole time.

'What are you doing up here?' Mona asked.

Cecilia held the grocery bag of whisky and cigarettes up one-handed and grinned. Curly stood, took the bag and shoved it in their usual hiding place.

'Good job,' Mona said to Cecilia, dipping her toothbrush back into the murky water and getting back to work. Curly joined her without another word. Cecilia stood watching them, her head tilted to one side.

'You're escaping,' Cecilia said.

Mona cursed under her breath.

'Do you want to come with us? Is that it?' she asked.

'I do!' Cecilia shouted, Mona and Curly shhh'd her.

'Keep your voice down,' Mona whispered. 'You can come. You know you're one of my favourite girls in here.' Mona stood so she was eye to eye with Cecilia. She put her hands on her shoulders. 'Tomorrow when we're switching up the new sheets with the old, you'll need to go and alert Curly. Once the two of you make it back outside just follow my instructions. Until then you mustn't breathe a word of this to anyone.'

Cecilia nodded her head as fast as she could.

'I'm so excited. I've been here so long,' she said.

Mona smiled and pulled her in for a quick hug.

'No more scrubbing floors, or sheets, no prayers or uniforms,' Mona said. Cecilia smiled and rushed back downstairs.

Curly gave Mona a disappointed look.

'Drats,' Curly spat as the handle on the toothbrush gave way.

'I'm surprised it lasted as long as it did,' Mona commented. An entire floor of scrubbing, hers had broken days ago. Curly had a lighter touch.

15

The next morning Mona and Curly hardly spoke at breakfast. No one spoke any more. Not even whispers. Not now Sister Margaret was around. Still it was the first time Mona and Curly had been out of the dorm in almost a week. Mona took in the sight of all the girls. Red shoving extra bread onto little Lucy's plate. Priscia staring blankly at the figure of Mary Magdalene on the wall. Isabel reading out the bible as if she were reciting a train schedule, the girls in front of her trying not to listen. Mona finally caught sight of Cecilia. She'd never seen her look so happy. It was hard to imagine what it must be like to be locked away for so long. Mona had only managed three months out of six and she'd already had enough. Perhaps you got used to it. Perhaps you came to enjoy the regularity of it all, the routine, the guaranteed feed and warm bed at the end of each day. She imagined why those things may be of comfort to some girls, they were no comfort to her.

When Charles and Robbie pulled into the delivery bay Mona took stock of both of them. She knew it would be the last she'd see of them. Robbie's tall walk with strides too wide, Charles' warm smile and shy eyes. As Mona leaned into the van to pull out the sheets she brushed her hand along Charles' shirt. He felt it and looked at her with surprise, he blushed, shifting his eyes to the ground. It had been so long since she'd picked a pocket. Three months of smiles and whispers between the pair had provided a buffer. He thought she was copping a feel, when really she was hunting for his wallet. She found it, sliding it up under her grey tunic.

Once the girls all returned with the fresh sheets and loaded them up, Charles and Robbie waved goodbye while Novice Anne gave her orders for the rest of the morning. Cecilia ran ahead to make sure Curly was on her way out while Red headed into the folding room. The Novice dragged her feet behind her, not looking back to see Mona waiting by the door. Curly and Cecilia slipped past everyone and back outside. The boys had just gotten back into their seats, Robbie was moments away from turning the key in the ignition when Mona whistled to the girls to hurry up. She opened the back of the van, hopped in and held the door, careful not to open it too wide so as to avoid being seen in the boys' rearview mirrors. Curly dived in next.

Just as Cecilia got to the van Mona smiled at her and said, 'Sorry love,' slamming the door in her face. The van drove off down the road. There was no window in back for Mona or Curly to see Cecilia crumple on the asphalt as they left her behind.

Curly leaned back to the side of the van, making herself comfortable on the fresh bags of linen. Mona could see she wanted to speak, but held a finger up to her mouth and pointed towards the front of the car. They could hear Robbie and Charles talking in front. They drove in the quiet of the faint conversation and tyres on gravel. The boys were mulling over the latest news. Mona was most interested to hear of the woman who tackled two housebreakers she caught stealing from her neighbours. The robbers were ultimately chased down by police. She chuckled to herself, imagining the ribbing the other inmates at Pentridge would give the pair, subdued by a young woman. Good on her.

The drive felt long though it couldn't have been more than five or ten minutes. Mona kept her eyes trained on Curly's face which seemed to be growing more distressed by the minute. Finally, the car ground to a halt. They could hear more traffic now and people passing by. They listened to the front doors open and shut, boots on the footpath. Mona opened the back door and peered out. Emblazoned on the side of the building across the street were the words 'Carlton Café'.

'Come on,' Mona said jumping out of the van, reaching her hand back inside to steady Curly as she too stepped onto the road.

More than a few passers-by noticed them emerge. A dog yapped at their heels as they ran around the corner, away from where Robbie and Charles might see them. They hurried, Mona keeping constant check on the road for passing taxi cabs.

'Where are we going?' Curly asked.

'We're not far from my old house, but we can't go there. It's the first place they'll look. My friend Stanley lives in Essendon, it's the safest place for the moment,' Mona said.

'Is that far?' Curly asked. The question stunned Mona for a second and then it occurred to her, Curly had said many times that she didn't know the city, had never been out on her own. She was looking around like a baby deer, eyes wide, jumpy, unsure. Mona wrapped an arm around her.

'We need a taxi. Keep an eye out,' she said.

'How will we pay for it?' Curly asked.

'I asked Charles to slip me a few dollars,' Mona said patting her side.

'That's so nice of him,' Curly replied. 'Nicer than what we did to Cecilia.' Mona rolled her eyes at that. There was no way she was going to let her come along.

***

Hutchison was stunned as Mona barged in the house. She greeted him with a quick kiss and led Curly into the bedroom.

'Great to see you. Please, Mona, no need for chit chat, just go right ahead...' Stanley called after them.

Mona giggled 'I'll introduce you later,' she said as she flung open Stanley's wardrobe. The left side was full of Stanley's old clothes. Mona doubted he'd bought anything new for himself since his wife left. She strummed her fingers over each item. Cream pants frayed at the bottom of each leg, faded striped shirts, one long black overcoat with shrunken sleeves. His old military uniform. Items half hung on hangers as if they'd been thrown and were desperately clutching for something to hold onto. Mona's hands moved quickly, drawing Curly's attention from the left of the wardrobe to the right.

'Ohhh,' Curly breathed a sigh of relief at the neat, clean and ironed lady's clothes.

'These are Stanley's wife's,' Mona said. 'I've pinched a few things from here before, Stanley doesn't mind.'

'Doesn't she want them?' Curly asked.

Mona's reply was cut short by the sound of Stanley trudging down the hallway.

'She ain't coming back,' he said. 'Made that pretty clear.' Stanley leant against the doorway, peering sadly in.

Curly nodded, giving him a sympathetic smile. He stayed in place watching as they rifled through his wife's things.

'Thanks Hutch, give us a minute will you.' Mona shoved him from the room as he argued.

'Just thought you might need some help, some of those buttons can be tricky, you girls just let me know if you need anything...' his voice lost to the other end of the house. Mona came back in, shoved a chair against the door and undressed. She reached for a polka dot frock first and threw it over herself.

'This one's mine,' she said to Curly. Curly nodded and continued to look through each item.

'She has lots of clothes, doesn't she? Why would anyone need so many?' Curly asked. Mona shrugged.

Curly settled on a white dress with capped sleeves and a ribbon at the waist. The collar on the frock reminded Mona of their Convent tunics, and she wondered, with all the clothes in front of them, why Curly would choose the one dress that most resembled the one she'd worn every day at Abbotsford. Both wriggled their feet into white pointed flats.

'The shoes are too big.' Mona could hear disappointment in Curly's voice.

'That's alright, just wear your Sacred Heart ones for now. When I see Lawrence, I'll ask him to pick you something up from the factory. He's a bootmaker. What size are you?'

'Four, last time I checked.'

They joined Stanley in the kitchen for sandwiches. It had been so long since Mona had made her own meal. She enjoyed cutting the bread and placing cheese on each slice as Stanley carved up some ham.

'Looks delicious,' Curly said.

'I like to get into the Christmas ham early. Lasts a while, only me to feed. When the kids were here this would all be gone in a couple a days,' he said. 'You know you can't stay here,' turning his attention back to Mona. 'Coppers will be here looking for you as soon as they know you've skipped out. If you ask me, you were stupid to leave. You only have a few months left, would you rather they throw you in Pentridge with Brown?'

'I love that you just assume I've skipped out. How do you know I wasn't granted time served or something?'

He laughed at that.

'Or something, or something,' he said.

'And you don't know what it was like in there. Pentridge would have been a damn side easier. We'll be out of your hair soon and out of town once the show season starts,' Mona said.

'Where will we go if we can't stay here?' Curly's eyes were wide with nerves.

'I have an idea,' Mona said.

'As good as your idea to rob that diamond shop?' A low voice came from the living room. Mona laughed and shouted out 'hello to you too Lawrie.'

Lawrence bundled Mona up in a hug.

'Glad you're out,' he said.

'At least someone is.' Mona motioned to Hutchison and he shook his head.

'You shouldn't a been in there in the first place. If you'd just done what I've always told you,' Lawrence started and Mona joined him for the chorus 'deny, deny, deny.'

'If you really want to help us you'll find us a room for rent and get a hold of some size four shoes for my friend Curly here,' Mona introduced the two. Lawrence took Curly's hand and placed a kiss on it.

'You're a young thing, aren't you?' he asked. Curly was about to tell him her age when Mona interrupted.

'You're observant, aren't you?' she said.

'So, what's your real name love, or am I stuck with the atrocious one Mona's obviously given you?' Lawrence asked.

'Mary, my name's Mary Duffy,' she said, blushing. It was the first time she'd said her full name aloud in a very long time.

'I thought Mary's what the nuns called you,' Mona said.

'My name was already Mary. And there wasn't another at Sacred Heart when I arrived, so I got to keep it,' Curly explained. Mona was flawed. She felt as if she knew Curly so intimately, they'd become so close, yet she didn't even know her real name. 'The nuns gave Mona the name Patricia,' Curly shared with the boys. Lawrence laughed.

'Patricia! I know of a lass in the Fitzroy back streets with that very name,' Lawrence grinned.

'What about that Patricia Ellis, now she's something…' Stanley chimed in. 'What I'd like to do to…'

'Alright, alright, I've heard just about enough. While you buggers are falling all over yourselves over that horrible bloody name, the coppers are probably driving round looking for me, to take me back to the Convent.'

'There's room at one of the boarding houses I know of in Carlton. I'll take you there now if ya like. Can't get you any shoes til tomorrow, sorry Mary,' Lawrence said.

'That's alright, these will do for now,' Curly replied before turning her attention to Mona 'didn't we just come from Carlton?' Mona nodded and sent her back to the bedroom to finish packing a bag of borrowed clothes.

'Am I a bad person?' Mona asked Lawrence.

'Yes.' He said and Hutchison laughed.

'No really, I mean, I didn't even know her real name. Am I a bad friend?'

'Yes.' He said again and lit her a cigarette.

'See, if *you* were a good friend, you'd reassure me. No, Mona, you're a wonderful friend.'

'But *I* never claimed to be a good friend. Or a good person for that matter. See, I know myself Mona, and I know you. You're no good, you're up to no good and you're as good a friend as any who'd choose a diamond over a mate.'

'Now, now,' Hutchison said, leaving the room to check on Curly.

Mona took a second to process this. She knew deep down she was good. A good person who didn't always pay enough attention to the finer details, like names. Who sometimes drank too much and gambled too much and did stupid things.

'Three diamonds,' she said. 'There were three.'

'Oh well…'

'Really pretty ones,' she grinned.

'Big too I expect.'

'Huge.'

'Well size is everything,' Lawrence was laughing now.

'Looked good on me too.'

'Why didn't you say so? That changes everything.'

With a bag full of clothes, including the bag and Robson's hat Mona had left there before her sentence, they bundled into Lawrence's stolen car. This time he'd chosen a brand-new black Pontiac. He filled Mona in on all the gossip she'd missed while away. Guggenheim was laying low after getting into a fight with a few blokes in Russell Street, he'd been stabbed with a carving fork! Though Stanley put on a brave show, Lawrence revealed they'd been to visit the ex in Mona's absence, Stanley begging her to return to Melbourne with the kids. Lawrence shook his head 'No dice.' And Brown was still in gaol of course. Lawrence went to visit from time to time.

'I can pay for your first week or two but after that you're on your own,' Lawrence said, attempting to flick his cigarette ash out the car window as they drove, but hitting Curly in the face with it in the passenger seat instead. She moved her head to dodge the grey and white specks.

'Thank you, Lawrence, I missed you,' Mona said. She hunted around the glove box, trying on sunglasses, and flicking through papers. She wondered who the previous owners were.

'You'll have to go rob another nice jewellery store or try your hand at breaking into those returned soldiers leagues,' he said.

'I'd never! Why would you suggest that?' Mona hit him in the arm causing him to swerve.

'My mate Albert Sharpe's been at it. Tilly's paying good money for wireless sets, and they leave 'em there unattended overnight.'

'Not interested,' she said. 'Besides the last time Tilly was supposedly paying good money for something, it didn't work out too well for me.' She looked back at Curly and shook her head. Didn't want Curly to think she'd ever steal from soldiers.

'Malvern shops, theatre patrons, RSLs, what's the bloody difference,' Lawrence said.

'There's a difference.'

'Maybe you aren't so awful after all.'

'Why thank you,' Mona said. 'Now you can save your advice, but for the money I'm truly grateful. I don't know what I'd do without you.'

'You mean that?' he asked.

'Sure,' she said.

'Maybe we could go for a dance at the Forty Club sometime, now you're back,' he said. By this point Mona wasn't quite listening. She was holding up a pair of round spectacles she'd found in the glove box, turning in her seat to show a giggling Curly. How funny she looked in them.

'Oh yes, sure,' Mona replied.

Lawrence drove them to a boarding house in Drummond Street. It had always been a favourite of Mona's. Not far from Hanover, only the park between them. But the dwellings in Drummond always appeared a bit fancier. More inhabitable. Fewer rats. The street was wider too with grass and trees down the centre. Lawrence dropped them out front with ten shillings and instructions to see a Mrs Grey.

***

'You can use the kitchen but leave your food there at your own risk. Dinner's at six. I don't cook all hours so ya miss it, tough titties. Toot's out back of course and you pay extra for a bath.' Mrs Grey reminded Mona of Sister Leoni, running through the rules of the house as she led them to their room. 'These are all full,' she continued pointing out closed doors at the tops of the stairs. 'Stay away from this one, he's a dirty old git. Will talk ya ear off too,' she said finger pressed against one door, her voice lowered. Finally, they got to the end of the hallway. Two rooms. Doors wide. One double bed in each. One set of drawers and a standing mirror.

'Ya have enough for a room each or d'ya want to share?' she asked.

Mona opened her hand revealing the cash Lawrence had given her, keeping the rest of Charles' money for the pub. Mrs Grey shook her head.

'One room it is,' she said, sweeping her hand across Mona's to collect the money. 'If ya want to stay on past next Friday…' she started.

'Yes we'll come see you about our situation once we're settled,' Mona said. Mona wanted to clear out of Melbourne as quickly as possible, but the sideshow would be on break until the new year and she wasn't sure how long it would take to scrounge more money together for the road.

Mona headed for the mirror as Curly leafed through the bag of clothes they'd taken from Hutchison's. There were no mirrors in the Convent and Mona wasn't sure what the months of hard labour had done to her. She felt smaller. She confirmed her fears when she looked in the mirror.

'I look haggard,' she muttered before turning her attention back to Curly. 'Don't bother unpacking,' she said.

'Why?' Curly had already allocated herself the top drawer.

'Because we won't be here long. And it's harder to run from the cops when you've got a bag to pack.'

16

For a week Mona and Curly lived off Charles' and Lawrence's money and the hospitality of the other boarders. Mona took to wearing her hair pinned up under a hat at all times, paranoid some cop on the street would spot her. There seemed to be so many more of them around town in the lead up to Christmas. Lawrence had been by the boarding house more than once, to let her know Collins had dropped in on him, Stanley and Guggenheim to see if they knew where she was. Collins, unconvinced they weren't in touch with her, had also asked them to pass on a message: that she wouldn't be in any trouble if she just returned to the Convent and saw out her last three months. Mona had to admit, the idea weighed on her. But she had escaped not just for her own sake, but for Curly's too. And what would Curly do without her?

By the time the weekend rolled around Mona was ready to show Curly a night on the town, the girl had just turned 18 after all. They met Lawrence at the Albanian club for a game of cards. They all won a few hands each, so when Lawrence tried to suggest they make a meal of one of the gentlemen seated beside Mona, she didn't see the point.

'Not in front of the little one,' she said, using Curly as an excuse.

'Little? You weren't much older than her when you started,' he said, but didn't push it. He was swimming in winnings and in a good mood. He was out with Mona and she was without a boyfriend. Mona pretended not to notice his sudden interest.

They went by the George N' Cafe for a late-night bite, then lay in the grass beside the Church in Lonsdale Street with a slew of other crims determined not to let 6 o'clock closing hours dictate when they could and couldn't drink. They fell asleep, drunk, under the hot summer moon. Mona woke in spurts as Lawrence and Curly bundled her into a Taxi and carried her to her room.

Mrs Grey had changed the sheets. The bed was draped in a rich red quilt which made Mona think of rose petals. She went to sleep in a glossy garden, but the blades of grass grew sharp and prickly as she faded in and out of dreams, kicking her sheets off and on again, pooling in sweat. By the time the sun peeked through the windows, the red of the roses had turned to blood, and she was swimming in it. Or perhaps it was pouring out of her? She threw the covers off. For a second when she looked up towards the end of the bed, she thought Cecilia was there, standing over her, pocket watch in hand. Mona felt haunted. By the police, by the Convent, her only recourse? Run away. It wasn't long before she had a plan in mind.

Curly woke to find Mona grinning over a copy of *The Argus*. Without explanation, Mona instructed Curly to wear a black dress and stockings and borrow a red lipstick from Mrs Grey.

'Tell her you need to look presentable, for a job interview,' Mona said tucking a pink short sleeved shirt into one of her new black skirts. Curly brightened.

'Job interview?' she asked.

'Don't get too excited,' Mona said. 'Just go and get some red lippy and meet me outside.'

All dressed up they strolled into the city without a word between them. Mona found it amusing. In the Convent they'd been desperate to talk, every chance they got, any time the nuns turned their backs. Now they were free of the nuns they hardly spoke at all. It had been over a week, but Curly seemed overwhelmed, though she tried hard to hide it. Mona watched her walk wide-eyed past the trams, office buildings and city workers. Melbourne was awash in Christmas tinsel, shop windows dressed in gift wrap and baubles. Mona enjoyed seeing it all through Curly's eyes. But it was the summer breeze she was enjoying most. The air around the Convent was a mixture of steam, detergent, and sweat. Back in the city, the air was fresh with the smell of summer and pine needles from Christmas tree littered street corners.

Mona stopped short just outside her old haunt, the Theatre. 'I need you to go in and buy one ticket for Saturday night's show.' Mona handed Curly the last of their money.

Curly did as she asked and returned with a ticket for *La Vie Paree.*

Next, she walked Curly around the corner to the printers. She waited nearby, within earshot, while Curly approached the shop owner as instructed.

'Hello there,' Curly said. Mona could hear her voice shake a little. She said a prayer under her breath.

'Hello, what can I d'ya for Miss?' the print worker asked, wiping his ink-stained hands on his overalls.

'I work up the road at the Theatre, we need to print some extra tickets for Saturday night's show.' Curly explained. She had a handle on her nerves now.

'Was there a problem with the ones I already done?'

'Well yes, it wasn't a mistake of yours I can assure you,' Curly pulled the ticket she'd just purchased out of her pocket. 'There's a misprint. It should read Parie with an ie, not double e,' she said.

The printer clasped his forehead in his right hand as if fighting back a splitting headache.

'I double-checked, spoke to Edelman, he said double 'e'.'

There was silence then, Mona said another prayer, c'mon Curly, you can do this.

'He got it wrong, I'm so sorry, we know it's not your fault,' Curly said. 'But my manager wants a fresh ream to replace the ones we haven't sold yet. He wants it today and I've been told to tell you to add an extra pound to our next bill for the rush job.'

'Huh, alright then. Wait a moment while I call Myer, if they can wait a day on their catalogue I spose I can fit this in now.' The printer walked out front to the pay phone. A moment later he returned with the good news. He'd have a fresh ream of tickets by close of business.

'I'll drop em in by five,' he said.

Again, Mona held her breath. Curly came through. 'Oh no, no, no, I wouldn't hear of it. We've put you out enough. I'll come back and collect them. Save you the trouble of delivery.'

Mona was impressed. Curly could think on her feet. She'd been worried Curly's nerves may be a hindrance to life on the road, but perhaps not.

They returned later in the day and collected the heavy roll of tickets. They jumped on a tram headed to Flinders Street Station. It was bustling with office workers heading home, and Friday night commuters coming into the city for a dance or a show. They deposited the roll beside the newspaper stand, lining their pockets with handfuls of twenty at a time.

'Due to popular demand the Princess has released extra seats for tomorrow night's sold out show, La Vie Parie!' Mona called out. She used to occasionally spruik tickets for the sideshows. She'd shout about Australia's hottest dancers, toughest boxers and most exotic amusements. She'd challenge passers-by to darts or to guess her weight. She loved it. She was good at it. Curly on the other hand, didn't need her voice it seemed. She sold just as many tickets as Mona simply by smiling and holding out her hand. They were halfway through the box, with enough to cover rent for a few more weeks, when Mona decided it was time for a break.

'Keep it up, I'm going to get us a drink and something to eat,' Mona said.

'Don't be long,' Curly begged.

Mona nodded. She headed to the bottle shop buying two bottles of wine in paper bags. She opened hers straight away and took a long swig. She'd sculled half the bottle by the time she got to the cafe, picking up two sandwiches. When Mona returned to the Station, Curly had sold almost the entire ream. Her handbag flush with cash. Mona handed her a bottle and a sandwich and ushered her to the street.

'Go take a break. I'll sell the last of em,' Mona said. Curly went down the street looking for somewhere to sit and enjoy her dinner.

'Only ten tickets left for La Vie Parie's sold out Saturday night show! One night only! Don't miss out!' she sang to the crowd. As she parted with the last tickets, she spied two uniformed police officers watching her. They couldn't know who she was, could they? Not possible. She knew there were no photos in her police file, yet. But still, they walked towards her, paces quickening. She kicked the now empty box behind the stand and ran.

'Hold up Miss,' they called out as they gave chase.

She tripped down the steps of the Station. Her long brown curls fell from beneath her cap giving the cops something to grab onto. She screamed.

'Hasn't anyone ever told you it's not polite to pull a lady's hair?' she said.

'Sorry Miss but it was the only way to catch hold of you.' The young officer held out a gloved hand and ran his fingers soothingly over her head. Mona stood still waiting for him to speak. Perhaps she was only in trouble for selling tickets in the station. Perhaps they didn't know who she was or that the tickets were fakes.

'We work out of Russell Street,' the shorter one said. 'Seen you a few times with the CI guys.'

Her hopes had been dashed. Mona's shoulders dropped in defeat. They knew who she was and where she was and wasn't meant to be.

'You're Mona Hayes. We've been told to be on the lookout for you. Absconding from the Convent, breaking bail...' Mona stopped listening as they moved to either side of her, taking one arm each and leading her towards their car. Her attention drawn back to their voices by the mention of Curly. 'The other lass with you?'

'Who?' she asked.

'The one you escaped with? Mary was her name. She's not in trouble, but her parents are looking for her.'

'I don't know where she went after we escaped. She's a young girl, not exactly the type I hang round with, as you would well know.'

'Well then.' The one who'd pulled her hair earlier sat her in the back of the patrol car while the shorter one sat in the driver's seat. He rubbed his hand over her head again. 'Sorry if I hurt you,' he said. 'Do you want to tell me about those tickets you were selling?'

Mona shook her head, for once heeding Lawrence's ongoing advice of denial.

'She works for the theatre,' the short one turned from his seat. 'I remember Collins sayin'. They mustn't a known she wasn't spose to be out.'

'I don't want to get them into any trouble. The Theatre Manager has been very kind to me. He didn't know,' she said, reinforcing the lie. Settling in for the short drive she took in the sights of Melbourne, watched as people milled around closed pubs sipping from their flasks, bartenders washing down walls. She thanked God that Curly still had her share of the ticket money. Hopefully she'd figure out what had happened and use it to get out of town. As the car rounded the corner and the Convent loomed large, Mona grew worried. She was back for another three months without Curly, but with Cecilia. She'd never really been scared of anyone before. Not even of the police. Especially not these police.

'What if I don't want to go back?' she said.

'What makes you think you have a choice?' the short one laughed.

'Well, I've broken my bail conditions haven't I? Shouldn't I be going back to Court? Or to Pentridge?' she asked.

'No, we've been told that so long as you return to the Convent without issue, you can see out the remainder of your six months, the escape won't be held against you,' the taller one turned in his seat to face her. 'You're being given a gift. Take it.'

So, she did. And she soon regretted it.

17

The police drove in through the delivery gates of Abbotsford Convent, dropping Mona, like laundry, at the feet of Novice Anne.

'She won't cause you any more trouble.' The tall officer leaned out of the passenger car window to address the Novice. Mona waited for a response, and it came in the form of a nodded head and a wave, and with that the officers took their cue to leave. Mona turned to watch the squad car drive out the gates and turn left back towards the city, where Curly was now no doubt in a panic as to her whereabouts. Mona followed the silent Novice up the stairs into the dormitory. The girls were readying for bed when she entered. They glared, too scared to acknowledge her presence in words in front of Sister Margaret, who waited with tapping foot by the end of Mona's bed. Mona was surprised it lay empty. She'd been gone now two weeks, yet it was as if, in the Convent, time had stood still.

The nun watched Mona with steely eyes, refusing to look away as Mona changed back into her grey garb. As she pulled the dress down over her head, she felt a sharp crack across her back. She refused to cry out in pain, instead continuing to dress herself as quickly as possible. The Sister greeted Mona's silence with another smack behind one knee, then the other. Finally, she spun Mona around to face her, needling her cane into Mona's neck, trapping her against the wall.

'Any more trouble from you and I go to the Courts - but not before beating the life from every one of your pale, pathetic limbs. Do you understand me?' the nun spat. Mona turned her head. The nun pushed harder on her stick choking Mona further. Mona coughed, struggling to breathe, until the nun loosened her grip once more.

'I said do you understand?'

'Yes,' Mona replied, making the snap decision to get through the next few months as smoothly as possible. From now on her favourite words would be 'yes Sister, no Sister,' and nothing more.

With that, the nun released her. Mona felt herself surrounded by relieved exhales from the beds around her. As the nun left she shouted.

'To bed! You'll be on menstrual towel washing from now on. And before you ask, there'll be no port for you tonight.'

Mona looked in the direction of Red's bed. Red leant down, lifted the loose floorboard and displayed a bare cavern where the alcohol and cigarettes used to be. Mona glanced around the room searching for the eyes of Priscia and Little Lucy. Isabel was gone. Unfortunately, Cecilia wasn't.

Mona couldn't think of a lie believable enough to warrant Cecilia's forgiveness. There was no way to get back on her good side. Mona didn't sleep that night. She sat upright in bed watching Cecilia. Her only distraction? Imagining the commotion that would take place when more people turned up at the theatre than there were seats.

Mona wasn't exactly welcomed back with open arms by the other girls either. Because she and Curly disappeared right after the morning delivery, the nuns suspected that Robbie and Charles had aided their escape. The next morning when the men pulled into the Convent, Sister Margaret greeted them. They denied any knowledge of course, though it suddenly occurred to Charles where his missing wallet had gone. Sister Margaret insisted on seeing inside the van for any sign Mona and Curly had been there. She searched thoroughly, and found the flasks and cigarettes they'd planned to smuggle in that day. She wasn't convinced when the men claimed the items as their own. She searched the dorms high and low and found the rest of the stash near Red's bed. Within the day both Robbie and Charles had been sacked, all delivery girls reassigned to new jobs and Red given twelve whacks of the cane. She still winced when sitting down for each meal.

'Well *you* got off bloody lightly, didn't you?' Red groaned.

'How'd you figure that?' Mona asked. She was relegated to the small laundry room washing the menstrual towels of every girl and nun in the entire Convent. It was the worst gig in the place and that was saying something.

'I couldn't help but do the math. You got three whacks last night, exactly nine less than I got after you left.'

'I'm sorry Red,' Mona said.

'Are you?'

'Not really,' they laughed.

'So, how's the kid going?' Red asked.

'She'll be fine. She's got a roof over her head, clean clothes, plenty of cash...'

'All legally obtained of course.'

'Of course. I just hope she isn't worried about me,' Mona said.

'I don't think anyone worries about you Mona,' Red laughed. The same cackle Mona'd grown to miss the past two weeks. Yet the comment it accompanied gave Mona a flicker of fear. No one worried about her. When it came to the rest of her time in the Convent, she could only count on herself. And her own instincts were telling her she was in trouble. As Red left the table, Mona could see the row of seats behind. Cecilia was staring dead at her. Locking fiery eyes with Mona she picked her knife up from the table, pricked her finger with the sharp tip and then slid it down the sleeve of her uniform. Mona glanced around the room. No one else had noticed. Not even Sister Margaret.

The only sunlight Mona saw was on the way to the refectory. Without the fresh air of deliveries and added distractions of sneaking sweets or whispered sing-alongs with Curly, the days seemed longer and more painful than before. Every step, every action took more effort. Two weeks of relaxation melted from her body as quickly as dirt from sheets. She was lucky the nuns didn't lock her in with the bloody undies for long, another girl needing punishment soon took over. Back in the main work room, Mona watched as her hands took on their dry, puckered, sheet-washing form. She could smell herself again. Feel the oil of her hair every time she ran her fingers through it. She followed Philomena's lead - leaning her left elbow on the corner of the washing tub to stop her falling over when the steam made her feel faint. Mona hadn't realised what a difference the couple of delivery breaks made each day. She wondered why she'd been given such a perk when she first arrived. Sister Leoni had told her it was because she was older and stronger than most of the other girls, more able to handle the heavy metal trolley. But that wasn't the case. Priscia and Martina were of similar age, Priscia much sturdier. The nun had been with her in court. Perhaps she had seen something in Mona? Wanted to give her some responsibility? An opportunity? She must certainly regret that now.

Whenever Mona's eyes began to flutter shut, as if she could sleep standing up, she felt a whack at her back. And when Sister Margaret left the room for other duties, Cecilia would take her place, staring Mona down with eyes as sharp as the Sister's cane.

***

'How do you know Cecilia wants to take revenge on you?' Philomena and Mona had been sent to clean the stairwell one evening, forfeiting dinner for rolling their eyes earlier in the day.

'Because it's what I would do,' Mona replied. 'At least when it comes to Sister Margaret I know what I'm in for. She couldn't do any worse than assigning chores, taking away dinner and giving me a whack. With Cecilia, it's the unknown that's killing me. I wish whatever she had planned she'd just get it over with.'

'I can ask her to speed things up for you if ya like?' Philomena laughed. Mona was certain she was the only one who saw the real Cecilia. 'Oh come on,' Philomena reasoned, 'She's nothing but a hollow-cheeked eccentric who spends more time dancing in circles than doing laundry. She's no harm to anyone. The Convent's just made her a little loopy that's all.'

'The Convent hasn't made her a little anything. She's the same little girl dropped off by her father ten years ago. This place is meant to be some miracle reformatory for fallen girls. But it's not. You can't grow or think for yourself or learn anything of use besides how to clean sheets and scrub floors.' Mona held up her scrubbing brush to make her point. 'The only difference between us and Cecilia is what was there all along. You and I want better lives than we have, Cecilia never learned to want a life for herself. All she ever wanted was to take one away.'

'Now you're the one sounding loopy. Honestly, I think you have her all wrong.'

***

Between the summer heat blasting through the high glass windows, and the steam coming off the soaking sheets, the girls were sweltering through an unusually relaxed day of laundering. The nuns allowed the girls to roll up their sleeves, take off their shoes and dip their hot limbs into a cold bucket of water between sheets. The nuns themselves found little relief in their own bulky habits and stepped out at regular intervals to catch a breeze outside. During one unsupervised moment, Mona noticed Cecilia coming towards her as if she were a ghost – pale, expressionless, floating as opposed to walking. Mona stepped behind a steaming pot as little Lucy, next to her, dropped a fresh batch of sheets into it, mixing them with a rod. It wasn't until Cecilia was within spitting distance that Mona noticed the string. Mona hadn't seen anything like it in the Convent, her mind flitted through all the places Cecilia could have gotten it, but she couldn't come up with an answer.

'What's that?' she asked, stepping back again, trapped between tubs.

Cecilia didn't respond. She moved swiftly. Bringing her arms up behind Mona, with the string between her hands. Before Mona could scream, Cecilia had wrapped it all the way around her neck. Lucy shrieked causing the other girls to look up. Some saw Cecilia strangling Mona, but others only saw what happened next.

Mona had about ten kilos on Cecilia. Alcohol weight. She used all her might to push Cecilia away, the wet floor creating a perfect storm. Cecilia's legs slipped right out from under her, and she landed on her backside on the floor. The back of her head collided with the side of the wash tub on her way down. Her pained squeal like nothing Mona had ever heard before or would ever hear again. Like letting the air out of a thousand coloured balloons. The other girls curled their hands around Cecilia's shoulders, lifting her from the floor. Blood poured from Cecilia's head down their arms as they carried her to the infirmary.

'She just fell,' Red told the nuns as the girls left behind nodded in agreement. Mona stayed silent, shocked but not sorry.

The nuns hot-weathered generosity came to an abrupt end. When knock-off time came, the girls were ordered to stay and continue working into the night. Dinner went cold in the refectory while the girls continued sweltering in the laundry. The nuns didn't leave them alone again. And Cecilia never left the infirmary.

The remainder of Mona's stay at the Convent was lonely. Most of the girls steered clear of her. She wasn't a violent woman, surely they knew that. Cecilia hadn't given her any other choice.

Mona was somewhat pleased that Red and Priscia warmed to her again soon before her departure.

'I wish I could say I'd be in Melbourne to meet you, but I plan to get out of town with the showies,' Mona told Priscia who was due out two weeks later.

'That's alright. You'll be back in September, won't you? For the Melbourne Show? I'll catch ya then.'

'Look up a fella named Stanley Hutchison when you get out,' Mona said.

Priscia agreed and gave her a quick embrace and tap on the back.

Red stood back from them both. Once they'd said their goodbyes she nodded quickly to Mona and begged her. 'Take care of Mary won't you?'

18

Mona readied herself for her departure the next morning. She tucked in her bedsheets with greater care and precision than ever before. She'd collected a couple extra bread rolls at dinner, hiding them in her tunic. She placed one under Red's bedspread and one under Priscia's. Sister Leoni led her out of the dormitory as if the day she arrived was a book being read backwards. As she reached the courtyard she turned to look up at the window where she'd first seen Curly. Instead of a grinning face staring down at her there was only an empty reflection of the building before her. Sister Leoni's keys clinked at her sides as she fumbled with the gate.

Sister Leoni took Mona back through the main Convent building, through hallways lined with crosses and girls scrubbing tiles. Sister Margaret waited for them at the main entryway. Mona eyed Margaret carefully as the nun pulled a piece of paper from her robe pocket and read aloud.

'To the judge, Dear Sir, Regarding Mona Hayes. During the time she spent at the Convent her conduct was quite satisfactory in every way except on one occasion, when on a sudden impulse'—Sister Margaret paused for effect—'she absconded from the Convent but was brought back after a few weeks and completed her term without giving any further trouble. We remain yours faithfully, Sisters of the Good Shepherd.'

She folded the paper and placed it back in her pocket. Mona couldn't hide her surprise. She was sure Sister Margaret would have taken great delight in telling the judge about her smart mouth, hidden alcohol and altercation with Cecilia. As if reading her mind, the Sister said, 'I think it's best for everyone for you to go now.' The old nun floated back down the hall and out a side door, back to the Sacred Heart to reign terror on the girls in the laundry.

'You've done good work here the last few months, hard work,' Sister Leoni spoke kindly. 'Sadly, some of the girls who come in through the courts, when they leave here, are destined to go back to the life in which they came. They've no real education behind them, they can't read or write. They have no skills besides the ones we've instilled in them.'

'Washing sheets, you mean?' Mona replied.

'I'd like to think you might have learned a little more than that. If you start to lose balance, just focus on one spot ahead of you, that's the trick.'

'If I ever want to stand still, I'll keep that in mind.'

'I hope you do, Patricia.'

'My name's Mona,' she said.

Sister Leoni smiled sadly, opened the wooden door and let Mona free.

It had only been a few months since she'd broken out with Curly, and still, the freshness of the air outside the Convent surprised her. No steamy laundry, no dirty smells of over-worked women. She was so busy looking into the clear blue sky that she almost didn't notice the dark figure leaning against his car on the road ahead of her.

'Well look who it is. Crime rate's dropped a good ten per cent since you've been in here.' Detective Collins grinned, threw his cigarette to the ground and walked towards her. She blinked twice, to make sure she wasn't seeing things.

'Good thing I'm out then – I'd hate to see you out of a job.' She waited for him to speak again, explain his presence, but he just looked at her. She grew impatient. 'So, don't tell me you're here to give me a ride?' She couldn't help admit, she liked the thought he'd remembered her release date. She didn't expect Lawrence or even Hutchison to show up. But a cop? Well, she was flattered, and nervous, and suddenly very concerned about the state of her appearance.

'I was just over at the Victoria Palace. They have a few vacant rooms. If you'd like I can give you a ride and spot you a night.'

'Why, you're not propositioning me are you Detective?' She knew he wasn't.

He laughed. 'Such a dirty mind for a newly reformed, good girl of the Good Shepherd.'

Now it was Mona's turn to laugh. She walked past him and straight towards the car, leaning down to open the back passenger door.

'What am I a taxi?' Collins slapped the door shut and guided her to the front passenger side. Though arrested many times, she'd never been in his car before. Technically not his, she supposed, but belonged to the CIB. Aside from stubbed cigarettes overflowing the ashtray, the car was pristine.

'I've never seen a car as clean as this one, who's your maid?' Mona asked.

Collins grinned in response giving Mona her answer. Must be a neat freak. 'You know, this may be the first and only time I've seen you completely sober,' he said as he started up the engine.

'That's not true,' she said, her earlier smile fading.

'It's a nice change. You might consider sticking to it for a while.'

Mona rolled her eyes. 'Now I understand what you're doing here.'

'No, you don't,' he replied.

She decided not to argue. Instead, she studied his face as he drove. He was a careful driver, focused, yet relaxed. He drove one-handed and tapped his other on his knee as if speaking to her in Morse code. If she only knew how to decipher it.

Though it had only been six months since she'd last seen him, he looked older. Perhaps it was simply that she'd never seen him so up close before. Sitting side by side in his car, she could home in on the smile lines beside his left eye and the crease of his cheek. Most police officers kept themselves freshly shaved, but Collins sported stubble, which Mona saw as a small act of rebellion. She wanted to tease him about it, ask him when his last haircut was and when he last shaved. But she didn't want him scrutinising her appearance in return. So, she remained quiet. A comfortable silence. When they came upon the Palace, Mona was almost disappointed. Collins got out and led her to the front desk. He paid for one night and handed her the key.

'It's so very generous of you,' she said. Collins looked a little too long at her hands. 'What manual labour does to a girl,' she said, twirling the key between her fingers. 'I'd cover them up, but I seem to have lost my best pair of gloves.'

She watched his face for recognition. To see if he remembered the gloves she'd lost in the robbery. He clearly did, he chuckled, taking a pair of black leather gloves from his pocket.

'Will these do?'

'I suppose they will.' Mona put both gloves and the room key in one hand and shook Collins' hand with the other. 'Thank you.'

'You're welcome.' He winked and walked away, glancing back at her just once before the door swung shut behind him.

Upstairs, Mona traced her freshly gloved fingers over the shabby hotel furniture. No bigger than a shoebox yet the room was her own. For one night at least. Mona couldn't remember the last time she'd been on her own. From the family home to rooming with Brown, sideshow trailers, boarding houses and the Convent dormitory. If only for that night, she had no one to worry about but herself. She thanked Collins again, silently in her head, as she turned to take a glimpse of herself in the mirror.

With no mirrors in the Convent, it had been three months since she'd seen her face in anything other than the crinkly glass of the dormitory windows. She kept her eyes low at first, saw the white quilt of the bed reflected before her. She promised herself that when she got her own place she'd buy a colourful blanket. Or black. Anything other than the stark white she'd grown to despise at Abbotsford. Her eyes trailed further up the mirror and focussed on the dust surrounding the frame. Finally, she saw herself. The beautiful new gloves Collins had given her were too big and out of place against her worn grey uniform. She cursed the nuns for not giving her her old clothes back. She'd go downstairs later and enquire after any lost property. Maybe she could secure herself a frock or coat at no charge. It would have to be a size or two smaller than she was used to. Her hands reached out to paw at her face. Her cheek bones had gained prominence in the last few months. The effects of irregular meals, pumpkin and porridge, and hard labour washing sheets and scrubbing floors. She'd seen the effects on her hands every day, but hadn't realised just how much weight she'd lost until now. She felt a ghost of her former self. Embarrassed that Collins had seen her in such a way. She'd never been around him without her hair done and eyelashes curled. Even without money, she'd always managed to wear nice frocks and coats. Some stolen, some not. Slight bags had formed under her eyes and her complexion had grown even more sallow. The only positive Mona could see in herself was the extra trimness in her legs. Her tired face aside, maybe she could make a few quid over show season with these new-found dancer's pins.

The bed she crawled into that night was more comfortable than any bed she could remember. Brown would be released from Pentridge soon, yet her mind didn't dwell on him long. She considered Curly's whereabouts only for a brief moment. Instead, as she drifted off to sleep, it was Collins on her mind. She wondered what his home looked like, what colour sheets he was slipping into, why had he come to pick her up and did he think about her once his shift was over? His smile was the last thing she saw before fading into dreams.

Mona couldn't remember the last time she'd slept without another person beside her. The hotel doors slamming, creaky corridors and late-night partygoers outside didn't seem anywhere near as loud as the sound of the inhale and exhale of a roommate. It had never occurred to her how much she loved the sounds of heavy breathing, coughs, sneezes, and shuffle of legs tossing and turning in hard-tucked sheets. She couldn't be alone, in the dark, with her thoughts. She needed the company of others.

By the time the sun came through the windows, Mona was already awake and dressed in nice new clothes - courtesy of a generous, over-packed,

Irish couple she met at breakfast - and on her way to Carlton. Just as she'd hoped, Curly was still in the same room at the same boarding house in Drummond Street. She explained to Mona that the night she'd returned to where they'd been selling tickets, one of the paperboys at the Station had told her that policemen had come and chased Mona away. She assumed Mona would either be returned to the Convent or sent to Pentridge to see out the next three months, so she'd waited for her return.

'Mrs Grey gave me a job cleaning rooms between tenants. Poor pay but I've been able to stay here for free, and what with the blokes always shouting dinner and a wardrobe full of clothes, I've not needed for much,' she said, opening up the cupboard and presenting Mona with the items she'd picked out at Hutchison's house months earlier. Mona's things remained untouched. Curly had kept it all just how she'd left it.

'I can't believe you waited all this time,' Mona said, pulling Robson's hat over her head.

'Well, to be honest, I almost threw it all out the window last night. Followed by a lit match. I thought you were to get out yesterday. When you didn't show I thought you'd forgotten about me.'

'I'm sorry, I did get out yesterday, but the nuns, they were generous, gave me money for dinner and a bus ticket, and put me up at a hotel for the night. They make sure you have somewhere to go. It's quite nice really, I couldn't say no,' Mona lied without knowing why. She told herself it was because she didn't want anyone to know she was on good terms with a cop. She also didn't want to chance blushing when she spoke of him. 'You surprise me Curly, and here I thought I was the vengeful one,' she said, glancing over at the window Curly had claimed to have wanted to throw her clothes out of. 'Don't tell me Lawrence and Hutch have been rubbing off on you?'

'I haven't seen them since you left. Word must have gotten back you'd been picked up by the police,' Curly said.

Mona tried not to let her disappointment show. She'd assumed her old friends would take care of her new one. 'Let's rectify that shall we.'

Mona headed straight for the wardrobe and flipped through her clothes. She picked out two outfits; one for her and one for Curly. It was a Saturday, and tonight everyone would be in Port Melbourne. Most likely at the home of Kim Sly, one of Hutchison's bandmates. There would be music, champagne, cocaine and dancing. The perfect way for Mona to celebrate her second night out of the Convent. They spent the hours before the party gossiping about the blokes Curly had met while staying at the boarding house. One gentleman in particular had grown quite fond of her. But for reasons Curly couldn't explain, she didn't care for him. In fact, she wanted to get as far away as possible, and soon.

'Well, I may have the solution for that,' Mona said. 'Show season.'

By the end of the day, Mona had convinced Mrs Grey to spot them two train tickets to Sydney. 'From there we hitch a ride with one of the troupes and travel right up the coast,' she explained to Curly.

'So, this is it then?' Curly said trying to hide her nerves. 'Last night in Melbourne?'

'That's right. Better make it count.'

19

Mona slipped into a white satin gown with shoelace straps for sleeves, a large flower at the right breast, sash around the middle with diamond-shaped panels down the front. She threw a black cape with white fur trim over the top.

Curly was all nerves in a ruby long-sleeved velvet gown Mona picked out for her. 'I'll stick out like a sore thumb.'

'That's the point,' said Mona.

The party seemed as if it'd been going on for hours by the time Mona and Curly arrived. Stanley Hutchison spirited Curly away to introduce her to one of his bandmates while Mona went straight for the gleaming liquor cart.

One thing was sure, that old Kim Sly loved green. Green curtains, green armchairs, green lampshades, even green alcohol. Three months without a drop of grog, Mona steered clear of the absinthe, pouring herself a tall glass of beer instead. It'd been so long since she'd seen women in anything other than habits and uniforms, she couldn't help but stare at the array of black long-sleeved dresses with butterfly clips at the waist, navy blue silk and girls in green who faded into the furniture. The men made an effort too. Was it someone's birthday? Criminals didn't normally look this good. Or had she just been locked up too long?

Outside, the Autumn air was chilly, but inside, the fire was roaring and the rooms packed. Discarded gloves, hats and coats littered every free corner. The smell of burning wood mixed with sweat and cigarette smoke, almost overpowered by the stench of cheap perfume worn by a few too many of the women waiting to dance by the firelight. Musicians with their instruments assembled by the window, ensuring the neighbours could all hear the brassy, boisterous swing jazz filtering through the dusty party out onto the street. Between songs there was clapping, shouting and drug taking. There was no doubt in Mona's mind, the cops would be breaking this party up by 1am. She'd have to make her escape before then, lest she want to end up locked up … again. She'd need to leave even earlier if she wanted food, typical men throwing a party, not so much as a jar of olives in the entire house.

'Hey, aren't you supposed to be holed up with the nuns?' James Lawrence sidled up beside her.

'My time's up,' Mona said.

'So tell me, what did the Sisters teach you then?'

'Hmmm, that mascara doesn't wash out?'

His tiny blue eyes crinkled in confusion, and she realised, he wouldn't know what went on at a Convent.

'Laundry,' she said, and he nodded.

Quickly distracted, he launched into a tirade about drugs and cars and keys and some other shit. He liked to talk with his hands, causing him to spill some of his beer on Mona's dress. She cursed; shouldn't have worn white.

'Serves me right,' Mona said as Lawrence, ever so elegantly, licked some of the spill off his fingers. Wouldn't want to waste it.

They turned their attention to the band. An argument erupted as a drunk, yet handsome young man pushed a pissed-off jazz singer aside so he could belt out a number. As the singer's male friends approached ready to rough him up, the young man grinned and winked at them, throwing them a pack of ciggies and shouting for more drinks for his friends. They laughed and accepted his offering. Those who weren't yet quite so charmed, he won over when he pulled old Lilly the shoplifter from her seat and danced with her. Mona had never seen her move, let alone dance, let alone smile.

'Who is that fool?' Mona asked Lawrence.

'That's Sharpe. The one I've told you 'bout. Almost as good a thief as you are when he's not half seas over. Doesn't get caught half as much.'

So, this was *the* Albert Sharpe. The gunslinger, robber, man of mystery she'd heard of yet never had the pleasure of meeting.

The fair-haired charmer finished his husky, warbling rendition of *Blue Moon* and took a bow for the crowd now gathered around the makeshift dance floor. He motioned for the jazz singer shouting, 'Over to you love, just warmed them up for ya.' Mona couldn't tell if the crowd's applause was because they enjoyed his performance or were glad it was over. The jazz singer was no improvement. Mona scrunched up her nose at the sound, Lawrence's hawk-like nose snorting, laughing at her expression.

'Well come on, she's using that horrible twill vibrato on every bloody note. Sounds like a kookaburra being slaughtered. Hutch would back me up. Shocking,' she said.

'Snob.' Lawrence laughed, 'Definitely not as good as you. But few are. Sharpe's not looking so bad now, is he?'

Mona looked across the room to where Sharpe now stood. He wasn't looking too bad at all. Two young women by his side giggled at his every word. He accepted a cigarette off one, a drink off the other, red wine, where did that come from? He caught Mona's eye as he took a swig. Shit he'd seen her staring, but she couldn't look away. Aside from Collins, he was the most handsome man she'd seen in a very, very, long while. Of course, she had just come out of six months in a Convent. Sharpe smiled and gave her a wink. He was all teeth, his grin taking up half his face, dimples on each cheek and chin. Like Cary Grant but with hair so fair that it, along with maybe another habit, earned him the nickname Snowy. She lost sight of him, a crowd had formed in front of the trumpet solo. By the time the pack parted, Sharpe was standing right in front of her. Her heart stopped.

'Lawrie, you going to introduce us?' Though directed at Lawrence, Sharpe kept his gaze trained on Mona as he spoke. She had to remind herself to breathe. Lawrence didn't answer at first.

Mona nudged him, 'Lawrence?'

'Albert Sharpe, meet Mona Hayes, Mona Hayes, Albert Sharpe,' Lawrence looked between the two.

'Pleasure,' Sharpe said. Mona gave Lawrence a quick nod and a smile, silently begging him to leave them. He frowned, his feet unmoving.

'Would you be a pal and go check on Curly for me? She doesn't know many people here and I haven't seen her in over an hour.' Mona nudged Lawrence towards the kitchen.

He hesitated, but finally gave Sharpe a nod goodbye and left them alone, surrounded by circles of smoke, swing dancers and the background sounds of that bloody awful singer.

'So, Mona, what's a lovely little thing like you doing at old Kim Sly's? Place is full of nothing but thugs, drunks and thieves.' Sharpe smiled and took a long sip of his drink.

'Then I should think I fit in nicely,' Mona said.

'No. You're much too pretty to be a thief. So, what do the cops make of you then?'

'Wouldn't you like to know.'

'Wouldn't I ever!' he said. 'Oi watch out.'

Sharpe grabbed her around the waist, his strong arms pulling her aside, then steadying her, as a couple of swing dancers barrelled towards them. Stains from Sharpe's red wine and her beer joined Lawrence's down the front of her dress.

'Now you've got my blood on your hands, and dress,' he said. Mona laughed as he patted her down, his sparkling eyes trailing his fingers. She instinctively covered her wet chest with her arms.

'Sorry, I don't usually get this handsy with a girl so soon.'

'Why don't I believe you?' she said. 'Don't worry it was already ruined.'

She'd never felt so nervous, so exposed, in all her life. What a state she must have been to him. Her white dress stained, her face a burning blush.

Sharpe didn't seem to mind. He poured himself another drink. Beer this time. Less clean up. Then they danced. The girls who'd crowded him earlier disappeared into the night, giving up, Mona thought. She had won him.

In between dances, she learned that he was a builder, when not stealing. He talked about dabbling in other things but wouldn't go into details. He'd served time at Pentridge for breaking and entering, once even breaking into a police detective's house, leaving fingerprints on an empty bottle of whisky on the kitchen table.

'Never has the drink been more to blame,' he said.

No matter how much Mona prodded, he wouldn't tell her who the cop was. Mustn't have been anyone she knew at Russell Street, or surely she'd have heard of it.

At some point in the night, between drinks, between smokes, between dancing and hand holding, Sharpe leaned in and kissed her. It was like in books she'd read, movies she'd seen, fireworks went off, music swelled – but not just any music, a full orchestra. She swore her heart was beating so loud he must still be able to hear the thrum, thrum, thrumming over it all.

'Come back to mine?'

She didn't agree right away, her own desire to say 'yes' so quickly, terrifying her. Instead, she lowered her gaze and asked for another drink. She felt like a nervous, virginal schoolgirl.

He waited an hour and said again, 'You're coming home with me.'

She nodded.

As they strolled from the party to the tram and back to Sharpe's room in Fitzroy, Mona could barely pull herself away from him. She took peeks at his darkened room between kisses and protested when he escaped her grasp. His room was small, with peeling wallpaper yellowed from tobacco smoke, the glint of full crystal ashtrays cluttering each corner. In lieu of a wardrobe, he had clothes piled on the floor. As he pulled the patterned curtains closed, a puff of dust filled the room, lit like snow by the outside streetlight.

He took off his coat and threw it on the pile. Then he was back in front of her, his chin brushing the top of her head as he slid her coat from her shoulders. He looked down at her, waiting for her response. She took a deep breath. This was happening. Her first time since Brown, her first time in a long time.

'Get on the bed,' he said.

Mona tried to make herself comfortable while Sharpe closed the door and turned on a lamp in the corner. She rearranged the skirt of her white dress, and lay back in an awkward half-lying, half-seated position. She couldn't shake her nervousness, fiddling with her hair, licking her lips.

Sharpe took off his shirt and kneeled on the bed, hovering over her, pushing her down. She was desperate to feel his lips on hers again. Instead, he trailed his kisses down her body. She could feel his tongue through the satin of her dress, shivers racing through her. She slid her hands up and down his bare muscled back and he grunted, grabbed her wrists and pinned them above her head. She tried to wrestle free, but he held her down. His hazel eyes sparkling, he continued kissing his way down her body. Once he let her wrists go, she tried to move again, run her hands through his hair this time, again he grunted and pinned them above her. She began to think she was doing something wrong.

'You're beautiful, Mona,' he whispered.

She felt more at ease hearing those words. It was a strange thing to her, to be with another man after having spent so long with only one other. He was so different. Unpredictable. She wanted to get out of her head, she wanted to enjoy it.

'Drink?' she asked.

He laughed and jumped off her. 'I thought *I* had a problem,' he said, throwing a flask her way. She took a big gulp, careful not to spill scotch on the blanket, as he took off his pants. She caught glimpses of his naked body between sips. Muscled and slightly bruised from getting in a few too many fights, but stunning. The kind of man who should be with someone truly beautiful. Not someone with the sunken, pale body that came from six months at Abbotsford. She finished off the flask. Then he was back on her. She loved the weight of him. The heaviness of his body on her slight frame.

Again, he pinned her wrists above her with one hand, the other grazing her cheek before his fingers tickled their way down her neck. She closed her eyes at the sensation, his breath on her ear. Her eyes snapped back open as she felt a sudden tightening. He wrapped his fingers round her throat and for a second her heart stopped. Then his hand loosened and continued its journey down to her breasts. Mona exhaled. He'd scared her for a moment. She just wasn't used to him. Didn't know his way. That would change. She giggled.

'What's so funny?' he asked.

'Nothing, just enjoying myself.'

He slid the skirt of her dress up around her waist, tearing at her undergarments and throwing them to the floor. Then, he was inside her. Thrusting fast, hard and deep. It felt better than she remembered. Better than Brown. She couldn't believe she could feel so much desire for someone she'd just met.

The room filled with the sounds of metal springs and moaning, heavy breathing and the occasional crack of knees and elbows. Sharpe bit her ear. She squealed in shock, and he did it again. Soon, his hand joined in on the torture, clasping her right breast and twisting so hard she thought she might cry.

He must have mistaken her pain for pleasure because he kept on biting and twisting, twisting and biting.

She wanted to tell him he was hurting her but didn't know how. Even the toughest of criminals could be fragile when critiqued. She gently pried his fingers free of her breast and held his hand.

He lifted his head and smiled at her. 'You're fucking incredible.'

All memory of any discomfort faded as pleasure spread through her.

He lit her a cigarette afterwards and offered her another drink. 'That was something Mona.' It was. Scary and exciting all at the same time. Just like stealing.

***

Mona gave up on sleep when he started snoring. Her eyes wandered around the bedroom. Work overalls, tool belt on the floor and boots kicked off in the corner. She leant over the bedside table and picked up a miniature ivory elephant that caught her eye, shiny and sharp, its trunk faced down. Albert stirred.

'Where did you get this?' she asked. 'It's beautiful.'

'Just a little memento. Though I think I should be rid of it - heard you should only have them trunk up, like a horseshoe, you know, better luck.'

'I make my own luck,' she said, desperate for him to tell her she could keep it. A memento of him.

'Have it,' he said.

She leapt out of bed and placed the elephant delicately into the side pocket of her already overstuffed purse.

Sharpe leaned up on his elbows and watched her, she'd thrown on one of his shirts during the night. 'Don't exactly pack light do you love?' He laughed.

'I'm meeting Curly at the station later, we're off to Sydney for the Easter Show, then all the way up the coast.'

His eyes grew cold. 'When will you be back?'

'Before you know it.' She began gathering up her clothes.

He got out of bed, grabbing her by the arms. 'Make sure to come see me as soon as you're home,' he demanded. She agreed.

Home.

Now she was kicking herself to have met such an exciting man right before show season. Gunslinger she'd heard him called, but she'd found no gun on him that night.

20

It felt like a lifetime since Mona had last been to an Agricultural Show. When she first followed the shows, her association with Brown and other tricksters saw her labelled a grifter rather than a legitimate showie. But over time, Mona had strayed from Brown's side enough to make herself useful among the other sideshow tents. She sold more tickets than any man going round and became so familiar with all the routines that she could fill in seamlessly when needed. Anytime a line-up girl ran off with one of the boxers or champion woodchoppers, she'd slip in line and dance as if she'd been doing so her whole life. When the piano player was too drunk to accompany the final annex show, Mona would have a bash, garnering more money in tips in fifteen minutes than an entire day of pickpocketing. When business was bad, she'd rejoin Brown and his mate Bennie managing the shady darts tent between stealing from enraptured and distracted patrons or from shops in town.

Mona knew Curly had never been to a show before, not even in Melbourne.

'Just wait til you see it all set up. Packed with crowds, spruikers, the smell of popcorn and fairy floss all around,' Mona said as they roamed the Sydney Showgrounds.

'Don't you mean the smell of…' Curly started, nose in the air.

'Horse shit,' Mona said. 'You get used to it.'

'Well, I do love animals.' Curly tried to console herself.

'We'll have to try make time to watch some of the jumpers,' Mona said, noticing Curly's enthusiasm wane as she explained further. 'It's the best place to sneak money out of women's purses, while they're focused on the horses and the cowboys. I'll teach you.'

It had only been a few short years since Mona was in Curly's position. Following Brown wide-eyed through the gates and round to Sideshow Alley. She had immediately loved the theatre of the set-up - the builders weaving around each other, avoiding horses and cattle, as they carried wooden planks and set up poles and tents, the sideshow stars practicing their acts, the spruikers warming up their voices. Brown shouted hellos to all and sundry, forgetting Mona was there, she had to walk around again on her own and introduce herself later. She'd learned that if she wanted a drink, she should ditch her boyfriend and walk by the boxing tent unaccompanied. Now it was Mona's turn to show someone the ropes.

Mona led Curly round the Royal Hall of Industries, built of red brick and arched windows. Men in cowboy hats walked cattle, sheep and horses towards the horse pavilion. Mona and Curly made way for a dusty green ute, accompanied by the loudest woman they'd ever heard, shouting to 'make way' for the carload of sample bags she was to unload.

'What's in store this year?' Mona asked, smiling sweetly at the woman.

'Oh, you're back again are ya?' the woman said, shaking her head. 'Come see me at the end of the run, I may have something for you.'

Sample bags were an important part of the Show, providing show-goers with delights from all the exhibitors. Perfectly wrapped miniature sweets, cheeses, even samples of perfume were packed into every bag. Any bag that wasn't up to snuff, cracked paper or damaged goods, were thrown out. And all perishables unsold by the end of the show were handed out to a lucky few. Mona made sure she was always one of them.

'How many people work here?' Curly asked.

'I don't know. Hundreds I spose, why?'

'And you know them all? They all know you?'

'My word no! We keep to ourselves usually. Unless there's someone worth knowing.'

Curly nodded, her mouth watering at the thought of the delicate cheeses and chocolates contained within each bag.

As they rounded the corner into Denman Road, they could see that the showies had arrived the night before and Sideshow Alley was almost set-up ready for the crowds. Canvas tents were lined up and down the space between the Royal Hall and the Horses. The tents were fronted by colourful banners with thick font that shouted about '54 stone Mexican Rose', 'Tim Tam the leopard man' and 'nature's greatest enigma Anna John Budd'.

Construction on staging was being finished by five strapping young men in singlets. A sign hung above them with the words 'Products of Jimmy Sharman's Troupe.'

'Those are the boxers,' Mona pointed out, her eyes also skimming over Penfolds and Bar 66. 'They practice all the bouts ahead of time. It's like a dance. It's incredible to watch. And finally, the ticket booth,' she said approaching a woman nearby. 'If ya need a hand with the tickets please let me and my friend Curly know, we'll be over with Bennie at the darto.'

The woman grimaced but nodded her head, throwing her cigarette in the direction of some of the other boxers who'd began choreographing a new routine nearby.

'We'll get a go,' Mona said to Curly. 'She needs food and toilet breaks same as anyone.' They went on to have the same short, one-sided conversation with every other ticket seller. Most were friendlier than the first, eager for a hand from someone with experience. Some recognised Mona from previous years. Most bristled at the mention of Bennie and darto. Their next stop.

Mr Arthur Bennett was only a couple inches taller than Mona, his unkempt hair rose another inch above his head in a sort of dark matted bird's nest. He never wore a hat. He lived in a pinstriped suit and tie loosened at the top. Mona would often tie it for him, then he would take it on and off by loosening it up over his head each day. He had quite a few scars on his face, one crossed his upper lip and there were other tiny ones on his forehead and chin.

'Bennie, meet my friend Curly. She's worked as a chorus girl before, we'll see if we can get her a few spots with the line-up,' Mona said, embracing him.

Bennie smiled a toothy grin, let go of Mona and moved in for a hug with Curly. Overly affectionate for a first meeting.

'Pleasure to make your acquaintance,' he said. 'I'd be pleased to put in a good word for you.'

Curly interrupted him. 'No please don't. I'll manage on my own.' If there was one thing she'd learned since arriving, it was that most people in the sideshow didn't like Bennie and his darto tent. It had never occurred to Mona her acquaintances were holding her back. Though Collins and multiple judges had warned her about the company she kept.

'Oh, the independent type,' he chuckled. 'Just like our Mona? Well very good. Very good. You know anything about darts?'

Curly shook her head. Mona and Bennie were happy to initiate her. There were tiny numbers attached to each section of the dart board. Prizes were attached to each number, yet with only Bennie able to see which number they landed on, paying punters had hardly a chance of winning. Occasionally when a crowd gathered round, Bennie would award a box of chocolates and spruik to anyone who could hear about how easy it was to win, enticing more to step into the ring. Sometimes Mona herself was awarded the prize.

'If a woman can win, any man can,' Bennie would say.

Mona picked up a dart with yellow feathers on the end. She stroked it to the sharp tip and motioned for Bennie to step aside. She threw it gently, moving her wrist so slightly that to Curly it seemed not to move at all. She landed a bullseye. Curly's jaw dropped.

'Now that, you'll have to teach me,' she said.

Mona smiled, but suddenly distracted, she dropped the second dart she'd picked up and ran next door.

'Stella!' she said, hugging a stout woman in a bright pink dress.

Kewpie dolls on sticks were scattered all around the tent, their big beady eyes and glittery scalps bobbing amongst a sea of rainbow coloured tulle and ribbon. Stella blew a strand of grey curls out of her flushed face. 'I want to set them up according to colour.' Stella skipped the pleasantries, her flustered determination getting the better of her. 'One of the customers suggested it in Glen Innes,' she explained, looking round the tent at strewn dolls of blue, pink, yellow and green.

'We'll help you for a cut,' Mona said.

Stella agreed. Her stall was one of the most popular in the show, no little girl attended without stopping by for a doll on a stick.

By the time Mona, Curly and Stella had finished, the rest of Sideshow Alley was complete. Behind the snake pit tent, some of the workers lit a fire and roasted meat delivered by the nearby butcher. Smart local business owners would introduce themselves to the showies early, garnering loyal customers who returned to the same shops and pubs each time they were in town. A slim young man with broad shoulders Mona hadn't met before patted the log beside him motioning for her and Curly to join him and his mate.

'Did you two just join?' he asked with a low husky voice.

'I've travelled the show season before but missed northern New South Wales this year, just arrived today. I'm Mona, this is Curly,' she said.

He gave both their hands a gentle shake.

'This is my first show,' Curly said.

'Well welcome, Curly was it? I'm Sid. This is my first too. And Barry's,' he said motioning to his silent friend seated awkwardly on the edge of the log beside them.

'Boxers?' Mona asked.

'What gave us away?' he laughed. Fit, young men in typical boxing singlets and shorts stood out amongst the pot-bellied stallholders round the fire. Sid winked and handed Mona a small glass bottle. She sipped, felt instantly drunk and handed it back. She sure was out of practice.

Sid handed his flask to Curly who surprised Mona by taking a big swig, barely flinching.

'I love boxing,' Curly said. 'My neighbour Johnny boxed, and he used to teach the boys in my street, but I was never allowed to join in.'

'I can see why; you'd get the shit kicked out of you.' Sid laughed, looking up and down her thin frame. When her mouth widened in protest he nudged her in the side with his elbow, sending her almost flying off the log.

'I think you're right,' Mona winked in Curly's direction before continuing. 'It would take quite the teacher to get this one up to scratch.'

Barry chimed in. 'Too much of a challenge for our Sid,' he said.

'Alright you lot. I'll show you all a thing or two.' Sid took the bait. He chugged the last of his drink, then pulled Curly up from her seat.

'You right or left-handed?' he asked. Curly held out her right hand. 'Righteo, you want to hold that behind a little, left hand forward, both facing up like you're ready to punch,' he went. 'That's it, feet in position, left foot forward pointing out.'

Mona and Barry watched on as Curly giggled through her lesson. Alternating punches for sips of drink. While Sid's technique declined throughout the evening, hers improved.

'Imagine how good she'd be if that neighbour'd given her a go when she was a kid?' Barry said.

'Anything men can do.' Mona liked the idea of Curly in a boxing ring. Unfortunately, the world wasn't quite ready for that. Darto, doll stands and dancing line-ups would have to do. Watching Curly and Sid boxing and flirting made Mona's mind wander back to the man she'd left behind. Sharpe and his piercing eyes, cheeky grin, and the excitement that coursed through her veins just by being with him. She hoped he'd still be around when she returned. Waiting in bed for her. Just where she left him.

By the time Mona and Curly returned to the tent Bennie'd set up for them alongside the Showgrounds, they were dancing drunken rings around each other, tripping over their own feet. Mona felt around in the dark for her canvas sack, flipping through it for her nightdress. Curly stiffened beside her. Mona giggled, shoving her, expecting that she'd fallen asleep before changing out of her floral day dress and boots.

'I can't find my sack,' Curly said, voice trembling.

'Don't worry,' Mona said, patting Curly's back. 'It's too dark in here and we're much too drunk, it'll be under here somewhere. We'll find it in the morning.'

Mona lied and helped Curly settle in among the bed covers. They lay on hard, dusty ground, but Benny had done his best to disguise the earth beneath them with a cloud of sheets and pillows. Mona waited for Curly's usual snuffly snore and picked herself up again. Things had a tendency to go missing when left unattended at the Showgrounds, if anyone knew that, it was Mona. But she'd never steal from a fellow showie or thief, and she never expected anyone to steal from her. Though, she wasn't really one of them, not a real showie, not part of any code they may have had between each other. She stood smoking her last cigarette in the chill night air, her eyes darting from the showies readying for bed by firelight, to the stallholders shuttled up in their vans, and back again.

'Bot one?' If Mona was the jumpy type, his voice would have startled her. The scruff of his boots sounded his close approach until finally Mona turned to see the outline of Bennie's face in the dark.

'It's my last. And don't bother asking Curly for one either. Her bag's been nicked,' Mona said. 'I wonder who took it?'

Bennie groaned. 'No point wondering a thing like that. You'll just start trouble and you're not one to be throwing it around. Bags come and go. What'd she have in there, anyway?'

'Just clothes and a bit of food, I think. I carry our money round with me, not that we have much.'

'Yet.' Bennie laughed. He nodded in the direction of the local shops up the road. 'Well, we can't have the little Miss running around with no clothes, can we? Unless you were thinking of more lucrative dancing roles for the girl?'

Mona didn't know whether to laugh with him or hit him. She went back to bed, getting up again just after sunrise. Curly's snores were still sounding. Without the regimented wake-up calls of the Convent, Mona had discovered Curly to be a late sleeper. She wouldn't be up for a few more hours. By then, Mona and Bennie would have a brand-new bag of clothes for her.

Mona and Bennie ran the same old routine they'd done many times with Brown. It was a large clothing store spanning two shop fronts. One side looked newer than the other, as if the owners had recently bought out their neighbour and expanded. Business was good.

'The little place across the street only has one shopkeeper,' Bennie whispered as they approached.

'No, I like this one,' Mona said.

He nodded, lit a cigarette and waited just outside the door while Mona entered. She stood tall, pursing her sore red lips together as she dusted the last of the showground's dirt off the edge of her skirt.

'May we help you.' two male shopkeepers had been talking at the front counter. When they saw her enter, they straightened and smiled.

'Oh, I hope so. I'm auditioning for a part at the theatre. It's always been my dream to be a singer, and they said they'd give me a try out today, but I need a frock,' she explained.

'We have plenty of dresses. The last of our summer stock is to the back, and there's some pleated dresses in red or black, even gold if that'll suit you,' one of the gentlemen said pulling a rack of gowns towards the change rooms.

'Will you help me too?' Mona asked the man who'd stayed behind the counter. 'I need to look my best. Two opinions are better than one, but three is even better, particularly from such stylish men like yourselves.'

The man grinned and followed Mona and his colleague to the back of the shop. While they fussed over Mona, Bennett snuck through the store. He slipped a winter shawl off a mannequin, a couple of dresses off hangers and shoes straight off the counter. He stuffed them into a large handbag he picked off the shelf near the front door and slipped out before Mona was done. Mona decided on a simple black frock with flowers.

'This is an audition-winning dress if ever I saw one. Thank you both so much for your attentiveness.'

Mona paid and was barely out the door, when one of the men shouted about shoes missing from the counter.

'Hang on a minute Miss,' he said.

She ran. She met Benny at the post office a few moments later, scolding him for taking something so obvious.

'You're one to talk Miss Diamond,' he laughed. Word had gotten back to him. She couldn't much argue with that.

21

Sideshow Alley was a world for people who didn't fit in to 'normal' society – whatever that was. It was one of the reasons Mona loved it so much; that and that easy targets circled like ducks in a pond. In the suburbs of her youth, she hadn't quite fit in; she broke too many rules for that. In the criminal world of Melbourne, she stood out, one of the few women among male thieves and drug runners. But at the sideshow, she felt at home.

Though Mona and Bennett had kicked off the Easter Sydney Show with a necessary swindle, they'd felt no need to pick pockets that first week. Show attendance was good on account of the 150th state anniversary celebrations. Some of the performers complained about low tent numbers, but Mona and Bennie saw plenty of action at darto. And Curly was making ends meet selling tickets for the showgirls – her two left feet having ruled her out of the show itself.

In her rare quiet moments, Mona daydreamed about Albert Sharpe, amazed by how the memory of one night could sustain her. She'd hold the little elephant he'd given her and use it like a talisman to conjure up images of him and his smile. When re-visiting their night together grew tired, she'd imagine their reunion. She'd design entire conversations in her mind. Plan outfits. Decide on songs they'd dance to and berate herself for being such a sap. She'd never pined for anyone before.

She wondered if Sharpe was thinking about her too. Did men do that? She'd always been under the impression the moment you were out of sight, you were out of mind where men were concerned. Yet, the Sharpe she was building in her head was waiting with bated breath for her return.

Saturday night was busy in Sydney which meant great business, but little time for breaks. Mona negotiated a deal with a couple of kids she caught with their heads buried under the canvas flaps of the showgirls tent. Little did anyone know how many shows she'd snuck a look at the same way, comparing the voices of the visiting singers to her own, wondering if she could do better. In the boys' case, she wouldn't tell their parents and in return, they'd run between the bar and the darto stall for the rest of the afternoon providing her and Bennett with a steady supply of booze courtesy of Geoff the generous bartender over at Bar 66.

'That's the last one Miss,' the eldest boy said, showground dirt still muddying his nose, as he handed over her fourth bottle within the hour.

'Gather round, gather round, kiddies, ladies and gents and who shall step up for a round? Hit 100 and this delectable box of chocolates is yours…' As Bennie drummed up business among the passing crowd, Mona grabbed the boy by the scruff of his shirt.

'Where do you think you're going? Do you want me to tell your folks what you've been up to?' Mona looked between the two boys dressed in matching blue shirts and tan slacks. The older boy she'd had hold of ripped his cuff from her grasp.

'Either we get a hiding coz we snuck into the sideshows, or we get one coz we're late home for supper, is all the same to us,' he said.

'Alright off you go then. See you next year no doubt, you little perverts,' she pinched the little one on the cheek and he giggled as he ran after his older brother.

Mona turned back to Bennett to find him propping the closed sign up against the side of the stall.

'We're not going to compete with the late boxing stoush and the Elders in the ring,' he said. 'May as well knock off now.'

Mona hadn't yet had a chance to see the Elders horse-riding act. Pearl and Ted Elder, like many of the performers, were also from America. Their trick roping and 'devil acts' were extremely popular. Mona took a quick glance of the show program. She still had plenty of time for another drink or two, then she could go to the ring and catch their performance. Mona knew Curly had been spending a lot of time at the ring after knocking off at the ticket stand. Mona hoped to run into her, though she knew the chances were slim with the size of the crowds that had been attending each night.

As she and Bennie headed to the bar, Mona noticed a couple of uniformed police officers asking for directions outside the Sharman tent. International act Mexican Rose was up out of her chair, pointing in Mona and Bennett's direction. Mona's mind flashed back to earlier in the day when she'd spotted one of the shopkeepers they'd robbed near the merry-go-round. He must have seen her too and sent the police after her.

'Damn it,' she muttered and grabbed Bennett's hand, leading him back past the horse training yard, pavilions and towards the Pygmy tent. They squatted there as they watched more police officers run past.

'They can't all be here for us,' Bennett said.

Mona clasped a hand over his mouth as two more police ran by, then four more, then five, then six. The sound of Mona's own heart pounding in her ears gave way to the distant sounds of screams and sirens coming from the Parade Ring.

'They're not here for us at all. Let's go to 66, c'mon,' Bennett said.

'Well, what are they here for?'

'Who the fuck cares?' Bennie huffed and headed for the bar, while Mona cut through Suttor Avenue. She headed west around the Ring towards the Grand Stand, the centre of the commotion. A crowd of onlookers watched on as police pulled people from the stands.

Mona found Ted and Pearl. 'What's going on?'

'All hell's broken loose in the stands,' Ted said.

Pearl finished his sentence as he shook his head. 'Too many trying to get in. A man passed out cold.'

Mona breathed a sigh of relief. The police were there for crowd control, not her.

Once all the commotion was over, Mona found Curly. They settled in for the Elder's show, remaining in the stands until after the fireworks. By the time they made it back to the tents, most of the showies had left for a night on the town. There were just a few of the boxers left, sitting around the campfire. Sid included.

He told them about the fight he'd performed earlier. He'd done his usual choreographed set – this time, it was his turn to win – and then a man from the crowd challenged him. The show's announcer had accepted the challenge for a steep fee, leaving Sid no choice but to stay in the ring and face the challenger.

The announcer pulled Sid aside just before the bout and whispered, 'It'll be better for business if you let this one win.'

Sid had his orders and was ready to see them out. Then the bell rang, the man – who Sid described as having a baby face on a tall man's body – punched Sid in the jaw. Sid barely felt it, but he put on a show. He fell back a couple steps for effect. The man then put his fists down and started fighting with his words. Sid wouldn't tell Mona and Curly what was said, but they could imagine, they'd heard some of the things shouted from the crowd during boxing matches. This time, Sid wasn't having it. He decked the guy.

Curly gasped.

'Don't worry, don't worry, I held back a little. Only knocked him out for a second. Some of the other blokes splashed some water over him and he was up, ready for his consolation prize.' Sid laughed.

Mona loved stories like that; someone getting what they deserved. She liked Sid more and more every time they spoke. She got the sense Curly did too.

With Sid, Curly was happier and more relaxed than Mona had ever seen her, even breaking into a campfire song at Sid's urging. Her voice was beautiful. Mona tried not to join in, afraid she'd embarrass herself by comparison. Curly was so young and delicate, with her wispy blonde Shirley Temple curls, yet her voice was sultry, husky, strong. Like it didn't belong to her.

Mona felt she was the opposite. Older and bolder in person, yet her voice had a fragility that somehow, smoke and alcohol had not yet spoiled. It felt weak next to Curly's, or so Mona thought. 'Solid voice but lacking soul' a judge once remarked at a teen singing competition, 'not enough emotion' another had said. Her teacher told her 'You just need more life to live, something more to sing about'. Every year Mona lived a little more, and each show season she told herself she'd try and angle a chance to sing. Every year, there was another reason not to. This year, that reason was Curly.

'I love her voice.' Sid nudged Mona, the other blokes whistling as Curly changed keys.

'Yes, she's really something,' Mona agreed.

'What about you Mona. Do you sing?' he asked.

'If the occasion calls for it.'

Sid smiled 'I can tell. You have a singer's chin.'

'Is that your cheeky way of saying I have a big chin Sid?'

'You're onto me, Mona,' he laughed. 'You can play piano too, can't you? I play.'

Sid stood, picking her up off the ground with him. Curly was bowing now, her song receiving a round of applause.

'I have an idea,' Sid announced. 'C'mon.'

Mona grew nervous as she followed him. In the Convent, singing was quiet, so as not to disturb the nuns, and self-conscious in front of Curly, who Mona felt was more talented than she could ever be. When anyone complimented Mona's singing, she didn't feel flattered, she felt a flop. She felt almost the same way about being single. One day she was happy to be free and the next she was daydreaming of Albert Sharpe's arms wrapped around her. She didn't know what she wanted more. Alcohol helped her forget she wanted anything at all.

Sid led Mona, Curly and a few of the other boxers through the unusually quiet Sideshow Alley, past the grand brick Royal Hall of Industries and towards Hordern Pavilion. Mona hadn't been inside this particular building, though she knew Nestle's had a set-up inside and had made a note to visit on the last day for leftover Easter eggs. As a kid, while her siblings rationed their eggs, eating them a few at a time, Mona ate all of hers within the hour, gave herself a stomach-ache and woke the next morning wanting more. An addict from an early age.

Sid opened the door with ease. 'They never lock it,' he explained, holding it open for all to sneak inside.

The lights from Sideshow Alley, lit to deter late night thieves, filtered through the long windows that lined each wall of the building. Reds, yellows and blues cast beautiful shadows over stalls filled with everything from chocolates to gadgets, radios and pianos.

'The occasion has called,' Sid announced.

He motioned for Mona to take a seat at a white baby grand while he sat on the bench of the biggest black piano she'd ever seen. Curly sprawled like a proper showgirl on a bench that sat between the two. The others scattered themselves around the hall, playing drums on anything they could find, in time to Mona's piano melody. She made something up on the spot. Sid played a few notes of his own. Mona and Curly sang nonsense about horses and cowboys and beautiful tattoos. Sid laughed and joined in with a joke or two between verses. By the end of the night, the combination of alcohol, singing and laughter left Mona without a voice at all. She'd never had so much fun doing something entirely legal – technically they hadn't broken in, the building had been unlocked.

Mona had to admit she was enjoying the 1938 show season more than any other. In years past she'd always felt more like a plus one. Brown's tag-a-long. And although he was surely out of Pentridge by now, she was relieved he hadn't shown up – possibly favouring the fish market now he only had his own mouth to feed. Not that Mona had ever been a burden. She'd always brought in her fair share. More than her share if she was being honest. And now she too got to experience what it was like to be on her own. No man to worry about. She'd barely even had to worry about Curly since they'd arrived. Curly had quickly taken to the show, making her own money and her own friends. For the first time in her life Mona didn't have to answer to parents, a boyfriend, nuns or the police ... she was free. But for how long?

22

Mona was devouring a bag of samples at the dairy hall when she saw him. The slicked back, almost dripping, hair and matching moustache. He saw her too. She flashed back to her first-ever run-in with Collins; he'd laughed at her for wearing the same outfit to the scene of a previous crime. Though the show season had been a good one so far, it hadn't been good enough for too many new outfits. She was wearing the same thing she'd worn when she and Bennett robbed slick's store.

He zeroed in on her, walking slowly at first, then, as she stepped back towards the stall door, his pace picked up. Soon they were both running. Her first instinct was to run to the darto booth to alert Bennett that she'd been spotted. But of course, she'd be leading the shopkeeper to both of them. So, she headed in the opposite direction, hoping to lose him among the bustling poultry, pigeon pavilions and cattle judging rings. He was a few paces behind her at first, as cowboys came between them, she drew further and further away. By the time she hit the edge of the Sydney Cricket Ground, he was gone. She pulled her hair under her hat and pinched a discarded men's shirt from the Vandyke tent to throw over her dress. She would be harder to spot now. She continued round Park Road to the sideshows. She'd alert Bennie. They'd get Curly to cover the tent and then hide out until the Showies went back on the road. They'd done it plenty of times, in plenty of towns. She approached the darto tent slowly. Curly was manning the stall with tear-stained eyes, while Bennie was being led away by a policeman. She turned on her heel and ran back in the direction from which she came, only to find herself smacking into the chest of the tallest man she'd ever seen.

'Ever thought about joining the Show?' she quipped.

He cracked a half smile. 'I have to take you to the police station Mam,' he said. 'You've been identified as a person of interest in a robbery.'

In the patrol car, she told the officers her name was Thelma Wilson. Bennie went with Arthur Stanhope. The police who picked them up were quite reasonable. Mona felt that an admission and apology would go over well, but she knew there was no point arguing the case with Bennett. He was of the same school as Lawrence. You don't admit anything unless the evidence is overwhelming. He apparently wasn't overwhelmed by two eyewitnesses. He spent the car ride to the station denying he'd done anything wrong, so Mona did too. The cops, and judge, didn't buy it. Both she and Bennie were found guilty. Mona was sentenced to five days hard labour at Sydney Gaol while Bennett got a whole month. She knew he'd appeal but for the meantime, he would be absent from the show tour. No doubt the bloke who owned the darto tent would have a male replacement within the day. She was out of a job and headed for prison.

***

If she ever again had to choose between a gaol and a Convent, Mona was now certain which was the better choice.

Gaol time in Sydney was not easy, but in comparison to Abbottsford it was like night and day. She had her own room, a light breezy uniform that cinched at the waist (the nuns would be mortified), she could wear her hair how she liked and chat to other prisoners over dinner without risking a whack of a cane. As she was only there for five days, she was given the simple task of sweeping common areas. This gave her a chance to move round the prison hallways and workrooms, meeting the women working in each area. By her third day, she was sure she'd met at least every girl there, twice. Unlike the Convent, there was also a visitor's area. She spoke to Curly through the glass with a white outfitted warder watching over her shoulder.

Though the time inside was relatively painless, it was costly. She'd lost her place in the Show and would have to find a new position. She resolved the rest of the tour would not be so rudely interrupted.

***

Though it was the beginning of winter, Mona hadn't been expecting Bundaberg to be quite so cold and dreary. The last time she was in Queensland, she'd sweltered through an almost unbearable heatwave. It was quite a shock to be pelted with rain when getting off the show train after boarding in warm and sunny Gympie.

'I thought it was meant to be a warmer climate up north,' Curly remarked on their way to the Bundaberg Showgrounds.

'It is,' Mona said.

Mona took on selling kewpie dolls for Stella and business was good, so she didn't need to worry about money. She also danced in the line-up more often, as many of the girls dropped out along the route to marry and start families. Though flush with enough cash to eat, drink and smoke her heart out, she was just shy of being able to afford drugs – which she hadn't much missed she had to admit – and clothes. The thin summer fabrics of her limited traveling costumes weren't quite cutting it as winter came on. It wasn't usually a problem. As the weather cooled, they travelled north on the show train, the sun generally warmer and brighter with each new town. But evenings were chilly. She hadn't realised just how much she'd relied on Brown's body heat in the past. Though she often shared close quarters with Curly, Mona risked being kicked in the side or punched in the face if she slept too close.

Since Mona couldn't rely on cuddles to keep her warm, she took to wearing a wool jumper to bed over her night dress. She often pulled thick socks on too. But the cold seeped through. She longed for her old, stolen, fur coat.

Mona and Curly took a rare day off and accompanied Sid and some other showies to the local race meet. Curly made quick work of extricating Sid's suit coat and throwing it over her shoulders. Mona shivered through

154

the first race in her winter frock and gloves. The small-town girls surprised Mona; they were as well-dressed and groomed as those in Melbourne or Sydney, though there was more tweed around the racecourse than she ever saw at Caulfield. Two women in the stands wore the most stunning fur coats she'd ever seen. She noticed them move places when the showies sat nearby and overheard one moan to the other about all the 'freaks the Show brings in.'

Mona flashed a disgusted look in their direction before heading off to stroll the course, perhaps sneak her way into the members' stand.

The sun was beginning to peek through the clouds bringing the mood of the races up a notch. It's amazing what sunshine can do. A few women seized the opportunity to peel their thick coats off and show off their dresses. Mona admired one group of young women in particular for a few minutes, their frocks matching pastels, before realising they'd left their picnic basket unattended a few paces over.

She bent down as if to fix the buckle of her shoe, reached her hand into the basket and pulled out a fresh dinner roll filled with cheese and ham. She bit in hungrily, looking back towards the chatting women to see whether or not they'd noticed. They were too busy swooning over a handsome young man at the betting counter up the hill. One of the women sauntered towards him, her best smile on, while the others watched. Mona took the opportunity to pick through the rest of the basket. She stopped when she got to a half-drunk bottle of Veuve Clicquot. She swept it up in her gloved hands and ran, careful not to spill any. She was at the other side of the members building when she felt safe enough to drink. She almost spat it out, as she'd shaken up the bottle so much the bubbles pricked her tongue. It had been a very long time since she'd had sparkling wine.

'Where'd you get that?' Curly had walked round the pavilion to look for her. Mona laughed and held out the bottle. She left Curly to finish off its contents as she went to find the ladies lavatories.

The toilets were attached to a large set of changing rooms. A young woman, who looked familiar, was sitting on a bench reapplying her lipstick with a hand mirror when Mona went into one of the toilet stalls. By the time Mona came out, the woman was gone, but she'd left her light grey fur and gloves behind.

Mona popped her head out the door and motioned to Curly to come over.

'What is it? No toilet paper?' Curly giggled, high on the champagne.

'No. Did you see that woman come out a few moments ago?' Mona looked around to see if she could find her.

'I didn't notice. Why?'

'It was one of those bitches from earlier. Remember in the stands?' Mona grinned, ran back into the change rooms and retrieved the coat. 'Someone's going to steal it, may as well be me. I'm bloody freezing.' She pulled the coat over her shoulders and felt around in the pockets. Unfortunately, the lady hadn't left anything inside. Still, sandwiches, champagne, fur, not a bad day at the races.

Curly fiddled with her hair and eyed the exit 'Maybe you should leave it.'

Mona shook her head. She was just too cold. Besides, if anyone deserved it…

As they walked towards the boxing troupe, sitting on the grassy knoll on the other side of the track, someone shouted. She and Curly turned to see the woman from the changerooms with a man.

'Run!' Mona yelled.

They bolted. Not fast enough. The now coat-less woman had seen both their faces and gone straight to a patrol car. Within the hour, the local police had pulled up outside the Showgrounds. Mona tried to pass the coat off to one of the boxers but was caught fur-handed. She admitted defeat and held out her wrists to the approaching officers.

'How did you know where to find me?' Mona asked them.

'The lady said she'd seen you with the showies, so we knew where to look. How about her?' He cuffed Mona then glanced towards Curly. Tears sprang to Curly's face. She hadn't been in trouble with the police before.

'She had nothing to do with it, officer. It was just me. I don't know what came over me.'

'What's your name, love?' The other officer pulled out a pad and pen and waited for her answer.

'Lena Williams.' Mona recalled one of her old favourite aliases without flinching, the name of her babysitter when she was young, the kind of girl every boy wanted to kiss, and every girl wanted to be friends with. She had this pull, people gravitated towards her. A bit like Curly. Lena invited blokes round and sat out on the front deck with them while Mona and her siblings were meant to be asleep. Mona would watch through the bedroom window as men took turns rolling and lighting Lena's cigarettes. Mona had wanted to be her back then. Now, here in Bundaberg Queensland, she was.

As the officers drove Mona into the police station and booked her for larceny, she won their favour by asking lots of questions, convincing them she'd never before been in trouble with the law.

'What happens now? Will I go to gaol? Will I go to court? Will the judge write to my mother?' Mona cried. She told them she believed the coat had been left behind, she didn't think she'd done anything wrong, that she'd learned her lesson. The police swore to the local Magistrate that they believed Mona to be a good citizen who had made a mistake, her first one, and would no doubt keep out of trouble from here on out. She was free to go with a fine. She was long gone from Bundaberg before the police realised that they'd had a habitual criminal in their grasp. But this time, she hadn't gotten away with a fur coat.

23

The show train had taken them up the coast of Queensland, starting in Gympie, and back.

'Once we get off, we have to decide whether we want to continue with the troupe down to central NSW or head straight to Melbourne, take a few weeks off before the Melbourne Show,' Mona told Curly.

Curly stayed silent. Her eyes cast down at her feet, flat on the carpet of the rumbling train, Mona's own feet laying comfortably on the seat across from them blocking other passengers from sitting down.

'So, you wanna take a few weeks off and head on back to Melbourne?' Mona asked.

'Actually, I think I'm going to carry on with Sid,' Curly said.

'What do you mean? I thought Sid was leaving the company after Gympie,' Mona said.

'He is. He's got a permanent boxing position in Sydney. And he's asked me to come live with him, as man and wife, he's going to get us a house and—'

'You're getting married? Why would you do that?'

'Well, not technically married in a church or anything. Anyway, why wouldn't I want to be with him? It's not every day a girl gets engaged; you've never been.'

Mona tried not to take it to heart, but a strange pang crept through her chest like a knot pulled tight around her.

'But you're only 18, you'll be stuck at home.'

'Better stuck in Sydney than in the sideshow.' Before Mona could interject Curly stopped her. 'I don't want to be doing this forever and end up a spinster in my twenties, in and out of court, running around with sideshow freaks and thieves.'

'You mean, you don't want to end up like me.'

'That's not what I meant.' Curly's eyes, temporarily on Mona, went back to her shoes.

'You were a performer before I even met you, singing backup for the biggest stars around.'

'My mother's doing, not mine,' Curly said.

Mona couldn't help finish that sentence in her mind – the sideshows were Mona's doing, not Curly's. She'd turned into Curly's mother, dragging her into a life she didn't want. Still, she was offended. The only way to win this argument was not to have it. No point ruining the end of what was a good friendship. Curly didn't want the life Mona had shown her. No respectable woman did. And Curly wanted to be a respectable woman more than anything. She wanted a home.

'I just want a normal life, don't you see?'

Mona did see. Curly didn't hate the confines of routine, she craved it. Craved the uniforms of the Convent, the security of the same bed each night, the warmth of the arms of the same man.

'I understand. Congratulations.'

Some birds simply preferred to be caged.

***

Mona celebrated, commiserated, her solo return to Melbourne with an impromptu visit to Stanley Hutchison's. She expected the house to be quiet as it usually was at 8 o'clock on a Sunday night. Either he'd be eating dinner in front of the wireless, or out making some extra change cabbing or dealing coke. Instead, she found Stanley's Hawaiian music ringing out into the streets, mingled with the sound of people chattering, laughing and yelling. She stepped inside, relieved to find the party as impromptu as her visit. Stanley, playing his ukele in the corner was wearing his dressing gown while his bandmates were in slacks and under shirts, suspenders slung down by their sides. Other men wore sweaters, no collars, the women in casual spring dresses and bare, dirty feet. Mona had just come off the train, she was tired, her hair long and untamed, her day dress crinkled at the bottom where it had been tucked between her bum and the train seat. She fit right in.

Stanley jumped up from his seat the moment he saw her, dropping his instrument hard on the thin orange carpet without a care. He picked Mona up in a bear hug. She'd never seen him so hyped. Not even on drugs.

'Mona! Home for the Melbourne Show!' he shouted to the room, and they all cheered. Mona glanced around not recognising anyone. The band played on with the very noticeable absence of Stanley's strings.

'What's going on? I've never known you to have a party here,' Mona asked. Stanley had always been paranoid about having people round his home, where he kept all his cash and cocaine. And the parties they liked to go to were loud and rowdy, just the kind of noise the police took notice of.

'Just a little get-together between friends.' He turned to the mantle nearby, took a half empty bottle of scotch off the shelf and handed it to Mona.

'Friends?' she said, taking a swig and passing it back to him.

'Lawrence should be round soon,' he said. 'And you know the band.'

Mona watched as his attention wandered and landed on the piano player. The guy was spending more time snorting cocaine off the lid than playing the keys. Stanley huffed. He trudged back to the band, cursing the pianist. This was more like him. Unfortunately, he'd taken the scotch with him.

'Can I get you a drink love?'

Mona spun around. Even from the quiet, sweltering halls of the Sacred Heart dormitory to the loud smoky drug den, she'd know that voice anywhere. Yet she hardly recognised her without the grey uniform.

'Priscia,' Mona said.

The large woman collected Mona in a velvety hug. They were wearing similar outfits, yet Priscia was in the brightest orange Mona had ever seen, lipstick to match. She outshone every casually-dressed crim in the room.

Mona chuckled as she remembered Priscia's criminal history – biting a policeman. She imagined that bright orange lipstick on the neck of someone like Collins and grinned. She accepted the cocktail glass Priscia held out for her.

'Priscia? God I haven't heard that name in a while. But you know what? I miss it.'

'You don't mind me calling you that?' Mona asked.

'Well, call me Patricia and we'll have a problem.'

'Who's Patricia?' Eddie from the Windsor approached and soon Mona was surrounded by familiar faces: Sandy and one of the Jones brothers, who stood with a deck of playing cards in hand, waiting for someone to offer a game.

Mona drank and chatted to the group. Criminals could be the best gossips. Mona had always loved to read fiction as a child. Grand stories of super sleuths, Victorian romances and books that could take her to every corner of the earth. *The Great Gatsby, Gentlemen Prefer Blondes, Gangs of New York...* She had no need for books now. Crime and booze and drugs, fascinating people and performers with stories from all over the world. Had she heard about Robert and his love affair with Jessie the coin counterfeiter? His wife sure hadn't. Had she noticed thief Jennie and her protruding belly? It wasn't long before conversation turned to her old friend Guggenheim. Had anyone told her, he'd been stabbed with a carving fork?

'I heard,' Mona said.

'Happened right in the middle of Russell Street. The bloke who did it'd be afraid for his life if Guggs wasn't now doing time at Pentridge for larceny,' Eddie said.

So, Guggenheim was out of action. Lawrence nowhere to be found. And Brown, well, exes were exes for a reason. And, having gotten through an entire show tour coke free, she was beginning to prefer the extra change in her pocket over anything Hutchison had to offer. Melbourne was like a stranger to her now. She was in a room full of people yet felt completely alone. She needed someone new to play with.

A hush fell over the group. Their heads trained on the front door as none other than Albert Sharpe walked in. Mona's jaw dropped. She noticed the same affection she felt swell inside her, marked on the faces of every other girl in the room. He was breath-taking. While the rest of the room looked ready for a sleepover, Sharpe looked as though he'd just come from the races. Black slacks and shirt with a bright yellow tie. Light hair slicked back, blue eyes piercing through the smoke. He walked with a confidence even the sharpest of criminals didn't possess. He moved slowly, nodding politely at the other partygoers. He took off his hat to shake the hands of the cigar smokers by the window and kissed the wrist of a woman seated on the carpet beside the coffee table. He knelt beside her to whisper in her ear.

'I hear he's a pimp,' Jones whispered.

'Nonsense,' Eddie said. As a hotel worker, he liked to think he knew a thing or two about pimps and sex workers. 'He's a hired gun slinger!'

'I heard he sells them,' Sandy said.

'What?' Mona asked.

'Guns!' Sandy replied.

'Probably steals them more likely. I heard he even once stole from the police,' Priscia weighed in.

'That's true,' Mona said, a little disappointed that the crime he'd confided to her the night they met was seemingly well known to the rest of the underworld, even those fresh from the Convent.

Sharpe flirted with the girl at the table. Blinking back her disappointment, Mona's heart shrivelled at the sight of them.

'How do you know him?' Jones asked, breaking through the jealous torment.

'I met him at a party in South Melbourne a few months back,' Mona said. She prided herself on her poker face, but Jones was too good a player.

'Like him, do you?' he said more as a statement than a question.

She shrugged.

'You know what they say about creatures with bright colours,' Priscia said pointing to the almost glistening shock of yellow down Sharpe's chest. The group shook their heads. 'Danger, stay away.'

The yellow tie swung against his suit as he stood and turned away from the girl. Mona pictured him as a soft honeybee, buzzing in her ear, tickling her cheeks, threatening to sting her. But bees aren't terribly dangerous, and if they sting you, they die.

The group were too busy gossiping about Sharpe to notice him approach. He slid his arm around Mona's waist and planted a kiss on her head.

'I was hoping I'd see you here,' he said with a grin.

The group grunted a few half-assed excuses and dispersed, leaving Mona alone with him. Sharpe slid his hand up and down Mona's side, the fabric of her dress changing shade under his fingertips. She smiled up at him, spying the woman he'd been talking to earlier skulking behind his shoulder.

'Why haven't you stopped by?' he asked.

'I just made it back today,' Mona said. 'Besides I wasn't sure what your current situation may be.' She nodded in the other woman's direction.

'Why, I've been waiting for you,' he said, ignoring Mona's reference to the woman behind him. 'I've thought about you a lot. And boy have I had a lot of time to think!'

'How's that?' Mona asked.

'You didn't hear?'

A guilty blush rose up Mona's face. She took a sip of her drink to try and control it. She'd heard many things, mostly in the last ten minutes.

'I've been in Pentridge,' he said. 'Just a couple weeks this time, but that's plenty enough. I'm not a very good thief Mona. There's gotta be easier ways to make money.'

By this time, he had a glass of scotch in his hand as if it had appeared out of nowhere. Mona had been so captured by his eyes, his low, silky voice and those fingers at her waist, that she hadn't noticed anyone hand it to him. She couldn't see anything but him. The room and everything and everyone in it faded away.

He clinked his glass with hers, proposing a toast to his newfound freedom and their re-acquaintance. Mona finished her glass and looked over his shoulder again. The skulking woman was gone.

That night, Mona was more wrapped up in Sharpe than in drink, yet she felt even drunker than usual. Her face hurt from smiling. Her neck and eyes tired from staring up at him. When he finally cupped her cheeks in his hands and kissed her, she lost all ability to speak. She'd seen girls behave like that before – giddy and in love. She'd never been like that though. Not with Brown, not with anyone.

She'd planned to crash on Stanley's couch that night but went home with Sharpe instead.

And there she stayed.

That first morning with him, the first since before she left town, she woke to the sight of him rummaging through her bag. His hair was sticking up in all directions, his Bonds singlet long and covering his bare behind as he delicately flipped through her things.

'What are you doing?' she asked, groggy yet petrified. It occurred to her, she may have gotten ahead of herself, thinking about him all season, swooning over him all night. Had she gotten him all wrong? Was he a thief of thieves? Not worth her time at all?

He gave a startled 'hmmph' and threw himself back on the bed, one hand behind his back.

'Curious,' he said.

Was he after alcohol or money? She had nothing else in there he could want, her valuables and clothes were with Stella, packed up with darto and kewpie dolls.

'Just wanted to see what a beautiful woman like you walks around with.' He kissed her head and she winced. He smiled and pulled the small elephant out from behind his back.

Mona sighed, relief flooding through her hungover body. 'Oh yes, I still have him. He's had quite the adventure, we've been all over.' It had been as if Sharpe himself was with her the whole time.

He put the elephant down on the floor and then got comfortable back under the sheets. They snuggled up and Mona smiled. He didn't want to steal from her, he just wanted to know if she still had his bloody elephant.

In turn, she very quickly learned a lot about him. She learned he could fry superb eggs and that he whistled at almost every free opportunity. She learned he was a light sleeper and that he talked, just a little, while dreaming. In those early days, she thought she'd seen enough to really know all of him. But she didn't know everything. Not even close.

24

While the showies set up shop at the Melbourne Showgrounds, Mona settled in with Sharpe. He'd moved since the last time she'd seen him. His new boarding place in Gore Street, Fitzroy, was a few streets over, and a few steps up, from her old haunt on Hanover. It sat in a row of identical brick terraces. The inside loomed long and large, well-kept and cleaner than any other boarding house she'd seen.

As Sharpe took her on a clumsy, kiss-filled, candlelit tour that first night, Mona began to wonder how he could afford it. Perhaps he was a better thief than he let on? Or maybe he was earning a good enough living on the tools?

Morning cuddles and breakfast in bed filled those first few days. She had a few weeks before the Show started, so he took time off too, he said, so he wouldn't miss a moment with her. She'd made so much money throughout the season that she needn't steal to keep them going on booze and food from the markets.

'I could get used to this,' Sharpe would say spooning mouthfuls of mashed potato in his mouth while she made seconds and thirds for him and the other boarders.

They'd have drunken nights by the fireplace in Sharpe's room. She'd dance naked for him in the flickers of light. And they'd have sex, fall asleep in each other's arms, and the next morning they'd start over and do it all again.

'I just have one question for you,' Mona said one evening as she twirled around the room in her white nightgown.

'What's that love?' He raised an eyebrow, lighting two cigarettes in his mouth at once before handing one to her.

She took it and twirled herself to the nearby wireless, turning the knob. Once she found a jazz station, she took to the next wireless on the shelf and turned that on too. She continued round the room turning on one after the other, after the other.

'Just how many wireless sets does one man need? It's like living at Kelvelectric.'

He was up then, dancing with her to the cacophony of music and radio hosts blaring from the multitude of speakers.

'Easier to fence than fur coats,' he said.

She snorted. She never fenced the fur coats she stole. How little he knew her.

A deep sombre voice on one of the radios soon caught Mona's attention. She shh'd Sharpe and they split the room turning off all other noise. The word 'war' cut through the romantic bubble they'd made. They sat on the bed and listened.

'Tensions between Germany and Czechoslovakia are now at breaking point with developing events pointing to a war in Europe of severity comparable to that of 1914...'

'Bullshit,' Sharpe stood and changed the radio station. 'Papers keep chopping and changing, war imminent, war not imminent...'

'Would you go?' she asked.

'They want common crims in the army? I'd be the best shot they got.' He laughed as he bent down, reached under the bed and produced a small black pistol.

It was true. He had a gun. All her time spent with criminals, and she'd never seen one.

'I'd show those Nazis a thing or two.' He twirled the gun around his finger taking aim, at Mona. She froze.

'Put that bloody thing down,' she finally sputtered, terrified.

A knock at the door saw Sharpe shove the gun under a pillow.

One of their housemates barged in, holding out cups of beer, urging them out of their room.

The entire house sat up all night listening to the radio. Every time Mona looked over at Sharpe, all she could see was the butt of his gun.

'Turn the music up, this is a good one,' one of the boarders shouted as another attempted to tap dance in front of the open fire.

'You should see Mona dance,' Sharpe said. 'Dance for them.' A glint in his eye.

Mona shook her head, exhausted, clouded by thoughts of war and guns and the uncomfortable feeling growing in the pit of her stomach. Sharpe didn't know her, and she really didn't know him. 'I think I'd rather see Joe here dance,' she said.

Joe continued tapping. The boys laughed and shared another round of beers before Mona slipped off to bed. She dreamed about Sideshow Alley, about safety. She was singing in the dream, and then she awoke, suddenly, painfully. She felt lightening bolts down the side of her body. She opened her eyes to find she'd been knocked off the bed and had landed hip first.

Sharpe stood over her. 'Next time I tell you to dance, you bloody do it.' He said kicking her in the side. The nail of his un-socked toe piercing her skin. She looked up at him, unable to speak. Gripping her stomach, rubbing the pain away, as he crawled into bed and fell asleep.

From that night, not knowing what Sharpe might do exacerbated her sleeplessness. Then morning would come, and he'd kiss her and flirt and make her breakfast as if the night had never happened.

Mona had been with Sharpe just a couple of weeks when the Melbourne Show finally opened. She began staying later and later at the Showgrounds to put off her evenings in Sharpe's room. She started early, took only short lunch breaks, and stayed until midnight. Some nights she'd get home and be relieved to find Sharpe wasn't there. Other nights he was already drunk, but hungry, having insisted on waiting for her to get home and cook for him. He grew more and more irritable with each passing day. He'd throw plates at the wall if Mona didn't butter the bread to the edges. If he wasn't satisfied with what she'd given him, he wouldn't let her eat her own dinner. She caught him going through her purse a few more times. She still carried round the little elephant, though she knew now that wasn't what he was after. She never confronted him about it – just felt a constant sense of relief that the boys had always taught her to split her cash between shoes, pockets, and friends. She wondered if he did the same with his guns.

***

'Staying for the fireworks?' Boxer Barry called to her from the troupe tent.

It was the last night of the Melbourne Show and Barry was carrying a bottle of champagne.

'Where'd you get that?' she asked.

'Some poor bloke's missus came by before this afternoon's stoush. Her husband was all geared up to volunteer a match. She gave us this and asked us to let him win,' Barry said holding the bottle proudly over his head.

'Did you?' Mona asked.

'Course not!' He laughed 'She'd already given us the bottle.'

Mona shook her head. At least the poor woman had learned a valuable lesson. Don't pay for what you haven't yet received.

Mona and Barry found a spot amongst the crowded stands. While watching colours stream across the sky, they passed the bottle back and forth between them. When they finished the champagne, Barry pulled out his trusty flask of fruit booze.

Once the fireworks finished and everyone else was gone, they reminisced over the last six months, and about Sid and Curly and the year to come.

'You know if we go to war, there'll be no more boxing troupe, maybe no sideshow at all,' Barry said.

Mona shook her head, unable to continue any discussion of war. She took another drink. Which led to another and another. Other showies joined throughout the night.

Before she knew it, she was waking up under the seats, on the hard concrete, at sunrise. She kissed Barry and a few of the other boys each on their heads as she left. Barry mumbled a sleepy good night and good morning in one.

As she wandered back down to Sideshow Alley, she could see that the other showies had already packed up many of the tents, stages and games ready for travel.

'Nice of you to show up, now that we've finished.' Stella jumped from a trailer containing the darto, guess your weight and kewpie doll stands folded up.

'Sorry, Stella, time got away from me. Anything I can help with before I head off?' Mona asked, knowing full well she was already too late.

'Generous of you to offer, would be even more generous if next time you don't disappear when the work needs to be done. Now go on, scoot. See you on the road.'

When she got back to Gore Street, Sharpe was sitting on the bed playing cards; she'd been hoping he'd either be asleep or still out partying. He threw down a 10 of diamonds and stood, eyes bulging, fists clenched.

'You smell like those dirty showies. I hope you at least got paid.' He ripped her coat from her shoulders, throwing it at the hat stand in the corner.

Mona's knees knocked together as she edged back towards the bedroom door. 'I've been working through the night, packing up the stalls with Stella. She said now they're touring Victoria, I could work on and off, just take the train and meet them whenever I need the money.'

She hoped this piece of news would wash over his mood. It did enough for her to relax, just a little, just for a moment.

Then he opened his mouth again. 'Did you make any money yesterday?' He motioned for her to sit down on the bed, and she did, perching herself at the corner's edge.

'Yes, business was good,' she said truthfully. 'Haven't had to pick a single pocket.'

Sharpe loomed over her and held out his hand, waggling his fingers as if to say 'gimme'. When Mona didn't respond, he said, 'So let's have it.'

'Oh, is rent due?' she asked pulling her purse onto her lap.

'Yep.'

'Alright,' she said, hesitantly, and handed him half her day's earnings.

He scoffed. 'That's it? Thought you said business was good.'

'Surely that's enough for my half of the board.'

That was how it worked. At least, that's how it had always worked with Brown. She kept her money. He kept his. They shared costs of living, a bank account – she was a woman after all. But Brown never demanded anything else from her. He knew she had her own stash of cash and left it at that. But she was very quickly learning that men are not comparable. No two relationships the same.

Sharpe ripped the purse from her lap and rifled his unworked hands through it, pocketing the rest of her cash. Well, the cash from her handbag in any case. The money in her pockets and shoes was safe.

But not for long.

The next couple of days, he insisted she pay for groceries, taxis, and give him any spare money she had. She waited for word from Stella who was meant to call through to the boarding house about when and where Mona should meet up with the show.

The call never came. Or maybe it had, and he'd answered for her. He wouldn't want her to go. He wanted her close, where she could look after him. She felt trapped.

And so, when he suggested they go along to a party at Lawrence's house, she just about burst with joy. The chance to see and talk to other people. To perhaps meet up with Hutch and arrange her escape. She took the last of her money and bought herself a new dress, ankle-length emerald green with pink and red birds and flowers swirling between blue printed leaves. It dipped a little low, which Sharpe liked.

'Not too revealing?' she asked him. She'd known him long enough now to know that she needed his permission.

'Just revealing enough,' he said.

He wore the same outfit he'd had on the night she returned to Melbourne. He whipped her around to the sound of the wireless in the next room, dipping her and kissing her. The Sharpe she loved was back. It was time to party.

25

Mona had never spent much time at Lawrence's house in Elgin Street, Carlton. He was a man who liked to be out and about. Home was where he went to sleep, that was all. If he wanted to see people, he went to them. She could see why. By the dim light of candles, guests sat on chairs topped with dirty clothes and put their smokes out on the floor alongside every cigarette Lawrence had smoked since 1935. Walking in arm in arm with Sharpe, Mona could see Lawrence, for the party, had at least dusted the wireless. He argued with another guest over what channel to tune into. They twisted and turned the knobs every which way creating a mishmash of music no one could dance to.

Mona attempted a circle round the room, like she usually did when first entering a party. Sharpe gripped her hand tight.

'Where do you think you're going?'

'Just seeing if there's anyone I know,' Mona said.

'There won't be, it's all Port Melbourne crowd,' he said.

'Ok well, I'll get us a couple of drinks,' she said.

At that Lawrence appeared, having won his argument with the other music man, two beers in hand.

'One for Snow and one for Mo,' Lawrence winked.

It wasn't long before Sharpe loosened his grip on her and was distracted enough by an old acquaintance for Mona to go for a wander. She went out back to the toilet and chatted to some women outside.

On her way back through the kitchen Lawrence cornered her.

'So, you've been spending a lot of time with Sharpe?' he said, more a statement than a question. But she answered anyway.

'Yes.' A part of her wanted to add that she didn't think she'd be seeing him much longer.

She wanted to ask if he'd seen Hutchison recently, perhaps she'd go live with him in Essendon until she could meet up with Stella and the showies. But she didn't know how best to ask, how to bring it up in such a way that it wouldn't get back to Sharpe.

'Look,' Lawrence said, his voice dropping to a whisper. 'Just don't let him talk you into doing anything you don't want to do. And tell him I said that, I'll deny it.' He hurried off as Sharpe returned with more drinks.

'What's Lawry after?' he asked.

'Just gasbagging,' Mona said. Maybe she could trust Lawrence. But then again, if he really cared for her, why hadn't he warned her sooner?

A man with a gaunt face and rounded back pointed a skinny finger at her and shouted over the music.

'Hey, aren't you the one who got into a fight with that British bastard Cavendish? Been ripping people off at his Sydney gambling house for years, one trip to Melbourne and he's on his arse.'

Everyone turned to look.

She shrugged, trying to pass it off as a drunk man's ramblings, mistaken her for someone else.

But Sharpe doubled down. 'That true?' he asked.

'He was ripping us off at cards, we had words, maybe a shove or two, that was all,' she said.

'I knew you liked it rough,' Sharpe growled in her ear with a grin, elbowing her in the side he'd kicked her in a few weeks before. Mona winced.

'C'mon, let's dance,' Sharpe dragged her into Lawrence's room and up onto the bed. Before she knew it she was jumping up and down with him, all giggles, watching him bounce around beside her, his light hair flying loose, his tie hitting his chin, grin bright, she wished he could be like this all the time. A young man, Henry James, was dancing beside the bed with a woman named May. He swung her, her legs flying into the air, catching Sharpe in the shin.

'Sorry mate,' Henry said, May echoing his sentiment.

But it was too late. A switch flipped. Sharpe leapt off the bed and within seconds, he'd knocked the poor young bloke out. On his way down, Henry crash-landed into Lawrence's bedside table, smashing the lamp Lawrence's mother had given him. Pieces on the floor.

Mona shouted, 'It was an accident, he said he was sorry.'

That was it, Sharpe's fiery hazel eyes and temper turned to her. He didn't wait to watch the other partygoers rush to Henry's side, or for Lawrence to discover the mess. He grabbed Mona's hand and dragged her out of the party. When she begged him to stop pulling her so hard, so fast, he took her over his shoulder smacking her ass as she tried to wriggle free. This must be where the expression to be 'dragged kicking and screaming' came from – a woman being dragged home by her increasingly erratic boyfriend. She avoided eye contact with the calm couples they passed, walking hand in hand home from other parties. The couples stared and even laughed. No one asked if she needed help. She probably would have said 'no' if they had, because not even she knew what was to come.

Back at the house, Mona couldn't hear the other boarders. Usually when arriving home late at night, she could hear talking from upstairs or pans clattering in the kitchen, one of the boys making a midnight snack. This night there was nothing. The quiet was deafening. As Sharpe dropped her with a thud to the floor. She rubbed her knee, which hit the ground first, while Sharpe undressed. He kicked a shoe off and flung it at her head.

'Hey!' she shouted, now rubbing her knee with one hand and her head with the other. She stood, eyeing the door, but he blocked her exit. 'Move, I've had enough, I'm leaving.'

'You're not bloody going anywhere,' he said. And lunged at her.

She dodged him, running around the side of the bed to the other end of the room. He chased her. Just when he had her cornered again, she jumped up and over the bed towards the door.

'Don't you dare go out that door,' he was louder now.

She hesitated just long enough for him to round the bed again. She jumped back on the bed and soon he was on there with her. It was as if they were back at Lawrence's but instead of dancing they were wrestling, then somehow, inextricably, kissing. She couldn't explain why she allowed it. Why she was hurt and scared by him one minute, aroused the next. Or maybe she was still scared. Scared to leave, scared to say no. It would all go easier now. They'd have sex. He'd fall asleep. And she could sneak out in the morning. No yelling, no chasing, no bruises – except for those under the hair he was now pulling from her scalp, and those on her breasts and hips where he grabbed her so hard she wanted to cry. As usual he mistook her pain and discomfort for enjoyment. Or did he? He pushed and pulled and pounded harder.

The next morning, cuddled up with him in the nicest boarding house she'd ever lived in, his hair tickling her face, expression sweet, face handsome, she second-guessed herself. Maybe this wasn't so bad. She stayed, then walked on eggshells. She made sure to spread his toast just how he liked it. Cooked and cleaned and questioned if she was becoming her mother, or his. Then they ran out of alcohol.

'You drank the last of it, you bitch,' he said, shaking an empty bottle at her as she sat on the bedroom floor, shaving her legs with his razor, a bowl of soapy water beside her.

'No, you did,' she said, honestly unsure which one of them was right. It didn't matter. It was gone. 'I'd get more but you already spent all *my* money,' she spoke almost under her breath.

He lifted her by the neck and threw her like a ragdoll across the room, the razor slashing one leg while she grazed the other on the rug beneath her. Crumpled in the corner, she saw the blood before she felt it. Then he was on her again. Lifting her up the wall, his face so close to hers he was practically eating the curls of her strewn brown hair.

'*Your* money? *Your* money? Who the fuck do you think you're talking to? After everything I've done for you!' he shouted.

She didn't understand what he was talking about. Perhaps in his angry state he'd reverted to an old argument with an old girlfriend. Someone who wasn't her. Someone who hadn't been supporting *him* ever since she moved in.

Sharpe dropped his hands from her throat. 'You'd do best selling yourself on the street.'

The pain of her leg and neck wouldn't set in for a few hours yet. She felt heady, like she wasn't really there. She laughed nervously then, certain he was joking.

'You think that's funny do you? Yeah, real funny. I'll be laughing all the way to the bank.' His eyes brought her back to reality, they were burning into her, scolding her, waiting for her to make her next move. She froze.

Every criminal has a code. Lines they will and won't cross. Sometimes those lines shift. But for the most part, Mona only stole from those who could afford it, disliked anyone getting hurt in the process, and never laid with men for money. Not that she hadn't considered it. But if she did that, it wouldn't be for Sharpe's sake. It would be her call, and money, to make. She didn't want to fight with him anymore.

'Alright,' she straightened herself, ran her quivering fingers down her wool skirt and walked as confidently as she could to the closet.

'Good, get yourself sorted,' he said, leaving the room.

Lawrence's words rang in her ears. He was good at that. 'Don't let him talk you into anything you don't want to do.'

Had this been Sharpe's plan all along? Was this what he did with all his girlfriends? Bleed them dry then send them to the streets? Pimp, she remembered. One of the crims at Hutchison's party had called him that. Danger, stay away. She hadn't listened. She packed a few items of clothing and was almost out the door when the black miniature elephant caught her eye, standing at the edge of the shelf over the fireplace, it's eyes white and gleaming. It was holding up Sharpe's wallet. She tucked it into her bag, pocketed the cash he had left, and hurried for the window. Cracking it open, she'd half climbed out when she heard him re-enter.

'Hey!'

She whipped around in time to see Sharpe's fist coming at her, causing her to fall from the ledge and into the bushes outside.

'You stupid bitch. Where do you think you're going?' He shouted out the window. But he didn't follow her out. He'd hurt himself hitting her. Good. She somehow managed to pick herself up and run, bag and all. She kept looking back to see if he was chasing her, but couldn't see him. Eventually she came to her old house on Hanover. She knew Gerry and Esther's schedules. Gerry would be at the market, Esther running her Wednesday errands, the kids at school. She snuck down the side of the house, lifted the bedroom window and slid in. She didn't feel the throbbing pain until she looked at herself in the mirror. It became real then. She struggled to decide what to tend to first, her hands dancing, shaking, up and down her body touching blood, bruises, broken skin. For some reason she decided it was her hair that needed the most attention. Like picking the low hanging fruit. She couldn't stop the black eye forming, couldn't mend the split lip. Not right away. But her soft wavy hair, the hair he'd stroked before she really knew him, she could smooth in an instant.

She slept in the shed out back for a few nights – didn't want the children to see her looking the way she did. Gerry gave her one week to move herself on. She couldn't go to any of her friends because Sharpe knew them all. She had no choice but to find a boarding place on her own. Live alone. Something she'd never done before.

***

'Any chance I could get a room further up the back of the house?' Mona asked the boarding lady.

She'd wandered up and down Carlton all day, ending up back at Drummond Street where she'd lived with Curly, this time number 155. She wasn't expecting the best room in the place. The one right at the front

177

with stained glass windows facing the road. She tried to shake visions of Sharpe finding her, banging on the glass in the middle of the night, wanting money, wanting her back.

'I don't like being so close to the street.'

'We're full up love but if you can convince one of the other boarders to switch with you, be my guest. I'm still charging you the same rate though, regardless what room you end up in,' the woman said, pulling a spare front door key out of her apron pocket.

'That's fine,' Mona said. 'I'll talk with them tomorrow.'

'Ahh yes, tomorrow I'm going to need a week's rent paid up front.'

Mona knew that was coming. She nodded in agreement, took the key and entered her room. A couple's room. She lay awake all night thankful she was no longer in a couple, yet scared to be alone.

Sleeplessness was more tortuous than usual. Her eyes adjusted to the dark and stayed wide all night. Every time the tree outside scraped along the windowpane, she jumped. Every pair of footsteps made her ears prick up, hairs stand on end. The late-night comings and goings of other boarders, sounds she would have ordinarily found comforting, kept her scared and alert. She didn't want to drink in case he found her. At least she'd stand half a chance if he was drunk, and she sober. Finally, she'd had just about enough. She couldn't stay in town a moment longer.

Before sunrise she'd left for the station. A handwritten note for the landlady begged 'Gone to the Bendigo Show. Will send money for rent as soon as I can. Please hold the room for me. Mona.'

26

Only a week or two later – she lost track – Mona returned in the dead of night, not letting anyone else know she was back in town. Her landlady had done as she'd asked, and Mona paid her rent. Business had been slow at Bendigo and Stella suggested Mona head home to Melbourne and she'd send for her if things picked up. Mona laid low for a while, steering clear of parts of the city Sharpe frequented. But soon enough, with a hungry stomach and lack of funds, she had no choice but to head out.

****

Mona swung her arms through the air and rolled her head from side to side, stretching her lithe limbs in front of the mirror in her new room – out the back of the house. She'd had an interesting conversation with a man named Tom Miller, a young pawn shop salesman who'd agreed to switch rooms with her. The deal was a better one for him than it was for her. He got a spacious room with a bigger bed and a fireplace, for the price of the smaller one. In exchange, he answered all her, what he thought to be, 'silly' questions about working in the pawn business. And he'd revealed what the most popular items in store were. They weren't diamonds after all.

'There those thousand thinkers were thinking how did the other three thieves go through.' Mona warmed her voice with tongue twisters, smoothing her fingers over the front of her pleated skirt and tightening the belt around her waist. She checked herself out in the bathroom mirror one last time before heading out for the day's performance.

'Good morning miss, what can I do you for?'

'Well hello there. I do hope you can help me. I'm Mrs Wilson from Balwyn Road Canterbury,' she said. 'I'm only 24 but I've been having some trouble with my eyesight recently, mainly when reading the paper. My husband said I should come in and have my eyes tested. You do that here don't you?'

She asked as if she hadn't very clearly seen the optometry sign on the way in. Her eyesight had never been better.

'Certainly,' he said, lifting the side counter bench and allowing her through to the back room.

He tested her eyes, and she misread enough letters and numbers on the chart for him to suggest reading glasses. She enjoyed their conversation, so she dawdled a little longer than she'd intended, browsing other items in front of the shop, ultimately deciding only to hit the one that day. She scooped a small bead out of her pocket and handed it to the man, whose name she now knew was Charles Wayman. She'd found the bead on the carpet of the boarding house after a party earlier in the week. A few girls had turned up wearing flashy beaded and sequined frocks that shed as they danced.

'While I'm here, I'd like to know how much to have this piece of jet made into a ring?' she asked placing it down on the counter.

He picked it up and studied it. 'Gold or silver?' he asked.

'Gold. Plated is fine,' she said.

'I could make something up for you for about 17 pounds and you can pay in instalments if you wish,' he said.

'Alright. I'll leave it with you. I have just one more thing.'

Wayman was practically rubbing his hands together. By this point he was under the impression he'd already made two expensive sales today, now a third.

'Do you have any lady's wrist watches? I promised my mother a brand-new watch for Christmas, but we have such different tastes, I worry she won't like what I pick out for her. I would bring her to the shops with me, but she's an invalid, and in such a sorry state that she can't leave the house,' Mona took a beat to check his reaction.

'Oh, that's no good,' he said.

'Would you mind if I took a couple of watches home to get her opinion, and then I'll come straight back and buy the one she likes? I'll also buy the glasses and put a deposit on the ring when I return.'

'So long as you promise to come right back with them. We close at 4.30 today,' he said.

'Oh yes, I won't keep you waiting.'

'Here let me show you our two most popular ladies wrist watches, surely your mother will like one of these.'

'Oh, thank you so much. Here let me leave my handbag with you until I come back,' she smiled. It always paid to offer to do things like that. People would believe you were sincere then, and refuse, as he did.

And so, a few moments later she was dancing out of the store with two of the most expensive watches in Camberwell. She never went back. The following Tuesday, she did the same again on Bourke Road nearby though she couldn't quite be bothered with the eye test. Again, she walked out with two watches more expensive than the last.

***

Detective Collins took his hat off as he entered the Carlton Hotel lounge. Women turned their stools to appraise his good looks as he scanned the room, a shorter young chap sidling up beside him. A couple of men whispered 'coppers'. Some got up and left. The Carlton Hotel was a favourite among Melbourne's criminals and the police knew it. It's why Mona didn't often go there. Why she knew Sharpe wouldn't be there.

He spotted her. And she instantly knew she was in trouble. Yet Canterbury and Camberwell were not his area. Surely, he couldn't be there for her? He was. He made a beeline, frowning, nodding at the young guy, he mouthed, 'There she is.'

It was a strange thing to feel almost excited at the prospect of being arrested. She hadn't seen Collins in months. Mona didn't wait for him to reach her before jumping out of her seat and shouting dramatically. 'It's all been a case of mistaken identity.'

'Unbelievable,' Collins shook his head and held back a smile. 'Don't start that now Mona, we know it was you.' He motioned for her to follow them out.

***

They walked in silence to the station. Every time they approached a busy street corner, Collins would reach for her hand. She soon found herself in the middle of CIB offices in Russell Street surrounded by policemen tapping away on typewriters, flipping through notepads and discussing cases over coffee. Finally, she got a proper introduction.

'Mona, this is Crawley, just transferred to CIB a couple months ago.' Collins watched on as short, young Crawley tipped his hat.

'You're a regular here at the station are you Miss?' Crawley asked.

'You could say that.'

'How goes the sideshows?' Collins called from the meeting room by the kitchenette, motioning both Crawley and Mona over.

'Very well – we just returned from Bendigo,' she said, omitting the few weeks in between. He wouldn't know the show dates off the top of his head. Surely.

'Really?' Collins' tone was teasing and disbelieving, ok so maybe he did know the show dates. She turned her attention back to Crawley.

'Do you like the theatre?' she asked.

'Certainly Miss.'

'You know, I worked as an usher for a time. Saw many of the best actors up close. You have a face for the stage.'

He smiled at the compliment before looking sheepishly over at Collins who was chuckling. Crawley was no match for Mona's charms.

'Sit.'

Mona sat down at the table while the detectives stood over her, arms crossed and waiting.

She shifted in her seat – if they thought their quiet stares would be enough to convince her to confess, they had another thing coming. For once she was going to heed Lawrence's advice. Then the door opened, and an officer brought in Wayman.

'Is this the woman who came into your shop the other day?' Collins asked him.

'Yes, that's her, no doubt about it.'

The clerk was escorted back out of the room as Mona jumped from her seat. 'That man's lying, he's never seen me before in his life!'

'Mona, Mona, Mona, whatever will we do with you?' Collins tutted pulling silver handcuffs from his belt and striding towards her. 'You're under arrest for larceny. Again.' He told her to sit and wait, an officer would walk her to the City Watch House. He was halfway out the door when he turned back with a dejected sigh. 'You know, you're going to gaol this time. Nothing to be done about it.'

'At least I'll be safe there,' Mona said. But he was gone. And she just couldn't figure out how to live the life she wanted, possess all the things she wanted, without stealing it.

***

The bus ride to the gaol was quiet. Mona sprawled across the back bench while another young woman sat a few rows ahead. Up the front near the driver sat five men shackled to each other. A bus in front was packed with around twenty other men. Mona tried to ignore the turned heads of the blokes as she studied the young girl from behind. She could see her head bobbing up and down and her shoulder's shake, Mona could only imagine the tear-stained face on the other side. Mona wondered what the girl did to be sent to gaol so young when Mona, a grown woman, had been granted time in the Convent two years before. Leniency. She would see now whether the Convent had been lenient.

Mona was already familiar with the high towers, brick walls and iron gates of the gothic Pentridge Gaol, having spent the odd day or two there awaiting bail in the past.

The other bus they'd been following pulled into the main gates first and the men filed out one by one. The young girl made a move to get up from her seat and the driver shouted back to sit down, they'd wait for the men to enter the prison first and then they'd drive round to the women's block. Mona watched as the men followed a warder through the doors of the dark building ahead of them. Some of the men looked quite young. Most had their shoulders slumped forward, defeated, scared. But a few older men looked perfectly confident, even content, as though heading home.

The bus driver closed the doors behind the men as they exited. He grunted as loud as the engine as it started back up. Mona looked out the window as they headed back in the direction they'd come in, turning left out of the main gate, straight up past the dark walls of the prison before turning left and left again. Finally, she could see the gates of the women's block. Though made of the same brick and stone, it wasn't as intimidating as the gates they'd just left the men behind. The bus entered through the south gate and stopped alongside the gaol.

'Aight you two, let's get movin,' a female warder with a blue coat shouted through the bus door. Mona got up and out into the chill evening air. She shivered, rubbing the prickling skin of her arms through her blazer. The summer sun seemed to have neglected Pentridge.

Though she'd mistakenly been quick to stand when arriving at the men's block, the young girl was now reluctant to move from her seat. The warder rapped her knuckle across the glass of the bus window. 'Hurry up, we don't have all day.'

The warder marched the two through the steel cloaked doors. Once inside the entrance she motioned for both women to stand against the brick wall as she looked down at her clipboard.

'Right so you would be Mona Hayes,' she said tilting her head in Mona's direction. 'Six months I see. And you there,' she said this time looking at the young girl, 'I spose you'd be Ruth Salinger. One month.'

Both Mona and Ruth nodded.

'Ruth you'll wait here with Warder June 'til you're called. Mona come with me.' The warder tucked the clipboard back under her arm and led Mona into a small office. There Mona was finger-printed, photographed, measured and appearance scrutinised. The warder wrote all the details down in a book. Hair colour, eye colour, build and complexion.

Mona couldn't help but allow the significance of this to weigh across her features. She knew those who served sentences of six months or more also have portraits taken when they leave, those, along with all the details now being recorded, go straight to the police gazettes, and CIB, and circulated right across the country. For the first time, police all along the show route would know what she looked like. Her history would follow her, aliases only useful until the officer flipped through his big book of criminals and found her. Convicted thief and prior Pentridge prisoner Mona Hayes. No more excuses would do. She'd be known as a career criminal wherever she went.

Next, Mona was taken to the changerooms. The warder bagged each item of clothing as Mona removed them; grey skirt, black shirt and heels.

'You'll get these back when you leave.'

Mona scoffed. 'That's what they said at Abbotsford.'

Naked, she was told to stand straight first, then bend over. She held her breath as the warder searched her head to toe before shoving her into the showers. The water was sharp against Mona's flush, embarrassed, skin. She washed quickly, then the warder handed Mona her new uniform.

'You'll go in and see the Matron, then I'll take you to your cubicle,' she pulled Mona by the elbow out into the hallway and through to the Matron's office. A sharp 'send her in,' came from inside. The warder opened the door, pushed Mona in and slammed the door behind her.

Mona stumbled towards the grand wooden desk as she straightened her uniform, the stiff fabric sticking to her still wet body.

'You a drinker?' The Matron didn't even bother to look up from her paperwork. She was a small woman, miniature mop of grey hair on her tiny head. Squinty eyes. But her voice was bigger than her body.

Mona stepped closer. 'Yes. Do you ask that of everyone?' she asked, unsure what gave her away.

'I do,' the Matron looked at Mona now, tipping her black rimmed glasses down her nose. 'The answer's usually the same.'

'Why ask then?' Mona snapped.

'Oh, you've got a mouth on you, haven't you?' the Matron stood now and walked around her desk, stepping in front of Mona. She could feel the Matron's hot stale breath on her face.

'Keep it shut while you're here and we'll get along fine.'

Mona bit her lip to stop herself answering back. The Matron smiled and stepped back towards her desk. 'Classic sign of addiction, when great lengths are sought in pursuit of drugs and or alcohol, to the detriment of all else.'

Mona didn't appreciate that the Matron could so easily boil her down. An alcoholic that talks back, is that really all she was? A memory of Collins observing 'this is the first time I've seen you sober' on the drive out of Abbotsford flashed through Mona's mind. Alcoholic. Alcohol had always been a constant in her life and had numbed the pain of her recently swollen eyes, bruised cheek. So yes, maybe she was an alcoholic. Yet wasn't she also so much more?

As if reading Mona's mind, the Matron cleared her throat. She shuffled more paperwork around, finding the sheet she was after. 'Tell me more about yourself. It says here you can read and write so I know you're educated.'

'Yes, I am,' Mona nodded.

'And? What else?' The Matron pried.

'I suppose I have six months to think about what else I am, besides a drunk and a thief—'

'Six months hard labour for larceny.' The Matron nodded her head as she read aloud from the paper in front of her. 'Not your first time in trouble with the law. Haven't learned your lesson yet?'

Mona shrugged, then couldn't help herself asking the question she'd been dreading hearing the answer too. 'What's hard labour for women?'

The Matron chuckled as a knock at the door interrupted their meeting. 'You'll find out soon enough. Off with you. Warder Stacey will see you out. Any trouble, and you'll be before the Governor, you hear me?'

Mona nodded. The door opened and in walked red-eyed Ruth. Mona hoped their beds weren't next to each other. She couldn't stand the thought of having to listen to the kid cry all night. The warder who'd stripped Mona earlier was back by her side walking her to the cells.

'The dorms are full, and since you're a stayer – here for six months I mean – you get your own cubicle,' Warder Stacey said.

'I assume that's a fancy word for cell,' Mona said as Warder Stacey walked her past the lined beds of chatty girls in the light-filled dormitory, and sure enough, into a dank dark hallway lined with cells.

'You missed dinner. I'll bring you something in a bit. You can have a wander round the cell block for a few hours but you must be back in your cubicle by eight.'

She led Mona into a corner cell.

'This one's yours.' She opened the heavy wooden door and nudged Mona inside. Mona was left alone to acquaint herself with the room she would call home for the next six months. Another couple of warders lined the corridor and eyed her suspiciously as she surveyed her surroundings.

An iron bed with a thin mattress, folded blankets, a small stool beside the bed with a copy of the bible on top, wash basin and toilet. Between the shared accommodations of the dormitory and the cells, Mona felt she had the better deal. At least here she had her own space. More space than she usually got in boarding houses and show tents. Dinner was announced with a thud on the end of the bed. Bread and dripping. Cold tea slid across the floor. She ate, she slept – or tried to – and the next morning after a porridge breakfast she found out what hard labour for women in Pentridge was.

27

The laundry was hot and crowded, yet familiar. Mona stated her name as she entered, and Warder Stacey made a mark on a file.

'For ya pay,' she explained before Mona had a chance to ask. The days in the laundry would be far less painful knowing that when she walked out of prison, she would be given a little bit of money. No doubt it wouldn't be much, but it was something.

Mona came upon many familiar faces, women she'd partied with and a certain someone she'd been at Abbotsford with.

Red's voice was as loud as her hair; it wasn't hard to pick her out amongst the crowd and steam of the laundry room. Mona muttered apologies as she weaved and bumped her way towards the familiar sounds of Red setting someone straight.

'You're just a bloody moron aren't ya?' she heard Red say to another girl as she approached. 'No wonder you ended up in here.'

'So, what's your excuse?' Mona shouted.

'What. The. Hell?!' Red screamed causing 'heys' and 'quieten downs' from every guard in the room.

Mona laughed and watched as Red stepped towards her, then back, then forwards again as if deciding whether or not to go in for a hug. Mona made the decision for her, grabbing her tight.

'So, what brings you to Pentridge?' Red asked.

'Apparently jewellers don't appreciate women taking their watches. And believe it or not, police no longer buy the mistaken identity spiel.'

'Did they ever?' Red laughed.

'Well apparently. Though I'd never tried it before. And won't, ever again.'

'You're too distinct, that's your problem. Aren't many women do what you do, looking as good while doing it.'

'Yeah, that must be it.' Mona said twisting her finger in a strand of Red's flaming hair. 'Talk about recognisable! So, what happened to you? Another raid?'

'I'd only been out of Abbottsford a couple days and the coppers came through. I'll be out of here by June.'

'I'm out soon after,' Mona said. She bit her lip too afraid to ask the question that burned within her. As if reading her mind Red spoke.

'Cecilia's fine you know.'

'Define fine.' Mona had often wondered if Cecilia might have died from her head wound, infection setting in.

'She had an almighty bump for a while but she's alright now. She was pretty well healed within a few days. Nuns said she could have come back to the dorms sooner, but she complained of other ailments, surprise surprise, until you left. Apparently, then, she was miraculously healed.'

'Huh,' Mona had mixed emotions at the news. On the one hand she was glad not to have severely injured the girl. On the other, she felt Cecilia deserved worse than what she got. Maybe not for the way she treated Mona but for hurting a baby? She deserved much worse.

'An eye for an eye,' one of the prison guards said soon after, when Thomas William 'Nugget' Johnson was hanged at the men's prison. A couple of the women Mona worked with in the laundry knew him and were upset. There was a strained feeling of nervousness around the prison that day. Not knowing what to do or what to say. Even some of the guards were on edge. It was the first hanging in three years. Guards whispered the off-hand comment between them, not meant to be heard by inmates. But Mona heard and inwardly agreed. He'd killed two people. Now it was his turn to die.

Red heard too and shook her head. 'Not everything should be so black and white.'

Prison routine set in after a few days. Freezing mornings in the cells, 6.15 starts, 7am breakfasts, midday and 4pm meals, lights out at 8.30pm. Painful and familiar. Yet Mona enjoyed the company of the other girls and even the guards. She was soon moved to the needle-room where she mended uniforms with treadle machines, learned raffia crafts and made blankets. The girls were free to talk and listen to the wireless in there. The only thing that quietened them was the Matron's footsteps coming down the hall. If behaviour was good during the week, a sewing class would be held with Mrs Beresford Jones and her raffia girls, the classes often becoming sing-alongs with visiting musicians.

In Mona's first class, Mrs Jones, the Raffia Lady as the other girls called her, pulled up a chair beside Mona and showed her the basic technique for sewing a purse. She spoke in a way that was kind but not condescending, her cheeks reddening with excitement as Mona followed her instructions. Expensive pearls dangled from the woman's neck as she leaned in close to survey Mona's handiwork. How easy it would be for her to lose that necklace in a prison full of crims. Yet Mrs Jones seemed to treat this as a class like any other.

'You can take this back to your cell and work on it in the evenings. Anything you finish I can sell for you and give you the money you've earned on your release,' she said.

'You're kidding,' Mona said.

Mrs Jones laughed. 'If I can help you ladies earn some money so you can start anew, my job here is done. Now, you've picked this up pretty quickly, I can see you must be a creative type. I can bring in paints one week if you fancy doing some artwork?'

'Oh no, I'm no artist. I can sing a little and play a few instruments but no, I haven't sewed or painted since school.'

'A singer!' Mrs Jones stood from her seat. 'Did you hear that girls? We have a singer here in Miss Mona Hayes. Maybe we should encourage her to start us off?'

The girls shouted and clapped.

'We like to sing while we work,' Mrs Jones explained. 'Do you know *Look for the Silver Lining* Mona?'

Mona cleared her throat. 'Um I can give it a go but you all must join in,' she said, waiting for them all to agree before beginning. The girls sat silent as she sang, but when she paused for what would have been the music break, Red broke into a poor piano impersonation 'dah dah dah' and everyone erupted into laughter.

One of the other girls started a second song, but the next song Mrs Jones said, 'Maybe Mona could do a nice solo on this one too?'

The following week, Mrs Jones had a piano brought in. She asked Mona to sit and sing for the entire class. Though she was making less money than the other girls who had the advantage of sewing throughout the session, selling an extra item or two each week in the process, Mona was overjoyed by her new role. Head singer. Star.

'You know you can't be writing letters in your cell without permission,' Warder Stacey rapped her knuckles on the bars of Mona's cell one night. Mona had managed to get hold of a pencil and pad. 'I'm going to have to write you up for a charge before the Governor.'

Mona stood to attention, holding the pad out for Stacey to see.

'I'm not writing letters, Warder, I've been enjoying our songs in the sewing room so much I thought I'd try writing one myself, to share next week. Please, look.'

The Warder took the pad and read it under the dim Pentridge corridor light. 'Hmm, nice words, but no notes, how will you know how to play it?'

'I'm sure I can figure it out.'

'Hmm,' the Warder said again, still holding onto the pad.

Mona waited. She couldn't get written up. She'd been doing so well.

'Yes, well right,' Stacey handed back the pad. 'Don't let anyone else see you with this.'

Mona wrote and hummed under the bedcovers from then on. Perfecting the piece. She knew Warder Stacey would be watching and if she didn't sing it that next week, the Warder may still write her up. She had no choice but to perform it, ready or not.

As she sat down at the piano, she told Mrs Jones she'd written something but would need to fiddle around with the keys for a bit.

Mrs Jones smiled grey teeth and wet eyes. 'Girls, while Mona warms up, I want to show you a new technique for sewing the corners together.' She gathered all the girls round a table at the opposite corner of the room as Mona played and took down notes on her pad. She couldn't read or write music, so her notes would only make sense to her. Finally, she felt ready.

The girls took their seats and Mona played. She felt embarrassed by her own lyrics. Words that told whoever was listening that she now had something to sing about. She'd lived a life of love and fun, felt pain and heartbreak. Like a child singing in front of her parents, she couldn't bring herself to look up from the piano, but she felt the air sucked from the room around her, all eyes on her.

When she finished, the room broke into applause. She felt Mrs Jones' hand on her shoulder as she looked up and saw her fellow prisoners standing, clapping, shouting and whistling.

'Good one. Yep. Bloody good one,' Red said.

'You should be singing professionally. You're a real chanteuse,' Mrs Jones pulled Mona aside later to say.

'I've always wanted to but it's not very realistic, is it?'

'What's not realistic? I know of many community groups who'd pay a good fee for you to play at charity galas and such, there's restaurants in the city who hire musicians on weekends, many opportunities out there for someone with talent like yours. You'd make much better money doing that than whatever it was you were doing before.'

Collins' voice ran across her mind 'if only you could use that brain of yours for better things.'

If she could steal from strangers, run away with the sideshows and entertain a gaol full of rowdy female crims, surely she could do anything. She'd never had the guts to give it a go before. Never liked the prospect of failing at the thing she loved the most. But failure was certain if she never even tried.

***

From sitting at the piano, to sewing and standing still in the laundry, the lack of movement was taking its toll.

'You could do to skip the dripping tonight Mo,' Red laughed, pinching Mona's side as they entered the dining hall. While midday dinners consisted of bread, dripping and tea – the dullest meal of the day – the atmosphere at teatime was anything but. The evening guards didn't mind a bit of mealtime chatter.

'Piss off.' Mona had already asked a warder for a bigger uniform.

'May as well eat while you can. At's what I always say,' old Beatrice snatched a couple extra pieces of bread and stuffed them in her pockets. Beatrice was a favourite of Mona's. She was in and out of Pentridge constantly. In her 60s, Beatrice looked older, with a two-toned mop of oily hair, black on the ends, grey at the centre. She was an alcoholic who'd spend every last penny on booze, or anything containing alcohol, in favour of accommodations. She'd drink herself sick, sleep out in the street, and then go right back to drinking the next morning. The only food she ate, or showers she had, were when the police picked her up for drunk and disorderly. Which was every other day. That was Beatrice's life. And she didn't seem to mind it. Too much of a drunk to care about anything other than the next drink. She'd been that way her entire life. Had hundreds of convictions. The most Mona had ever heard of. Mona liked the old woman while being terrified at the same time. She saw her future. 60 years old, still in and out of prisons and Convents. Drinking, stealing, moving from boarding house to boarding house never knowing when her next meal would be. Not to mention contending with cheating boyfriends, abusive ones, crooked ones. At least when Mona travelled with the sideshows she was working, seeing different towns and cities, meeting new people – most of them *not* of the criminal variety – and she was free.

On the way out of the dining room Beatrice took a couple of apples from the fruit bowl. But unlike the bread, she didn't hide them in her pockets. Mona looked around and noticed others peeling mandarins and oranges, slurping down pears, as they too headed back to their beds. The guards didn't so much as bat their eyelids. She'd been in for weeks, why hadn't Mona noticed this before?

'Wait, they let us take fruit back to our cells?' Mona asked. Even in gaol in Sydney, food stayed in the dining hall.

'Yup. It's the excess grown over at the men's prison,' Red said.

'Goes rotten if not eaten right away, guards know that,' Beatrice said making her way to the dormitory.

Red shuddered, leading Mona back to the cell block. 'I don't know why you talk to her.'

'Who? Old Bea?'

'Old Bea. Not as harmless as her wrinkles make her look. She'd give Cecilia a run for her money. Turn on you in a second. I heard she once beat a cellmate to a bloody pulp.'

Mona shrugged. She'd already been beaten by a man. What could a little old woman do? 'Better to keep on her good side then, hey.'

Mona's mind swirled watching as girls licked fruit juices off their fingers, tossed mandarins at each other and ate apples whole. She could tell them how to turn that fruit into wine. If the staff were lax on the fruit, it wouldn't be too hard to sneak a bottle of water and some sugar back to the cells. Mix it all together. Home grown potent Pentridge prison alcohol. No delivery men needed. It took everything in her not to mention it. Hell, it took everything in her not to do it for herself, not to spring into action and start an entire production line. Prisoners could smoke freely in Pentridge, they got *paid* in Pentridge. Imagine all the cigarettes. Imagine all the cash I OWE YOU's in her future. Simply by dealing homemade fruit booze to the long-suffering locked-up alcoholics – herself included.

She thought about it all night. Tossed and turned in bed. She thought about how long it would take to brew something good enough to drink. She thought about the space under her bed, way up the back where the guards didn't look. She thought about drinking again. The next morning, Beatrice was led away from the dining hall.

'See you in a day or two Bea,' a couple of girls shouted after her. She cackled.

Mona's interest in introducing alcohol to the Female Prison left with Beatrice. And it didn't return when she did a few days later. As far as Mona was concerned, the women were doing well enough without any alcohol, her too. And her voice had never sounded better. She thought that maybe, rather than using this time trying to find a way to drink or escape, she should accept her punishment. Sit in a cell. Do laundry. Sew. Sing. Think. She'd robbed people of their things, their money, and she should be sorry. She'd had it partially right all along – when caught out, red-handed, she acknowledged her guilt. She'd put her hands up and say, 'Ok I'll make a statement' without argument. Then she spent too long believing stealing was ok so long as she was poor and stole from those with more. She spent too much time listening to people like Lawrence. But she was right to admit her guilt back then. Now she just needed to feel it.

28

'Hayes, Mona,' one of the guards called, her shrill voice cutting through the chatter of the needle room. Mona stood. 'Matron will see you now.' The other girls nudged her 'what have you done?' They watched as Mona followed the guard. She hadn't set a foot out of line while incarcerated, so confusion and worry spread across the faces of those she'd grown close to – if Mona was in trouble, what did that mean for the rest of them? They needn't have worried.

Sitting at her desk, Matron's head was barely visible behind teetering stacks of paperwork, just a mop of grey hair peaking between large leather-bound volumes. She stood when the guard announced Mona's entrance.

'Right, right, Mona Hayes. Come in and shut the door behind you.' She took the largest stack off the desk and dropped it to the floor beside her with a thud, disturbing dust laden carpet. It was warmer in the office than the rest of the gaol, large windows soaking up the afternoon sun. Mona sat in the chair opposite the Matron, who remained standing as she opened another file and flicked through it.

'Looks like you've been behaving yourself in here.'

'Yes, Marm,' Mona said, fidgeting, nervous.

The Matron sat, the leather of her chair belching beneath her. 'Wasn't a question. I see your mouth still works.'

Mona smiled, mouth closed, and waited.

Once the Matron was done reading the guard's notes in front of her, she eyed Mona, pushed her glasses down her nose and nodded.

'Alright, so why did you ask to see me?' The Matron asked. For it was Mona who requested this meeting weeks ago.

Lawrence had visited Mona on his way out of the men's prison after a three-month stint. Caught stealing scrap iron not long after Mona's charge. He told her Albert Sharpe was in gaol too, coincidentally due out at the exact same time as her. Lawrence thought it funny, the two love-birds serving time at the same time, divided by just a few walls.

'Spose that'll be some reunion when you get out,' he'd said, taking a long drag of his cigarette, blowing smoke in Mona's terrified face.

'It's as you said, Matron, I've behaved well in here. I've become one of the best seamstresses in the needle room, entertaining the Raffia girls with singing and…'

'So I've heard,' Matron said.

'And I believe I'm an outstanding candidate for early release based on such good behaviour.'

Mona didn't expect the Matron to take long to think about it. The main reason prisoners asked for an audience with her was to beg for early release, Mona knew. She usually had a response ready before they even sat down.

The Matron looked back at her notes and read for a moment more before she spoke. 'When you first came in here, I asked you to tell me about yourself and you couldn't seem to come up with much of an answer. So, Ms Hayes, what can you tell me about yourself now?'

This time Mona knew what to say.

'I'm hard working. Resourceful. I can clean, sew, sing, dance, play piano, read, write, and…'

'And…?'

'And I know I'll be alright on my own,' Mona finished. Pleased with herself. She would be alright. So long as she could get out of prison early.

'Do you have any plans for after your release?'

'Yes, I think so.'

'You could give singing a try. From all I've heard you're very good at it.' The Matron smiled at Mona for the first time. Crooked brown teeth on full show.

This was the time for Mona to say her dreams out loud, finally admit them to herself and everyone else. 'Yes, I think I will pursue a career in singing.'

'Alright then. I'll recommend the Governor give you seven days special remission,' she said. 'If it goes through, one of the warders will call you up for your exit photograph in the next week, and you'll be scheduled for discharge on the 23rd of August. How does that sound?'

'That sounds wonderful,' Mona said, hoping seven days difference would be enough to avoid a run in with Sharpe, his empty wallet and his raging fists.

'Guard'—Mona rose as the guard entered—'Take Mona back now. And tell Marta on your way out that I'm ready for this paperwork to be re-filed.'

***

Often, when criminals were released from Pentridge, a welcoming committee would wait at the gates, re-introducing them into society with cheers and hugs, and bottles of bubbly. Mona herself had greeted many acquaintances at the gates over the years. Once, when Brown was released from six months in Pentridge, Mona, Guggenheim and Hutchison assembled with instruments and played *Happy Days Are Here Again*. Mona had dropped her ukele and jumped into his newly buff arms.

'Brick breaking,' he had said as she traced the muscles beneath the thin fabric of his suit. Rather than rushing off to the nearest groghouse, as they'd planned, Brown had insisted on adding their instruments to the fanfare assembled across the road for a newly-freed bank robber about to make his way home. The guards had tried to hide amused grins at the repetition of the song.

'You should come back every day!' one had laughed. Another spoke to Hutch, asking him questions about the music, the ukuleles. He said his son had been wanting to take lessons. He wrote down Hutch's number.

The day Mona left Pentridge, she braced herself for a rather lack lustre welcoming committee. If she'd been leaving next week when she was meant to, maybe Collins would have been sitting in his car, across the street, making sure she had somewhere to go. She couldn't help but feel disappointed that, as planned, no one was there at all. The Matron and the guards had kept quiet about her early release and, thankfully, Sharpe hadn't found out.

A few steps out of the gates, she swivelled around, staring up at the dark walls and pocked bluestone of Pentridge. She promised herself she'd never be back. If she didn't want to live in fear and captivity, she needed to steer clear of Sharpe and the criminal circles he ran in, keep her nose clean. She was lucky in a sense. So many of the women she'd grown to know at Abbotsford and Pentridge had no life skills besides the ones that had gotten them in trouble in the first place. Whereas Mona could do many things. She was finally ready to give those things a try.

29

Mona went straight to Carlton to pick up the suitcase kindly kept by her old landlady. She got a tip on lodging at a boarding house just up the road and found a domestic job in Regent Street, Fitzroy.

She spent her days washing laundry, mending curtains and sweeping cigarette butts off the front steps, indulging in just one beer at dinner on the way home. Then she'd spend the evening drawing out ideas for show tents and costumes. She wrote song, dance and joke routines and rehearsed until she was hoarse, or until knocks and cries from the other boarders shut her up. She even cut down on smoking to help her reach the high notes. She used to put this kind of time and effort into stealing. But now, she would be ready to audition for her own tent when the showies arrived in Melbourne in September.

This wasn't usual of course. An unknown solo singing act. Women performers were in the sexy dance troupes and strip teases, they rode stunt bikes or horses, or were sideshow curiosities – big, small, tattooed. Occasionally a singer or musician would accompany other acts, or sing in a troupe, but it had been a while since Mona had seen a tent devoted to a single female chanteuse. She knew it could work though, and be successful, if given a shot. No more Convents, prisons or boarding houses. No more cleaning, sewing or stealing. She'd go on tour and be the boss of her own life, keep her own money, perform for people she wasn't robbing. She just needed to survive long enough to see it through.

Mona received her first pay on the Friday afternoon. She went straight into town to buy a dress she'd seen in the Myers catalogue. The perfect dress for an audition. A black satin bias cut, floor length, sleeveless, with matching gloves. Easy to mend for dancing. She'd make large slits up both sides, so she could go from sweet to sexy with just the flash of a leg. She went in and made a deposit on the outfit, then stopped by a hotel for dinner. Seated at the counter, with the other single diners, she ate steak. Then stayed. Too long. Lingering to chat to the staff.

One of the waiters was about to serve her scotch in a teacup, when a hand reached out, gripping Mona's shoulder from behind.

'It's well past six, and that doesn't look like coffee to me.'

The waiter froze. Mona couldn't even bear to turn and look at the man breathing down her neck. Instead, she jiggled in her seat, trying to edge away from him.

He gripped her shoulder harder. And laughed. 'Relax, I'm no cop.' The waiter breathed a sigh of relief, placed the cup in front of Mona, and went back to work.

Mona pushed the cup aside, stood and turned to face Sharpe. She couldn't tell from his face what mood he was in. She tried the only trick she had. Charm.

'Well, hello there.'

'Well, hello there,' he mocked. 'I heard you were in Pentridge, meant to be out this week, I waited for you.'

'The Ladies' prison Matron was very generous with me, asked the Governor to let me out early, good behaviour.'

Sharpe laughed again. He smelled of the scotch she'd just rejected. Mona thought about her next move. She'd tell him she had to go, meet up with a new boyfriend. Or would he see right through that? She could tell him she was late for work. A waitressing or usher job. More believable. Just as she began to speak, he reached out and gripped her wrist, pulling her to the door.

'You're coming with me.'

'Really, I have to get going. I got a job nearby and my shift starts—'

'You'll make more money if you come with me,' he said.

She broke free of him and ran up Bourke Street trying to flag down every passing car and taxi.

He chased after her. 'Get back here, you thieving bitch. I want my money. You're coming with me.'

The money she took with her when she left him. She'd almost forgotten. He caught up with her, grabbing her again, slamming her up against the wall of an office building. People whispered as they passed, some even looked concerned, but no one stepped in. As she tried to make space between them, Sharpe smashed her head against the wall. She'd heard the expression of seeing stars but never before believed it. Yet the details of Sharpe's face disappeared, and white spots, golden stars and shadows danced across her vision.

'Please. Can't you leave me alone? I'm not the only girl in town.'

She heaved, releasing what felt like a hiccup, and she realised she was crying. Her vision returned as Sharpe's nose pressed against hers. He'd bent his legs, leaning down so she could see the whites of his eyes under the streetlight, the dark ring around the iris with blue and green streaks fading to brown at the centre. She'd loved those eyes once.

'The only one to steal from me though aren't ya? I want my money. I want you to come back and live with me. Work for me,' he said, still pinning her to the wall.

'I want nothing to do with you.' She was feeling braver now. People were starting to mill around. She could see behind Sharpe's head that two men were approaching, hesitantly, they would soon intervene, and she could get away.

He slammed her head against the wall again. This time, no stars.

'Everything all right here?' one of the men put a hand on Sharpe's shoulder and he let her go.

'We've hailed you a cab Miss, if you need it,' the other man said.

'Perfect, gentlemen, we're on our way to a party.' Sharpe said shoved them out the way as he pulled Mona into the waiting cab. He told the driver to head to an address in Fitzroy, on King William Street. She'd been there before. Many times. Couldn't remember whose house it was, just that there was always a big crowd. She'd get away from him then.

'A party,' she said.

'We can talk more there. I know after a few more drinks, some snow, you'll come round, won't you darlin',' he said putting his arm around her, pulling her close on the back seat.

She nodded, tears prickling her eyes.

'Well, you might want to fix yourself up. It is a party after all,' he laughed.

She wanted to tell him to go fuck himself. Easier to just go along. For now. Until she could get away. She took her pocket mirror out of her purse. She'd lost her hat. Her hair half fallen out of its low bun, strands strewn wildly around her head. She let her hair down and combed through it with her fingers. As she did so she found blood on her hands. The back of her head was cut. She couldn't do much about that now. But she could straighten the collar on her coat. She could lick her lips and pinch her cheeks and wipe the streaked mascara from her skin.

As they entered the party, out of the corner of her eye she saw Lawrence on the doorstep with a group of women she didn't recognise. He called out to her, but she ignored him, staring straight ahead. He was, after all, not just *her* friend anymore. He was Sharpe's too. And men side with men. Once they entered the house, Sharpe started a round of hellos and followed a drug dealer out the back of the house.

'Come,' he commanded Mona.

She nodded, then ran out the front door the minute his back was turned. She didn't think he'd notice her gone until he got outside and by then he'd be more interested in the coke than her. Surely.

She was wrong.

He shouted her name as she broke into a run. She lost one shoe, then the other, but she kept running, asphalt like pins on the soles of her feet. She'd just about reached the street corner when she felt his hands at her back. He pushed her to the ground.

'Don't think you're leaving without giving me my money,' he said.

Blood pooled in her eyes as he pulled her up by her coat collar and punched her in the head, flattening her back on the road again. He was kicking her in the stomach when she heard a horn honking. Headlights. She opened her eyes, wiping tears and blood and hair from her face. Her voice hoarse from screams.

'What's going on here?' a man's voice broke through the night.

Next she knew, Sharpe was gone, and three men were loading her into a fruit truck, one of them delicately placing her high heels back on her feet. As they drove up the road and past the party house, Lawrence lit Sharpe's cigarette on the porch. Someone called for a cold cloth as Sharpe cradled his fist in his lap and sat down.

'We'll get you to the hospital in no time Miss.' She turned her attention back to the men. Three skinny fruit pickers squished along the front of the truck, her closest to the passenger door.

'You'll be right,' the driver said. 'Probably looks worse than it is.' How bad did it look? She touched her face, blood smeared. She didn't feel much pain. Yet.

'That bloke your husband?' the one next to her asked.

'No,' she whispered.

'What'd you do to piss him off?'

She stared out the window, her mind whirling. They were taking her to St Vincents Hospital. Sharpe would figure that out. He'd go there to find her.

'No, no hospital,' she said.

'You need it Miss,' the driver said.

'I'd rather go to my friend's place,' she said.

'Where's that?'

***

His house wasn't quite as she'd expected. Well-groomed shrubs, pansies and daphnes lined the little path leading up to his bright white door. Unlike his neighbours' darkened driveways, light filtered from his windows out onto the street. She knocked and stood back onto the lower step, ready to run if courage escaped her.

Detective Collins opened the door with a curious raised eyebrow. Though it was now almost 11pm, he didn't seem concerned by the late-night visitor. He leaned casually by the open door, cigarette dangling from his lip, half empty glass of beer in hand. Mona's eyes travelled across his bare, muscular arms, white singlet stained with cooking grease, a kitchen towel slung over his shoulder. Warmth from an open fire filtered out the doorway.

'Mona?' he questioned into the darkness.

She stepped up into the light flooding the porch.

'Looks like I'm not the only night owl,' she said.

He grimaced as he saw her. She knew blood was pouring from her forehead and she was having trouble keeping her left eye open. He placed his hand on her chin, lifting her face to get a better look.

'What happened?' His cigarette now littering the freshly swept stoop.

'I'm alright, I just need to clean up and I didn't want to make a fuss going to the hospital. Can I come in?'

He leaned back as though trying to decide what to do. Mona felt like maybe she'd made a mistake coming to him. He'd once let slip where he lived. She assumed that to be an open invitation. If she ever needed him. But maybe it wasn't.

'Never mind, I shouldn't have come,' she said.

He grabbed her hand before she had a chance to leave. 'No, it's alright, come in.'

He let her hand go and opened the door wider, allowing her entry.

'Thank you,' she whispered as she passed him.

Inside, his house was as neat as the outside, and quite feminine. The wallpaper was patterned mossy green with curtains to match. A gold-trimmed mirror hung over the roaring fireplace, doilies lay across round tables on either side of the couch.

'You have a wife,' Mona said.

Collins shook his head, motioning for Mona to sit while he retrieved his first aid kit.

'I did,' he answered from the bathroom.

Mona took a seat on the couch and took off her coat. You wouldn't know it was winter from the temperature of Collins' sitting room.

When he re-entered, he grabbed a nearby footstool and sat across from her, their knees touching. He had a wet cloth and an old tobacco tin in his hand. He opened the tin and placed it carefully on the coffee table next to them, took the wet cloth and pressed it to her forehead. His touch was soft, as if he was waiting for her to wince in pain.

She didn't. 'It's ok, it's not hurting. Still in shock I think.'

He pressed a little harder, wiping the drying blood. They didn't speak as he cleaned her head. She kept waiting for him to ask what happened. He didn't. Maybe he was afraid he'd scare her off. Or perhaps it was some new police interrogation technique, drive the crim crazy with silence til they can't wait to spew their guts out. It was kind of working.

'I like this,' she said pointing to the wireless.

'The music?' he asked.

'Yes. There's no mistakes in jazz, only choices.'

He smiled, placing the cloth on the table. He took some pre-cut bandage strips and tape out of the little tin. 'I'll just put this across this gash here. It should do in lieu of stitches.'

He got up and went to the kitchen, coming back with a large metal spoon. He placed the curve of the spoon over her eyelid. She shuddered from the cold contact.

'So that's where all the cold air's gone,' Mona joked. 'The kitchen.'

Collins chuckled. Once he finished packing up his kit, he took a deep breath, clasped her shoulders in his hands and looked her square in the eyes. As he went to speak Mona stopped him.

'Please don't ask me what happened,' she said.

'I already know what happened, you don't get bruises like this any other way,' he said. 'Someone beat you Mona, who was it? Can't I take you to the station? Press charges?' Pent-up questions poured out of him.

'Why? I'm just a liar and a thief. What good will it do?'

His shoulders slumped as he took the spoon and placed it on top of the tin, stood up and walked out of the room. Mona remembered seeing a phone on the table in the hall. She could see it from the open doorway. She watched it like a hawk, ready to jump up and remove the receiver from Collins' hand if he picked it up. She didn't want him to call into Russell Street. Again, she began to doubt her decision to go to his house. But again, he came through for her, passing by the phone as he re-entered. He had another glass of beer.

'Don't worry I won't force you to tell me anything you don't want to. What *can* I do for you?' he asked.

'Well, I've been here almost a full twenty minutes and I'm yet to be offered a drink,' she said, motioning to the beer in his hand.

'Here,' he smiled as he handed the glass to her, sitting down beside her on the couch. Suddenly she wasn't thirsty. Mesmerised by his eyes, so close to hers.

'You have really handsome smile lines here,' she said touching his face, 'and here. That must mean you've had a happy life.'

'Or I smiled through an unhappy one.'

Smiling through it. Mona was good at that too. When learning to sing, Mrs Hart taught her a little trick she'd remembered her whole life. If she was having a bad day, singing flat, she should lift her cheeks. Mona was surprised the first time she tried it. It worked. The simple action of lifting her cheeks, lifted her spirits, and pitch. And when she lifted her cheeks even higher, producing the fake smile usually reserved for distant relatives at Christmas, she could more accurately hit the highest notes. Anytime Mrs Hart pointed at the ceiling, Mona would lift her cheeks, smile while singing, sharpening the note. To this day, she did it. But not just for singing. Whenever she was feeling flat, she'd force a smile to feel better. She'd smiled her way through poverty, a cheating boyfriend, arrests, Convent life, and gaol time. Now her smiles had brought her a Sharpe she couldn't get rid of. Maybe smiling through it wasn't always the answer.

'Smiled through it, or drank through it?' she nodded towards the brass liquor cart in the corner, full of almost empty bottles of every kind. 'We're not so different, are we?'

'I'm not being beaten up in the middle of the night.'

She knew he didn't mean to offend. All the friends she drank and did drugs with, robbed shops and picked pockets with, all the boyfriends, thieves, addicts and sideshow stars, they were all gone. The only one she felt safe with, the only one she could rely on to clean up her blood and soothe her bruises, was a man on the opposite side of the law.

'Do you think you'll ever be happy living this way?' Collins broke the silence again.

'Is anyone ever really happy? Are you happy, as a detective?' Mona asked him.

'If I didn't have that, I'd have nothing,' he replied.

His feelings about policing shocked her, came so close to how she now felt about singing. Her dreams were all that were holding her together. Yet she didn't have the energy to explain that she'd been trying, trying so hard to lead a different life. Besides, wasn't he the one who'd just poured her a drink?

'I'm sorry,' he said. 'I just don't understand why you would come here and not tell me—'

'I can't press charges,' she interrupted. 'Things will just get a lot worse for me.'

The jazz cut out, and silence filled the room. Mona held back tears knowing she would soon get up from his comfortable couch and leave. He was staring at her again. Their faces so close. His eyes, dark brown.

She felt a charge of electricity between them, like she hadn't felt since her first night back in Melbourne. With Sharpe. A policeman was just as dangerous. Maybe that's why she'd always liked him. Maybe that's why she'd come here. In that moment, as the current drew them closer, their lips almost touching, she hated herself. Why must she chase the things she shouldn't? She pulled away. He did too. Perhaps he was having similar thoughts. A rule-breaking, risk-taking police detective. Why else would he welcome a criminal into his home? Beaten or not. Maybe he was just as big of a mess as she was.

They stood at the same time. He shook his head, as if shaking her, but begged again, 'Let me take you to the hospital to get checked out, or the station to press charges.'

Her turn to shake her head.

'At least tell me who did this to you, maybe I can help in some other way.'

She shook her head again. 'Thank you for everything. I was so nervous coming here but you're really the only one...' she blinked back tears as a sob escaped her lips.

He pulled her into a hug. 'You can always come to me,' he whispered in her ear.

She felt his lips at her neck, his breath warm and smelling of beer. They reluctantly extricated themselves from each other's arms. Mona startled as she spotted a familiar black ornament on the mantelpiece.

Collins turned and caught her eyeline. 'I used to have another. They come as a pair, but it was stolen.'

It was a black elephant, trunk down, glinting eyes. Mona was stunned. She wasn't the first criminal to enter Collins' home, Sharpe had been there too once, before she knew him. The policeman's home he'd once robbed, it had been Collins'.

'It's beautiful,' she said, heading for the door. 'Thanks again.' A moment ago, she hadn't wanted to leave, now she couldn't get out fast enough.

Collins called after her, 'Wait!' He caught her at the front gate and slipped a week's worth of board into her hand. 'For a room, somewhere safe, please Mona.'

'Don't need it,' she said, handing it back. 'I'm working in Fitzroy, living cheaply, at 33 Drummond.' Now he had her address too. He put the money back in his pocket, nodded a goodnight and walked back inside.

30

Mona couldn't look in the mirror as she dressed the next morning, carefully pulling her coat over her throbbing arms and side. Swelling throughout the night, coupled with the raw heat of tears, welded her left eye shut. A velvet hat placed low over her head hid some of her bruises. Mona had an appointment with a music shop in the suburbs and no one, not even Sharpe, would derail her. She was to talk to the owner about options, instruments suitable for taking on the road. If she aced the show audition and got herself a gig she couldn't rely on borrowing other musicians' pianos and guitars. She was contemplating the ukele. Hutchison had taught her a little of the instrument over the years. Or perhaps she could afford a spinet with her domestic work earnings? One small enough to fit in the back of Stella's van.

Noticing stares on her walk through the city, Mona pulled her hat down and fanned her curls around her cheeks. Still, the stares continued. She gave into the temptation and turned to look at her reflection in a shop window. She'd barely registered just how bad she looked, when she spotted a familiar shadowy figure approaching. Mona froze, blinked a few times, were her bruised eyes deceiving her? She looked again and could still see his reflection coming towards her. Turning to look at him in the flesh then, she could see him smirk, his stride quickening. She broke into a run, forgetting the pain her body was in, fear taking over. He ran up behind her, but the gap between them was growing. He was tall, legs too long and slow, he was bumping into people, tripping over himself. He was drunk. Her legs were small, quick, nimble, and she sober. Slipping into a hotel on the corner of Elizabeth Street just opposite the train station entrance, Mona found a place on a chair at the bar and watched the window. She'd wait for him to run past, looking for her. Then she'd duck into the station right as her train pulled up.

'What'll you have Miss?' asked the bartender, his eyes lingering on her bruises. Mona glanced at him briefly, pointed to the beer tap and looked back out the window. She'd been distracted for just a second, but it was too late. He was right behind her.

'Thought you could run from me, did you?' he said.

The bartender put the drink down on the counter and asked, 'You paying for the lady?'

'No,' Sharpe yelled, the force of his voice causing the bartender to stumble backwards. Mona mumbled an apology to the man as Sharpe pulled her off her seat by the scruff of her coat. She tried to stay put as he ripped the fabric and punched her in the back. She fell to the floor. One moment she was flailing about, trying to stop him from picking her up and dragging her out of the pub, the next she was running from him. Sharpe was hot on her tail. Then, a familiar policeman approached. Sharpe didn't notice, he continued to shout at Mona as he caught up with her. He pushed, he shoved.

'You better stop, here's the police,' Mona spat, nodding towards the officer walking towards them. She couldn't remember his name, but recognised him as one of the men who'd returned her to the Convent what seemed so long ago.

Sharpe grabbed her by the neck pulling her ear towards his lips. 'If you give me up, you will see what you will get. If I do any gaol over you, you see what will happen. I will kill you stone dead you fucking bitch.'

'Everything alright here? Miss Mona isn't it?'

Sharpe let her go then, spinning around to cut down the officer with a grin.

'Oh, I spose you two know each other?' Sharpe held out his hand.

The officer waved his hand away, refusing to shake it. 'You want to give this man in charge? Looked like he was harassing you?'

Sharpe laughed as Mona tried to find words to explain this away. She couldn't decide what terrified her more. Sharpe not getting in any trouble, or Sharpe getting in trouble.

'You know how it is,' Sharpe said. 'Just keeping the little woman in line. Trying to get her to come home, where she belongs.'

Again, the officer ignored Sharpe. 'Do you want me to charge this man?'

Both men glared at her now. Sharpe's eyes angry, challenging, the officer waiting for her to say the word so he could take out his handcuffs.

'Just an old lover's spat,' she said. Sharpe's grin grew wider. 'I've no interest in charging him. I just want to go on my way. If you'll help me get the train?'

'Alright.'

He held out his hand to Mona and she took it, trying to avoid Sharpe's gaze as the officer led her to the station.

'You look pretty banged up,' he said to her as they waited for the train.

'It looks worse than it is. Nothing too serious.' Mona tugged at her hat again.

'You come down to Russell Street if he causes you any more trouble.'

She was late getting to the music shop, the owner gone. She banged her gloved fist on the door a moment, then cried. Told herself to calm down. She could get another appointment. She'd find her instrument. And if worse came to worst, she always had her voice. Sharpe could not take that. Radios blasted from open windows, breaking news accompanying her tearful walk home. Crowds formed to listen from pub corners.

'Fellow Australians, it's my melancholy duty to inform you, that in consequence of a persistence by Germany in her invasion of Poland, Great Britain has declared war upon her, as a result, Australia is also at war...'

She tried not to listen, to selfishly think of what the news might mean for the show. No, she would get her show season. She must. She spent the next few weeks head down, focused on her act. She decided to do a four-song set with impromptu chats to the audience between each song. It would go for about 20 minutes. Perfect show length. Yet the

Melbourne Show wouldn't roll around until the 19th of September. She couldn't audition until then, and if she got a gig, wouldn't be able to leave town until the 29th. That was a long time for Sharpe to get to her. How could she keep him at bay just long enough to be on her way? What was the one thing that could scare the only gun slinger she knew? She settled on a gun dealer. Better than that, a gun dealer Sharpe knew. Word would get back to him she was packing, and he'd leave her alone she was sure of it. If he didn't, she could wave it in his face next time he came around and he'd back down. She just needed to stave him off until she could audition and get out of town.

***

'Troops Advance Under Fire: Heavy Guns in Action' *The Argus*.

'Nazis Worried By French Progress' *The Age*.

'Allies Prepare to Attack' *The Herald*.

War was everywhere and yet show season grew closer. Mona plastered her healing face in makeup and checked out a few houses she knew the showies stayed at, chatting up tent owners. She arranged an audition with one man, Walter in the white suit. He ran a number of tents, all sorts of acts.

'Solo singer in a tent on your own? Highly unusual for someone unestablished,' he said, twirling his grey moustache between his fingers. 'Come on in then and show me what you got.'

'Now? I thought I'd just schedule a time with you,' Mona said, nervous.

'This is the only time I have for the next few weeks. Audition for me now or not at all,' he said.

She nodded, smiled, followed him inside. He motioned for her to take a seat at the piano in the corner of his front sitting room. She sat, angling the chair so he could see her – nothing worse than a performer who doesn't face their audience. She sang the song she wrote in prison. She'd always wanted to be one of those singers whose notes touched your heart, sound piercing your skin and shattering inside until goose bumps cover arms, tears spring to eyes. That day she felt she was. It was the performance of her life. The biggest thrill, too – so much better than dope, more exciting than stealing.

Walter stayed quiet for a moment. If she didn't get this job, she didn't know what she'd do.

Finally, he stood, eyes squinted, smile wide. 'Well, that was quite something, quite incredible. Well done indeed.'

'Thank you.' Mona stood, hands by her sides, waiting for some good news. The kind of news that could change her life.

'A powerful voice for such a little lady. You're pitch perfect?'

'Not quite,' she admitted, then kicked herself. He wouldn't know. Talk yourself up. 'Almost.'

'Pretty close then. Yes, very good, very good.' He paced the room, fondling his moustache, Mona could hear the cogs grinding away in his head. He hadn't been planning on her being good, perhaps. Maybe he was quite sure, after inviting her in, he'd end up turning her away. He was wrong.

'You would be open to some line-up dancers accompanying you?' he asked.

'I can fall in line. Whatever you think would make the show worthy of your tent and investment.'

'Splendid, wonderful. Well, I won't say yes just yet. Let me go away and take another look at our schedule, crunch some numbers, you know what I mean. Leave your address with me, and I'll come by in the next day or so to let you know. But I must say, I'm impressed. And I do hope to find a place for you in my line up.'

Mona tried not to get ahead of herself but couldn't stop the smile stretching from one ear to the other. He whole body buzzed. 'That would be wonderful, Walter I look forward to seeing you shortly.'

She skipped out of his house, mentally running through final set lists and outfits. She imagined the sign above the tent 'Mona Hayes, singer, songstress, songbird?' Maybe a stage name? She'd have to think of the best way to promote herself. Until then, she decided her audition alone was worth celebrating. She went in search of Stella.

'Are you signing up for the Red Cross?' Stella asked her.

'What?'

'A few of the other girls are going to enquire about working for the Red Cross on Monday if you want to go with them?' Stella poured Mona a beer as the two sat, chatting in the small kitchen. They'd been to see a late picture show and managed to arrive back at the showies' house in time to nick a few bottles from the boxers.

'No, I told you,' Mona said. 'I auditioned for that fellow Walter.'

'Well, you might be in luck there,' Stella said. 'With so many signing up for the war effort, extra show hands will be needed.'

'Not a show hand, I told you, I'll be performing,' Mona said, again.

'I know Mona, honey, I'm just sayin' if this Walter lead doesn't pan out...'

Mona was growing tired. It was as if Stella didn't think she could land a performing gig and was already planning other jobs for her – Red Cross, show hand. She looked at her watch, 3.30am.

'Do you have any food in this place?' Mona asked, already knowing the answer. An excuse to leave.

'With a house full of bloody boxers with big appetites? I'm afraid these cupboards are bare.' Stella stood, laughing, opening the cupboard to reveal a lonely jar of pickles.

'Well, I'm going to love you and leave you. I'm gonna get a feed and go home to bed.'

The two kissed each other good night with Stella trying one more time to convince Mona to visit the Red Cross with the other girls. 'Just to see what it's all about.'

Mona shook her head all the way down the street.

She was at the corner of Lonsdale and Exhibition Streets when she noticed the back of a familiar head. Seeing him out of the smoky, dimly lit Albanian Club caused her pause, she almost couldn't remember his name. As she sped up to catch his stride and tap him on the shoulder, she could see he still had his nametag on. Berktash. But he went by Baby, or Bebe, one of those. She'd give Baby a try.

'Baby? From the Albanian Club?'

'Yes, Mam. You're familiar.'

'Mona. We've met a few times. Where are you off to so late, or early?'

'I closed up. Now going to George's for steak and tea. Want to join me?' his thick accent cut through the night air.

'George' N Café? Yes, I was headed that way myself.'

They walked without much chatter. Berktash yawned twelve times; Mona counted. Though he was a tall man, with legs almost twice the size of hers, he walked slowly, struggling to stay awake. Mona walked ahead a few steps, stopped and waited for him to catch up, then walked a few steps ahead again, continuing in that way until they reached the café. Small square tables were adorned with fresh white tablecloths, Worcestershire sauce in the middle of each setting.

The sound of steaks sizzling on the grill in the kitchen filtered out to the dining area. She loved that they did things that way. They had food ready to go twenty-four hours a day. She and Berktash ordered at the front counter and by the time they'd hung their hats and coats on the wall hooks by the table, the waiter was serving their meals.

'Bebe,' came a voice from one of the taxi drivers seated in the other corner. Berktash pulled Mona's seat out for her and then went to greet the man. 'Never seen you without your Carlton scarf, where is it tonight, Bebe?' The old man chuckled.

'Not tonight,' Berktash said and chatted politely yet briefly to the man before returning to the table with a smile.

'Nice man. I see him here most nights. His driver friend Ernie will take us to Drummond Street if you're that way?'

'Yes, I am,' Mona said. It occurred to her that Berktash may be one of the Albanian Club staff members living in her building. She knew there were a few but had never seen them on account of their work schedules.

'What time did you start work today?' Mona asked, tucking into her steak.

The waiter put a coffee down on the table in front of Berktash.

'I ordered one too,' Mona reminded the waiter.

He nodded and headed back to the kitchen.

'I start early in the day, around lunchtime, and work until the last of the night. A long day,' he yawned, again.

'I'll say it's been a long day,' a familiar voice came from behind Mona. 'An even longer night.'

Sharpe and his old mate Charles Clarke, notorious Sydney confidence man and card sharper who often visited friends in Melbourne, approached. Her breath caught in her throat. Berktash looked at her as if to ask whether she knew the men.

'We'll eat here,' Sharpe shouted back to the bloke behind the counter.

'No, don't sit here, I want nothing to do with you,' Mona said.

Clarke laughed and pulled up a seat.

Sharpe grinned 'I've got you now,' he said and pulled up the chair alongside her. He left his wool coat and light hat on. His little mate, Clarke, ignored the row of hooks along the wall, placing his hat on the table.

Berktash and Clarke introduced themselves, shaking hands, engaging in conversation about Sydney. Berktash had never been.

'Running round with the Albanians now?' Sharpe sniggered in her ear.

He hadn't tried to pull her from her seat, hadn't hit her, this was an improvement. Maybe he would be civil in front of Clarke. Maybe he knew she had a gun in the little purse she now held at her lap. Or maybe her new mate Berktash made him nervous.

'It shouldn't matter to you.'

'Why shouldn't it matter? You're mine, remember. And you won't get away from me now bitch, I'll make sure of that.'

'Why won't you leave me alone?'

'Because you're going to work for me, remember? You need the money, don't you? And you owe me the money you stole.'

'I don't need money and anything I took from you was mine to begin with. Earned at the show.'

She tried to think about driving off into the sunset with Walter, being free of Sharpe for good. It was as if he could read her mind. 'Oh, you think you're going on the road with the showies, do ya? Like a real performer? You're nothing but a common whore, and now you'll work for me and make money like one.'

She stared at him, wide-eyed, tears forming.

'Did you hear me? You're not getting out of here. You'll come with me.'

Why couldn't he just leave her alone. Just for a few more days. That's all she needed. A few more days and she'd be gone.

Instead, here she was, three men surrounding her, one her violent ex and two she knew very little of. She realised then that Clarke was glaring at her. She tried to remember what Sharpe had said of him. Was he violent? Was Bebe? As the waiter placed two more steaks at the table, in front of Sharpe and Clarke, she jumped to her feet. 'Hurry up with the coffee and let me get out,' she shouted.

'Bugger, sorry Miss, I forgot, one more moment,' the waiter sputtered and headed back to the kitchen.

Mona couldn't wait. Leaving her hat on the hook, she gripped her bag tight and ran for the door. Sharpe leapt from his seat and followed her onto the empty street, grabbing her wrist and pulling her out of view of the café windows, alongside the hotel next door. She struggled with him, hitting him on the chest as he crowded her.

'I've had enough of this. I can't stand any more of it. Find someone else and just leave me alone. I want to go home.'

'I'll take you home alright, you fucking bitch.'

His fist hit her face so fast she never saw it coming. She felt his middle knuckle between her eyes, stumbling back. Yet somehow, she didn't fall. Was she getting too used to being hit?

Berktash's deep voice pierced through the pounding pain and darkness. 'Mona, still coming?'

He was with the taxi driver he'd spoken to earlier, Ernest, getting ready to leave.

'Yes, I'm coming, I'm going home that way,' Mona said. She tried to push past Sharpe as Berktash and the driver got in the cab.

'Better yet,' Sharpe said, pulling her arm and twisting it back in the direction of the hotel. 'I know somewhere we can go right now, they won't mind the bruises.' He laughed. 'You'll make me some money and then you can be on your way.'

He kept trying to pull her back, keep her away from the taxi. They struggled like this for what felt like an eternity. Still the cab waited. As Sharpe pulled and pushed her, slapped her and yelled at her, she waited for rescue. She felt Berktash and Ernest's eyes on her. But they weren't interfering. A lover's squabble. She knew if she didn't get in the cab soon, they'd drive off and leave her and then she'd be in real strife.

'Leave me alone,' she screamed, cried, pushed Sharpe so hard he tripped over himself.

She had one over him. Or a few. She was no longer using drugs and had only had a couple of beers with Stella that night, Sharpe had clearly had more. His stumble gave her a second to flee. She lunged into the open door of the cab.

He reached for her hair and pulled but lost his grip as she dove lower onto the backseat.

'I will bash your brains into the gutter, you fucking bitch.'

'If you don't leave me alone, I'll shoot you,' she cried, her threatening words undermined by the quivering of her voice.

'That ain't nothin' to what I'll do to you.' He snaked his rough hands around her ankles and began trying to drag her from her seat. When that didn't work, he went for her hair instead. She felt her curls being ripped from her head as she found herself half in and half out of the taxi. Half in and out of Sharpe's grasp. Half in and half out of her old life.

She cried out, trying to break free of him.

'Leave me alone, I want to go home.'

He kicked her square in the stomach.

'Fuckin' bitch.'

Pain reverberated through her. It was as if Berktash in the back seat, and the taxi driver disappeared. So too did the café, the shops, the hotel. The street was bare but for him and her. She scrambled back inside the cab. Her right hand reaching for her purse, now nestled under the front passenger seat. 'I warned you,' she said.

She produced her small black pistol and aimed it just below his chest. He laughed and lunged at her again. She pulled the trigger, and he staggered backward, falling to the ground. She saw flashes and red, blood like the wine he'd spilled on her so long ago. Her ears rang from the sound of the bullet, her vision shaky, unsure if it was all just a dream.

'Get me a gun!' he screamed back towards the café, to his mate Clarke still dining inside. No, not a dream, and he was still after her. She aimed the gun at the driver, and shouted 'go!'

31

Mona found the driver as unhelpful as he'd been moments earlier, when she was being kicked to a pulp on the side of the road. Rather than start the engine, he got out of the cab to check on Sharpe. She looked beside her. Berktash was gone too, his door hanging open. She got out of the car and ran, the sound of Sharpe's voice playing over and over in her mind. 'That's nothing to what I'll do to you… Get me a gun!'

Mona arrived home after sunrise and climbed into bed. She lay awake, trembling under the covers and licking her lips raw. It didn't happen, she told herself, rubbing tears from her eyes. It didn't happen. By the time she heard a knock on her door, she was surprised to find her face washed, body freshly dressed, bag and pistol nowhere to be found. Maybe it had all been a dream.

'Mona there's a man here to see you.' A fellow boarder shouted from the hallway. She felt nauseous, panicky, her hands still shaking, she wanted out of her own body. Sharpe had found her, she was sure of it. Her window was too small to climb through. The only way out was down the hall. Turn left and out the back to a fenced in yard and outhouse, or right and out the front. Either way he could see her, catch her. She didn't know which way to go.

'All right,' Mona shouted, not recognising the sound of her own voice. She took a few shaky steps out of her room and turned towards the front door.

There he was.

'Collins,' she collapsed against the wall in relief.

His glassy eyes widened at the sight of her bruises – new ones mingled with the old ones he'd cared for a few nights before. He took his hat from his head and held it across his chest as he motioned for her to step outside. She obeyed, shuffling out onto the porch, wincing as sunshine hit her face.

'Mona Hayes?' a detective she'd never met greeted her at the bottom step. A little shorter than Collins with darker hair and buggy eyes, his glare intimidating, like the headmaster to Collins' vice principal.

'Yes,' she said.

'Come with us to the detective office please.'

He pointed towards the car where another detective was waiting with the door held open. Three detectives, all there for her.

'What for?' She held a cold hand to the bruising on her cheek, shielding them from the sun.

The headmaster tilted his head, examining her as he answered. 'A man was shot dead outside the George' N Café at about 4am this morning, and it's alleged that you were there at the time.'

Dead.

He only said it once, but it rang in Mona's ears over and over again. Time slowed.

Dead.

She shook loose a sudden pounding in her head. How could it be? He wasn't dead when she left him. She could still hear him calling out for a gun.

Collins was standing beside her now, his hand on her shoulder. The two other detectives watched closely. Sharpe couldn't be dead. They were lying. He was fine. Maybe in hospital with a few grazes no worse than hers. But he couldn't be dead.

'That's a pretty heavy one you're trying to tack on me – murder,' she tripped over the words, her whole body shaking.

'You need to come with us,' the headmaster replied.

Mona looked up at Collins, towering over her. She blinked back tears as he nodded towards the car, not saying a word, not until the last moment.

Out of earshot of the other detectives he whispered, 'Just tell them the truth, Mona. It'll help you now.'

She knew then. It was true. Albert Sharpe was dead. She had killed him.

***

She waited in the all-too-familiar interview room at police headquarters. She wasn't handcuffed, which she thought strange. She could hear officers making a fuss outside the door.

Then the headmaster entered. He cleared his throat as he sat and placed a folder of papers on the table between them.

'Where's Collins?' Mona asked.

'Attending to other cases I expect. I'm Detective Delmenico.' He launched straight in, all business, his eyes trained on hers. 'Do you know a man named Albert Sharpe?'

'Yes.'

Delmenico was taking notes, left-handed scrawl in a notepad small enough to fit in his pocket. Mona had once mistakenly pickpocketed a notepad instead of a wallet. When she'd realised the man had his entire life jotted inside, she'd raced after him, discreetly slipping it back where it came from. She wondered if that man too had been a cop.

'How long have you known him?'

'Collins?' she asked. She'd never been without him in a police interview before. She kept looking past Delmenico to the door.

Delmenico coughed. 'No. Albert Sharpe. How long have you known him?'

'A long time.'

Delmenico put down his pad and pencil and watched her intently as he spoke. 'At about 4am this morning Albert Sharpe was shot dead outside the George' N Café in Russell Street. You were there at the time.'

It was a statement, but she supposed he was asking for an answer.

'Yes.'

'It's alleged that you shot him.' He emphasised the word alleged almost like he was singing it. Alleged meant that she was the last person he was speaking to. She held her own shaking hands, trying to steady them on the table. She stared down at them as tears plopped one by one onto her skin. Delmenico placed a handkerchief by her right hand. She couldn't make her fingers move to pick it up. She couldn't formulate words to express what she was feeling or even what happened. She wanted to convince him, and herself, that she'd done nothing wrong. Yet the words came cold.

'He's in his place,' she said. 'It's my blue and I will take it.'

Her throat was sore, closing up at the admission. She closed her eyes for a moment and tried to cool her burning face with her cold un-gloved hands.

When she opened her eyes Delmenico was gone. Had she imagined the whole exchange? She began to question herself as she waited. Was she going crazy? When did she first sit down? How long had she been in this room?

'Excuse me,' she called.

A young detective walked in and offered her a cup of water, said Delmenico would be back soon.

She closed her eyes again, put her head down on the table in front of her. By the time Delmenico returned, she couldn't tell whether he'd been gone five minutes or five hours.

'Ok Mona we have the taxi driver and the man Bebe who were present when the shooting took place. We'll arrange for you to be lined up with some other women for the purposes of identification, or you may stand alone.'

He motioned for her to stand, but she couldn't make her legs work, didn't need to, there was no point.

'I don't want any line up. Those men know me well.'

'Fair enough.' Delmenico popped his head out the door. 'Right,' he called. In walked the taxi driver Ernest.

'Do you know this woman?' Delmenico asked him. Another officer was peering in, watching over the identification.

'Yes,' Ernest said.

He looked nervous, shifting from foot to foot, not looking Mona in the eye. She thought he might have been scared. She had, after all, held a gun to his head, shot someone dead right in front of him. Watching him reminded her of the night Sharpe had pointed a gun at her, how scared she'd been. She was just as bad as Sharpe. Worse. He'd never killed anyone.

'Is this the woman who was in your taxi this morning when the man was shot outside the George' N Café?'

'Yes.'

Next, the detective brought Berktash in. He was wearing the same clothes as when she'd last seen him. Hadn't shaved. He looked scared too.

'Is this the woman who was in the taxi with you when the man was shot?'

'Yes.'

Again, she was left alone in the interview room. What was Delmenico waiting for? Couldn't he just send her to the City Watch House? She felt as though he was dragging it out on purpose, torturing her, just the beginning of what was to be her punishment. She deserved it. She never wanted to hurt anyone. Yet she'd killed someone, a man she once loved. A man she once spent days and nights under the sideshow stars dreaming about, a man she'd danced with, been to bed with. The woman who once couldn't bear stealing a damn notepad, had now stolen a life. She was an idiot to think she would ever grace a real stage, the only one she'd ever know now would be in prison.

Back Delmenico came with his pad and pencil, the other detective watching from the doorway.

'We are going to ask you further questions. You need not answer them unless you wish. Anything you say now may be given in evidence.'

She nodded. She knew the drill.

'Who was present when the shooting took place?'

'Sharpe, the taxi driver, Baby and I. Baby was sitting in the back of the taxi. In the right-hand corner.' She was having to picture it now, see it in her mind's eye like a motion picture, and she knew she'd be replaying and reciting it over and over again for a long time to come. This day, the longest day, was just the start.

'Were there any other persons about at that time?' Delmenico pressed on.

'No.' If there had been, Mona hadn't seen them, hadn't noticed, she was wrapped up in that taxi, in Sharpe.

'Did anybody else have anything to do with the shooting?'

'No.'

'Why did you shoot him?'

'I have my reasons.' Her voice shook, hurt.

'What are they?'

This part was the hardest. How could she possibly, properly, convey what had been going on for the past few weeks. Longer. Since she met him.

'He has been following me about, and knocking me about, and he has been trying to get me back to live with him, make money for him,' the words caught in her throat. She held her cool hand to her face to try calm herself, hide the redness and heat pooling in her cheeks. A lump the size of Sharpe's fist formed in the back of her throat.

'Were you drunk at the time or had you taken dope?'

She wished she was drunk now. Had Delmenico been talking to Collins? Maybe. But he also had her file, and it was all in there no doubt. Drunk, addict, thief and now murderer.

'No, I had a few drinks, but I knew what I was doing. I remember everything.'

Unfortunately.

'It's alleged that at about 4am this morning, Bebe met you in Lonsdale Street. You went with him to the George' N Café where you sat at a table and were served a meal. Afterwards, Sharpe and another man entered and sat at the same table. You and Sharpe spoke; you got up and left the table and went outside. Sharpe followed you out. Shortly after Bebe went and got into a taxi. You called out to Bebe that you were going with him, and you went and got into the taxi. Sharpe also got in the taxi, and you and Sharpe started to struggle, and Sharpe was shot. Is that right?'

'Yes. Nobody else had anything to do with it. Did Baby make a statement?'

Delmenico handed her a set of typed pieces of paper. She didn't need to read the whole thing, the odd word and phrase jumped out at her like knats. 'She was carrying a small bag. Two men came in. The fair man took the woman outside. He was pulling at her. I heard a shot.'

'What he has said is true,' Mona said, pushing the papers back across the table.

'Ok. Do you wish to make a written statement? I'll take it down in writing and it will be tendered in evidence.'

She agreed. He prompted her with a few more questions. She spoke about the past few weeks with Sharpe, told him as much as she felt he needed to know, and he took down her statement. She couldn't bring herself to go into too much detail about Sharpe's punches, his kicks, the hair pulling, the blood and bruises – over so many days, weeks.

'He kept persecuting me … threatening me.' She said, continuing. 'Sharpe started to argue with me and said "You are not getting out of here. You will come with me." I got up and said "Hurry up with the coffee and let me get out." As soon as I got up Sharpe's meal was placed on the table, he never touched it but chased me out of the café on to the footpath. I said to him "I have had enough of this. I can't stand any more of it." He started to struggle with me. I said "If you don't leave me alone I will shoot you." He said "That will be nothing to what I will do to you." I saw Baby in a taxi outside the café and I walked to the taxi and said to Baby "I am going home that way." I got in the taxi and sat next to Baby in the back seat and Sharpe jumped in after me, and started to pull me about, I said "Are you going to leave me alone or I'll shoot you." He persisted in struggling with me and trying to stop me from going home. I had the pistol in my right hand and I pointed it at him, I pulled the trigger and the pistol went off. I said to the driver "Drive away quick." He did not drive away and I jumped out of the taxi and ran up towards Little Lonsdale Street. I don't know where I went, I just ran.'

Once she'd finished, she was asked to check the statement and sign between sobs.

'Mona Hayes, you will be charged with the murder of Albert Sharpe at Melbourne on the 15th day of September 1939.'

Charged with murder. This was real. This was the end of her. The end of Sharpe. He was really dead. Now so was she. Trying hard to compose herself, she asked 'Do you want me to go over now?'

The Watch House. Finally, an end to the questioning. Finally, out of the interrogation room.

'Yes.'

She got a glimpse of the time as she was escorted out of the building. 5.30pm. She'd been there all day.

***

In her cell in the City Watch House, she cried so hard she struggled to breathe. For the police, she'd relived the worst parts of her relationship with Sharpe. Yet suddenly all she could think about were the good parts. The sweet, charming young man she danced with. The man who touched and held her, who kissed her, made her knees weak. She cried for the love she lost while he was still alive. But the Sharpe she fell in love didn't ever exist, did he? The real Sharpe was the one who kicked and punched her, spent her money, wouldn't leave her alone. She needed to remember that.

'You get a phone call, Miss.' A uniformed officer unlocked her cell door. She wracked her brain for someone to ring. Hutch was in gaol, Lawrence was Sharpe's friend. She couldn't stand the thought of calling Stella, her doubts about Mona's future confirmed. She couldn't think of a single person that could help her now. Not one single, real, friend. She stayed seated on her cot.

'Up ya get, c'mon, the phone's out this way.' He pointed towards the front office she'd been walked through half an hour prior. She was about to tell him she didn't need a call when the officer held out a card. 'Don Collins said to give this to you.'

Mona took hold of the small white piece of paper with gold

lettering. Maurice Goldberg, barrister and solicitor, 305 Bridge Road Richmond, J 2446. She'd never had a lawyer before, always represented herself.

'Don't worry, lawyers work late, he'll answer,' he said, walking her through to the office.

She sat down at the desk, picked up the phone and dialled the number. The officer busied himself with paperwork, pretending not to listen. She could almost hear him later, Collins asking, 'Did she call him?'

'Yes. Yes, she did.'

32

It was Wednesday 27 September 1939. Mona re-tied the loose flowing bow on the top of her shirt, shifting uncomfortably in the back seat of the police car transporting her from her holding cell to the Coroner's Court at the City Morgue. The Coroner's name was Tingate, he would make the final decision as to the events surrounding Sharpe's death and whether Mona should be tried for murder.

Mona wore a grey skirt and white silk shirt Stella had dropped off at the gaol. She'd worn a red woollen jumper with the outfit when appearing in the City Court for bail a few days earlier.

'Not exactly a sombre colour, is it?' her lawyer remarked. 'Don't wear red again. A white or black shirt, patterns are fine, but nothing bright.'

That was her first interaction with him. The famous Goldberg. With his thick black-rimmed glasses and gravelly voice. If he believed the case hinged upon her wardrobe, she was in serious trouble. Though she was remanded at that hearing, Goldberg impressed her none the less, and he was confident she wouldn't go to trial for murder.

The inquest was just like being in a court room, filled with police and reporters. The first person called was Sharpe's brother. Mona could hardly breathe as he spoke. Their voices were so much alike. If she closed her eyes, she could swear it was him. Very much alive.

'My name is William Arthur Sharpe, and on the 15th of September this year at the City Morgue, I identified the body of Albert Sharpe.' At the mention of Sharpe's name, Mona could see William's bottom lip quiver, hear the catch in his throat. He took a moment, waved away a cup of water offered by one of Tingate's staff, and continued. 'He was 24 years of age.'

A parade of medical professionals, experts and police followed. The ambulance driver who took Sharpe to hospital, the doctor who tried to save him, the surgeon who performed the post-mortem, the analyst who received Sharpe's clothes after his death, a detective who photographed the crime scene, and even the police officer who accompanied the body to the morgue.

Then, a familiar face, the man from the front counter of the George' N Café, Nicholas. English not his first language, he spoke through an interpreter. He relayed everything that had happened in the café that night, adding, 'I saw the fair man come and fall in front of the window.' Mona closed her eyes and saw it too, Sharpe clutching his stomach screaming out for a gun. But according to Nicholas, Sharpe never made a sound.

Goldberg asked him follow-up questions. Did he see Mona leave? Did she hurry? Did she run? Did Sharpe chase after her? Nicholas didn't notice those details either. Mona began to worry, and question her own memory. Sharpe had threatened her, hit her, called for a gun. How did Nicholas not see or hear any of that?

Then Berktash was called. He, too, had an interpreter allowing him to speak fluently in his Albanian tongue. The interpreter relayed Berktash's description of the evening, much the same as the written statement Mona'd seen at the detective office. Berktash seemed tired, dark rims around his eyes, he squinted under the harsh lights of the room. Goldberg asked him follow-up questions about that night. What threats did he hear Sharpe make? Was Mona upset? Did Sharpe strike her? Or kick her? Berktash's version of events matched Mona's.

'He dragged her out of the taxi by the hair of the head and kicked her.'

A man named Mornane, assisting the Coroner, found it strange that Berktash and Mona lived in the same house without knowing so prior to that evening. He asked about it.

'I was working at night, and I do not know whether the girl was living at that address prior to the shooting, I know nothing about it,' Berktash said.

Mornane pressed harder, and Mona could see Berktash grow distressed, as if worried he was being accused of something he didn't understand. 'I still swear that I did not know that Mona Hayes was living there.'

Goldberg nudged Mona in the arm, 'anything to this?' he whispered.

'No.'

He nodded. Satisfied with the answer. Even she couldn't quite believe the coincidence. She'd been living with Baby for weeks and hadn't known it until running into him that night.

Goldberg followed-up, asking Berktash to explain the living situation further.

'This house at 33 Drummond Street is a house that only has rooms to let. There are about eight rooms in the house, but I do not know exactly,' he answered. 'I do not know the various persons who live there, I do not take any notice of them.'

Mornane continued asking questions, unconvinced, perhaps wondering if Berktash was involved in the shooting more than had been said.

Mona looked around the room. He seemed to be the only one under this impression, the journalists appeared bored, lighting cigarettes, chattering amongst themselves. They understood the lives of boarders better than Coroner's Court staff.

Next was Berktash's taxi driver friend, Lionel, who he'd chatted to briefly in the cafe. Unlike Nicholas, he confirmed that Sharpe had called for a gun. Relief waved over Mona at that, she hadn't imagined it, her mind wasn't playing tricks on her. Lionel was followed by taxi driver Ernest.

'The girl appeared to be trying to get away from the chap,' he said. 'The chap was using some bad language towards the girl ... I looked straight ahead. It pays to mind your own business and not be too sticky nosed.' Though he wasn't looking, he could hear everything. He described Sharpe abusing her, threatening her, then he heard the gun go off. Again, he reiterated that Sharpe called for a gun as he staggered away. But Mona's heart sank as he recounted her pointing the gun towards him. 'It was put against my neck … I was told to drive off.'

As he stood and headed out of the room, Mona tried to catch his eye, she wanted to convey in some way just how sorry she was. He wouldn't look at her.

Prior to the inquest, Goldberg had asked Mona about witnesses to the other instances of abuse she had talked about in her statement to Delmenico. Lawrence's name came to her mind. Goldberg had passed the name onto the Coroner's Court only to find him already due to be called. What about the young Constable, who'd seen her with Sharpe that day? No, she didn't know his name. What about Collins, who'd cleaned up her bloody cuts and iced her bruises? He'd have to admit to having a known criminal in his home. He could lose his position. Not to mention, he'd have to say how he knew her, that she was a criminal. It wouldn't make a difference in the inquest but if this went to Court, and he was called again, it would look bad for her in front of a jury. She decided to keep his name to herself a while longer.

Lawrence wore his best suit, the dark blue one, with the shiny light blue tie that she liked. He winked at her and smiled. She refused to smile back. She felt like he'd chosen Sharpe over her months ago, that men would always side with their mates. What would he say today? The truth, she hoped.

'My name is James Henry Lawrence, and I am a bootmaker residing at 68 Elgin Street Carlton. I knew the deceased Albert Sharpe. He was at a friend's place with me about 8pm.'

Mona hadn't known that. Lawrence was with Sharpe that night? Just before he died? That's why the Coroner called him.

'A man named Eric and two men named Norman and Alan were there at the same time. I and Sharpe and those other three men were drinking beer, between us we drank more than about 11 bottles. That 11 bottles was the last lot bought; there may have been more drink earlier. After drinking that beer Sharpe asked me would I go to the George' N Café for supper. I refused…'

Oh, how different things might have been if he had gone with him.

'He then left on his own. I never saw Sharpe again.'

Goldberg asked about Sharpe's demeanour that night.

'He had a good quantity of beer and was fairly drunk. When in drink he was a very excitable man, very quick-tempered and ready to pick a fight. I have never had any violence with him; but in his cups he was not particular with whom he fought. He was very excitable.'

'Did he have a reputation as a gunman?' Goldberg asked.

'A man can be reputed to be a lot of things. I have heard he has had a gun in his possession at times, but I never saw him with one.'

'What do you know of his relationship with Mona? Did you know they lived together?'

Lawrence looked a bit startled by this, raised his eyebrow in Mona's direction. Hadn't he known they lived together?

'I have seen the deceased and Mona Hayes together frequently. I never knew they lived together. Within a few weeks prior to his death, I heard deceased threaten Mona Hayes one night in King William Street, Fitzroy.'

The way he described that night wasn't quite how she remembered it. Did she have it wrong? Did he have it wrong? One thing that married up was the abuse she suffered. That part, at least, they agreed on.

'This man tried to go get Mona Hayes.' Suddenly he was some strange faraway man. Not Sharpe, not the deceased, but 'this man'. 'She refused to go with him. He assaulted her. I stepped in and tried to stop him, but he went on hitting her. She was knocked to the ground. Someone there picked her up and put her in a taxi.' Mona didn't remember him stepping in. And it was a fruit truck. Wasn't it? He continued on.

'I heard the next day she had two black eyes and a split on the forehead.'

She wondered who he'd heard that from. Just when she thought he might have finished his testimony, he went on to explain Sharpe's further harassment, which she hadn't realised he knew about.

'I have seen her run from the deceased several times,' he said. 'Whilst he has been with me, I have heard him say he would like to see her and give her a couple bangs, or something like that, that she had done something to him or something of that kind. I have heard him say he would like to see her dead.'

The words of the taxi driver echoed in her head. It pays to mind your own business. That was it wasn't it? How else could Lawrence remain friends with a man who threatened and hurt her, how Baby and the driver could sit and watch her struggle?

As he left the room, Goldberg nudged Mona again. 'That was helpful. His criminal history might be a problem if this goes to trial. Start thinking about other names, people who might have seen the abuse, your injuries, anyone that can give testimony like that who isn't a con.'

Mona nodded and turned her attention to Delmenico, next to testify. He went over everything they'd talked about from the time he picked her up at Drummond Street, through to the end of their interview at the detective office. He then read out her statement in full.

Goldberg asked him what he had known of Sharpe prior to that day.

'I had known the deceased, Sharpe, by repute. I would not say he was a reputed gunman. He was not reputed as a man of violence that I know of.' As if he would know. 'I did not know him personally; I only knew him as a thief. He had several convictions for stealing and other minor offences.'

Goldberg asked about how long Mona had been in the police interview room. Was she exhausted? Was she given breaks? How was she treated? Mona had told Goldberg she'd been interviewed all day, and he wasn't impressed.

'We first saw her at 11.30am and I think she was charged about 5.30pm. She made a statement between four and five I would think. As to whether she was questioned from time to time during that time, we saw her at intervals as I have related in evidence. We had interviewed the others in between. She was upset at the finish.'

'Was she upset to begin with?' Goldberg asked.

'She appeared to be a woman under great mental stress, no I think when we first saw her, she was trying to be brave.'

Some other detectives got up then and confirmed Delmenico's version of events, then Mona was asked to address the Coroner.

'I do not wish to say anything now,' per Goldberg's instructions. Goldberg argued that after all the evidence, murder should not even come into question. Mona had clearly acted in self-defence. And so, that was it. All witnesses done in one day. The Coroner concluded the proceedings, ignoring Goldberg's plea to find in self-defence.

'Having inquired upon the part of our Lord the King, when, where, and how and by what means the said Albert Sharpe came by his death, I say that on the 15th of September 1939 at Melbourne, in the Royal Melbourne Hospital, the said Albert Sharpe died from the effects of a bullet wound in the abdomen wilfully and maliciously inflicted at Russell Street Melbourne by one Mona Hayes and I further say that in the manner aforesaid that said Mona Hayes murdered the said Albert Sharpe.' Murdered. Not killed in self-defence. Murdered. Goldberg had been wrong.

Mona was committed for trial. She was granted bail. Goldberg didn't apologise for getting her hopes up, didn't express any shock, instead he looked her up and down and frowned. 'Now, to prepare you for trial.'

33

Just like his business card, extravagant gold lettering fronted Goldberg's office on Bridge Road 'Maurice Goldberg Barrister and Solicitor'. There were no chairs in his window-fronted waiting room. Mona tapped a rusty bell that sat atop an unattended reception desk, then leaned awkwardly against the counter, reading her folded newspaper as she waited for Goldberg to emerge. He didn't, instead bellowing for her to come into his office. He didn't stand as she entered, too busy wiping sweat from his flushed face and shuffling files around his desk until he came to one with her name on it.

'Sit,' he said, still not looking at her. The chair in the corner of the room was heavy, Mona pulled it closer to his desk and sat down. The smell of wet wool and cigar smoke overwhelmed her as the dark leather screeched beneath her shifting legs.

'The way you present yourself is important,' Goldberg lowered his thick black glasses and dived straight in. 'We need the jurors to like you. When you take the stand, make eye contact with His Honour and jury. Answer only what's asked. Avoid any mention of your criminal history, it has no bearing on this case, and we don't want it to poison the jury's minds against you. Don't elaborate unless instructed. The words 'Yes' and 'No' are your best friends. Don't try to answer a question you don't understand. If you don't know, don't guess…'

Mona sat nodding. Goldberg sighed, 'You might want to take some of this down,' he said handing her a pencil. She scribbled notes along the edges of her newspaper. He didn't offer her a pad. If she got this wrong, if she lost the case, it wasn't a short stay at a Convent or Pentridge that awaited her.

'I know this must be overwhelming Mona, but you need to stop imagining the worst.' He continued, telling her he'd tried many criminal cases and was not at all concerned about this one.

But Mona didn't like her luck. 'What's the worst I could get?' She already knew the answer. Everyone found guilty of murder got the same sentence. But she was different, wasn't she?

'If found guilty, you will be sentenced to death.' Blunt. He paused long enough to see her shudder. 'But we'd appeal for leniency. Then you'd be looking at ten years, most likely a lot less,' he said.

Mona dropped her head to her hands. Her body shook but no tears were left. It had been days since she'd shed one. He got up from his seat then and perched himself on the desk in front of her, leaning over, hand on her shoulder. 'But that's worst case, Mona. This was self-defence. I'm certain you'll be acquitted and sent on your way.'

'You said something similar before the inquest, yet here I am answering a case of murder.'

'I'm not worried,' Goldberg said, slapping his legs and standing again, as if to say 'case over.'

Only a handful of women had been executed in Victoria. Mona could remember the names of two of them: Martha Needle and Frances Knorr. They'd killed seven people between them, babies, children. Men were hanged far more often, two in the past year. They'd killed two people each. Mona remembered what the guards at Pentridge had said to her the day the 'Nugget' died. 'A life for a life.' Was she just like these people? The 'schoolgirl strangler' and 'Brunswick baby farmer'? She didn't believe she was, but maybe they didn't either. Maybe they had their own reasons for doing what they did. Maybe they felt justified, as if they had no other choice. Kill or be killed. Then, be sentenced to death anyway. No, she had to keep telling herself, she was different. They were wicked. She was not, was she?

By the time she returned home, her belongings had been packed into a hessian bag. One of the boarders explained that it would make everyone in the house more comfortable if she found somewhere else to live.

'I can stay with my employer. I'll be fine,' she said, unsure if she was trying to convince the boarder or herself. He nodded and handed her a letter that had arrived that morning, then sent her on her way. She understood Berktash was afraid of her, and so too the other boarders. She'd come and gone from many houses but had never been removed before. Since her release from Pentridge, she'd tried so hard to be a good boarder, a good citizen, a good singer. To be more than what she was, and now would never be. The letter brought tears back to her long dry eyes.

'Dear Mona, I've seen the papers and heard all about your predicament. I understand there were circumstances not yet reported but at this juncture I'm unable to find a place for you on tour. If things get sorted with the courts, you may wish to try your luck with the shows overseas. My brother James runs tents in America. No doubt this messy business hasn't made the papers over there. Walter.'

Her dreams were dashed. Her voice roared uncontrollably, and it took everything in her not to collapse right there on the street. She had nothing left to live for. And if she did live, Sharpe would always be with her. Guilt and pain were inescapable. Mona had spent all day talking about herself, *her* court case, *her* house, *her* career. Yet it was Sharpe she was always thinking about. She did deserve to die. She threw the letter, and her note covered newspaper, away.

***

Thursday, 23 November 1939. The sandy stone of the Supreme Court stretched as far as the eye could see. Mona was early. She entered the thick double doors slowly, knowing she may not be exiting that way. Out on bail, Mona didn't have to stay in the holding cells below. Instead entering the same as everyone else.

Mona had rarely seen Goldberg in his wig and robe. So, when he approached ready to walk her into the courtroom, she almost didn't recognise him. The black cloak floated behind him, reminding Mona of the nuns at Abbotsford. The length cleaned the black and white ceramic tiles of the Supreme Court foyer floor, leaving a polished shine in his wake.

'Ready?' He asked.

Mona shrugged, held out her arms, and waited for Goldberg to critique her all black outfit.

Instead, he checked his watch, whispered to a passing guard and then greeted his colleague Cullity, who barrelled towards them, sending folders full of papers flying.

Mona felt the hot rush of her breakfast moving its way up her stomach, to her heavy chest, saliva invading her mouth quicker than she could swallow. She excused herself and ran to the restroom to throw up. Her stomach settled but the hammer of her heartbeat refused to ease. This was it. She could be headed for a lifetime at Pentridge or a death sentence. She tried to calm herself, told herself not to think so far ahead. She'd spent her whole life living in the moment, she needed to do that now. Just focus on five minutes at a time. In this five minutes, she needed to fix her face and get herself seated in the court room.

'Ready?' Cullity greeted her next.

'Yep,' she replied, this time.

'That's an improvement,' Goldberg said. 'Before we go in, as we said during prep, it would be helpful to have a witness to more of the abuse you suffered. If you have a name, now's the time. Cullity can round them up while the prosecution presents their case.'

She shook her head 'I don't know.'

'That's ok, there's still time.' Goldberg must have known she was holding out on him. There were witnesses to Sharpe abusing her on the night of his death – surely that was enough for self-defence. Would the court even allow testimony related to past abuse? Goldberg seemed to think it was worth a try.

Goldberg and Cullity headed to the front of the court while an officer escorted Mona past them to her place in the dock. She could see the trap door to the basement cells below. Reporters filed into the right of the room. The jury would soon fill the seats to the left. Behind her whispers.

She turned around to see some of Sharpe's mates, ones she'd partied with only a year before. She sat low on the leather, her heels catching on the red carpeting beneath her feet, bright as blood. The chandelier above lit up the polished dark wood circling the room, climbing halfway up the walls, trying to escape.

She looked ahead to Goldberg just in time to see George Sproule enter and shake his hand. Crown Prosecutor Sproule appeared older than Goldberg, more serious, dark eyebrows and straight upper lip. He was tough, but not as tough as the Justice, so she'd heard.

Longing to see a familiar face, she braved the whispers and slurs of Sharpe's friends to turn again and look at the gallery behind her. Seeing Hutchison, even Brown, Lawrence or Guggenheim would have provided some comfort. None of them were there. Half already in gaol themselves. Then she saw him. Even seated in the very back stall he seemed taller than every other man in court. Hat still on. Brow furrowed. Detective Don Collins. It would be so easy for Goldberg to call him up. Have him tell the jury about the blood and bruises he'd cleaned up for her that night. She caught his eye. She could see from his eyes his silent plea 'let me take the stand for you.' Even if he didn't bring her criminal history into it, his bosses knew well who she was and would be watching his testimony closely. Admitting to consorting with criminals, having one alone in his private home, would not bode well for his position on the force. He could lose his job, at a time when jobs are hard to come by. The job he'd once told her he couldn't live without. Hadn't she ruined enough lives already? She just didn't think she could do it to him. Even with her own life on the line.

'Have a name yet, Mona?' Goldberg approached again and leaned up to whisper the question.

'Maybe. Let me think on it a little more. Once I've heard the prosecution's case.'

He nodded and returned to his place at the front of the room.

And so it was, in the Supreme Court of Melbourne, on Thursday the 23rd of November 1939, before his Honour Mr Justice Martin and a jury of twelve, that Mona's fate would be decided.

34

The Justice appeared, waiting for quiet before taking his seat. Goldberg had told her that Justice Fred Martin was one of the harshest you could get. He warned that Martin abhorred swearing and smoking, so she should do neither. Mona studied Martin's flushed stern face. The man appeared beyond charm and already against her. He practically scoffed at her plea 'Not guilty.'

Mr Sproule began by addressing the all-male jury. They dressed as though in uniform, a gaggle of grey suits. One man couldn't keep still, his knees jiggling, feet tapping. Another looked concerned as the juror next to him pulled out a pad and pencil. 'Are we meant to take notes?' he whispered to those around him. He didn't get an answer.

Sproule called the first witness.

Horace Finn Tucker must have been given similar advice to Mona before taking the stand, or he'd been there before. He repeated the oath to tell the truth, then kept his answers short and to the point, projecting his voice over the tapping of the court reporter's loud black Gibson typewriter. He introduced himself and his profession as a doctor at the Royal Melbourne Hospital.

'On the 15th of September was a wounded man admitted?' Sproule asked him.

'Yes.'

'What was he suffering from?'

'He had a small penetrating wound on the upper part of his abdomen. He was unconscious and at that time, he was very nearly dead.'

As much as she had hated Sharpe towards the end, as scared as she'd been of him, she was relieved to hear that he was unconscious in the hospital and therefore, not in pain. Regardless of the pain he had caused her.

Tucker explained that he died at 5 o'clock that morning.

'Will you put your finger where the wound was?' Sproule asked next.

Mona shifted her gaze from Tucker to the jury, watching their eyes follow the line of his finger as he pointed to his abdomen. Sproule thanked him and he exited the witness box, rushing out the door to get back to work.

Next, after taking his time to shuffle through the court, the Coroner's surgeon spoke. Mona recognised him from the inquest. His name was Mollison and he had 50 years' pathology experience behind him. Mona knew him as having worked the case of Squizzy Taylor, famous in the Melbourne underworld, killed twelve years earlier.

'I found that the body,' Mollison said referring to Sharpe 'was that of a young man five feet eleven. There was a small bullet wound of entrance on the right side, four and a half inches below the nipple.'

Upon hearing of Sharpe's nipple, Mona recalled him twisting hers their first night together – the way he'd hurt her even then. Now he was a body being spoken of in terms of 'its' individual parts. She struggled to follow as Mollison spoke of Sharpe's blood, abdominal cavity, and the amount of alcohol in his system. As the direction of the bullet was discussed, Goldberg must have sensed her discomfort. She wiped sweat from her forehead, and he turned in his chair to glare at her. Sweating didn't look good, made her seem guilty, she remembered.

She turned her attention to the red carpet and concentrated on breathing from the diaphragm, as if warming for a performance – in 1, 2, 3, 4, 5, hold 2, 3, 4, 5, out 2, 3, 4, 5.

When she looked up again, the famed Coroner's surgeon was gone. In his place was Sharpe's brother. If she'd seen him on the street, she would have thought she'd seen a ghost.

'On the 15th of September did you see the body of Albert Sharpe at the City Morgue?'

'I did,' William Sharpe said, a lot more composed than he'd been at the inquest. He explained to the jury that he was Sharpe's brother, that Sharpe was 24 when he died. That was all Sproule needed from him. Identification. Sproule offered no condolences, no comfort as he handed the witness over to Goldberg for cross examination.

Goldberg stood but remained behind his desk. He would be quick too. 'Sharpe was rather tall, nearly six feet?'

'He was.' William shifted from foot to foot, standing tall on the stand as though reaching for the six feet his brother had left behind.

'And very strong?' Goldberg asked.

The brother hesitated, knowing why the question was being asked and perhaps, not wanting to answer it. But eventually he did, quietly. 'Yes.'

'Nothing further.'

The judge directed him to leave the stand. As he did so, William looked straight at Mona, his eyebrows pulled down tight, nostrils flaring, just like she'd seen Sharpe so many times before. Perhaps, if the court had been empty, he would have hit her. Sharpe would have hit her full court or not. Maybe that was what made these brothers different? Or maybe she had him wrong. Maybe he was just like she'd always wanted Sharpe to be: kind, gentle. Maybe he had no idea his brother had been violent at all.

Next was the Ambulance driver. He introduced himself as Michael Samuel Jackson of Barkly Street, St Kilda.

Sproule passed a photograph round the jury as the Ambulance officer spoke of arriving at the George' N Café at 4.35am and seeing Sharpe on the footpath.

'He was lying outside the small pillar at the entrance.'

'Was he conscious when you got there, or did he show any signs of consciousness?'

'None at all.'

The Justice asked Goldberg if he had anything to ask, Goldberg declined. Mona was disappointed. She'd wanted him to ask how much time had passed between getting the call and the ambulance arriving on the scene. Wasn't that important considering she would testify that Sharpe was still shouting threats when she ran? He wasn't unconscious then.

Next was Government Analyst Charles Anthony Taylor. A striking man, big and balding. Mona felt the entire courtroom hold in a breath as he took the stand. He was practically famous. The policeman's secret weapon.

'On the 16th of September did you receive a parcel of men's clothing from Detective Delmenico?'

'Yes.'

Sproule picked up a familiar coat.

'Was this in the parcel?'

'Yes. I examined this overcoat and found a bullet hole just above that button in the position that I have marked with a ring of chalk,' he said, holding the coat high so the jury could see where he'd marked it, see where the hole was, the hole Mona had put there.

She couldn't look at it, focused her eyes on the floor. His voice continued like a wireless playing in the house next door, she could hear sound but couldn't quite make out the words. A bead of sweat dropped from her forehead, hitting the point of her shoe. She snapped up, afraid Goldberg had heard the thud of perspiration. Reporters were fanning their faces with their notepads. The smells of sweaty men wafted across the room with each flap of paper.

'I examined the fabric against the bullet hole and found that the fibre of wool had been singed. I am of the opinion that the discharge of the gun or revolver that produced it would be up to about three inches away from the cloth, that is, within the distance of the flame.'

Goldberg questioned him next: 'When you say up to three inches, you mean within three inches?'

'Yes.'

She didn't know what good that question was meant to do and was beginning to wonder whether Goldberg would be the death of her.

35

Berktash, through his interpreter, testified next. He looked better than when Mona had last seen him at the inquest. Better rested. She was glad. She knew that he would regret accompanying her to dinner that night for the rest of his life. He introduced himself first before arriving at Mona and the events of September.

'Do you know Mona Hayes?' Sproule asked.

'No.'

Mona watched as the jury members' heads snapped quizzically between Berktash and Sproule, Sproule and Berktash.

Sproule reclarified. 'Do you know this woman?' he pointed in her direction, his black robe hanging from slender arms.

'I know her now.' He wished he didn't.

'Do you remember the morning of the 15th of September?'

Berktash explained their run in after closing the Albanian Club on Exhibition Street.

'Had you met her before that?'

'I had never met her before.'

Sproule shook his head and checked his notes. He tried again.

'Had you seen her at the Albanian Club?'

'I had never seen her before.'

Mona couldn't understand why Baby would deny knowing her except that perhaps the inquest had filled him with fear. They'd gone in hard asking about his living situation, questioning how well he knew her. He was scared, she could tell. Mona knew though, he had nothing to worry about, no one had any interest in attaching him to the crime. It was on her and her alone. But he was experiencing a trial second hand, in a foreign language.

Evidently the detail of their knowing or not knowing each other didn't matter much to Sproule, wouldn't help or hinder his case, he moved on.

'How did you come to go with her to the George' N Café?'

'I met her at Lonsdale Street, and she asked me where I was going. I told her I was going to have a meal. She said she would come with me.'

'When you went inside did you sit down at a table?'

'Yes, we went in and sat at a table. After five minutes two men walked in to our table.'

'Did you know them?'

'I saw them once before.'

This was new. She had been so wrapped up in Sharpe, so terrified when he'd walked in, she hadn't realised that Sharpe and Clarke were familiar to Berktash – they must have met him at the Albanian Club too. Though she was sure she remembered Clarke introducing himself that night.

'Did you know their names?'

'I did not know their names. They were talking to the woman.' Berktash avoided looking over at her while the interpreter stared as he spoke.

'Was there any quarrel between either of these men and the woman? Did you understand what they were saying?' Sproule asked.

'The conversation was very quiet. I could not understand a word they were saying. The girl got out first and the man followed behind. The man that got shot.'

'Did you follow out immediately?'

'After two or three minutes I left. I saw them outside twenty feet from the café. Near the hotel. I could not hear what they were saying. I called a taxi.'

'When you got into the back of the taxi was the driver at the wheel?'

'Yes, he was sitting at the wheel.'

'Did you drive away at once?'

'No, I was waiting for Mona because she was living in the same direction, and I waited to drive her home. After 20 minutes they came up towards the taxi, and the girl was trying to get in and the man was following her.'

'What did the man do when she got in?'

'The man was half-way in the taxi, and he was standing up and trying to drag the girl out. They were talking very angrily. The girl was telling the man to leave her alone as she was going home, and he was trying to drag her out.'

'Did he drag her right out of the car?'

'After they had been talking for five minutes, he dragged her out. As soon as he got her out of the car, he gave her a kick.'

At that Mona winced, feeling the pain of Sharpe's boot all over again. She noticed movement among the jury, a couple looked shocked, shaking their heads. This was the first they were hearing of Sharpe's violence towards her.

'What happened after he had given her a kick?'

'After he gave her a kick the girl was screaming, and it seemed to be very painful.' It was. 'And after that I heard the gun fired.'

'Where was the girl when you heard the gun fired?'

'Just outside from the taxi.'

Justice Martin interrupted. 'Was she standing up?'

Berktash replied, 'Yes.'

Mona could see Goldberg flinch, better if he'd remembered her struggling on the ground. She had been, hadn't she?

Sproule continued. 'Did you see where the man was when you heard the gun fired?'

'They were facing each other and as soon as I heard the shot, I saw the man get away.'

Get me a gun! She thought she was dead in that moment.

'What did the girl do?'

'After I heard the shot, I got out of the taxi, and I got away and did not see the girl afterwards.'

'Where did you go when you got out?'

'I went home to 33 Drummond Street?'

'Does anyone else live there?'

She could see Berktash stiffen, back straight, shoulders tense.

'I did not know anyone living there.' Concern spread from his temples down to his now trembling lips.

'Are you Albanian?' Sproule changed topic.

'Yes.'

'Do you help in the management of the Albanian Club?'

'No.'

'Did you before it closed down?'

Mona was confused, she didn't know it closed down. But then, on bail she kept herself segregated, alone, out of trouble.

'I was only giving help there,' Berktash said. Justice Martin clearly had no interest in Berktash's dealings at the Club. He interrupted again. 'Where was the girl kicked?'

'I could not say exactly but it seemed to me that she was hit somewhere in the stomach.' Correct. 'I would not like to have that kick myself.'

Sproule picked up again.

'When this man was trying to pull out the girl who was going home in the same direction as you, did you try stop him or defend her in any way?' Mona was surprised Sproule asked this. Perhaps trying to prove the beating couldn't have been so bad if no one stepped up to help her.

'No.'

Goldberg stood, giving Berktash a reassuring smile before cross examining him.

'When you first met the girl, you went to the corner of Lonsdale and Exhibition streets?'

'Yes.'

'And she addressed you as, 'Hello Bebe'?'

'I did not call her Bebe.'

'Did she call you Bebe?'

'She said 'Hello' but not the name.'

Not true. He didn't want to know her. But the jury knew, as well as Goldberg and Sproule, she didn't accompany a stranger to dinner.

'This girl asked you where you were going?'

'Yes the girl asked me that.'

'Did you tell her you were going to the George' N Café for supper?'

'Yes, I told her that.'

'Did you ask her to come with you?'

'Yes.'

'When you went into the George' N Café you sat at a table, did you not?' Goldberg surveyed the jury as he spoke, all listening intently, eyes trained on Berktash's interpreter for an answer.

'Yes.'

'Who else was in the café besides you and the accused?'

'A few taxi drivers.'

'How long were you in the café before the deceased and his companion came in?'

'Just about five minutes.'

'Did you or the accused invite either of these two men to join you at your table?'

'We did not invite them. They walked right in and sat at our table.'

'And did the taller of the two men enter into a conversation with the girl?'

'Yes.'

'As a result of that conversation with the deceased man, did the girl, Miss Hayes, appear to be upset?'

'Yes, she seemed to be upset.'

'Did she get up and say, 'I am getting out of here'?'

'Yes, she said that and walked straight out.'

'At the time she walked out was the deceased's meal served to him?'

'It had been served.'

'Would it be true to say he did not even start his meal when he got up and followed the girl outside?'

'He never touched his meal at all.'

'How long had the girl and the deceased left the café before you went outside?'

'After two or three minutes.'

'Did you see the man pulling the girl about outside the hotel?'

'I saw them talking there.'

'When you were sitting in the taxi, did you see the man grab the girl by the hair and hit her?'

'After the girl came into the taxi he grabbed her by the hair and kicked her.'

'Did you see him hitting the girl before she got into the taxi?'

'I did not see that.'

'Did you see the man jostling or crowding the girl?'

'Yes, I saw that.'

'Did the man appear to be trying to stop the girl going to the taxi?'

'Yes, it appeared that way.'

'Was there another struggle between the girl and the man in the taxi? And was he trying to drag her out?'

'There was some conversation in the taxi and he was trying to get her out and the girl was saying, 'Let me go, I want to go home, leave me alone.''

'When he pulled her out of the taxi, did he appear to be angry?'

'Yes, he seemed to be very, very angry. He grabbed her by the hair and dragged her out.'

'Did he kick her?'

'It seemed to me as soon as she came out from the taxi he kicked her.'

'Was it a heavy kick?'

'It was so hard it made the girl scream.'

'And it was a kick which would have hurt you a great deal if it had landed on you?'

'No human being would not feel it the way the kick was given to her.'

Mona teared up as the jury shuffled in their seats, she could hear pencils on paper, journalists taking down every word.

'After he kicked the girl, did he grab her again by the hair and pull her towards him?'

'I saw her kicked and heard her scream and after that I heard only the shot.'

'Was the girl crying and saying, 'Let me go'?'

'She was crying all the time.'

Goldberg again, 'Was the man swearing at her? Do you know swearing when you hear it?'

'I can understand the swearing. In any country the first thing you learn is swearing.'

'Was he swearing at her while he was trying to pull her out of the taxi?'

'Yes.'

'The deceased was the aggressor throughout, was he not?'

'Yes.'

He deserved it did he not? Mona thought. Yes. No. She didn't know anymore.

'The girl told the man she did not want to go with him, did she not?'

'Yes, she told him she did not want to go and did not like to know him at all.'

She wished she'd never known Sharpe at all. Then he'd still be alive, and she'd be singing with the sideshows.

Berktash sighed loudly as he left the stand, his interpreter walking him out. Mona felt the jury was on her side, but she'd also felt, just a few short weeks ago, that she was free of her old life with Sharpe. Like the bee Priscia had once compared him to, Sharpe had left his mark. He stung her and died, but his stinger remained. And if the men on the jury took his side, that sting could kill her too.

36

Nicholas Haskas, the George' N Café waiter, was sworn in. Like the inquest, he described the night of the 15th of September. He said they'd been quiet at the table, but that Mona had left first with Sharpe following close behind.

'After four or five minutes I saw the man who was shot sitting in front of the door, and he was holding his stomach with his hand,' he said.

Mona realised that the timing of the events between leaving the café and her shooting Sharpe was different for everyone. For Berktash it felt like twenty minutes, as he waited in the taxi for her. For Nicholas it was five. Mona had lost all sense of time.

Cullity stood for the cross examination. Goldberg had explained to her the difference between his role and Cullity's but Mona still didn't understand it. She saw Cullity as a bit of a loose cannon, a bit like her. He had been reprimanded in the past for using slang in cross examinations, and he often appeared in the Court Sidelights of *The Herald* for his humorous quips in court. She wasn't pleased he was questioning witnesses in her case. She didn't want to be in the Court Sidelights. She was already in every news column in the country. *Domestic on Murder Charge, Murder in Taxi.*

'How many tables are in this café?' Cullity started, receiving a soft thirteen in reply. Unlucky for some. He asked about the other people there that night. 'Were the only persons in the café the Albanian, the accused, the deceased and another man, plus some taxi drivers?'

'Yes.'

'You said you saw the deceased four or five minutes after he left the café. Might it have been as many as twenty minutes?'

'It might have been five minutes, or it might have been more. I am not certain about that, because I did not look at a watch.'

He looked at his watch on the way out, surprised he'd been in court so long.

Next was taxi driver Ernest. Sproule stood again giving a nod to Cullity.

'At about four o'clock on the morning of the 15th of September did you go into the George' N Café?'

'Somewhere round about that time,' he answered, describing the scene at the restaurant.

'When you went outside did you see the accused? Down towards the hotel?'

'I did. He was trying to shepherd her that way. She was trying to walk to the right, and he was bumping her and pulling her towards the left.'

'Did you go out and sit in your driving seat?'

'Yes, I followed big Bebe up to my car and sat waiting for directions.'

'How long did you sit there from the time you got in till the time the shooting occurred?'

'Somewhere about ten or twelve minutes.' Different again.

'When the deceased and the accused got near your car what happened?'

'He was trying to obstruct her from getting into my car. He was swearing, threatening and pulling at her.'

'Did you look around to see what was going on in the back?'

'No, I was minding my own business. There was struggling and wrestling going on, but what exactly was happening I could only see on the sharp side in his corner.'

'Did you hear a shot?'

'Yes. I glanced at Sharpe as soon as the shot went off. He staggered back on to the centre of the footpath. He grabbed his stomach and sang out something about 'Give me my gun' or 'Give me a gun' or words to that effect.'

'What happened to you?' Unlike the inquest, this time, he looked at Mona. She lowered her eyes in shame.

'I was told to drive,' he said.

'Who told you to drive?'

'I could not swear. It was in a high-pitched voice.'

Her voice. They both knew it. But for some reason his memory must have faded, he'd gone over and over it all in his head too many times, he was questioning his own mind. She knew that well. She was doing it too.

'Was it in a foreign voice?' Sproule asked, referring to Berktash.

'It was all in a whirl in one minute.'

Or was he protecting her? Did he feel sorry after all that was said at the inquest and in the papers? Did he feel guilty for not trying to help her? Was he trying to help her now?

'What did you feel?'

'I felt something pressed against my neck and I got out as fast as possible.'

Goldberg cross examined.

'You say you saw him shepherding her and he was jostling her. Was she trying to get away from him?'

'That's the impression I got.'

'How long would it be before they rejoined you at your cab from the time you left the café?'

'I would say somewhere about ten to twelve minutes.'

'And then you saw them for the last few yards as they approached the car?'

'Yes.'

'Was he still jostling her and crowding her?'

'Yes.'

'Was she pleading with him to let her alone?'

'Yes, she was saying 'Leave me alone; let me go home.''

'After she got into the cab, he followed her?'

'Yes, they were arguing the point at the door for a second and then he got in.'

'In the cab did you hear him using foul and filthy language towards her?'

'Yes.'

'Did he say 'I will belt you into the gutter and I will bash your brains in'?'

'Words to that effect.'

Hearing those words spoken by Goldberg in a quiet court room, jurors eyes wide and mouths agape, journalists scribbling madly, her eyes welled up. She could almost feel heat coming from where her welts had been in the weeks before the shooting. Feel Sharpe's kick, her hair being pulled, and knowing, truly knowing, that he would kill her before she ever got her chance at a normal life.

'And he seemed to be in an ungovernable temper?'

'I would not have liked to cross him at the time.'

'And because you did not like to cross him at the time you lay on the seat so that you would not see what was happening?'

'That's correct.'

Guggenheim once told Mona that the more witnesses to a crime, the more likely you were to get away with it. She'd never been game enough to test that theory. Guggenheim reasoned that if there were lots of people around, all would stand back and wait for someone else to step in, expecting someone else to run and call the police. But if there was only one witness, they were more likely to feel responsible for what was happening. They were more likely to step up because they were the only one who could. Perhaps Ernest was waiting for Berktash to help her, and Bertktash waiting for Ernest.

'And the next thing you heard was a shot?'

'Correct.'

'Can we take it the man was definitely the aggressor throughout?'

'Yes, I got the impression that if he had went away, she would have been only too glad to get rid of him and would have willingly gone away.' At least Ernest was helping her now.

Goldberg sat, satisfied.

The Justice adjourned for a short break. Mona felt faint, she went to the bathroom thrice, smoked a cigarette and nibbled on the corner of Cullity's sandwich.

'Next are the cops and their case is done,' Cullity said.

'We'll be able to present this afternoon. We probably won't get another break Mona. It might not be too late if you have someone you want me to call?'

She'd been torn about Collins. He was still there, in the gallery, ready. She'd spent all her life not wanting to fly alone. Grasping for companionship. Waiting for help. Yet she'd shot Sharpe on her own, now she wanted to face the consequences on her own. She could do it herself. She could do as she'd intended upon her release from prison. She could turn her life around. And she didn't need a man to help her do it.

'No, I can do this.'

'The jury's with you,' Cullity reassured her of her decision.

'Alright, we'll call you and then rest. We should be done by the end of the day. You ready for this?'

She thought she might throw up again. 'Ready.'

37

Delmenico entered looking more dapper than Mona remembered. Sproule gave him a familiar nod and smile. Mona's case was going to rely on her testimony, and Sproule's case would come down to this.

'Your name is Frederick William Delmenico and you are a detective stationed at Melbourne?'

'Yes.'

'Come to the 15th September.'

He'd done this many times before, no need for all the questions, Delmenico went into his spiel.

'At about 11.30am on the 15th of September with some other detectives, I went to a house at 33 Drummond Street, Carlton, where I saw the accused. I said to her, 'We want you to come to the Detective office.' She said, 'What for?' I said, 'At about 4am this morning a man was shot dead outside the George' N Café in Russell Street and it's alleged that you were there at the time.' She said, 'This is a pretty heavy one you are trying to tack on to me now, murder.''

Mona's face flushed, having forgotten her over-active mouth when faced with the detectives at her door.

'She accompanied us to the Detective Office, where I said to her, 'Do you know a man named Albert Sharpe'? She said 'Yes.' I said, 'At about 4am this morning Albert Sharpe was shot dead outside the George' N Café in Russell Street; were you there at the time?' She said, 'Yes'. I said, 'It's alleged that you shot him.' She said, 'He is in his place.''

He is in his place. Reporters' heads dropped to their pads again, they liked that detail. She began to second guess herself. After Delmenico's testimony maybe she'd need Collins after all. But it was too late now.

Delmenico went onto describe everything the way it had happened in the interview room. Berktash and the driver being brought in to identify her, everything that was said, their entire conversation as if played back word for word. He remembered everything the same as she did. He produced her statement on a piece of paper. He went on to describe what happened after she was taken to the City Watch House.

'I took possession of the clothing of the deceased and conveyed it to Mr Taylor, the Government Analyst. The bullet was given to me as evidence by Dr Mollison. I saw the deceased at the Melbourne Hospital on the morning of the 15th September and saw the body again when Dr Mollison was conducting the post mortem examination.'

Sproule appeared uninterested in this, getting straight back to Mona. 'Did she say anything about being kicked?'

'No.'

Goldberg cross examined. 'Sharpe was well known to the police was he not?'

'He was known to me by repute. He had some convictions.'

Not as many as her, she bet Delmenico was dying to say.

'What time was it you first spoke to this girl and took her into custody?'

'About 11.30am.'

'And it was 5.30pm the statement was taken?'

'It was somewhere in the vicinity of 5pm.'

'And she told you she got the pistol to protect herself?'

'She did.'

'Did she tell you this man was persecuting and assaulting her?'

'Yes, she told me in the words of her statement.'

'When you brought her to the police station, she appeared to you to be a woman labouring under mental stress?'

'Not at the time we brought her to the detective office. She seemed to be a person probably who was trying to be brave. Later on, after she had made the statement, she then appeared to be in distress.'

'And did she not appear to be a woman who was trying to get control over herself, trying to refrain from breaking down?'

'Up until the time she made the statement I would say, yes, she was.'

Delmenico looked over at her, gave her a slight nod.

'Did she tell you that she had been kicked and had her hair pulled?'

'No.'

'Did she tell you this man wanted her to come back and live with him? And for an immoral purpose, that he wanted to use her to make money?'

'Yes.'

Mona heard a few gasps from behind, noticed a few jurors shake their heads. That hadn't come up before. Surely the jury saw that she wasn't a cold-blooded killer, Sharpe had forced her hand.

Sproule concluded his case after one of the other detectives confirmed Delmenico's testimony. Justice Martin then called on Goldberg.

'The accused will give evidence on oath, and there will be no other evidence called,' Goldberg announced to the shocked court.

Mona again flipped, questioning herself, was she doing the right thing? She turned around to look at Collins, his eyebrows furrowed in confusion. He thought she'd call him, or at least call *someone*. He was wrong. This would be one of the shortest trials in Victoria's history.

38

Mona was led from the dock to the front of the court. She felt small walking through the space. Everyone's eyes on her. No one made a sound. She was today's entertainment, singing for her life. She put her hand on the same bible that everyone else had sworn on. She swore too. Thinking of the nuns as she did so. Goldberg gave her a smile of reassurance as she found her place on the stand, hoping no one could see her knees shaking. Sproule sat seated now, and watched as Goldberg stood, cleared his throat and began.

'What is your name?'

'Mona Hayes.'

'Where do you reside?'

'35 Regent Street, Fitzroy.'

'What is your occupation?'

'Home duties.'

'How old are you?'

'26.'

'Do you know the deceased, Albert Sharpe?'

'Yes.'

'When did you meet him?'

Her throat caught as she said the words 'March 1938' remembering the night they danced and went home together. Just over a year ago, yet it felt like a lifetime. They'd gone over this many times. She knew Goldberg would ask about her relationship beginning with that night, yet no matter how much they'd practiced, her voice quivered with the memories.

'When did you again see Sharpe?'

'September of that year. I was going with him for a couple of weeks, and he persuaded me to go and live with him in Gore Street, Fitzroy.'

They'd talked about that word, persuaded. The living situation had been at Sharpe's suggestion, mind you Mona had nowhere else to go at the time. Goldberg had stressed, 'Yes but it was still his idea, right? He persuaded you.' She surprised herself by remembering to use the word. A lyric memorised.

'How long were you living with him there?'

'Three weeks,' she said, but really wasn't sure. That period was now lost to time and trauma. All she knew was that in one minute she was happy, the next she was fighting for life.

'During the first week what was his treatment of you?'

'He was all right to me.'

'What was his treatment of you whilst you were keeping company with him prior to going to live with him?'

She'd practiced this too. Couldn't tell Goldberg or anyone else that she hadn't known him well at all before moving in. That she'd only known him a few hours before first sleeping with him. A fool rushing in.

'He was all right to me then.'

'After that, what happened?'

'The next couple of weeks he treated me very differently. He assaulted me on several occasions.'

'When you say that he assaulted you, what did he do to you?'

This part Goldberg hadn't wanted to rehearse too much. He told her it would be ok, helpful even, if she went into detail and showed emotion while doing so.

She took a shallow gulp of the stuffy courtroom air, unable to calm her nerves, and exhaled a shaky vibrato. Her eyes watered as she spoke. 'He knocked me down'—she looked at the floor as if looking down on her own battered body on the roadside, fruit truck driving by—'he kicked me and ill-treated me in every way.'

'Of what did the ill-treatment consist?'

'Punching and kicking me about on the body. Twisting my arms behind my back.' She stopped short, rubbing her wrists together remembering how he'd pin her down in bed, hold her wrists so tightly they burned if she moved.

'Why did he do this?'

'Because I would not do what he wanted me to do.'

'What did he want you to do?'

She kept her eyes trained on Goldberg now, unable to look around the room, unable to face the probing, judging eyes of a certain someone in the gallery. 'He wanted me to go on the streets.'

'What for?'

She coughed, rubbed her hands over her eyes, wet with tears. She croaked out the words, 'For an immoral purpose.'

'Who for?' Goldberg handed her a handkerchief which she wiped her tears with and handed back, he shook his head and mouthed, 'Keep it.'

'Myself, I suppose. He said that if I did that, he would look after me.' She said the words slowly. She'd said them to Goldberg before, but in that moment, it was as if she was finally understanding what they meant: Sharpe had never wanted to be her boyfriend, or husband, had he? He'd wanted to be her pimp. All along. And he thought she'd go along with it if he made her love him first.

'Did you agree to the suggestion?'

'No.'

'What happened then?'

'Well, I eventually got away from him.'

'When did you get away from him?'

'About three weeks I was with him. That would be in November – some time in November; I cannot say for sure.'

'When did you next speak to Sharpe following November 1938?'

'I did not see him again until this year.' Because she was in gaol. She worried she'd be found out, the jury who seemed so sympathetic to her now would change their minds if she revealed the truth. She was a common criminal after all.

'Can you fix the date?'

'Yes, it was the 25th of August.' This date she knew. She remembered well.

'Where did you meet him?'

'In Bourke Street.'

'Was it an arranged meeting?'

'No.'

'What happened?'

'He tried to force me to go back and live with him again. I tried to get away from him. He chased me a little further up the street, and we were arguing the point. We both got into a taxi together. I thought it best to go with him than to be assaulted. We went to a house in Fitzroy. King William Street. He went out the back after we had been there for about a quarter of an hour.'

'What did you do when he went out the back?'

'I went out the front. I thought it was my opportunity to get away. I got almost to the corner of the street, and he caught me again.'

'What did he do when he caught you?'

'He knocked me down. First of all, he punched me in the head, and then he knocked me down and kicked me.'

She couldn't help but start tearing up again as the Justice added in his own question. 'Was this in the day time, or at night?'

'This was at night.'

Goldberg continued. 'Did anyone come to your assistance?'

'Yes, three men in a fruit truck or a utility truck. They wanted to take me to the hospital.'

'Where were you taken?'

She looked to the back of the gallery then. 'I went back to the city. I would not go to the hospital.'

Collins' head bowed. He rubbed his hand over the stubble of his chin, his eyes catching hers. She remembered his hand caressing her face that night. Easing her wounds. She looked away, refocusing on Goldberg pacing in front of the jury.

'As a result of that assault, did you suffer anything?'

'Yes, I had two eyes.' Her words felt like they were falling into each other now. She knew she was stumbling, spitting out her words in the wrong order, but she couldn't get her tongue to work.

As if reading her mind, the Justice called for a glass of water. She thanked him and he smiled, not so tough, nodding for Goldberg to continue.

'What do you mean by two eyes?'

'One eye was closed altogether, and the other eye was black. I also had a cut forehead here.' She traced an imaginary line on her head and felt herself calm down again as she remembered Collins gently blotting her blood with a cloth. She tried her hardest not to look over at him again.

'Following that, did you see Sharpe within a day or two?'

'Yes. The next time I saw him was going down to the railway station.'

'Tell the jury about that?'

She realised then that she hadn't looked over at the jury in quite some time. Goldberg pointed at them. She turned her gaze towards them. 'I ran into a hotel and he followed me in there and pulled me from a chair and hit me in the middle of the back and was struggling with me. He tore my coat.' She felt her tongue getting heavy again, took a sip of water. 'He came in there and pulled me from the chair.'

'Was there anyone else in the dining room?'

'Yes.'

'How many people?'

'Three or four. I had only just sat down when he came in. He pulled the chair from underneath me and dragged me out of the hotel. We were arguing the point all the way up the street and a constable was coming. I said, 'You had better stop because here are the police.' He said 'If you give me up, you will see what you will get; if I do any gaol over you, you will see what will happen."

'Did he say what would happen to you?'

'He said 'I will kill you stone dead you so-and-so'.'

'Did you give him in charge to the policeman?'

'No, he came over and said, 'Do you want to give this man in charge?' I said 'No."

'What did you do on the 11th of September?'

'I went and bought a gun for my protection. I bought it from someone who knew him, and he would find out I had it and would probably leave me alone.'

'Do you remember the evening of 14th of September this year?'

'Yes.'

'Did you meet the man Malig at about 4am on the 15th of September?'

'Yes. I said to him, 'Where are you going?' and he said, 'I am going to the George' N Café.' I may have said, 'I will go with you.' Or he said, 'You can come if you like.''

'Had you known this man before?'

'Yes, I had seen him on one occasion before.'

'When you got to the George' N Café, what happened?'

'Bebe and I were having our meal, when Sharpe and another man named Clarke came in.'

'Did you invite them to sit at the table?'

'No. Nearly every other table was empty. I said, 'Don't sit here, I do not wish to speak to you at all.' He said, 'That will be alright I have got you now.' Or something like that.'

'Will you tell the court the circumstance in which you left the café?'

'I was going to wait for coffee, and I sang out to somebody – I don't know who – 'Will you give me my coffee; I want to go.' As soon as they put the meal in front of the other two people, I did not wait.'

'You mean the deceased and Clarke?'

'Yes.' It played out in her head in slow motion as she described it. Like it never happened to her. Like she was watching a play from the stalls. 'I left that chap there sitting at the table with the two of them, and when I got to the door he was behind me.'

'Who was behind you?'

She stumbled over the words 'the deceased.'

'What happened then?'

'He punched me straight away, as soon as I got outside the door. Then he tried to drag me around the corner of the George' N, round into the next street, we were fighting and struggling there. He was pulling me about. He said, 'You won't get away this time."

'Did he tell you what he wanted to do to you?'

A shiver of fear ran through her. 'He said he knew where I could get money.'

'You refused to listen to this suggestion?'

'Yes.'

'Then what happened?'

'We struggled in the street. Then I saw Baby and the taxi driver come out, so when they got into the taxi, I ran up and tried to get in. He stopped me in the first instance from getting in. Eventually I got into the taxi.'

'You say he stopped you in the first instance from getting in. What did he do?'

'He punched me.'

'Did you ultimately get into the taxi?'

'Yes, I did. We struggled and fought there in the taxi.'

'When you say we struggled and fought, what did he do to you?'

'He kept punching me all the time and he said, 'I will bash your brains out'.'

'What kind of temper was this man?'

'He was a maniac.' The journalists were busy, pads filling up fast.

'He pulled me by my hair first. He tried to get me out of the door, and I would not go. I put my foot on the side of the taxi and would not get out. Eventually he got me half out and kicked me in the lower part of my body.'

'In the private parts of your body, is that it, when you say the lower part. Will you indicate that portion, with your hand?'

She stood on tiptoes as she ran her hand down her pelvis. 'The bottom of my stomach.'

'And following that what happened?'

'Then he pulled me by the hair again, and I could not stand any more of it.'

'What did you believe he was going to do to you?'

'I did not believe at all, I am quite certain what he was going to do.'

'What are you quite certain he was going to do?'

'I am quite certain he was going to carry out his threat. That he would finish me.'

'What did you do then?'

'I know what I did, but I don't know how I did it.' Suddenly, all she could see was a haze of hands and coat and feet. All she could feel was pain in her side, pain at her head, pain in every place he was pushing and pulling her. She could see flashes of her purse, she could see her hand reaching desperately for it. She could see footpath and then … bang.

'You admit firing the shot?'

'Yes.'

'At the time you fired the shot, can you tell the jury why you fired it?'

She looked over at the jury again. Scanning the eyes of each man as tears ran down her cheeks. 'I was in terror of my life.'

'How far away would you be from him?'

'I must have been close, because he had his hands on me at the time.'

'Did you have any intention of killing him when you fired the shot?'

'I did not know what would happen.' She had been living in a world where mates like Guggenheim could get stabbed in the street, go to hospital and be out two days later. No one even charged. When deciding in that moment to shoot him, her only thought was getting away.

'Then what did you do?'

'I ran. I realised that I had done something, I did not actually know what I had done.'

'What did you do with the gun?'

'I threw it away.'

'Did you tell the police about these various assaults on you?'

'Yes.'

'Did you tell them about the constable?'

'Yes, I think I did.'

Justice Martin interrupted. 'What constable?'

Goldberg answered for her. 'About the constable who spoke to her after one of the assaults.'

'Oh some days before.' Martin nodded, remembering back to the beginning of Mona's testimony. How long had she been up there?

Goldberg asked Mona, 'Did you tell the police about the kicking?'

'As far as I know, I think I did tell them.'

'What was your condition that day?'

'I was in a terrible state.'

'Were you in fear of this man?'

'Yes, in terror of my life.'

Goldberg gave a reassuring smile and returned to his seat. Sproule took his time, checking his notes and adjusting his robe as he stood. He cleared his throat to begin.

39

'Miss Hayes, you, having lived with this man, eventually left him and did not see him for some months from November to August?'

'That's true.'

'And then on that day in August you went off with him to some house?' Attitude crept into Sproule's voice, as though he wanted to phrase his question 'So you're trying to tell me that he abused you, yet you still went with him to a party? Were you just asking for it? Were you stupid?'

'Yes.'

'Why did you do that? Intending to take up your life with him again?'

'No, I went with him because I thought he was going to assault me there and then.'

'Why did you go to a house where he could assault you with much greater safety?'

'It was not a house we were going to take, but a party where he knew people. I was not going to a house to live with him.' She worried now her testimony hadn't been clear. If he'd misunderstood this point what had the jury misunderstood? She looked over at Goldberg, he gave her a nod, he wasn't worried. She finished her glass of water.

'You were safer surely in Bourke Street than in any house with a man like that?'

Spoken like a man.

'Not on this occasion.'

'You ran out of the front, and he assaulted you like this in the street?'

'Yes.'

'Why didn't you go to the police then?'

She took a big breath. 'Because I had been threatened by him that if I did go to the police what would happen.'

'Did you prefer to shoot him rather than go to the police?'

'No, I did not prefer to shoot him.'

'Apparently every time he saw you, either in a public place or not, he assaulted you for several meetings after that?'

'Yes.'

'And you were still afraid to go to the police?'

She thought he was trying to trick her. He wanted her to slip up, to say she hadn't bothered with the police because she, herself, was a criminal. Goldberg told her that Sproule had once spoken in court about an accused's criminal history when he wasn't supposed to. Was he trying to do that here?

'Yes. What would be the good of my going to the police? I would have had more damage done to me.'

'You might have had him locked up for assaults?'

'I did not wish to do that.'

'On September 11th you went and got a pistol? Was it loaded when you got it?'

'Yes.'

'And you carried it with you just in case you met this man? With no intention of using it on anybody else?'

'No intention at all; no intention of using it on anybody.'

'Why did you carry it?'

'Merely to frighten him.'

'To let him see it, or was it you thought he might hear you had got it?'

'I obtained it from a man I knew would tell him straight away I had it.'

'So long as he thought you had it, you did not need to carry it, if that was going to be the deterrent?'

'Oh yes, it was quite essential to carry it. I know that he always carried one.'

'Were you afraid he would shoot you?'

'My word.' He was getting to her. She could feel her face and neck reddening, her whole body shaking. She was sputtering her words again.

'What?'

'Yes.'

'He had never tried to shoot you up to date?'

'He has pulled the gun out at me.'

'You never told us that. How is it you did not tell us that when you were telling us all about it?'

'Telling who?'

'Tell the court or your counsel. How is it you did not tell us about his pulling a gun out and threatening you. How did you come to miss it? Had you forgotten?'

'No, I had not forgotten at all.' In truth she had. Him showing her the gun while they were together, aiming it at her, all seemed to pale in comparison to the pain of his fists and feet. That's what she focused on when talking to the police, when talking to Goldberg.

'It's one of the worst things, I suppose?'

'It does not matter how one is going to injure you one way or the other.'

'Excepting that shooting is worse than punching?'

She was worse than Sharpe then? She stayed silent, her mouth dry, no more water in front of her.

'You carried your gun because you knew he had one?'

'I carried it in the first instance. I got it because I wanted somebody to tell him I had it.'

'That is all right; but why did you carry it?'

'What was I going to do with it if I did not carry it? How could I frighten anyone if I did not have it?'

'So long as your friends told him you had it. Did you have it to show it to him?'

'Yes, to produce.'

'That night when he came to you in the café and was threatening you did you show it to him in the café?'

'No.'

'And when you got outside, and he was trying to get you around into Lonsdale Street, did you then show him the pistol?'

'No, but I said, 'If you don't leave me alone, I will shoot you."

'And was not that your attitude, if he would not leave you alone you would shoot him?'

'No, I had no intention of doing anything like that. I just thought I would try to frighten him.'

'I suggest it was this, that because he would not let you alone and was trying to pull you out of the cab that you did shoot him?'

'I beg your pardon?'

'It was because he would not let you alone and was trying to pull you out of the cab that you shot him?'

'No.'

'As you said to him, 'If you don't let me alone I will shoot you'?'

'I had no intention of doing anything like that.'

'Did you hear Malig's statement read out today in court?'

'Yes.'

'Did you notice there was nothing in that about kicking or hair pulling?'

He had talked about kicking hadn't he? Hadn't he said he himself wouldn't have wanted to experience that kick? Was she remembering wrong? Did she imagine it? She'd also told it to the police when questioned.

'To my knowledge I told the police that.'

'Do you remember having the statement read out to you in the detective office?'

He was talking about Berktash's original statement? She couldn't distinguish what was in that from what he said at the inquest to what he said in court that very day. 'Yes.'

'Did you notice there was nothing about kicking and hair pulling?'

'I heard a statement read, but I did not know actually what was in it…' No that's not right, she read it, it wasn't read to her, her mind was spinning. 'I did read his statement at Russell Street.'

'The detective tells us you said that was true. Did you notice it left out the worst things, the punching, the hair pulling and the kicking?'

'I did not notice that.'

'And your own. Did you notice when you read your own over and when it was read out to you?'

'I was in a state that I did not know what I said or what I had written.'

'Do you think you might have left out all about the punching and the kicking and the hair pulling?'

'I will not contradict that I did not tell the police but to my knowledge I did.'

'Is it this, Miss Hayes, someone has said to you 'you had better make it as hot as you can, it will make it look as if it were a more dangerous assault' and you have improved on your story since you told it to the detectives?'

'No! My story is this. To my knowledge I did tell the police everything. If they say not, I would not contradict it.' She dropped her head, rubbed her forehead with her hands.

'You were in the cab when you fired, were you not?'

'No, I was half-in. I do not know where I was.'

'You were not standing on the footpath?'

'I was half-in and half-out.'

'You were certainly not standing up facing him on the footpath?'

'No.'

'Did you get back into the taxi after the shooting? You told the taxi driver to drive off quickly?'

'I think I did.'

'You would be in the taxi then?'

'Not necessarily.'

'You did not want him to drive away without you did you?'

'Want who?'

'The taxi driver, when you said 'drive off quickly'?'

'No I think I told him to drive away.'

'Did you put your pistol up against him in some way.'

'I may have done that.'

'And when he jumped out, you jumped out, is that right?'

'I do not know that I was ever back in again to jump out.'

'I suggest that you must have been in the taxi when you told him to drive off quickly, and you wanted him to drive you somewhere?'

She wanted to be driven away. To get away, from Sharpe. But she didn't know what it mattered. Sharpe was dying outside the taxi regardless of where she was or what she remembered about where she was. She thought she was half-in, half-out, but why Sproule thought this was important enough to question over and over again she just didn't know.

'I do not know whether I was in or out.'

'I want you to remember and think now. You told the taxi driver to drive off quickly. You say that you must have meant him to drive you somewhere?'

'Yes, but it would not be necessary for me to be in the taxi to tell him that.'

'No, if he drove off quickly, he would leave you behind if you were not in the taxi.'

'I do not know whether I was in or out of the taxi. I cannot just think, and it's no good me saying whether I was in, or out.'

'Did your memory cease after you fired the shot?'

'Yes, temporarily.'

'You do not know where you put the pistol, or anything of that sort?'

'I threw it away.'

'Was it lost, or was it where you could find it again. Where did you throw it?'

'In the street.'

'Which street?'

'I cannot say.'

'Why can you not say?'

How could she explain what was happening to her, how her mind was spinning like a top, how that night she ran around in the dark like a mad woman for hours? How could she explain she remembered lifting her arm up and releasing but didn't remember where or when or what happened after?

'Because I do not know for sure. I was running and running around.'

'And you eventually found your way home? You were living at 33

Drummond Street then, were you?'

'Yes.'

'Was Bebe living there too?'

'I could not say.'

'Was anybody else living there?'

'There were several people. It's an apartment house. I did not know whether Bebe lived there or not.'

Goldberg had told her to use the word apartment over boarding. Sounded like a better living situation, he'd said.

'You had only seen Bebe at the Albanian Club; is that right?'

'Yes.'

'On this evening was he to pay for your supper?'

She'd run out without thinking of paying. Trying to get away from Sharpe. She knew how it sounded, like a date, but who cares? What did it matter?

'Yes, he paid for it.' She supposed.

Mona was surprised when Sproule sat down then, questions over. Sudden. Abrupt. She looked across at Goldberg and he nodded. The judge told her she could leave the stand. She felt tired and relieved but mostly scared. It was all over. Now it was in the hands of a jury of men. Men like the ones who turned their backs while she was being beaten? Or men like Collins? Who sat at the back of the room bewildered, simmering, mad even, that she did not call him. That she wouldn't let him help her.

Once she'd returned to her place, Goldberg stood. 'At this stage, is Your Honour going to put anything to the jury at all?'

'No,' said Martin.

Sproule and Goldberg gave their final addresses. Sproule reminded the jury that Mona hadn't claimed she was punched or kicked in her initial statement, insinuated she was exaggerating for self-defence. But Goldberg focused on the statements that had been made in court. Berktash and the driver both corroborated her tale of violence and threats. She was in danger for her life.

Cullity handed her a cup of tea as they waited in a nearby office for the jury to return. She jiggled the teabag, but had no energy to lift the cup.

'It may be a while,' Goldberg said.

'You did great on the stand, Mona. The jury were on your side the whole time,' Cullity said.

'Even after Sproule laid into me?' she asked.

'Yes, I'm certain of it.'

She didn't feel like it had gone well. She thought Sproule had made her look a fool. She was regretting not calling witnesses to back her up. She could have called Collins, hell Goldberg may have even been able to find the constable who'd helped her, or the men from the fruit truck.

A knock at the door startled them, she spilled the tea over her skirt. 'Jury's back.'

Goldberg looked at his watch.

'Twenty-eight, no, twenty-nine minutes. That was quick.'

'Must be a record.' Cullity used a handkerchief to blot Mona's skirt.

'Is that good?' Mona asked.

A guard came for Mona while both men returned their wigs to their heads. They had been expecting it to take longer. They had been expecting to go home.

Mona slowed to a crawl as the guard led her back to her seat. She couldn't lift her feet from the ground, they dragged along like dead weights. Her hands trembled as they gripped the rails. She couldn't hear any sounds coming from behind her, though the courthouse was again full of journalists, police and onlookers. Everything slowed except the beating of her heart.

'All rise.'

Mona could barely hear the words, but as everyone stood she took that as her cue to stand too.

She watched Justice Martin's mouth move, something like, 'On the charge of murder what say you?'

One man from the jury stood, cleared his throat and straightened his tie with a shaky hand.

She could swear the word 'guilty' left his lips and reverberated around the room. Her heart stopped, but her ears finally awoke. There was a 'not' in front of the 'guilty'.

'And on the charge of manslaughter?'

'Not guilty.'

Not. Not. He'd said 'not'.

She looked down at Goldberg and Cullity shaking hands.

She turned her attention to Sproule gathering up his papers, shaking his head, shoulders slumped.

Not guilty.

She was free. She screamed silently, collapsing, her voice trapped in her chest.

Behind her, the gallery emptied. Reporters rushed off to file their stories. Sharpe's mates glared and spat in her direction on their way out the door, Collins was already gone.

40

Mona wrote to Walter's brother James about the overseas sideshows.

While she waited for his reply, she laid low in Fitzroy, living and cleaning at 35 Regent Street, teaching neighbourhood children to sing, and saving every cent for travel. She never saw any of her criminal friends again, not Lawrence, not Hutchison.

The only encounter she had with police was when she happened to pass a two-up game while walking home from the store. She could spot a cop a mile away, so when she noticed a couple six-foot, clean shaven, well-dressed men approach, she laughed and walked on, knowing full-well what was about to unfold.

James wrote. He trusted his brother's opinion more than anyone's. If Walter agreed Mona belonged on a sideshow stage, James would put her on one in America.

***

The ship was smaller than she'd imagined, the crowds lining up to board made her wonder how they would all fit. She noticed one man on the dock casually bumping into people in line, his hand swiftly, expertly, slipping into pockets. He slid the wallets he'd collected down his socks. She laughed, nudged the nice family behind her and said, 'Watch out for that one if you don't want your ticket stolen.'

On the outer deck of the ship, children danced at her feet and sang about finding a land beyond a rainbow. Their voices carried on the summer wind, swirling round the ship like leaves. Other passengers joined in, as if there'd been some rehearsal she hadn't been invited to, they'd all learned the lyrics ahead of time.

'Haven't seen it yet, have you?' A gentleman tipped his hat and lit himself a cigarette, offering her one in the process. She shook her head no. She had her own.

'Seen what?' she asked.

'Wizard of Oz,' he said. 'A picture about a girl lost, trying to find home.'

Maybe that's what she was doing, and home was where the singers were, where the sideshows were. She wasn't running away, she was finding her way home. As the ship pulled away from the dock, and people tried to push past her to line the deck's edges, she held her ground. Just because she didn't have anyone to wave goodbye to didn't mean she should miss the view. One final farewell to good old Melbourne.

Then she thought she spotted him. His long coat, hat on, clearly a cop. Collins? Whoever he was, he wasn't waving, just looking up at the ship. Finally, he took his hat off and held it to his heart as they sailed away. She imagined it *was* him. That he had received her parcel in the post and had come to see her off – or perhaps, make sure she was really leaving. One less criminal file he'd have to keep.

She'd held onto the little black elephant for two years believing it was Sharpe's, once she'd known it was Collins' she'd held it even tighter. She wondered if things could have ever been different between them. If he had met her one day, at the races or a show, and she had not been committing crimes on the side, would he have liked her? Could they have been friends? Probably not. But at least now the little elephant was where it belonged. Soon, she would be too.

END NOTES

This fictional book is inspired by the true crimes of Mona Hayes. According to public records, Mona Hayes (also known as Ruth Norbury, Mona Wilson, Mona Williams, Lena Williams) was a thief who often worked as a theatre usher and domestic and travelled with the sideshows. It's unclear from public records what jobs she performed during show season. Inconsistencies in the public records include her state of birth and religion. She held many arrests – mainly for theft – in Victoria, NSW and Queensland. Police attributed her criminal lifestyle to drugs and alcohol. She lived with Arthur Wilson (also known as Albert Brown among other aliases, I have used Wilson Brown as his name in this book) on and off for around five years and was acquainted with criminals Daniel Guggenheim and Stanley Hutchison. She was sentenced to six months in Abbotsford in 1937 (in which she escaped for a period of two weeks with an 18-year-old named Mary Duffy) and six months in Pentridge in 1939. She briefly dated Albert Sharpe who also had a criminal record as a thief including stealing from a policeman's home. Mona shot Sharpe outside the George' N Café in 1939. She was tried for murder and acquitted. Lawrence, a friend of Sharpe's, testified at the inquest about Sharpe's assaults on Mona though he did not testify at trial. Parts of this book contain excerpts from criminal trial briefs held in the collection of Public Record Office Victoria.

- Excerpts in relation to the theft of diamond rings in 1937: PROV VA 667 Office of the Crown Solicitor, VPRS 30/P0 Criminal Trial Briefs, 581, 1937.

- Excerpts in relation to the theft of a fur coat in 1937: PROV VA 667 Office of the Crown Solicitor, VPRS 30/P0 Criminal Trial Briefs, 628, 1937.
- Excerpts in relation to the theft of watches in 1938 (trial in 1939): PROV VA 667 Office of the Crown Solicitor, VPRS 30/P0 Criminal Trial Briefs, 34, 1939.
- Excerpts from The King V Mona Hayes for Murder 1939: PROV VA 667 Office of the Crown Solicitor, VPRS 30/P0 Criminal Trial Briefs, 806, 1939.

The rest of this story is my imagining of what life may have been like for these people at the time, building on research into Australia in the 1930s including, but not limited to, Abbotsford Convent, Sideshow Alley and the suburbs of Carlton and Fitzroy. Many of the characters in this book are entirely fictional including the women of the Convent, friends on the sideshows, and Detective Don Collins. Don was named in memory of my late father Don Oldfield, late grandfather Don Mackie, and for my pa Don Oldfield Snr. Despite years of research, I unfortunately have not yet discovered what happened to Mona beyond 1943. Due to the theatrical nature of her thefts, and close proximity to the theatre and sideshows, I have imagined her to be a performer and given her a hopeful ending here.

ACKNOWLEDGEMENTS

So many people have helped me throughout the researching and writing of this book, in both big and small ways. Thank you to: Firstly, Mona Hayes for inspiring me to write.

My mentor and friend Susanna Lobez, Debbie Lee and Ginninderra Press for believing in this book and making it happen! Graham Davidson for a fabulous design.

To everyone at Public Record Office Victoria, especially Kate Follington, Asa Letourneau, Natasha Cantwell, Andrew Joyce, Jenny Rout and Sebastian Gurciullo for your encouragement and enthusiasm.

Lee Hooper and Born and Bred Historical Research, Dr Madonna Grehan, Emily Boyle and the Abbotsford Convent Foundation, Loreta Tabellionc and the National Archives of Australia, Amber Evangelista, Tracey Manallack and the Victoria Police Archives, Ann Swain and the Queensland Family History Society, Frances Cairns, Peta Browne and Bundaberg Regional Libraries, Karen Finch, Nicole Rawson and the Royal Agricultural Society NSW Heritage Centre, staff at the Supreme Court of Victoria, Vikki Petraitis, Michael Shelford, Gideon Haigh, and Hazel Edwards.

My appreciation and gratitude to everyone in the Bayside writers group especially Andrea Barton, Virginia Cairns, Kate Murdoch, Bella Ellwood-Clayton, Cassie Lane and Daphne Briggs.

Thanks to Elizabeth Astley and Dorothy for insights and recollections of 1930s Melbourne.

A special final thanks to all my family and friends especially Jess, Mum, Jason, Eleni, Jalen, Gran, Pa, Kate, Daniela, Jen, Petra, Dana, Caroline, Megan, Benn and Jax for all your love and support. I miss you Dad, Nanny and Grandpa – I hope you can read this wherever you are.

ABOUT THE AUTHOR

Tara Oldfield is a PR and communications professional from Melbourne. In her current role at the State Archives, she delves into fascinating files of Victoria's past, writes regular history articles and presents episodes of the award-winning Look History in the Eye podcast. Tara has written for publications such as Traces Magazine and Ancestor. In 2024 she won a Mander Jones Award for her short historical fiction Bitter salts. Her journal article examining the life of Kate Rounsefell, fiancé and almost victim of serial killer Frederick Bailey Deeming, was published in Provenance in 2025. Through Tara's work with archives, she happened upon the files of a fascinating 1930s criminal, inspiring her first novel - Diamonds, furs and murder: The many crimes of Mona Hayes.